CATA

BY VAL P GOULD

AbgrundBooks

Catalyst

Published by AbgrundBooks, Sandwich, Kent, UK (michael@abgrundrisse.net)

Cover painting 'The Low Copper Sun Lit the Moor with Flame' by the pastel artist Cheryl Culver PPS RBA (www.cherylculverpaintings.co.uk / cherylculver@btinternet.com)

Layout and design by michael pennamacoor of Abgrundrisse (michael@abgrundrisse.net)

Printed by Lulu (www.lulu.com)

ISBN: 978-0-9555869-3-4

Dedication

For my sister Cheryl and my daughter Ellen and in loving memory of my dear Mother, my mentor and my friend.

Acknowledgements

I would like to thank Jane Gardam for taking the time to read my book and for giving me encouragement to proceed with my story. I would also like to thank Geff and Annika Sneller who waded through my third draft with a red pen!

My special thanks go to my sister Cheryl both for donating her painting for my book cover and for her invaluable input and for being a sounding board for my ideas. And to my daughter, Ellen, a special thanks for her honesty and sometimes harsh but justified 'trashing' of my early drafts. Thank you for making me behave like an adult in the face of criticism.

Finally I extend my gratitude to my publisher and designer michael pennamacoor for his tolerance and for a job well done.

Val seen here with her three dogs in Sandwich, Kent.

CHAPTER 1

A BLACK EMPTY ribbon stretched out in the headlights of the car. She flipped the Pink Floyd tape to play.

The first strains of Atom Heart Mother swept through the car. She drummed her fingers to the beat on the steering wheel.

Damn! The tape stuttered. As she reached down to eject it something flashed in her peripheral vision. She glimpsed a man's face, pale and ugly in her lights, heard a soft crunch, a shudder ran through the car. The screech of her tyres merged discordantly with his scream as he fell.

Pin prickles of shock raised the hairs on her arms and the back of her neck. She gripped the steering wheel in horror. Where on earth had he come from? They were in the middle of the moor, not a car or house in sight. It was as though he had just dropped from the sky! The man staggered to his feet and shot a look in her direction. He lurched, limping away, his raincoat flapping open as he went. She sat frozen and watched him try to run, then fall and then run again into the night. She couldn't believe what had happened, traumatised she stared after him. What a bloody disaster! *I could have killed him!* She had certainly injured him, how bad was he? She would have seen him had she not been fiddling with the tape... she couldn't drive on pretending it hadn't happened.

Oh Christ what shall I do? What shall I do? Sandy jiggled her legs up and down in agitation scrabbling her hands through her cropped spikey hair. *He can't be that badly hurt or he wouldn't be able to run.* She started the engine again which had stalled in her emergency stop. The car, still in gear lurched and stalled again. *SHIT, SHIT, SHIT! I can't just go on, damn him to hell!* Taking a deep breath, she grabbed her torch and started to run after the limping figure calling out to him to stop.

"Wait, please wait, I'm sorry, let me help you!" He lurched on, arms flailing and one leg dragging. She shouted out again

"Stop you bloody idiot!" He hesitated enough for her to pick out his face in her torch light; pale and flat, his piggy eyes glinting, then lumbered on. *Sod you then!* Sandy stopped and began to return to the car, *can't say I didn't try.* A cry of pain made her hesitate and playing her torch across the flat heath she searched for the figure. At first she could see no sign of him, then, he rose up out of the heather, and looked back at her. However, in spite of her calling to him once again to wait and that she would help him, he staggered on.

For Christ's sake! Sandy made one last attempt to reach him, reasoning that he might have hit his head and be confused.

She put on a spurt but he had a head start and in spite of his injury he kept a distance between them, her plimsolls slipped and slopped; the evening dew coating the soles as if with oil, and she cursed that she had worn them. Her destination had been for warmer climes than the moor! Thank goodness she hadn't worn her flip-flops.

Very soon her thin jacket and sweatshirt were soaked with sweat, a hot late summer day had handed its mantle to a sultry night. Quickening her pace she called again, he hesitated and seemed about to stop, but didn't and veered away crashing through some bushes. She heard a muffled cry as he stumbled again. The man was still running away, *why doesn't he wait? The idiot!* It was becoming stupid, what the hell was she doing? He didn't want her help or he would have stopped. On he went through heather and springy tufts of grass and angrily she made up her mind to let him go but, noticing that his pace was flagging she changed her mind yet again and continued her pursuit. She began to catch him up.

It may have been a rock or a rabbit run which caught her foot as she scrambled her way through the scrub, as all of a sudden Sandy was sprawled face down in the heather, a cloud of mosquitoes, disturbed from the foliage whined in her ears. Every ounce of breath had been forcibly expelled from her lungs. She couldn't breathe, the pain was intense and Sandy was sure she had broken a rib. After what seemed an eternity of suffocating she managed to gulp a breath; gasping, she rolled off the rock which had punched her in the stomach when she fell. The heather was coarse and scratched her face and something sharp was pressing into her thigh. As she sucked air back into her winded lungs, the moist peaty soil pervaded her senses in its heady aroma. Sandy curled her head to her knees and closed her eyes waiting for the pain and fainting sensation to pass. *Fuck him! I don't need this!* He could go to hell and she would get back on with her journey.

Wearily and still in pain, Sandy struggled to her feet and metaphorically giving him two fingers she shone her torch into... white. A blank wall of mist. Sandy couldn't believe how utterly blind she had become and how suddenly it had happened. She was shrouded in thick fog. Only moments before the moor had been eerily lit by the moon and stars, which were now completely obliterated by the fog; the temperature had plummeted *I can't see a bloody thing!* She stood stock still, shivering a little and pulling her jacket closer, her eyes straining to see and her mind racing. All thought of helping the stranger forgotten, she concentrated her mind on finding her way back to the road; it can't be far away. Feeling around Sandy found the hazard that had tripped her; a branch lying across her path and stepped carefully back over it in the knowledge that this was the direction in which she had come. Now she had to concentrate and try to orientate herself in the direction of the road. She cautiously began to attempt to retrace her route. Running through the moor in the dark had been difficult enough but now it was far worse, there was absolutely no visibility and Sandy tripped and fell countless times bruising her knees on stones and adding further scratches to her face. Snagged on a thorn bush, her jacket tore as she angrily ripped it free. Still trying to remain focused Sandy ploughed on when suddenly from the depths of the mist she heard a frantic cry. She instinctively turned in shock trying to see where the noise had come from; it had to be the injured man. It sounded so close, but the torch light bounced off the fog, droplets of suspended water danced in front of her eyes. He was wailing and muttering then whimpering, each new cry seemed to come from a different direction and it set every nerve ending in her body on end. Her heart crashed and, her hands shook. The noise stopped suddenly. Who or what was this man? He sounded like a madman. Sandy was terrified. Thank goodness she hadn't caught up with him, why on earth did she go after him in the first place? The sweatshirt, now icy cold clung to her back, her hair was wet and dripping into her eyes. It was silent but for the sound of her breathing and the drip, and crackle of the moisture in the air. The fog had smothered all sound and light. She had to get away from him, back to the car. Like a punch in the stomach, it hit her that she had no idea which way she was now facing, having instinctively turned at the sound of the cry. She stood rooted to the spot trying desperately to remember which way she had turned but it was hopeless, pure guesswork. She spun round and round in abject panic. *Oh Christ, help me!* Sandy berated herself for her recklessness in following him, she was chilled and shaking, everything was ruined. She crouched down into the heather and tried to get a grip on her panic; he could be a mere yard away and she wouldn't know it. Would he attack her? His behaviour wasn't normal; there was no telling what sort of maniac he might be. Thinking of men she knew, she asked herself if they would have behaved like this and the answer was no. They wouldn't have run off like that. She couldn't imagine anyone she knew behaving so irrationally. She asked herself again why on earth she had followed him. Sandy remained silently huddled into herself, her knees ached from crouching and she quietly eased herself to sit and listen. She felt the cold wetness seep into her jeans and soak through to her skin. The smell of wet foliage and wet plimsolls briefly took her back to her childhood running wild in the woods and dens around her home and tears sprung to her eyes. Soon her teeth began to chatter, to her ears they sounded like a drum tattoo. An owl's cry, far away, a rustling close by, the minute sound of a sudden release of moisture from an overladen leaf, in her imagination were all made by him, as he crept upon her. The fog showed no sign of lifting and Sandy remained, too scared to move.

She had no idea how long she sat in fear, straining her ears, making herself as small as she could. It seemed like hours. The man didn't appear, thank God; hopefully he'd wandered off in a different direction. Her panic subsided a little and she began to think more rationally again. Numb with cold and so stiff she could barely move Sandy knew she couldn't remain here for ever, she had to get her circulation going again; she had to make a decision. Very cautiously, with the torch shielded inside her jacket, Sandy flicked it on and off to see the time. It was 10.30pm there was still a chance she could make it to the train if she could only get back to her car. But there was no way she could be sure she was going in the right direction, she supposed that it made more sense to stay put until the mist lifted. Chances were that it wouldn't lift 'til dawn and it would definitely be too late to catch the flight then. But surely it's better than wandering and getting further lost. After all it's bound to clear when the sun comes up. Could she last that long shivering and soaked? People *did* die of hypothermia under these conditions. If only there was some sort of shelter, some bracken or something. She groped around, in half-hearted hope, for something she could use for warmth but of course everything was soaking wet; no point looking any more. Sandy hunkered down in the wet grass and heather, cradling herself with her arms, and hugged what warmth was still remaining in her body. Praying that the madman would be as unable to see and find her as she was unable to see him, she began her vigil. The mist and darkness combined, imprisoned her in a muffled cocoon. It was strange how the fog stifled noise, yet amplified it at the same time. Every drip of water seemed loud and her breathing was raucous in her ears. The rhythmic drumming of her heartbeat accompanied each breath she took, so loud that she was sure it could be heard reverberating across the moor. Holding her breath she listened intently for any sound of footfalls approaching. A distant thrumming made her sit up, it was growing louder. It was getting closer. Oh my God is it a car? Sandy leaped to her feet, cocking her head to catch the direction of the sound. She turned slowly, tuning into the engine noise. It certainly wasn't far away but difficult to pinpoint exactly where. Apart from the fact that the car was moving, the moisture seemed to hold sound and one time it appeared to be coming from behind and the next in front. The gear changing was altering the pitch, it was accelerating away, yes, it was going that way. Sandy fixed her blind gaze on the invisible car and without hesitation made the decision to find the road. *Yes! I can still make it. I'm buggered if I'm missing my holiday for that loser!* She stopped herself as she began to rush headlong in her excitement and forced herself to move cautiously. Her mind firmly fixed on her perceived direction of the road; she concentrated on following the noise of the car as the throb of its engine became fainter and fainter until she could no longer hear it and silence fell once more. Unnerved by the silence and consequent lack of guidance, although she had been expecting it, Sandy felt a jolt of anxiety. Causing her to pause and breathe deeply to steady herself before proceeding. She walked, arms outstretched, like some story book ghost, to feel for any hazards which could trip her. She couldn't risk losing her sense of direction again now that she was so sure she knew where the road was. She planted her feet as carefully as possible, testing the ground for sogginess; break a leg and she could die, fall into a bog and she was definitely dead. The concentration was more wearying than the walking, her breathing, short and shallow with stress seemed not to feed her lungs. She rubbed her eyes to clear them of moisture, the scratches on her face from brambles and shrubs smarted as she scrubbed her hands over them. Her jeans and plimsolls chafed painfully on her cold legs and feet and her eyes ran with tears which she was unable to control. Striving to keep going in as straight a path as possible, she kept her mind fixed firmly on the path which would lead her to the road, praying that another car would pass which would confirm her route. But she neither heard nor saw anything other than her laboured breathing and the dense white mist, no tiny glimmer of light filtered through. The car she had heard was probably the only car to pass that night, it was doubtful that any more would come by at this time. How long had she been on the moor? Doggedly ploughing on half expecting to stumble on to tarmac any minute, sure she had gone the right way; Sandy fought back the doubts which kept forcing their way in. Weariness of body gradually became weariness of spirit when no firm ground greeted her stumbling steps. Yet still she staggered on, it can't be far away now. Travelling in thick fog was akin to walking with your eyes closed and with nothing to guide you. Had she wandered off course, even in a circle? The air was thick with moisture and she gasped for oxygen as though through a wet flannel. Tripping and falling and shaking with the cold and fear she wove her haphazard course in her search for the road. Scared to stop and scared to proceed, panic built up and up, her head felt as though it would burst. It was no good pretending any more, the going remained heath-land; no hard gravelled road welcomed her tread. As sure as she could be, the route that she had taken was straight; she didn't think she had swerved to any great extent, so why hadn't she reached the road by now? She had definitely heard a car and she was positive she had discerned the direction it had come from; she hadn't rushed headlong at the first sound but had carefully listened to be absolutely sure before moving at all. Sandy recalled how hard it had been to pinpoint the car, apart from the fact that it was moving all the time, there had been a sort of echo — no not an echo, more as though the moisture in the air had sucked up the sound, swilled it around and spat it out again. It reminded her of that frustrating semi-deafness one gets with a head cold, where you hear noises in the ears and your head feels sort of unbalanced. With her vision gone and sound muffled, she realised with a sinking hollowness that she must have fooled herself into believing she was going in the right direction in her desperation to get off the moor. A coldness ran through her, a coldness which had nothing to do with the temperature. It was the chill of utter despair.

The fog was still dense, the faint light from the moon quenched. Her torch was useless; seeming to intensify the opacity of the saturated air. She should have stayed where she was when the mist descended, and waited for it to lift, but the fear of the close proximity of the man whom she now was sure was a madman and her determination to catch her flight had made her act impetuously when she had heard the car and now she was lost. Madman or not, she desperately needed someone, anyone; she cried out for help into the sodden air, but it was like shouting into a cushion; her muffled voice seemed to bounce back at her. Sandy crouched shivering against a boulder and stared into the mist, little sparks of light flickered in her vision. Clothes soaked and fingers and feet numb with the cold she fought in vain against sleep for fear of dying of hypothermia. She jolted as she felt sleep claiming her, forced her eyes open and attempted to stay alert but finally she succumbed and her head fell forward and awkwardly to the side, the cold wet rock 'cushioned' her cheek and she slipped into sleep.

Sandy jolted awake with a cry of pain, her neck had cricked and for an instant she was unable to move it. The pit of stomach clenching which floods in when reality dawns on first awakening, when despair creeps in as you remember something tragic that sleep has put aside, hit her bodily. The realisation of where she was, so very cold and hopelessly lost was unbearable. Wincing with pain she eased her neck loose, stretched her cold, stiff body and despondently looked up into the mist – it had completely cleared and she was greeted by a clear night sky. Other than her sopping wet clothing it was hard to imagine that there had been a mist at all. A chill breeze walked icy fingers over her. Rigid with cold, she tried to stand but her legs were numb. She rubbed them furiously with her hands which were also numb and managed to restore some circulation. Shining her torch around, all she could see was moorland, no lights from cars moving on the lost road, just an expanse of scrub and heather; no glint of moonlight on the roof of her car. *Oh shit, where the hell am I?* Sandy staggered to her feet, she shone her torch at her wrist but her watch had stopped, it had been her grandma's watch, a delicate little thing more suited to dresses and evenings out than the damp atmosphere on the moor. Mum had told her to leave it at home but Sandy had insisted that she wear it. Now it was buggered. She had no idea of the time except that it was still night. The moon was a wedge of yellow light, a thin outline of its full self faintly glowing around it; the rest of the sky was pitch-black, save one or two random stars. Through the darkness, lit only by the small torch beam, and the thin moonlight Sandy trudged, stumbling over tufts of grass and small prickly shrubs, shouting expletives as she tripped. Her eyes constantly searching the horizon, the darkness blurred through her tears as she soundlessly wept, the tears trickling down her sore scratched face. Gradually the scrubby grass thinned and gave way to bracken and gorse, each plant reaching out and deliberately scratching or tripping her. In spite of her fear that the man may be near-by, she shouted for help again, but the darkness had a density which seemed almost physical. Sandy wanted to lie down and sleep. Where was the road? Where were the houses? If she had been walking in the right direction surely she should have reached somewhere man-made by now!

She sank down onto the ground exhausted and in spite of the cold she slipped into the arms of Morpheus.

When Sandy woke again the night was unfurling and a ground mist swathed her, its tendrils caressing her body like a ghostly shroud. Grey light suffused with mauve and pink painted the sky in a Turneresque glow. A morning chorus began with a single blackbird's note and as the music swelled she thought of her father and their country walks which made her cry like a child. She looked around her at the moorland, the heather still held on to its bloom of purple which in the morning light sparkled with moisture. One or two windswept trees stood starkly against the sky and far above her a falcon hovered, its wings barely moving as it scanned the moor for its morning meal. A faint whiff of fox drifted into her nostrils, somehow comforting in spite of its unpleasantness; living creatures were all around her, some visible and some unseen, life was there and she felt less alone. She was very cold and still scared but she was alive. She searched the horizon and in the distance made out a jumble of rocks which she realised must be a tor. She may be able to climb up and get some idea of her position, you could see for miles from some of them. But her body refused to move, her jeans and T-shirt were clinging like icy rags to her flesh, her jacket was sodden and her hair dripped moisture down her neck. As she cuddled her arms around herself desperately trying to get warm, the sun slowly rose further above the horizon. Yet still she sat huddled and shivering. Every move she had made had been the wrong one so far, she was scared to try again. She sat and wept for mum. After a while, Sandy, having cried herself dry, noticed that the morning was growing finer, she forced herself to struggle to her feet and set off stiffly and stumbling often, in the direction of the tor. The act of doing something rather than just giving in renewed her hope. As she moved onwards Sandy felt the warmth of the rising sun and relished it. Her limbs loosened and her numbed extremities came back to life. The rocks on the horizon were much further away than she had supposed, the sun had risen to its full height and still they appeared distant. She was desperately thirsty and a gnawing hunger pain persisted, causing her on more than one occasion to double up with stomach cramps. There were peaty puddles here and there but Sandy was scared to drink from them, she had never been in a situation such as this before and was totally uneducated in survival skills. However, the thirst became so overriding that finally, when she came across a slightly clearer puddle she knelt in the spongy turf, her wet jeans cutting into the back of her knees and scooped a little water into her mouth. It was icy cold and surprisingly didn't taste too bad. She waited a while to see if she felt any adverse effects, then, re-assured that she felt none, she cautiously drank some more. She then scooped some into her cupped hands and splashed it over her face, her cuts and scratches stung but she felt better; fresher. As she travelled, the scrub began to grow thinner and the way stony. Tripping and stumbling Sandy, to her joy arrived at the jumble of stones at the base of the bigger rocks. Confident that she would see a house or a village from the top she scrambled up the loose gravel and on to a bigger outcrop, taking great care; the rocks were wet and slippery. Sandy imagined herself arriving in habitation, knocking on the door of a house and begging to use their phone. She would have quite a tale to tell them all when she got home. Dad would come and pick her up and they would probably have a laugh on the way home about Sandy's innate ability get herself into trouble, sobering up before they reached home where Mum would definitely throw a wobbly and say that she knew she was right and that Sandy should have taken a taxi. They would have a cup of tea and something to eat and go and retrieve Sandy's car, *must remember to take jump leads, did I leave the lights on? Can't remember.* Surely the airline would give her another ticket when she explained what had happened and she would still have her holiday. Laughing to herself in spite of her sore feet and legs and her grinding hunger she clambered up the last outcrop and excitedly looked around her. The sun was in her eyes and she squinted to see better. Stepping into some shade her wet plimsoll slipped on some moss and she lost her footing completely, slithering down the rock, gaining momentum as she scrambled for a hand hold. Sandy hit the ground with a soft thud. Her head whiplashed and crunched back down as she landed and fell unconscious.

CHAPTER 2

A PITIFUL KEENING woke Sandy and she opened her eyes to blackness and pain; it was she who was crying. Her right arm hung twisted. The arm was useless and dislocated from the shoulder, the pain was excruciating. She passed back into oblivion. She dreamed that she was loading her milk float (her holiday job that summer) and the crates of bottles were heavier than usual. She found that lifting them gave her such pain in her shoulder that she had to ask for help.

The foreman at the dairy, Geoff, fat, middle-aged and gruff, hadn't wanted to employ her.

"You're too small, not strong enough; you'll be loading your own float..."

He had given her a trial run and a big heavy diesel one ton van to drive, told her to be there in the morning at 3am and no later. He was grinning smugly to himself, she noticed, confident that she wouldn't last the day.

She had loved the country round and over the summer months she would drive directly into the sunrise, clad in shorts and T-shirt, tanned and healthy, running between houses; leaving the van at the end of the road as it was so noisy and her first delivery would be at about 4.30. Compliments came back to the dairy about her considerateness and friendly demeanour. Elderly men and women offered tea and cakes and were grateful for a chat. Some single men invited her in also, but, she suspected, not for a chat. At *these* houses Sandy crept silently up the path and 'unchinking' the bottles ran quickly back to the van to avoid any uncomfortable attention. Half way through the round a pint of gold top was a personal treat; sitting in the morning sun glugging straight out of the bottle. Only once did she oversleep, and the foreman, having grown to regard her as his favourite roundsman, had loaded her float for her and delivered it to her flat, throwing stones at her window to wake her. That, according to the other milkmen, was a first.

"He must be going soft", one said.

"No, it's her hot-pants" re-joined his mate.

"It's because she's a bloody good milkman" growled Geoff as he walked into the depot. She loved being one of the boys and although it was good to be admired, fancied or whatever, it was also good to be appreciated for the job.

"I say, are you okay?"

She jumped involuntarily and screamed in pain.

"You fucking idiot" she screamed "what the hell were you thinking?"

Anger at what had befallen her and the agony in her arm smothered any other emotions she might otherwise have felt — like fear; had the man she hit come to attack her?

"Sorry, I didn't mean to startle you."

Sandy realised immediately that this was not the man. He wore hiking boots and a parka anorak; in fact there was no similarity at all.

"Sorry, I thought you were someone else."

He pointedly and mockingly looked around

"I didn't see a coach tour! Is there one hiding behind the rocks?"

Sandy had no energy for banter, she groped around to pull herself up and screamed with pain, as if someone had grabbed all the nerves in her arm and neck and twisted them together at the same time as kicking her in the back.

"My God, you need help" he said, blanching at the sight of her dislocated shoulder, "can you stand, can you walk?"

He smiled a little boy smile, apologetic and disarming which, oddly made her wary. But in her agony she slumped to the ground and pleaded

"Please help me I can't bear this pain any longer," and doubling over she was violently sick at his feet. She slumped to the ground, the soft perfume of the crushed heather where she fell, rose and dispersed around her. When she came round, the man in the anorak had disappeared. Had she imagined him? She had no idea.

Sandy was sure she was running a fever. Her thirst was ripping at her throat and in spite of the now hot sun she was shivering. Looking up through blurred eyes she almost screamed with relief as she caught sight of a hazy figure in the distance. It put her in mind of films she had seen when travellers in the desert see a mirage of an oasis.

"You came back! Please can you get an ambulance or something, I am really ill!"

Sandy felt desperate and very frightened, the pain was intense and every slight movement induced her to black out.

"Where the hell did you go? You just buggered off and left me for hours!"

"It's not been that long, I'm sorry I left you but I needed my back-pack." Sandy shook violently and retched again with the pain.

"I think I can re-locate your shoulder, if you'll let me." He was a bit grubby and she shrank from his helping hand; but then, so was she grubby, and wet! She shook her head wildly,

"No I need a doctor, not some tramp, piss off!"

"Will you let me try? I *do* know what I am doing" he earnestly insisted. "I've got some water and some pain killers in here somewhere." He rummaged in his back-pack and produced a shabby lemonade bottle which looked as though it had been used as a rugby ball, half filled with a rather yellowish liquid. At her expression of distaste he said reassuringly

"It *is* water; the peat makes it look like weak tea." Sandy wasn't so sure; it looked more like weak pee! But it was cleaner than the water she had drunk from the puddle and she gratefully reached for the bottle. "Drink some now and take the pain killers." He waited, holding the pills out to her. "I'll try to be as quick and gentle as I can." He pushed the pills into her good hand and held the water, ready for her. Sandy was in agony; although she doubted the man's ability to re-locate her shoulder she could stand the pain no longer. Should she let this stranger loose on her shoulder? What if he made it worse and tore all her ligaments? She could lose the use of her arm for ever couldn't she? She screwed her eyes tight and tried to ride the pain but it was overwhelming. Feeling almost delirious, she took the pills and put them in her mouth, he handed her the water, she gulped it and swallowed them down. He insisted they waited a while for the pain killers to take the edge off her pain. Twenty minutes or so later she smiled grimly at him.

"Okay do it."

She passed out yet again with the pain when he pulled her arm and the socket slipped into place.

Later when she woke all she could see was blue. Her arm was in a sling which appeared to be part of a T-shirt, again rather grubby, and torn in places, she could smell a musky male smell on it, like skin smells when sun-warmed and slightly sweaty. It was a bit too personal and Sandy was ready to be disgusted by it but found instead that it was reassuringly pleasant. The pain in her shoulder was a lot less, and in comparison to the former agony, bearable. Her rescuer was nowhere to be seen but a note was tucked into the sling.

"Gone hunting, stay here and rest." Turning her head she

realised that she was in a blue tent. All was quiet excepting sounds of nature, bees buzzed in the heather and the occasional bird called overhead. Totally exhausted, Sandy fell deeply asleep.

Out on the moor, people were hunting and others were being hunted, but Sandy was oblivious.

Two boys in a stolen van discovered Sandy's car, its door open.

"Must 'ave gone for a piss." The other laughed, replying

"'E'll piss hisself when 'e comes back fur it. C'mon!" Being practised in the art of car theft, they quickly fired the engine and took off, racing each other on the deserted road.

At some point Sandy's car was rammed by the van, driven off the road into a ditch and torched. Her suitcase, packed for her holiday was in the boot. Her bag on the passenger seat, containing her ticket and passport, now relieved of its cash, also perished.

That morning as Sandy slept in the little blue tent, the connecting flight for Mauritius took off with one empty seat.

The following evening, June, leaving her dinner untouched, was hovering near the wall phone in the hall, an improvement on the old Bakelite one they had had since 1960.

"Sandy should be arriving in Mauritius any time now."

"Not yet, don't forget it's about a twenty hour flight. She'll ring as soon as she can, make a cup of tea or pour a glass of wine and stop worrying," replied her husband Tim. Sandy's parents had seen her off from their home in Cornwall. She was travelling by train overnight and due to catch a connecting flight to Ostend and from there a charter flight to Mauritius. This was to have been Sandy's first ever flight and it being such a long haul, they were naturally anxious to know she was okay.

The following day, Josie, Sandy's friend from college met the flight in Mauritius and assumed in the casual way of students who hitch-hiked their way to and from college and changed destinations on a whim, that Sandy had changed her mind. She hailed a rickety taxi and spent the day snorkelling at the beach. No doubt her friend would be in touch sometime.

In Cornwall, that evening, June and Tim struggled between anxiety and annoyance that Sandy was so oblivious to their concern that she hadn't bothered to phone them on her arrival.

It was deep dark night when Sandy awoke, hungry and very alone. Her exhaustion from the pain and her fruitless hike over the moor had depleted her energy. Thoroughly disheartened at the realisation that she had definitely missed her flight and that she had no idea where she was or who the hiker was or where the madman was, she lay back down on the bedroll and stared vacantly into the darkness. *Fuck everything!* She slept, but her sleep was light and filled with anxiety, she jolted into wakefulness on and off imagining she heard someone creeping up to the tent. In the end she was so edgy that she gave up on sleep and rummaged in the tent looking for a torch but found none, she must have dropped hers when she had fallen. So she sat at the open flap in the faint moonlight staring at the sky and listening all the time for any sound of the man returning. There was something about his boyish apologetic smile that reminded her of the promiscuous lecturer who possessed a similar boyish charm and over whom she had agonised as he worked his way through the nubile and gullible nineteen year-olds in the first year.

All through her grammar school days, Sandy had been passionately in love with the classically unobtainable — a teacher; Tom. The elder brother of a friend, he had taught at a different school and when Sandy had first met him she was fifteen and he was twenty five. The day on which school finally ended in 1968 he had asked her out. The summer was a dream; she had found her future partner and his feelings were the same. Tom wanted to marry soon and to settle down near home. However, Sandy had been accepted at art college in Nottingham and she was determined to go. Reluctantly Tom gave in and they became unofficially engaged with a view to marry when Sandy had finished her course. Tom had balked at the four year wait but as he had no option other than breaking the engagement, he acceded. At the end of the autumn term he had arrived with the top down on his sports car and presented her with a huge fur hat and gloves. A light snow lay on the ground and there had been a hard frost but brilliant sunshine and it was a most exhilarating drive home. She remembered her mother being annoyed that she could have 'caught her death of cold'. Oh Mum, I do love you.

Tom had started to drive to Nottingham to see her or to bring her home for the weekends. Every weekend! This had been fine at first, but it meant that the student experience, which is all part of going away from home, was missing in Sandy's life. She missed out on parties, trips and dances. Her work suffered because she had no time outside of college to do the extra painting the course required. It had felt as though she were still a child being chaperoned and smothered. Tom began to change; he wanted Sandy to leave college in Nottingham and train for teaching nearer home. She was an artist and the last thing she wished to do was teach under-elevens. Sandy's stubborn and independent nature, hitherto unprovoked, had started to break through. Tom seemed to think that his ten year seniority gave him the right to dictate which direction her life should take; ignoring the fact that she was a person in her own right, with a talent, and not just an appendage to him. Sandy had suddenly visualised herself; a middle-aged junior school teacher with 2.4 children, pandering to what had now become apparent; a rather bullying man already set in his ways.

Sandy became desolate, she realised that getting engaged so early had been hasty and that she had had no yard stick with which to measure her relationship with Tom. But, she had loved him for all this time, how could she not love him now? She shivered as she thought of never making love with him again, how could she bear to lose that? They were so right together, but...

Tom had been the first, he had taken her virginity. Tom had arranged with Sue and Greg, his married friends, to let them spend the evening at their house whilst they attended a party. The fire burnt welcomingly in the open grate and wine and nibbles had been left for them. It was a very romantic setting and they were both excited and Sandy, very nervous. Tom had had relationships before and had come prepared with condoms, though he confided, he'd love to make her pregnant so that they would have to marry immediately.

"I love you Sandy, I've loved you for years without being able to declare it." Tom whispered as he slipped her jacket off her shoulders. He handed her a glass of wine and beckoned her to sit beside him on the sheepskin rug in the flickering firelight.

"Are you sure you want to do it?" He asked her softly. "I'll understand if you think it's too soon, though I admit I have a job keeping my hands off you." Sandy put her wine glass on the hearth and traced her fingers lovingly over his face. As he smiled down at her she melted with love for him.

"Oh Tom, I have dreamed of this moment for years," she replied, "I am nervous, it's true, but I really do want you."

"I'll be gentle, I promise." He pulled her to him and kissed her. The logs in the grate crackled and the flames lit their bodies with an amber glow as they made love on the sheepskin rug. Tom was gentle, as he had promised and afterwards, as they lay in each other's arms, relaxed and happy he had asked her to marry him. It had been the beginning of a relationship filled with love and desire for each other, every opportunity to be together, to make love, was grabbed unashamedly, wherever and however. They refused invitations out so that they could go to bed; their friends despaired of them,

“They’re just jealous.” Tom laughed. “I know at least three of my rugby mates who would give a lot to be where I am now!” Then the summer came to an end and kissing feverishly right up until the train left the station, they said their goodbyes as Sandy began her art course.

To his surprise, Sandy sadly ended the relationship. The relationship they had been building up to for four or more years had in fact lasted a mere six months. She thought she had loved Tom, but realised that she really had not known him, it had been an infatuation, the attentions of an older man, the little notes he had sent her, the Valentine cards, having to wait years before dating him because he was a teacher, all had served to intensify her obsession, and then, when they had made love, it had been so good that she had often closed her mind to little things he had said or done which had made her sit up and sometime bristle with anger. However, now she was twenty and no longer the romantic little girl of fifteen who was hooked on Jane Eyre and he was not the storybook Mr. Rochester but an ordinary bloke. That was fine; after all, life isn’t a story is it? She had grown out of fictional romance and he being an ordinary bloke was not the problem. The problem was that they were worlds apart in all other aspects than physical attraction, how long could that last when he was determined to dominate and plan her whole life for her?

The following term found Sandy missing Tom but not wanting to go back. She was emotionally vulnerable, she had never dated anyone else; she felt empty and lost. She also felt like a bird released from a cage! Two contradicting emotions; a longing for the security Tom had given her and indeed, for the passionate love making they had shared, and a whooping of joy for the freedom of spirit she now had. She very soon appeared on the radar of that sweet smiling boyish predator and he had homed in. She didn't want to remember the humiliation she had felt when it had become apparent that he had been seducing every first year student he could as well as her.

Sandy pulled her thoughts back to the present. She had waited all night for someone to return to the tent and was hungry, confused and becoming very scared. She still found it difficult to use her right arm and an unpleasant bruise had spread from the shoulder down to her elbow. What should she do? If he returned he would find a way of getting her home, surely? But what if he didn't return, or worse, he came back but turned out to be some sort of maniac. Her imagination started to create dreadful scenes, no one knew where she was and she would not be missed for ages. By the time she was, she could have been raped and murdered and buried deep in a bog! She pulled herself together with a mental slap; he'd hardly bother to fix her arm were he going to murder her would he? Anger burned in her at the stupidity of the situation. She couldn't make sense of it all. Why did that man run in front of her car? Surely he could see her lights approaching along the flat moorland road and there were no other cars. If he'd wanted to cross over he could have waited or gone long before she had reached him. What, she wondered, was his problem, was he trying to commit suicide? Normal people didn't run about at night on the moor. Or run in front of cars.

Dawn came and still she sat there debating what to do. An eerie grey green light misted the heather, tiny muted sparks of golden gorse flowers hung like fairy lights on invisible Christmas trees. All was still, no wind, no sun; that haunted hiatus between night and day. The landscape was identical all around her, heather, gorse, heather, gorse, an occasional blackthorn. She stared at the sky to try to determine the sun rise, and there it was; a faint orange glow bleeding into the clouds. Daft exploits and dare-devil adventures were all very well when she was surrounded by friends in a familiar environment. They had done some stupid and quite dangerous things during her time at college but this was different; the vastness of the moor was daunting and she felt so alone. Where had 'the anorak' gone? Had he abandoned her and his tent and gone home? How long should she just sit there and wait? What if he didn't come back, what then? If I just do a recce... she thought, and snatching the impulse before uncertainty made her hesitate or change her mind she set off with the haze of sun to her left, the shortbread biscuits she had found in the tent and the bottle of water he had given her, stuffed into her jacket pocket. It was daylight after all and there was no fog, she could always come back to the tent if needs be.

There were no tracks or paths with the exception of a few small rabbit runs. The heather was springy but concealed ruts and soggy puddles. Sandy travelled very slowly and cautiously. She felt somehow that she should head south, though she couldn't say why, only that she seemed to remember that the northern side of the moor was less inhabited. But of course she could be totally misguided...

Later that morning, with a couple of rabbits slung over his shoulder the man with the tent returned. He had not intended to be gone for so long but, finding himself the wrong side of some very marshy ground he had taken a circuitous route back. With the dimming light and unknown territory travelling had become dangerous, consequently he had spent the night in the open: something he was quite used to doing; his parka had kept him warm and the night had been fine. The dawn had heralded, and kept its promise of, a beautiful hot day, he hummed contentedly to himself as he gathered tinder for his cook fire. Assuming Sandy was still sleeping, he shrugged off his parka, rolled up his sleeves and skinned and gutted the rabbits. Soon he had the meat spit roasting over a peat fire. From his back pack he took some wild mushrooms and cooked them in a small billycan. He gently pulled open the tent flap and removed tin plates and cutlery, plastic cups and some salt.

"Food's ready" he said. There was no response.

"Hello?" he called, and pulling back the tent flap fully, he saw that the sleeping bag was empty, the tent was empty. Maybe she had gone for a pee, he called out

"Hello! I'm back!" There was no response; he waited, expecting her head to rise up out of the heather, her face blushing with embarrassment. But she didn't appear. Where the hell had she gone? He called out numerous times and circled his camp site looking for any sign of her. She had completely disappeared. It was only the absence of the biscuits and water bottle, when he looked more closely, which convinced him he hadn't imagined the whole episode. Well, that and the ache in his back from his trek with her draped across his neck, like a slaughtered fawn. He scanned the horizon but saw no sign of her. The heather had sprung back into place in her wake and he had no idea in which direction she had gone. *My God, she'll be completely lost, the stupid girl!* An unwelcome memory forced itself into his thoughts, of that dreadful night when his brother Alistair had run away.

"I've got to find her" he said out loud. Oliver shivered; oblivious to the noon heat. The sun was glaring but seemed far away as though painted in the sky. Could he find her before dark? Could he find her at all? Trying to maintain some plan in his head he dug deep in his pack to find his compass. He reminded himself that he was experienced in survival, having taken part in many such exercises when he was a member of the CCF. At school he had loved the exercises with the junior cadets; he had excelled at the survival test and his orienteering wasn't bad either. Oliver's love for the wildness of the moor; his chosen place for meditating, writing and testing himself against the elements, soured in his thoughts. *A God-forsaken death trap for the unwary.* The bright green sphagnum moss looked solid but often covered mires in which one would sink, unable to swim or to gain any purchase. Oliver, as a local, knew them as "quakers" because they shifted as you walked on them and he usually knew how to avoid these areas, last night being the exception. Also, at this time of year in particular there was the chance of fog, another deadly hazard; the sudden descent of mist so dense you couldn't see a foot in front of you, just like the one the other night. Oliver had been glad he had been back at his tent when that one had come down. He decided to leave the tent, as, if he took it and the girl returned, she would have no shelter. In fact she would probably wander even further into the moor looking for it, and him. He decided that speed in finding her was the priority and hell, what's a tent when someone's life could be in danger! He wanted to travel light and quickly. Oliver upturned his bag, emptying out all unnecessary weight, slinging it all inside his tent. He grabbed only Ali's rope — which was always safely stowed in his pack, a compass, his sling shot and his folding shovel and flung them back in his pack. He was trying, in his haste, to be practical, taking just the necessities, in case he had to carry the girl. He planned to head for the soft, dangerous ground first and go on from there.

The sun-warmed heather and gorse scents, the bees and butterflies, the occasional sighting of a rabbit, a falcon hovering overhead; the beauty of the wildness was wasted as Sandy watched the sun getting lower in the sky. Still not having found the road, she was lost; again! What was the use of wandering further and further? She needed help to get home, she couldn't do it alone. Resignedly she turned with the sun to her left and hoped that she could re-trace her route back to the tent. Realising the pointlessness of the day's slog, all her hopes were on finding the tent and the nameless man who owned it. When darkness fell completely, and the night-time sounds replaced the buzzing bees and the cry of the buzzard, Sandy could no longer chance travelling, she had looked for a stick or branch with which to prod the ground in front of her as she walked but there were no trees and no sticks. Every step had been a testing pressure with her forward foot before putting weight on it and she was exhausted. The clear blue cloudless skies, of the unusually hot day, darkened, the sun dropped beneath the horizon and the temperature dropped with it. She found a thick mound of heather and curled up in it, drank the last dribble of water and ate the last biscuit. She was desolate, cold and tired. She closed her eyes and prayed. Something she hadn't done for a long time. A spider walked across her face — *Ughshitgetoff!* She leaped up brushing frantically at her face and hair, shuddering at the creepy sensation of those eight hairy black legs. She was cold; the cloudless sky was bright with stars millions of tiny winking sparks in a blue black canopy. Unable to contemplate the thought of lying down again with spiders crawling all over her, Sandy stood up, chilled and still trembling from her aversion, she started to walk, almost in a daze, seemingly uncaring as to which direction she went, but hoping desperately to find the tent in spite of the darkness. She stumbled through the heather, not bothering to test the ground for bogginess, just wanting to keep moving for warmth and a futile sense of purpose. A strong wind suddenly blew across the moor, ragged purple clouds swathed the moon which slowly faded and was extinguished. The first heavy raindrop splashed in her eye as she gazed blindly upwards. It was as black as if her eyes were closed. And then, God emptied the skies. *Shit! That's all I need!* It was like standing under a waterfall. The rain was solid. She battled on however, her plimsolls rubbing and slipping; threatening blisters on her heels and toes. She tripped and staggered, gained her feet and then tripped again, falling. Soaked through to her skin she lay in the heather and swore like a fish-wife. One of her plimsolls had come off when she had fallen and in the dark and wet she felt around to try and find it, all the while crying and cursing her situation. It was then that she found what had tripped her; a fine rope was pegged into the ground. *Oh God, yes, please...* She reached out, and there it was — the tent; the tension of the smooth synthetic fabric giving under the pressure of her searching hand.

CHAPTER 3

TIM FOUND JUNE in the study furiously writing on airmail paper. On hearing him come in she stiffened and hunched over the page, turning away from him. As he approached, she looked up at him, a mixture of anger and anguish; her eyes were moist but flinty.

"She should have made contact by now!" she gripped the pen tighter as though Tim intended to snatch it away from her. She stabbed her forefinger on the letter in time with her words

"I am writing to Sandy!"

"I can see that" Tim replied sharply, "why so aggressive?"

"She hasn't phoned! Why didn't she give us a phone number?"

"Because it's a 'campement', remember? They don't have phones. They were doing it on the cheap." Tim replied, fighting the urge to be impatient but also trying to hide his growing anxiety. He disguised it with indignation.

"She's probably having a great time and has forgotten her promise to communicate, what did you expect? She's always been inconsiderate." Tim paced the room, picking things up and putting them down again. "Don't worry so much. There haven't been any air crashes reported, and we haven't had the police knocking at our door." He stopped pacing and turned to June "Remember, no news is good news."

"Don't quote stupid maxims at me!" snapped June. "She's my beautiful little girl and I want to know she's alright. I didn't want her to go, you know that. But you insisted that she needed to see a bit of the world, and kept on about what a fantastic place Mauritius was when you were there in the Navy." June's eyes sparkled with un-shed tears as she turned her face away from him.

A simmering atmosphere was growing between them. June had always, in Tim's opinion, been over-protective of Sandy, that's why, he knew in his heart, Sandy had chosen to go so far away to college in Nottingham rather than closer to home like Exeter where she had in fact been offered a place. June was incredulous when Sandy had chosen not to take it up. Sandy loved her mother, it was without question, but she had to gain her independence and Tim had been all for it. However, he felt for June, he understood her feeling of loss, knowing that Sandy would probably never actually live at home again once she had completed her studies. He placed his hands gently on June's shoulders and massaged them with his strong warm fingers. She raised her face to him; he looked lovingly into her eyes and kissed her. Pulling up a chair, he sat beside her and quietly read through what she had written.

"I'll just add my love" he said reaching to pluck the pen from June's still rigid grip, "and then I'll go into the village and send this off. Give it a couple of days to arrive and I guarantee we will get a very contrite phone call. I love her too you know."

Oliver, despite his respect for the hazards of the moor, travelled swiftly, on his quest to find Sandy, trusting to his luck that he would not step into a bog. His knowledge of tell-tale signs of wet soil hidden beneath surface growth enabled him to move relatively confidently, though not incautiously. The bright hot light of the day hurt his eyes and he told himself that that was why they were watering, though he knew this to be untrue. His memories of Ali and that night would remain with him for ever and he was helpless to control his silent tears whenever he dwelt on them.

He headed immediately for the areas he knew were marshy; there was no sign of her. He was sure that he would have seen some evidence had she fallen foul; perhaps the sling he had made her would be lying on the surface of the morass had she fallen in, or a plimsoll, lost in her struggle against the ever-hungry liquid peat. Taking heart from the lack of any of these things he extended his search northwards to where he had found her. As day moved into dusk the air cooled considerably: *could be rain tonight and no shelter, damn I could do with my parka.* His thoughts extended beyond his immediate personal comfort to the feisty girl. Oliver mused that her gutsy attitude and boyish mannerisms were a pleasant change from some of the girls he had known; not all feminine and simpering, but down to earth and not averse to a good cuss. In spite of himself, he smiled as he recalled his encounter with her at the base of the tor and her first words to him.

As always on the moor, night came swiftly once the sun had dipped behind the heather and good sense told him he could go no further that night in spite of the faint neon-like light from the sliver of moon and its accompanying firmament of stars. He sat and thought about Alistair. He had been a rather rebellious boy of thirteen, and had run away from home after an argument. It had been late in the evening when it was discovered he was not in his bedroom at the farm as the family thought, but had disappeared leaving a scrawled note.

"You all hate me, you'll be glad I've gone."

With their mother's anguished tears and self-berating cries tearing the silence of the night, they had searched for Alistair, calling him and begging him to come to them. They seemed to have searched for hours, Oliver's mother had been hysterical with guilt as it had been she who had sent Ali to his room, when he had sworn at her and been unforgivably offensive. Her usual common sense, phlegmatic approach to adversity with which she had always kept the family in check had vanished. Barely able to walk, anguish sapping the strength from her legs she had collapsed sobbing when suddenly in the distant dark they heard a faint call,

"Help me, Oliver, Dad, someone please!" They rushed in the direction of the voice, Oliver crying out to his parents to be careful. They were only just in time. Alistair was up to his chest in a bog when they found him and the bog did not want to give him up. Their father was prepared to sacrifice himself in order to save Ali.

"I'll go in and he can climb over me" he had insisted, and started to lower himself into the sucking black mess.

"Wait!" Oliver shouted "I've got the rope."

Oliver had been a fit young man of nineteen and he loved his wayward brother in a way only siblings can. "Let me go, I'm stronger than you Dad." And without waiting for a reply he had tied the rope around his waist, given the other end to his parents with a warning to stay away from the edge. Lying down, he eased himself towards Alistair, his weight spread over the surface and grabbing him by the arms he called to his parents to pull like hell! Oliver shuddered in the morning air at the thought of that girl sinking slowly out of sight, thick brown sludge gradually reaching her mouth and then her nose, and he could imagine the terror in her eyes as she sank beneath, vanishing as if she had never existed.

Ali had been dragged out of the bog, sobbing with relief and terror, but true to form attempting to be brave. They had said nothing of his note, pretending that they had not found it. When they had finally reached the farm and Ali was safely in a hot bath, Oliver put the note on the floor by Ali's bed; as if it had blown off in the breeze from the open fanlight. Ali could dispose of it quietly and pretend that he had gone on an adventure, albeit a foolhardy one and no more would be said.

Thankfully as the years had passed since then, he had managed to control his hormones, and on reaching his late teens his puberty madness and aggression receded, though he was prone to impatience and sudden outbursts. Ali was now studying criminal law at university. On his visits home though, he seldom ventured on to the moor. Oliver had invited him on one of his foraging trips, hoping to lay the ghost of Ali's experience, but he had declined, his excuse was that he had exams and needed to study. Oliver had known what his brother was meant to be studying and it wasn't The Stones, Bob Dylan or science fiction! In Oliver's opinion, Ali spent too much time in his room and he was getting rather tubby, his preference for biscuits and fizzy drinks over fruit and juices, along with lack of exercise didn't help.

Oliver glanced up at the sky as a shadow moved above him. A barn owl, silently, spectre-like glided over him; its white wings seeming too large for its small body. It dropped, and glowing in the lunar light, plunged into the heather. *At least you have some supper.* The spit roasted rabbits were probably a culinary treat for a fox by now, his hunger was becoming an over-riding sensation and he berated himself for not eating the meat or at least bringing it with him. The lemon-yellow sleepy eye of the moon was becoming hazy and the pin-pricks of light from the stars were disappearing as though someone had swept a paintbrush of blue black pigment across the sky. A sudden breeze caused his skin to goose-bump, the moon became a dirty brownish purple and very soon was no longer to be seen. The darkness was intense and with it came the storm. The heather gave forth a brief refreshing aroma of rain-watered foliage after a hot day, and then succumbed to its battering as the rain hissed down. Then Thor clashed his cymbals in the distance and a vivid fork of lightning momentarily turned the darkness to brilliance.

As Sandy groped her way to the tent opening, fumbling in the rain to find the ties, she heard again those cries that had so frightened her before. They were coming from inside the tent! It was the injured man, she was sure. He must have followed them. Hearing those wailing noises again terrified her, he sounded demented! She stumbled away from the tent and slipped on something. She reached down to feel what it was and felt fur and next to it a sticky mass of guts. Adrenaline suddenly surging through her, she edged away from the tent as quietly as she could, poised ready to run. And then, compounding all her fear, the sky lit up with electricity as the tent flap was opened from the inside. A face now confronted her. It was bizarrely and horribly small, flat and ape-like. Their gazes locked. Sandy screamed and so did he, but the sounds were swallowed up by the storm.

"STAY AWAY FROM ME!" he shouted scrabbling back inside the tent. Terrified, Sandy quickly backed away from it.

"HELP ME SOMEONE!" Sandy screamed into the night, knowing there was no-one to hear her.

"GO AWAY!" he shouted from inside the tent.

Sandy hurriedly retreated waiting, tensed and frightened, but prepared to fight for her life. Thunder crashed and flashed all around her, the tent luminously pale blue one moment and darkly ominous the next. This was not an irrational fear of the supernatural, for Sandy had, even as she had screamed, recognised that pale face. She wasn't scared that he was a demon, but that he was some kind of maniac – *my God, he must have eaten that rabbit... raw...*

He did not come out of the tent. Was he waiting for her to go away, or was he waiting for her to enter and then to attack her? She edged further away slipping once more on the guts, lightning flashed and thunder rolled and still the rain fell torrentially. Where the hell was the hiker? If only he would come back, he would know what to do. Scared to approach the tent but having no other place to go, Sandy moved quietly to the back of the tent, away from the opening, partly to try to find a little shelter and partly to remain out of sight should he come out. There she sat guardedly and waited. Clothing literally saturated, every movement squelched and she could feel water gathering around her waist, inside her plimsolls, inside her shirt and in her underwear. It cascaded down her face and into her eyes, stinging and blurring her vision. Would it never stop?

Gradually, the rain eased and the wind lessened, and finally, having spent its anger, the storm wrapped its clouds around itself, and quietly grumbling, moved away. All it left was the drip, drip, drip, of gravity relieving the sodden heather of its load.

From inside the tent, there came thrashing sound, the blue nylon walls bulged as if being kicked and punched. This was accompanied by a strangled crying, a breathless sound as of a creature in the throes of an agonizing death. He sounded demented. Just as quickly as the thrashing started, it stopped. She should get the hell out of here while she could, but where?

Cautiously she approached the tent and listened. She heard stertorous breathing from within the tent and relaxed a little, *He's asleep?* Quietly and with trepidation Sandy pulled back the flap a fraction and peeped inside. In the darkness she made him out, curled in on himself like a dog might lie. She opened the flap and crept in. The man jumped up with a cry of alarm and backed himself against the wall of the tent, releasing water from the sodden walls. "Leave me alone" he said, "I'll smack you if you come any closer." Sandy jumped with surprise; she had not been expecting this reaction. He crouched like a frightened animal, visibly shaking. He didn't make any move to attack her, but she was still wary; a cornered frightened animal could turn vicious, and so might he. Keeping the tent flap open and remaining close to it she tried to appear calmer than she felt. The storm had cleared completely and a wan moon lit the sky, its light thinning as dawn approached, but inside the tent all was murky grey.

"Do you remember me?" she asked quietly. She discerned a slight nod of his head in the gloom, "I was the person who ran into you." He looked so pathetic, huddled up and trembling.

"You didn't stop" he said pitifully.

"I'm really sorry, I didn't see you, I could have killed you! It was all my fault, Oh God how badly are you hurt? Is there anything I can do?" Sandy gabbled on, her guilt making her garrulous.

"My leg hurts." He replied, his voice breaking a little. And then, forcefully and angrily,

"And I'm not going back there!" His anger re-awoke Sandy's wariness of him. She remained where she was, on guard, saying nothing. He didn't enlarge on his comment, neither did he make any aggressive moves, so Sandy, keen to keep his anger at bay, changed tack and commented vaguely and casually, that it was useful he had found the tent and did he by any chance have anything to eat or drink as she was ravenous.

"I ate the rabbit" he said "it was cold and wet." *My God he did eat it raw!* He added "I think you burned it, is that why you left it?"

"N-o," she replied hesitantly, "I didn't cook it; I wasn't here." The speech patterns of the man were odd, Sandy thought, his way of stating facts was somehow childlike. She cautiously moved from the entrance on her hands and knees, and settled herself on the floor of the tent and emitted, as best she could, a feeling of calm and kindness.

"The storm has stopped now. Lucky you had the shelter of the tent; I'm wetter than a fish!" She gave a self-depreciating laugh and was thrilled to see a faint smile on his face.

"That's funny." He said and suddenly he was laughing like a little boy. Gently she said

"Do you mind if I stay in here for a while until the sun comes up and I can dry off a bit. Then we will find our way home."

"NO! You can't go, we can stay here, it's safe here." He paused and looked at her pleadingly, "Please? You're kind, I like you, do you like me too?" He trailed off into silence and turned away from her. She thought she heard him swallowing as though fighting off the desire to cry. She remained silent, a friendly presence which did not threaten.

It was the second full night on the moor and so far all that Sandy had eaten since she left home, where luckily she had had a huge roast dinner and pudding to follow, was half a packet of biscuits. She was starving and worried. She had a strange man in her care, for that was how she was beginning to see it, and nothing to eat or drink. Glancing around the tiny tent in the faint dawn light, her eye fell upon a heap of clothing; a waterproof, a parka and a jumble of other items. She shuffled over to look closer. Tucked under the clothing she saw a tin of baked beans, *I hate baked beans!* Her head dislodged more rain from the roof of the tent as she scrambled to her knees and rummaging deeper she found more beans, crackers and some cheese. *Wow, food!* Sandy even found some matches but abandoned any hope of lighting a fire; everything outside was waterlogged. She quietly busied herself pulling out a tin plate and mug and some camping cutlery which luckily, included a can opener. Finally when she had prepared the 'feast' she whispered close to his ear,

"Breakfast is served."

The smile that greeted her was as gentle and sweet as a cherub. As he smiled his face looked fuller and younger. He ate, rather clumsily with the bent fork and Sandy scooped out beans from the tin with a cracker. She watched him covertly, not wishing to alarm him. She still was a stranger to him and could inadvertently do something to change his mood. To her surprise and shock he suddenly lunged across the tent to her. She recoiled in fear. But, instead of attacking her as she had feared he placed himself clumsily beside her and rested his head on her shoulder.

"You are kind" he said "not like the others." Sandy looked down at his face with its contented smile and stroked his hair. She found herself wanting to say *there, there,* and stroking his head she was reminded of stroking her dog's head when she laid it in her lap. This poor man, what was he doing running across the moor, and why was he so frightened? Sandy wanted to know but was cautious of asking. Where did he live and why did he not want to go back?

She needed to treat him carefully and with kindness and sensitivity.

"Shall I look at your leg and see what the damage is?" She said quietly, looking down at his head with its lank dull brown hair as he contentedly lay against her. He didn't answer immediately but nestled in closer. Then he reached down and pulled his trouser leg up.

"It hurts there." He pointed at a huge bruise emanating from an angry looking graze. Relieved that no bones appeared to be broken, though she knew that this was highly unlikely; given that he was able to run as he had, Sandy inspected the leg.

"That looks very sore, but luckily I don't think anything is broken, thank goodness. You'll be right as rain soon, just try not to knock it." Sandy pulled the trouser leg gently back over the bruise; he winced as it rubbed the graze but didn't pull away. Although she still felt a tremendous guilt over his situation her conscience was eased a little, at least she hadn't done any permanent or serious damage. The question now was what to do with him?

Whilst Sandy sat nursing the strange man, Oliver, having been caught in the storm in his failed attempt to find her, was soaked and weary. He followed his compass and his memory and trudged disconsolately through the heather, its scent rising with his every step began to make him nauseous. Small flies clouded around his face and he breathed some up his nose. His eyes puffy and sore from mosquito bites on the lids felt like a boxers might after a thrashing in the ring. He truly wished he had not come out on the moor this late in the summer. The flies were always worse in the autumn, as were the mosquitoes. Apart from these immediate physical irritations he was depressed and angry. If that bloody girl hadn't appeared as if from outer space he would not be trudging, ill equipped through sodding wet heather. He had found her in the middle of nowhere and had not had time to question her as to what she was doing there; she was in such pain and extremely angry. All he had thought about was fixing her shoulder and he was pleased with himself that he had remembered the training he had had in the CCF. He knew that they were a long way from either his farm or a town as he had been trekking for a week now, surviving on his foraging, trapping and slingshot skills. He hadn't touched his iron rations of beans and cheese. At least they would be there when he got back. He had obtained drinking water from natural springs and, when necessary, trapping the rain and even the dew. He had given the girl his last bottle of water and his hikers' flask was empty. Last night's deluge had been wasted as he had left the tent in such a hurry that he hadn't rigged up his rain collecting gear. His attitude towards Sandy was rapidly changing from admiration for her courage to anger at her foolish recklessness. When or if, he found her he would not let her out of his sight until he got her to habitation. After that, he told himself, he would be glad to see the back of her and happily she would be someone else's problem. A voice in his head asked him why he didn't just give up on her and get on with his trek. After all she wasn't his responsibility and he didn't even know her name. Why should he care? Oliver knew that these were not his own thoughts, but those of a devil over his left shoulder. He trudged on.

Josie was having a good time in Mauritius, or so she told herself. But she had no one to share it with. The Mauritians were friendly and she had been invited to a barbeque on the beach that night. However, when she got there they were all locals and though they made her welcome, she felt out of it. The French she had learned in school had sort of come in useful though as they seemed to mix French and English in a language of their own. But she still found it difficult to understand them. However at one of the parties, she was introduced to a young American couple who were taking a year out from university to travel before 'real life' as they put it, took over. They took her scuba diving and water skiing, Josie had only ever snorkelled and suddenly she really did begin to enjoy herself. She no longer felt so alone and out of place. Josie was a dark haired girl, olive skinned and small boned. Having been sunning herself for a month before Sandy was due to arrive she had begun to tan a deep brown. Her blue-green eyes were the only thing which differentiated between her and a native Mauritian. She soon found that she was not being scrutinised as a tourist but she was being regarded as an inhabitant of this paradise island. Now she had some friends it would be great to stay here for maybe a year, find work of some sort. Maybe she should make some enquiries. Shame Sandy hadn't come she'd have loved it.

Oliver, deeply lost in his thoughts, was startled when one, two, and then a third partridge flew up from under his feet as he slid down from a rock into the gorse. He quickly reached into his pack for his sling shot, fumbled and dropped it. The partridge flew squawking into the distance. *Shit. I could have got that big fat one easily!* Looking down he realised that one had not got away, he had inadvertently stepped on its wing and it lay pitifully broken at his feet, flapping in its terror to get away. Sorry mate. He stooped down, grabbed it and swiftly rung its neck. Feeling a trifle happier and more like himself he strode on quietly whistling through his teeth.

As Oliver walked, his eyes alert for signs of the girl, he was also aware of the sun sinking lower. The days were getting noticeably shorter and glancing at his watch he saw that it was already 5pm. He quickened his pace, not wanting to spend another night with no shelter and he was still some way from his tent. In spite of the clear skies, the air had a heaviness which hinted that the thunder was merely lurking in the distance, waiting to ambush him as soon as darkness came. It was, therefore, a huge relief when, finally, he saw in the distance a little blue mound, crouching, as if hiding in the heather. Oliver felt ridiculously emotional as he approached the tent. He was 'home'. All was quiet, just as he had left it. There was no sign of the girl. *God knows where she is.* He had failed her and he didn't even know her name. All he could do now was to pack up the tent; head back home and inform the police. He could search the moor for weeks and never find her. If she hadn't perished in a bog by now, she could starve or die from exposure. She didn't appear to have any survival skills, or possessions and only thin clothing. A few yards off, Oliver flung his pack down in the heather and wandered a distance from the tent. He sat watching the last hazy light withdraw from the sky. As the sun settled into the clouds on the horizon, staining them with a peachy glow, Oliver heaved himself to his feet and walked a little way to where his water harvester was sited. *Better set this up.*

For the remainder of that day Sandy had sat quietly whilst her companion dozed against her. Uncomfortable in her still soaked clothing she shivered involuntarily as every movement pressed her cold clothing against her skin. She should really have taken it off and laid it out in the air to dry off a little. But with him there that was out of the question. The dwindling light filtered through the fabric of the tent and colour washed the face of the man as he lay against Sandy's bruised shoulder. He was awake but motionless. Sandy moved gently to ease the ache caused by the weight of his head. He sat away from her and seemed to be pondering a thought. And then, as if reaching a big decision,

"I didn't do it." He said adamantly. "They were cross with me and hurt me."

"What didn't you do?" Sandy asked, imagining a small misdemeanour he might have done as a child.

"I don't want to talk about it. You will be cross with me too." They sat quietly for a while, each in their own thoughts.

This is bloody crazy, what the hell am I going to do with him?

"I'm called Sandy, what's your name?"

"Mummy calls me Paulie." She remained silent, as did he. Sandy was very worried; she had made herself responsible for a man with Down syndrome. She recognised it now, the almond shape of his pale blue eyes, his tiny ears, the floppy way he moved, the childishness, the unselfconscious display of affection. One of the girls at school had a young brother who was Downs. Charlie was his name and he was sweet, he was happy and very loving. She had first met Charlie when she had gone with her school friend to see a play he was in at his special school. What struck Sandy the most was how happy all the pupils were. She remembered that he sounded vaguely effeminate and his speech had a sort of lisp. He had been so excited about the play and had hugged and kissed Sandy when she had told him how well he had acted. When she hugged him back she became his special friend for life!

What was making this man, Paulie so unhappy? He was obviously affectionate, his desire for a kind gesture and the way he snuggled up to her were all so like Charlie. But Charlie had been loved. Paulie was unhappy, frightened, and seemed without love.

We can't stay here like this. I don't know what to do! For some reason this man was scared of people, until she knew why, she wouldn't know what to do about him, she was stuck with him! *Oh Christ what else can possibly go wrong for me?* This ridiculous situation was quite unbelievable. Whoever would believe her story?

"Okay, I'll call you Paulie." He smiled and hugged her. Sandy, feeling a bit awkward gently extracted herself from his rather constricting arms and suggested,

"How about we pack up and go in the morning?"

"Where?" Paulie liked Sandy; she didn't look at him strangely like some people did.

"Somewhere safe."

"Oh yes, somewhere safe, we can hide and they won't ever find us!"

Sandy was slightly alarmed by his response.

"Who won't find us?" she asked, attempting to make her voice light.

"The mean ones. I didn't like it there, people were nasty." Paulie was beginning to get upset and very agitated. He fidgeted in a jumpy way and started chewing his nails, one after the other. Sandy thought perhaps she could gently extract from him more information and very carefully she said

"I won't take you where people are nasty, but who are these people, where are they?"

"I don't know!" wailed Paulie and he began to cry. He sobbed and Sandy quietly moved to sit beside him

"Look Paulie, we can stay here and when that the man who owns the tent comes back..."

"No, I don't want him to come back; he'll be nasty to me."

"I don't think he will, he helped me when I was hurt, he knows the moor and can help us."

Sandy wished with all her heart that her rescuer would return and help them all get home. She was sure that when Paulie met him he would realise that he was kind.

"I think we should sleep now and pack up in the morning and then perhaps we can get you back to your mummy."

To her surprise, with abject panic on his face, he lunged past her and scrabbled to open the tent, his flailing arms catching her across the face with an eye-watering blow. She could taste blood and her nose gave an enormous throb. Sandy cried out in pain. He was mindless to his having hurt her and was wrenching the tent open, sobbing

"I hate you, I hate you!"

Sandy, still holding her nose cried out

"No Paulie!"

Oliver, having set up his water harvester, was approaching the tent when he heard from inside sounds of pain and alarm. He heard her calling "No Paulie" and immediately rushed to her defence. As he opened the tent flap a man crashed out, bent over and charging like a rhino on his hands and knees, butting Oliver with his head and knocking him backwards.

Semi-winded, he sprawled on the ground. The man ran blindly off into the darkening moor, sobbing, *I hate her, I hate her!*

"Paulie wait!" shouted Sandy scrabbling out of the tent.

"What the hell is happening?" Oliver demanded, getting to his feet, "Who the devil is that, are you alright?"

"Yes, No oh I mean yes, but *he* isn't!" replied Sandy wildly running her hand through her damp hair.

"Will you please explain what is going on?"

"Oh Christ, thank God you've come back!" Sandy cried, seeming only now to be conscious of Oliver's arrival "We have to follow him!"

"Why?" Oliver demanded "Who is he? Has he hurt you?"

"No he hasn't hurt me, well he didn't mean to. *He's* hurt though!" she shouted.

"What the hell are you talking about?" Oliver was angry now. He grabbed Sandy and swung her round to face him. Oliver had spent the best part of a day and a night looking for Sandy; he was wet, tired and hungry.

"Just get this bloody straight" he said fiercely, "I am not chasing after some bloke you have picked up! And if you go after him you're on your own. Get it?"

"But you don't understand, he's vulnerable, he's not normal..."

"What do you mean, not normal? He seemed pretty normal to me, two legs two arms a head and a body in between!" Oliver was really losing his patience with Sandy. "You expect me, after finding you cosily tucked up with some bloke in *MY* tent, to go looking for him in the dark?!" Oliver felt his fingers dig into her arm and her struggle roughly away.

"That bloody hurt, how dare you!"

"There you were all snug and intimate while I'm out all bloody night looking for you, you stupid girl. Do you take me for a fool?"

Sandy felt tears threatening at the injustice of what Oliver was saying and his anger made it difficult for her to express herself.

"I *was* lost, I was stupid to go off alone I realise that now." She stammered, "But it's complicated, you don't understand."

"No I damn well don't!" Oliver spat the words at her, his eyes hard in the grey dusk light.

"We've wasted so much time with you shouting at me he could be anywhere by now!" Sandy was beginning to return Oliver's anger. "Look, we have to go after him, he's hurt, you callous bastard, I will explain later!" Oliver was completely confused and extremely angry.

"NO," he shouted. "I am not chasing after yet another bloody idiot!" Spittle sprayed from his mouth. He was flushed, with his ginger hair and freckles and an image of a pelican crossing beacon flashed into Sandy's mind, incongruously, she nearly laughed as the thought flitted very quickly out again. Seeing the hint of mockery on her face, Oliver reined in his ranting and attempting to regain some dignity he reasoned,

"We can't look for him now, let me at least have something to eat or I shall die from hunger. You can explain then." Oliver didn't wait for an answer but crawled into the tent only to come storming out again;

"You've eaten my bloody beans and cheese!" The guts and skin from the rabbits he had cooked caught his eye; the rabbits on the spit were gone. He turned furiously to Sandy

"Why the hell did I worry about you, you ate the rabbits *both of them* and then gorged on my iron rations! Your boyfriend must have given you some appetite!"

"Oh God, I'm so sorry." Sandy felt dreadful that she had raided his store; but she had been ravenous.

"I did eat the beans and cheese but I didn't eat the rabbits, Paulie had eaten them when I got here." Everything she said seemed to make things worse.

"*Paulie?!*" Oliver sneered. "How sweet. I trust he enjoyed them!"

"Actually he said they were a bit burnt." Sandy bit back her words but it was too late. Oliver couldn't believe what he had just heard; this bloke had had the cheek to eat *his* food and then to criticize it! What had become of his meditative trekking holiday? His peace and solitude completely destroyed and the whole situation was actually getting worse! He sat down in the heather, put his head in his hands and through his gritted teeth he said

"This has gone far enough. Firstly I need to know how you got here and why. Then you owe it me to explain about this 'Paulie'."

"You don't get it do you? You're typically male tunnel-visioned!" Sandy was sick of being in the wrong and apologising for things which had been out of her control. Oliver bristled at the insult but retained his cold manner,

"Then," he continued "I will decide whether to leave you here to find your precious Paulie on your own, or I will look after you until I find a way of off-loading you into civilization."

"I *will* explain and then you can bloody well judge me and piss off and leave me if you want!" Sandy flung back at him. Oliver was un-moved,

"I am going to attempt to light a fire and cook and eat this bird." He held up the sorry looking and pitifully small partridge by its feet then flung it angrily to the ground and said "While I eat *my* meal you can begin your explanation. With that he rummaged around and thankfully found a small amount of dryish bracken and heather from the more sheltered area behind the tent, he then tore, reluctantly, precious pages from his notebook. Finally he managed to produce a flame which he coaxed to catch the dry peat block from his store in the tent.

"Keep that fire going while I deal with this bird." He abruptly instructed Sandy. As he plucked and gutted the bird, Sandy fed the fire and was glad of its warmth and light. Still shivering in her soaked clothing she moved as close as she could until steam began to rise from her jeans, then, pulling off her plimsolls she placed them near the fire. Struggling out of her clinging jacket and sweatshirt she wrung the water from them, very nearly quenching the flames. Quickly, dropping to her knees she blew hard on the smouldering peat and thankfully it sprung back to life. Red faced and embarrassed she glanced at Oliver, the flickering orange glow reflected off his face as he worked, studiously ignoring her. Gone was that boyish charm. His face was set and hard.

What a bloody mess, Sandy watched him as he spitted the bird and put it over the glowing peat fire, she wanted to say sorry about the beans and the cheese and explain about Paulie. But he looked so stern that she didn't know where to start, she also thought that at that moment she hated him. How could she start to explain the bizarre sequence of events to this heartless man, especially with so much anger and dislike between them? She remained mulishly silent.

Sandy thought back through the events of the last few days:

I should be on a beach on the equator, not on this bloody moor. What luck, she thought, to start out full of excitement (and a lot of apprehension about her first flight) and to end up here with this unpleasant man. She had tried to help Paulie after he had stupidly run in front of her car, guilty about hitting him due to her lack of attention, but it had been his fault hadn't it?

She started, brought out of her thoughts, when Oliver handed her a cooked leg of partridge. She looked up at him standing over her.

"It's against all my instincts to even think of sharing this with you, but *I* was brought up by people with respect for others!" Water still dripping from his hair, Oliver took off his sweater, wrung the worst of the water from it and draped it over his backpack near the fire, he then removed his boots and socks and, shivering slightly he sat opposite her in the warmth of the fire. Taking a huge bite from his meat, fat dribbling over his large hands he sighed,

"Okay I think it's time we introduced ourselves, I'm Oliver, who are you?" And as they ate the meagre repast she recounted everything that had befallen her. Sandy told him proudly how she had worked on a milk round after finishing art college, to save money for her trip to Mauritius and how excited she had been. Oliver grunted his approval.

"That's tough; getting up at a God awful hour."

"I know, but I really enjoyed it. I was on my own and I had a country round." She shrugged as she nibbled the last bit of meat from the bone. "I don't know if I'd have liked it in the winter though."

"That's true, at least the dawn comes early in the summer, the thought of getting up in freezing cold dark delivering ice cold bottles doesn't appeal." Oliver had spent many freezing nights and days in the open, not enjoying them especially; it was more a test of himself, than a pleasant outing. He fed more peat on the fire and they shuffled in closer to the warmth.

Sandy had left a tearful mother and a beaming father waving to her as far as she could see them. Her night drive to catch the overnight train had been argued against by her mother

"We'll take you or pay for a taxi" she had insisted,

"Don't be ridiculous, it'll cost a fortune, I can leave the car in the free car park at the station." Sandy hugged her mother tight, breathing in the faint smell of cooking which hung in her hair and reached up for her father's embrace, he hugged her against his slightly tubby stomach which she prodded playfully, "I'll be okay and it'll be there for my drive home." And off she went.

The air was cooling now and a chilly breeze clapped the loose tent flap making them both jump. Sandy told Oliver how she had been happily driving and listening to music when Paulie had rushed into the road.

"I didn't see him until it was too late, I tried to catch up with him, I could see he was hurt but he just ran away. Then there were these dreadful noises when the mist came down they hardly sounded human." Sandy shivered involuntarily as she recalled the panic she had felt.

"What I mean is: I can't imagine what animal would have made a noise like it. Anyway," she shook herself mentally, "I heard words so it obviously wasn't an animal." She paused as she sensed that Oliver was thinking her a bit stupid. His reply, laden with sarcasm confirmed this,

"No, I admit I have heard wild animals on the moor making strange noises but can't say I've had any conversations with them."

"Okay. So I'm talking rubbish!" she answered with some pique. "But you weren't there, it was bloody creepy. After the initial shock I knew it had to be Paulie; after all he can't have been far away. It was a sort of keening, like a child crying but mixed up with a man's voice." She glanced at Oliver to see if he was still mocking her. He still had that patronising smile on his face making her feel stupid and feminine. She stood up and looked down at him, hoping her elevated position would make her feel less pathetic.

"Sit down; you're giving me a pain in the neck." Oliver was aware of the double entendre and continued to grin at her discomfort. Sandy flounced down a little further away from Oliver, her face flushed and angry, taking a moment, she continued

"I tried to find my way back to the car, until the mist came down I knew exactly where it was." Sandy thumped her fists on her knees in retrospective frustration, "But, what with the fright, I only turned the once when it startled me and that was enough to get myself completely lost." She knew she wasn't expressing herself very well; she was rushing through it and tripping over her words. "When I found the tor after the fog had gone, I was sure I would be able to get an idea of where I was... but I slipped." He smiled wryly and said

"And then to my misfortune and your luck, I found you!"

"Okay drop the sarcasm. I was grateful for your help but I had been scared out of my wits." It all seemed so melodramatic now. There had been no monster, no supernatural being just a poor man crying in the dark.

"I can't believe it. When you found me, for a second I assumed you were the man who I'd been chasing, it didn't cross my mind that there would be someone else in the middle of nowhere." She shook her head at the memory of her fleeting confusion. "You must think I'm mental!"

"No, I don't" said Oliver becoming more serious, "You were in a great deal of pain, alone and frightened," he paused,

"I haven't imagined monsters when I've been on the moor, but I *have* been scared, it happens to all of us. Anyway, you certainly weren't too scared of me; I seem to remember being called a fucking idiot!"

"Put it down to delirium." Sandy laughed. Oliver smiled at her, it was the first time he had seen her laugh and kindness was beginning to replace the hard look in his eyes. After all, she was well out of her depth here in the middle of nowhere and credit to her, she had been brave. The knife-laden atmosphere between them started to soften. They talked into the night about things that they had done in their lives. Oliver told her about Alistair and the terrible night when they thought he was lost.

"I stayed calm on the outside for my parents' sake, but my insides were jelly. Ali was going through his teenage angst. I can't remember if I was as bad, I probably was, but life with Ali at the time was a mine-field. He would lose his rag over any authority and storm off." He put his arm gently and protectively round her shoulder,

"What a bloody awful mess!" His anger had subsided after hearing Sandy's story and he began to feel compassion for her. However, his attitude regarding Paulie's safety was more ambivalent. Sandy had a feeling that he was not wholly convinced that Paulie was harmless and moreover, he showed a distinct reluctance to attempt to find him.

"He knew what he was doing; he must have known where he wanted to go."

"I don't know if he did." Sandy was thoughtful, "He seemed confused and scared, and as I told you, he has Downs. I'm sure he has Down's, so he might not think like you and me."

"But in spite of that you don't know him, you have no idea what sort of person he is, he could be a murderer or sex maniac for all you know," continued Oliver. "And do you think we could stop calling him Paulie? Sandy grinned,

"Yes, I agree — Paul." Continuing, "If he was a sex maniac don't you think he would have attacked me by now, or killed me if he was a murderer? He had plenty of opportunity. He's just a guy with a problem, why do you assume the worst?"

"But why do you want to go after him? Let him go and let's get you home."

"Because I think he is harmless and needs help."

Sandy was sure that Paul was a Down syndrome sufferer and that his adult body contained the innocent mind of a child. To her, Oliver seemed hard and unfeeling and she didn't like the way he just discounted Paul and the danger he could be in.

"It's okay for you, you're normal, young and fit, we both are. Paul may be an adult but he doesn't necessarily reason like one! He was terrified of something, I think it was something I said, and I don't know what."

"Was that why he ran off?"

"Yes at one moment he was calm and sort of loving," then seeing Oliver's expression she added "as a child might be, and then the next he was crying and shouting that he hated me."

"Well, he's obviously unbalanced. These mentally disabled people are unpredictable; we don't know how to find him because we have no idea where he is trying to go. And if we did, how would he behave? He could be violent."

"I'm sure he isn't violent!" Sandy reposted. "He needs help."

"That's why the best thing we can do for Paul is to get to civilization and alert the rescue services and let them find him. After all, they have helicopters and sniffer dogs. All we've got are our eyes."

It was pointless arguing with Oliver, Sandy was still not convinced and becoming a little annoyed but she felt impotent. She began to smoulder silently,

If Paul was a girl, he'd look for her! Bloody men!

They sat silently for some long time in the remaining warmth of the fire, watching its embers slowly die. Oliver dampened them and scuffed over the ashes to make sure they were completely dead and, getting to his feet he said

"We should get some sleep and make a move in the morning."

Sandy sighed

"Okay."

"You can have the bed-roll." Sandy began to protest "No arguing" continued Oliver, "I'm used to roughing it, come on, bed." Sandy crawled over to the bed and lay down listening to Oliver's steady breathing as he slept. *He has already wiped Paul from his mind. But I haven't.*

CHAPTER 4

THE MORNING WAS fine, Sandy moody, Oliver cheerful. Confirming Sandy's thoughts of the night before he announced

"Right, let's pack up and head for home."

"And what about Paul?" she demanded.

"There is no chance of us finding him." Oliver said with exasperation. "We don't know which direction he went in and it's pointless looking." In spite of her concern for Paul's safety, Sandy knew that Oliver was right. The odds of finding someone on the moor were slim, especially if they didn't want to be found but she still was reluctant to give in

"But I want to help him; it's my fault he's here."

"You tried and look where it left you? Let him go, someone will find him." He didn't give voice to the thought: *maybe.* Reluctantly, Sandy donned her still damp sweatshirt and jacket and with difficulty pulled on her squelchy plimsolls, breaking the blister on her heel which had blown up to the size of a shilling.

"Hang on; put a plaster on that or it'll be agony." Oliver dug into his pack and extracted a first aid kit, from which he took some lint and a strip of plaster. "Pad it with the lint to take the pressure off. If it starts to rub again shout and we can re-dress it."

"Thanks, you're very well equipped aren't you?"

"I like to think so!" Oliver burst out laughing.

"Men! That's all you think of."

They set off, following Oliver's compass, heading south.

He reckoned it would take two, possibly three days to reach

habitation, travelling at a sustainable pace and taking time to forage and hunt for food. Sandy trudged along beside him, in a quiet and pensive mood. Oliver, a lover of solitude, would have appreciated the lack of someone chattering inanely as they travelled, had it not been an uncomfortable silence. He knew that she was, although futilely, looking out for any sign of Paul and it put him on edge.

Why can't she just leave it be!

When they were making camp for the first night Sandy had suddenly shouted

"There he is!" Oliver had spun round, ready to fight off an attack or something. "Look, over there!" cried Sandy. He looked but could see no-one. Then, gazing into the low sun he saw a shape and laughed.

"That's a rock."

"Are you sure? I saw it move!"

"Positive, or are we seeing trolls now?!" Sandy turned on him angrily

"Don't be such a shit!"

"It's 'Bower-man's Nose'; a rock formation. Some of the rocks can look like a person from a distance." Oliver explained. Then seeing the scowl on Sandy's face, "I'm sorry I didn't mean to mock you I was only joking." Sandy accepted the apology but did not acknowledge it. She did not like the way he laughed at her concern for Paul, or being made to feel ignorant. She preferred to be cognisant of her situation and disliked her dependence on someone who, she felt, had no compassion for someone such as Paul. She turned away and, muttering to herself she continued attempting to light a cook-fire. Another thing she was not good at. My God she hated this.

"I am bloody good at lots of things which you are probably rubbish at!" she threw at Oliver who was smiling at her attempts.

Patronising git.

"I'm sure you are, but at the moment I'm the only one who can get you home so just hack it will you!"

"Okay Mr. Smug. But there may come a time when you need what I have to offer, just remember that."

"I will look forward to that!" Oliver gave her a salacious wink, then, seeing her glare, followed with "Sorry but that sort of comment left you wide open!" The innuendos were just innuendos, they both knew that but Sandy bristled and Oliver blushed.

"Sorry, sorry," he held his hands up,

"Hmm, right, that's cleared up; so, what are we eating tonight?" Sandy asked ungraciously.

"Wild mushrooms so far, keep the fire going while I go hunting before it gets dark." Oliver gathered his sling shot and went to the back of the tent and after a bit of scrabbling he held, to Sandy's surprise, a shotgun.

"Where did you keep that hidden?" she asked in alarm.

"Under the tent, tucked right at the back, just for emergencies, like now, when we have nothing to eat and it's getting late, I'm off, back soon."

"Will it still work after all that rain?" Resisting the urge to laugh he replied,

"A waterproof case does wonders!" He'd done it again; there was no missing the mockery in his voice.

"Of course; how stupid of me." Sandy snapped turning away from his grinning face. "You'd better get going then!"

Oliver was right, the light was beginning to fade and they needed to eat something, Sandy's stomach was sore with hunger. She watched him silhouetted against the low sun as he strode confidently away, sling shot stuffed in his pocket and the gun, broken for safety, in his hand.

If I had to be stranded with anyone, Sandy thought grudgingly, I suppose I'm lucky it's someone so competent even if he is an arsehole.

She had to admit to an unwilling respect for Oliver, he was a survivor and, even if she didn't like other aspects of his, as she saw it, chauvinistic character, in fact didn't like him at all, at least she knew he would keep her safe and would, in time, see her home. Although they had walked at a sensible pace throughout the day, it hadn't been a comfortable, leisurely stroll. There were no footpaths as such, merely animal made tracks or naturally formed areas where the springy marsh grass was quite pleasant to walk on. Sandy was tired and her shoulder ached. Being of small build and wearing inadequate shoes, she had found the going tough, especially with the blister breaking through the plaster and soaking her plimsoll with blood. It was strange, when walking without fear she had become more tired than when she had been running scared. It must be a delayed reaction, now that danger had passed. Her adrenaline, having returned to its normal level was allowing her body to register its weariness. Glad for the rest she sat and waited, nursing her arm across her knees.

Oliver moved quietly across the moor, the tor on the horizon was too far to go tonight, but he knew there would be grouse feeding in the scrub around its base. *Tomorrow.* He couldn't decide whether he liked Sandy or not. She was feisty, arrogant and damn rude, but, he acknowledged, an attractive girl, well, not pretty, far from it, with her hair much shorter than Oliver liked on a girl and her very slight boss-eye. But at least she had some character and given more amenable circumstances he imagined she would be good company. He recognised the fact that she had been landed in a dilemma not completely of her own making. Oliver could understand her huge disappointment at missing her flight and her consequent bad temper. But he couldn't understand her concern for the bloody man who had caused this to happen. If it had been him he would have happily throttled the guy! This Paul, where had he come from, what was he about? She seemed sure he was harmless, suffering from Downs or something, but was he harmless? It didn't add up. No sane person runs heedlessly in front of the only car on the road unless he's running from something. If he is sane, what was he running from? If he wasn't 'all there' does that automatically make him harmless?

Oliver turned it over and over whilst keeping a keen eye out for prey and also watching the dusk creeping like a ghost across the flat landscape.

Well he's gone God knows where and good riddance. He closed his mind on Paul and, seeing a rabbit darting for its burrow he sighted and shot. Bull's eye!

A thin grey mist was dampening the ground by the time he returned to the camp. To his pleasure and, he added to himself, surprise, Sandy had a good hot cook-fire glowing.

"Great fire" he complimented her, she gave him a withering look.

"I'm starving" was all she said.

Paul lay shivering in the lee of the tor; the ground was wet with mist. He was hungry, lost and scared. The girl he had liked and trusted had turned on him. She was going to take him back. He had told her he wasn't going back there but she and that man were going to give him back to those nasty people. It wasn't fair. He had called out for Jimmy but he didn't come. He was glad Jimmy hadn't come because he had said horrid things to him and made him scared, but he wanted someone. Paul closed his eyes and wept. Dankness seeped into his clothes and despair into his mind. Exhausted, he slept.

Oliver and Sandy ate the greasy rabbit, slightly undercooked this time Sandy noticed and smiled to herself, and mushrooms. Surprisingly, they felt satiated and content. Sandy thanked Oliver for the food, quite politely. He nodded in acknowledgement. They watched the moon shrug its way out of the cloud, the heath was illuminated through the ground mist, it was quite beautiful. Oliver was beginning to relax when Sandy said

"I do hope Paul is alright." Oliver's hackles momentarily rose and he bit back his rejoinder of "*I don't bloody care*" saying instead

"I'm sure he is. Rest assured, we'll send out a rescue party as soon as we can." It was odd, Oliver felt sort of possessive over Sandy, or was it just protective, or jealous? She seemed to really care about this weirdo and here he was; a normal, dependable, fit guy and she couldn't care less about him. It wasn't that he fancied her or anything but why did she care more for Paul than she did for him? *Women! I put her shoulder back, tore up my favourite T-shirt for her, I fed her, I am going to get her home, I gave her my bed and she barely gives me a second glance. Paul, Paul, Paul! Damn him to hell!*

Oliver slapped himself mentally telling himself to get a grip.

"Let's sleep and start early." They slept as they had the night before, Sandy on the camp bed and Oliver on the ground.

Sandy flatly wished Oliver a goodnight and silently, *keep safe* to Paul.

Sandy took a while to fall asleep, she felt that she needed to hear Oliver's steady breathing of sleep before she could think. Apart from Paul, for whom she felt a sort of responsibility, though why she wasn't sure, she was desperately concerned about her parents. It had been three, four or was it five days, she had lost count, since she should have let them know she was safe. They must be going mad with worry. She had promised them, especially her mother, that she wouldn't leave them wondering, as she had done in the past. She was more mature now and *did* consider other people's feelings. Dad would be okay; he was laid back, but mum, she would have started worrying as soon as the car was out of sight. She distrusted fate, expecting the worst to happen as had so often happened before. Hopefully all they were thinking was that Sandy was a selfish inconsiderate cow. However, if Josie had got word to them that she hadn't arrived; God knows what hell they must be going through! *Mum, I'm sorry. I'm coming home as quickly as I can.*

With this thought she rose the next day and to Oliver's surprise was anxious to pack up the tent and get going.

"Take me home please." Was all she said.

"Yes Ma'am." He cheerfully replied, wondering what had caused this sudden turn-about, touched his hand in salute to an imaginary cap and set to dismantling the tent.

CHAPTER 5

THE MORNING BROUGHT no comfort to Paul as he sat huddled in misery on the damp ground. He hugged himself and cried. He sobbed and shook until he was exhausted. He had no idea where he was or what he was going to do.

"Mummy" he cried, over and over, but no mummy came as he knew she wouldn't. Should he try to find Jimmy? But Jimmy had been cruel to him, he had said horrible things to Paul and at one point that first night on the moor he had thought Jimmy was going to kill him. That was what had made him run away after Sandy had hit him with her car. He didn't understand, Jimmy asked him to go with him and he had promised to look after him. Jimmy had known how unhappy Paul had been and he had seemed kind. But, so had that girl Sandy, she had seemed kind as well, but both of them had betrayed him. In his experience, people were either kind, not kind or they just ignored him, oh, yes, sometimes they laughed at him.

Paul had been so happy living with his mummy, just the two of them. She loved him and cuddled him. His thoughts of his mother brought the tears to the surface again and he quietly wept. As he sat miserably thinking of what had happened to him over the last month, trying to make sense of it all he realised that he was no longer cold and had stopped shivering. His raincoat which was now torn and stained, gave off a faint smell of sun-drying grass cuttings. He took it off, carefully spread it over a rock to continue drying, and leaned back soaking up the early autumn sun. Birds sang high up in the herring-bone patterned clouds. He listened to them wistfully, remembering summer days at home as a small boy when he and his mummy would lie flat on their backs on the little lawn at the back of their house and watch the clouds form shapes in the sky. They saw all sorts of things, from dragons to trains, faces and animals, it was endless fun.

Suddenly, a vicious pain in his chest jolted him back to reality and he belched, then retched and bile rose in his gullet. He had not eaten anything since 'breakfast' which Sandy had found in the tent. He had drunk nothing for a long time and his mouth felt vile. Mummy had always insisted that he cleaned his teeth after eating his breakfast but he hadn't cleaned them for days, not since he and Jimmy had run away. Paul's gaze took in the landscape around him, there was scrub and gorse and the occasional wind stunted small tree. His eye fell on some brambles and a sparkle of raindrop in the sunshine beckoned him. The brambles were covered in fat blackberries, rain-washed and ripe. Jumping to his feet and after a spell of hunger and thirst induced dizziness; he steadied himself and lumbered over to the fruit. They were juicy and sweet. As he stuffed handfuls into his mouth, the black juice trickling down his chin, he became calmer and regained some small vestige of optimism. He would try to find the girl. She *had* been kind; she had comforted him hadn't she? Jimmy obviously wasn't going to look after him like he had promised in fact Paul was now quite certain that Jimmy hadn't really liked him at all or he wouldn't have said those horrible things about his mummy. Paul was really scared, he was alone and lost and the blackberries though temporarily assuaging his hunger and thirst, had increased the sore bile in his stomach. He needed someone and that someone had to be Sandy. He didn't want to consider the big ginger man; all he wanted was to have someone to keep him safe. With this in mind, Paul started to walk, repeating over and over to himself, 'Sandy, Sandy, Sandy,' as if this would somehow help him to find her. His raincoat lay drying draped over the rock.

His passage was noted and quietly and stealthily, he was followed. In the distance the faint chop, chop, chop of helicopter blades merged with the humming of bees gathering their last harvest of heather nectar before winter.

Oliver and Sandy chatted amicably as they walked, he was glad to have a purpose and she was anxious to get home and relieve her parents' anxiety. Oliver still wondered what had changed Sandy's attitude but decided to stay mum for fear of her reverting to her former mood. Although Sandy was increasingly eager to get home, her thoughts still strayed to Paul and she hoped that the rescue services would be in time to find him safe.

"Tell me about yourself," said Sandy after a while, "what do you do for a job?"

"Well, actually I'm not working at the moment," Oliver replied ruefully "I chucked in my job at the end of the summer term. I was teaching biology at a secondary school in Exeter." He didn't continue so Sandy prompted him

"Why did you leave?" He glanced at her and she was sure he was blushing; he mumbled something about another calling and abruptly changed the subject.

"It's about time you learned to forage; I'm hungry for lunch aren't you?"

"Yes, a bit peckish, but," and she hesitated before her curiosity made her prompt him again, "what sort of calling, religious? Have you had a vision?!" She was mildly mocking him and he found surprisingly that it didn't offend him. He had been mocked by Alistair and one or two of his more macho friends with whom he had experienced survival courses in the youth cadets. He had responded angrily to the scathing comments they had made and resented being called a wimp and a pansy. However, he had a feeling that Sandy would perhaps understand, being an artist.

"I quit teaching because I wanted to write poetry and the stresses of the teaching just stifled my creativity." He laughed derisively at himself and pulled at the ginger curls at the back of his neck. "I come out on the moor for peace and solitude." He gave an enormous laugh, "What a joke!" They looked at each other and an infectious laughter took hold of them both.

"Right," Oliver gasped as he caught his breath, he couldn't remember when he had last laughed himself helpless, it felt good after all the angst of late, "lunch. Are you willing to learn survival?"

"It would have been useful earlier, but yes, teacher sir, learn me."

"Grammar!" laughed Oliver. "Firstly the easiest survival foods are berries, nuts and fungi. The edible nuts are generally well known to most people as are the commonest berries such as blackberries, elderberries, wild strawberries etcetera. and most people know not to eat yew berries."

"Yawn!" Sandy waved her hand in front of her mouth, "Boring. I'm hungry, what else can one eat, especially in this sort of place?"

"Well, I was coming to fungi, they are the most nutritious are also potentially the most deadly."

"Can't think why you gave up teaching, you almost look as though you are standing in front of a blackboard in mortar and gown. I am in thrall!"

"Tell you what, we'll just forage as I'm hungry and you can learn hands-on as it were."

"Okay, lead on." Sandy watched Oliver as he immediately picked some mushrooms hiding in a clump of grass. He separated one from the others, "Why did you do that?" she asked, "Was it too small?"

"No, it's deadly poisonous," he replied, "look, see this yellow tinge, that's the thing to look out for, also it smells different, sniff." Sandy reluctantly sniffed the mushroom,

"Yes, It smells sort of..." she searched for a word, "yucky, sweet."

"Well that's as good a description as any; yucky is what you would feel if you ate it. You would have sickness and diarrhoea and then you'd start to feel better.

"Well that's not so bad..." Sandy started to say but Oliver cut her short,

"Then it would come back, destroying your organs until you died. It's called the Death Cap and has no antidote." Oliver plucked the rest of the mushrooms saying "Can you tell if any of the others are the same, just look at them first, don't smell them."

Sandy studied them and was amazed at how alike to a mushroom they were but there were quite obvious differences when you looked for them. For a start, they looked vaguely wet but were in fact quite dry, there was a ruff of white underneath the crown and the gills underneath were much paler than an edible mushroom.

"They are all Death Caps!" she exclaimed "But if you hadn't told me I could quite easily have thought they were okay." She shuddered and her mind briefly flicked back to Paul, he wouldn't know the difference, but then, he probably wouldn't think to look for mushrooms as he had no means to cook them.

"It's quite unusual to find them in this sort of terrain," mused Oliver, "they mostly grow in woodland under deciduous trees." He brushed his hands in a disgusted sort of way down his trousers, "I need to wash this off." He knelt at the near-by pool and scrubbed his freckled hands in the water and rubbed them with coarse grass. Sniffing his hands he said "That seems to have got rid of the smell. Come on let's move on and look for something edible."

Soon they came to some blackberry bushes and ate their fill but their stomachs cried out for something more substantial. Oliver decided that they needed meat and he also desired a vegetable of some sort. He spotted a tall plant with curled reddish leaves,

"Ah, curled dock, brilliant. You can eat the stalk cooked or raw, leaves as well but they need boiling several times to get rid of the bitterness."

"We'll give the leaves a miss then shall we?" Sandy looked sceptically at the plant, it didn't look edible but what did she know? Oliver pulled up the dock and shook off the dirt,

"What about that plant, it looks like a carrot?"

"Could be arrowroot but it could also be hemlock. Go carefully with foliage like that." Oliver warned her.

"This dock stalk will go nicely with a bit of rabbit or partridge and some tasty mushrooms." He shot a glance at Sandy's face with its 'I don't fancy mushrooms' expression, her nose was wrinkled up with a look of extreme distaste, he grinned at her, "Trust me I'm a biologist." He laughed.

The route Oliver had planned took them through some rocky terrain, peat coloured pools in the hollows seethed with mosquitoes which took a delight in their fresh blood on the menu. Water boatmen skimmed across the surface of the water and the occasional frog croaked in the scant shelter of the rocks. Further on they came upon a clear stream running through the rocks. Oliver filled his flask, offering Sandy a mouthful, he asked her to describe the taste.

"Well, it's beautifully cold which is great but it has a slight tang to it as well, why's that?"

"It's from a natural spring. We're not used to spring water at home; it's all been treated and recycled. Delicious isn't it?"

"Yes, it is; no faint smell of chlorine and its coldness is really refreshing. Look, there's some watercress, maybe that's giving it the tang!" Sandy was thrilled to have seen a plant she recognised. Oliver knelt at the edge of the shallow stream and putting one hand on the bottom he reached out and picked a handful of cress.

"Brilliant. Now all we need is some meat." As they followed the stream along the springy sun soaked verge Oliver warned her

"Watch out for adders; this is perfect for them, they warm up in the sun and if you're bitten by one it can be fatal."

"Great! You go in front with your big boots. Or you could piggy-back me!" she said, laughing.

"Well, it wouldn't be the first time!" Oliver smiled. "My back still aches. You may be small but after a mile or so you start to weigh a ton." The stream got wider as they followed its course and the verges more foliated.

"Bullrushes!" Exclaimed Oliver

"I beg your pardon, was that an expletive or a sneeze?"

"Bullrushes — food." Oliver laughed. "The rhizomes, the stalk, the leaves and earlier in the year, the flower can all be eaten boiled or even raw." He pulled a few up by the roots and strapped them across his backpack. "Now, somewhere to camp and then food."

As they walked, Oliver told Sandy about other edible wild plants and flowers and how there were some really delicious fungi, quite often the ones which looked the most disgusting. His descriptions of them and which parts were the best and which should be cooked, soon became too much for her to take in.

"Stop! My brain is exploding with information. One plant at a time please!"

As it was the middle of the day, rabbits were not in abundance, as they tended to feed at dawn and dusk. Sandy wasn't displeased at this as rabbit had been their last meal and she wasn't that fond of the taste. She recalled visiting her grandmother one day when she was cooking rabbit stew and remembered how revolting it had smelt; nearly as bad a smell as that of boiled tripe, which had been another of her grandparents' favourites. Being country people they knew how to live cheaply and healthily. However, the sight alone of a piece of tripe, looking like a bit of rubber matting was enough to make Sandy heave, she could never bring herself to try a taste. Tongue had been another meat which squeamishly Sandy had refused to try. They used to serve it up at the primary school with beetroot and mashed potatoes. The beetroot would bleed into the potato and the tongue would become a ghastly purple red, as though still alive. She could never understand why such an unappetising combination of foods was given to children under ten. Half of the class regularly left the meal untouched and consequently were refused pudding. And compounding this, there was only tea to look forward to at home as, having cooked dinner provided at school, it was assumed that she would not be hungry. On these days Sandy would use some of her pocket money and buy a tuppeny-ha'penny cream bun from the little shop on her way home, getting icing sugar powder all down her dress.

"You'll get fat if you keep buying those buns!" her mother would warn her. She thought lovingly of her mother and an urgency to get home made her fidgety.

"Come on" she cried, "we can carry on heading for home and we will be sure to find a bird of some sort you can shoot."

"Okay, whatever you want but it's important to keep your strength up. I would like to head off track a little towards those rocks, there's quite a lot of scrub there and that's where we'll find grouse if we're lucky."

"That's a sky-lark isn't it?" Sandy squinted up at the small bird singing high above them, "Daddy used to take me out on nature walks when I was small, he knew all the birds and their songs."

"Yes, it's a skylark, wonderful little birds aren't they," Oliver stopped and listened to the song, "it's amazing how such a small creature can make such a loud sound."

"Daddy collected birds' eggs when he was a boy. I know it's frowned on these days but he had a super collection." Sandy's father had made a box and lined it with saw-dust, and all the birds' eggs were neatly and safely displayed. He had shown Sandy how to blow eggs and how to identify the birds which had laid them. Sandy remembered the first time he had shown her a wren's nest; a perfectly made round house covered with moss and a tiny opening for a door. It was thrilling, as inside the nest they could hear the chicks cheeping for food. The mother had been perched on a branch, a grub in her mouth watching them warily as they inspected her nest. Not wishing to frighten her away from her brood, they had quickly moved on.

"Daddy, how can all the family fit inside such a tiny nest?" she had asked "It must be very squashy!"

She smiled at the memory of her childish wonderment. Life had been so carefree then.

As the morning progressed into afternoon the autumn sun turned the moor into a tableau of colour. Purples and yellows of late flowering plants and bright red berries of hawthorn and shining orange hips on a wild briar rose were offset by numerous shades of green and brown. All was quiet and Oliver's appreciation of the moor began to reassert itself. A slight mist rose from the evaporating moisture on the foliage.

"This will never change," he said, his waving hand encompassing their surroundings, "a beautiful wild and unspoilt piece of the planet." He sighed, "I could happily live out here away from the noise of civilization and the prattle of people especially at this time of the year, in spite of the mosquitoes."

"'A season of mists and mellow fruitfulness.' To quote the obvious." Sandy smiled. Oliver smiled in agreement as he stripped a handful of wild rose hips from a briar and put them in his bag.

"Rose hip syrup!" Sandy exclaimed, "I had that as a little girl."

"You're not very big now." Oliver teased.

They wandered on, Oliver sometimes leading, at others walking alongside Sandy, as they made their way in the direction of the tor.

"Is there a flight path over the moor?" Asked Sandy as she stopped suddenly. "Can you hear a plane?" Oliver cocked his head and listened.

"No, that's not a plane, I believe it's a helicopter but a long way away, maybe the air-force is doing manoeuvres."

"I can't hear it any more, can you?" Sandy walked on, her attention taken by a wind-sculpted hawthorn tree, "I wish I had my drawing materials with me; that beats any man-made art." Oliver smiled to himself.

"You understand why I love the moor so much don't you?"

"I think so," she paused, "yes I do, I just wish I could be here under different circumstances and better prepared. I'm lucky you found me. I just wish Paul hadn't run off like that, he could be heading for safety along with us now."

"I wondered how long it would take you to bring him into the conversation." Oliver muttered. He didn't let his previous irritation colour his response, in fact he found that he felt no irritation at all. Paul was gone and wouldn't bother them, they would alert the rescue services thereby doing their best by him, done and dusted! "You know I didn't take to him in the brief time I knew him, being knocked flat on my back and winded wasn't the best introduction." Glancing at Sandy's petulant expression, he gave a placatory chuckle, warding off any angry exchanges. "But, had he not run off I assure you I wouldn't have turned him away. Anyway, we'll have the rescue people out in a flash as soon as we get home."

"Gosh! The rescue services; that could have been the helicopter we heard. I wonder if he's been reported missing. I was so wrapped up in my own missing person role that it didn't occur to me that someone was missing Paul!" Sandy thought back to her conversations with Paul in the tent. *Of course, his mother would be frantic by now.* "His mother must have reported him lost. Thank God, that means he'll probably be found before we even get home!" Sandy visibly relaxed, her guilt taking a back seat now that she had convinced herself that Paul would be alright. She did a sort of hop and skip, much to Oliver's amusement, and linking her arm in the crook of his she sang "'Oh I love to go a wandering my knapsack on my back,'" finishing the verse with raucous "VALDEREEEEEE VALDERAHAHAHAHA" and collapsed in to a giggling heap when Oliver playfully deposited her in a bed of heather.

CHAPTER 6

PAUL'S BRUISED LEG was aching and he stopped to rest it. Rolling up his trouser leg he inspected the graze. It was still very angry looking and some blood had stuck the fabric of his trousers to the wound. As he pulled it away, the graze began to bleed again, very slightly, but the sight of his blood frightened Paul and he reached for his handkerchief to wipe it away. But his hand didn't find the pocket of his raincoat and he realised that he had left it behind. Panic swept up on him. Should he go back for it? It was warm now, but he had been cold last night even wearing it, what if it was colder tonight, or it rained? Indecision sent him into a frenzy. Mummy had always told him what to do and what to wear. Paul sat on the ground and put his head between his hands. He started to shake and then he cried out, a pitiful wail. His anguish echoed around him bouncing back from the rocks and merging with the startled squawks of disturbed grouse.

"Well, well, what seems to be the matter?" Shock at the close proximity of the voice made Paul leap up. He spun round and stumbled on a large stone, landing on his face at the feet of the man he most feared.

"Where are you heading young Paul?" The man said. He stood with his hands on his hips, his shaven head shining with sweat in the sun. Paul noticed the stubble on Jimmy's chin and unconsciously rubbed his hand across his own face. There was barely a growth of beard. He rarely had to shave, which pleased him as he hated the sensation of the razor scraping his soft skin, but he did wonder why he was different from other men, like Jimmy for instance whose beard grew dark and coarse.

"Come on get up!" He kicked Paul in the ribs making him gasp.

Whimpering, Paul edged to his knees and then slowly to his feet. "Why are you so horrid to me? You said you were my friend."

"And so I am, young Paul, as long as you do as I say." His eyes glinted and his mouth twisted in a smirk. "Well, are you coming or not? Because if the answer is no I shall have to hurt you won't I?"

"I'm coming, I'm coming" stuttered Paul "please don't hurt me!"

"Good, you'll be my pawn." Paul didn't understand what the man called Jimmy meant. All he knew was that he had no choice. Jimmy had already shown how cruel he could be and Paul still carried the barely healed small round scars from Jimmy's cigarettes. He bowed his head and prepared himself for whatever Jimmy had in mind. His raincoat forgotten, he shivered but couldn't recall why.

"I am really hungry" Sandy held her stomach as it rumbled and gurgled, "when are we going to find something to eat?" Oliver agreed that he too was ravenous and suggested that they hurried towards the rocks and stopped fooling around.

"There's bound to be some fowl roosting there and I think we should make camp as soon as we reach the rocks, it'll be sheltered there if it rains or the wind blows up." They picked up some speed and with a purpose veered to the west. The sun dropping lower in the sky was beginning to turn from gold to copper. Sandy, following behind Oliver, picked out his tall silhouette against the sun. A golden haze outlined his dark form, giving him an ethereal look. He turned to Sandy and beckoned her to keep up. "Nearly there." He said. He gave an intake of breath "You really should look behind you, it's spectacular!" Sandy caught up with Oliver and together they faced the way they had come. The low copper sun had lit the moor with flame. Everything glowed; grasses had become golden, berries luminous, greens vibrant. Sandy stood gazing at the scene completely wrapt. Oliver turned to face her, the sun reddening his ginger hair and beard like polished Egyptian pure gold. His tanned face also glowed a ruddy gold. "You look like a Viking warrior!" she laughed, "All you need is a horned helmet and the image is complete."

"Except for the parka!" he replied. Reluctantly Sandy turned her back on the beauty of the moor and they pushed on. Finally, after a tiring climb up a slight but long incline they reached the foot of the tor. It was surrounded by large rocks, and Oliver was thrilled to find one with a deep cavity in which a well of rainwater had gathered.

"First things first," Oliver said, "I'll hunt, do you think you can put up the tent?"

"I'll give it a go." She replied. Oliver had not patronised her, she felt no need to prove herself, they were working as a team, "Off you go then, I'll try not to hang myself with the guy-ropes."

Sandy surprised herself with the speed with which she erected the tent, only one false start when she had not chosen the site well enough and the tent sat at a frightening incline and rather too near the beginning of a steeper slope. She checked thoroughly before starting to assemble the tent on the next choice of site. Not too many stones and relatively level, she tested whether she could bang in the pegs in various spots to ascertain any underlying rocks. Satisfied with her spot, she had it up in a trice.

Oliver returned soon after, a brace of grouse in his hand.

"I didn't hear a shot" she questioned, "did you use your sling?"

"Yes, it seemed like sacrilege to disturb the peace and anyway grouse are so dumb you could almost catch one bare-handed." He tossed the birds on to the ground and heaved his pack from his back. From inside he pulled a string bag containing some revolting looking fungi, the bulrushes, cress and dock he had gathered earlier and another bag containing blackberries.

"Don't suppose you have any double cream about your person? That would put the finishing touches to our forthcoming feast."

"Sorry, no I ate it all as soon as you were out of sight. Anyway I prefer fruit au naturelle. Shall I light a fire while you prepare the fowl?"

"Yes, thanks, you'll find the furze burns well if a little quickly so be prepared with the peat blocks." They worked companionably preparing the meal and by the time the sun had slipped its fiery way behind the rocks, they were enjoying the best meal they had eaten since being together. Sandy took a little persuading to eat the fungi but after using Oliver as her court food-taster, nibbled a little and, finding it surprisingly pleasant, finished the remainder on her plate.

"That was very filling," she grunted, easing her jeans' waistband, "I think I shall have to wait a while before pudding."

"That would be thc fungi, it's very dense and meaty and full of goodness, a brilliant survival food. We've got enough vegetable to last us a couple of days, that was a good haul we got back there."

"Yes and I surprised myself that I actually enjoyed it, well, nearly." They relaxed in the warmth of the fire, Oliver leaning against his backpack and Sandy sprawled out on his parka.

"You know, I am actually beginning to enjoy this survival lark." Sandy said as she rolled over to warm her other side. Her clothing had begun to dry quite well, both from her own body warmth with the exertion of hiking and from the sun and breeze of a glorious September day. However, her tight jeans, still a bit damp, rubbed behind the knees. To ease the soreness she stretched her legs out, grimacing as they rubbed her chafed skin.

"Why don't you take them off and get them completely dry?" Oliver suggested, "With the heat this peat is throwing out it shouldn't take long." Seeing that she was embarrassed at the thought of this he fetched the bedroll from the tent and suggested she slipped into it by the fire whilst her jeans were drying.

"Thanks, you know, I think I will, my legs are quite spreethed."

"Spreethed?" Oliver questioningly raised his eyebrows.

"Sorry, it's one of my gran's expressions, it means chafed." Oliver moved discreetly away from the fireside whilst Sandy struggled out of her jeans and gratefully pulled the bed roll over her legs.

"Chuck them over here; I'll rig up a line from the tent to that bush over there. It should be high enough, Can't have them catching fire!" He laughed. "Mine are still damp as well, so is my sweater, may as well take advantage of the fire to get us both warm and dry." His long legs, Sandy noticed, as he unselfconsciously peeled off his jeans, were lightly bronzed and covered in fine, slightly curly, ginger hairs. "That's better." He spread his jeans and sweater on the rope alongside Sandy's and resumed his place by the fire, their clothes gently roasting in the heat.

"I still wish I had made it to Mauritius, and I fully intend to get there somehow, but this experience has been good for me," she rummaged her hands in her hair, self-consciously, "sort of maturing." She looked shy and Oliver raised his eyebrows in question, "I would like to stay in touch with you when all this is over, if you'd like it, that is." She felt her face glow but her blush was disguised by the firelight.

"Yes, I think we should," Oliver said without hesitation, "I'd like that. Most of my female friends are 'feminine'..."

"Hey," Sandy bristled a little, "I'm not butch!"

"No, you misunderstand me" this time it was Oliver who blushed, "I didn't mean that, I like your tom-boyishness, you're not fussing over your nails or your hair all the time, you're like one of the lads." He trailed off feeling a little silly. Sandy laughed and shoved him playfully

"Fat lot of good fussing over my appearance stuck out here! However, I can assure you that I do scrub up well!"

"I'm sure you do, I look a bit smarter as a rule as well, especially when I've had a shave." Oliver handed her a plate of blackberries, "Here, pudding, tuck in and then we can wash the plates and tell campfire stories." The blackberries had a vaguely earthy taste, they were sweet yet tart; a refreshing taste after the heaviness of the fungi and they made appreciative noises as they ate.

"Talking of scrubbing up," Sandy said after they had eaten, "I feel filthy. I haven't washed or cleaned my teeth for days, I must stink!"

"Can't say I've noticed other than your hair being a bit stiffer and bog-brushy than when I first saw you." Oliver ran his big freckly hand through his own curls. They pinged back into place like springs. "My hair feels a bit stiff too and this beard is itching, I think I have a nest of mozzies feeding off my chin!"

"Well what do you usually do about washing?" Sandy started to feel itchy too at the thought.

"When I'm on my own I usually have a strip wash every other day, but we don't have separate rooms in the tent and I didn't think you'd react well if I suddenly took all my clothes off!"

"Too right!" Sandy recoiled in mock horror. "But surely we could work out a discreet way for both of us to scrape some of the dirt off. I don't suppose you have a spare tooth brush?"

"As a matter of fact, I have. I always bring a couple, just something I am fastidious about; clean teeth."

"So you've been cleaning your teeth every day and didn't think to offer me the spare?" Sandy retorted, "Please let me have the spare, we'll be home soon and I'm sure your old one will see you out."

"I'm sorry, I didn't think, I suppose I had too much on my mind regards getting you home safely, of course you can have it." He got up immediately and dug deep into the small pocket of his rucksack and pulled out a toothbrush still in its packaging. "We can boil up some water now if you like and I will wander off out of sight while you have a wash, after all you're half undressed already! Then you can do the same for me."

Later that evening, washed, and feeling a lot more like themselves, Oliver and Sandy settled for the night in their usual sleeping arrangement. Wearing her jeans, now dry and warm Sandy slipped into a more restful sleep than she had hitherto done, relishing the minty taste of toothpaste as her last conscious thought before her eyelids closed peacefully in sleep.

CHAPTER 7

IT MUST HAVE been just before dawn, though it felt like the middle of the night; she was so soundly asleep, when Sandy woke suddenly to find Oliver alert and listening.

"Ssh!" He whispered. "There's someone outside." A soft footfall near the back of the tent made them freeze. "Stay here, I'm going to check it out." He barely whispered, but indicated his intentions clearly. Sandy sat rigidly in the bed roll her heart thumping wildly. Oliver quietly undid the fastenings on the tent and crept outside. Sandy heard a muffled shout. She extricated herself from the bedroll and clambered out of the tent, she was no coward and wasn't prepared to leave Oliver to deal with whatever or whoever was out there alone. Then there was another cry which she recognised as Paul's. He must have come to find her. She was no longer frightened for Oliver, but was more concerned at what Oliver might do to Paul. Sandy, still on her hands and knees saw Oliver in the moonlight, struggling with Paul. She called out, "Paulie is that you?" Oliver threw the man to the ground and stood over him, large and dominant in the pale light.

"What the hell do you think you are doing?" Oliver shouted at the slumped form. He nudged him none too gently with his foot, which luckily was not booted.

"Sandy help!" Paul cried squirming away from Oliver. "I want Sandy!"

"I'm here Paulie" Sandy called "stay still and he won't hurt you."

"You don't know that!" Oliver snapped back. "What does he think he's doing, sneaking round, why didn't he just call out? He's up to something!"

"Oliver, calm down, you know he's not as rational as you or me. Give him a chance to explain." Oliver was fuming and his green eyes shone like a cat's in the moonlight. Paul lay huddled at his feet whimpering and mewling. He looked dreadful, in the moonlight his face was so pale as to be translucent and he was very dishevelled. Sandy was not sure but she thought she caught a whiff of excrement as she came closer. Oliver must have caught it at the same time.

"He's shit himself, the dirty bastard!" he cried. Sandy was horrified, she had begun to like Oliver and now he had shown himself to be as cruel and insensitive as she had first thought him to be. Paul was in need of help, he was a lost soul, frightened and helpless. How could Oliver be such a callous pig?

"Oliver!" She shouted, "Stop it! Leave him alone!" Trying not to gag on his smell she approached Paul and spoke softly to him,

"Paulie, it's okay we aren't going to hurt you," Paul wriggled closer to Sandy and away from Oliver, he clung to her leg and pressed his face, soaked with tears and grime against it.

"He made me." He whimpered. Sandy crouched down to be closer to him, noticing a stiffening of Oliver's posture as if he were about to protect her,

"Who made you do what?" Sandy tried to coax him to explain, gently stroking his hair from his greasy forehead.

"Jimmy, he made me, he's going to hurt me." Paul started to sob.

"Oh for Christ's sake!" Oliver shouted, "The bloke's an idiot, he's talking gibberish." He stamped his feet in anger: a petulant child. Sandy totally ignored him and turning her back to him she continued to try to comfort Paul. "There's no one else on this bloody moor surely!" Oliver said in an exasperated voice, "Don't tell me there's more like him sneaking around; it's beyond belief! What is it, an outing for idiots? Everybody meet up at the little blue tent and we'll have a mad party!" He ranted on hardly taking a breath until Sandy jumped up and grabbed him fiercely,

"Please will you just stop?! You're the one behaving like an idiot!" Oliver angrily shook himself free but fell silent. "One thing I know is that Paul doesn't tell lies, it just doesn't occur to him to do so. It's part of what he is. So just back off, okay?" Oliver grunted something which Sandy chose to ignore,

"True, something odd is going on," she said quietly to Oliver, "but if we want to find out what, we have to handle Paul very gently, he needs to trust us or we'll never get anything out of him." Oliver took a deep breath, exhaled slowly, his shoulders relaxing and his fists unclenching he muttered grudgingly

"I'm sorry, you are right. My temper sometimes goes on overdrive; I see red and nothing else."

"The Viking warrior?" replied Sandy more gently, "Just try and keep it in check for now okay?" He nodded and glancing over Sandy's shoulder he spoke directly at Paul

"Look here, I don't want to hurt you or anyone, but you must admit it's a bit odd to come sneaking around in the middle of the night!"

"Better..." Sandy commented, "but still too confrontational. Leave me with him a while, you get a fire lit or something and we can have a cup of your emergency coffee."

"How did you know I had coffee?"

"I found it when I raided your baked beans and cheese stash, I would have drunk that too if I could have lit a fire." Oliver glared at her,

"My peace and solitude; where did it go?" and grabbing his torch from inside the tent he set to preparing a campfire.

Sandy, positioning herself slightly up-wind of Paul, gently spoke to him,

"Tell me what's been happening to you Paulie, I'm sure we can help." Paul made a move towards her and she involuntarily drew back from his smell. He shrank into himself, rejection reducing him to an unwanted child, she thought he was about to cry but he just sat with his head bowed and said nothing. She could hear Oliver scrabbling in the dark to light the fire, muttering under his breath, *talk about a petulant schoolboy!* She, who was the rescued one, relying on Oliver's competence to get her home safely, now felt as though she had two under tens who had squabbled in the playground, on her hands. Paul, she knew, could not help himself, but Oliver had no excuse.

"Oliver," she called in as sweet a voice as she could bring herself to muster, "be a sport and stop complaining." She was answered with a grunt and an expletive as the fire guttered and failed. Sighing, she turned back to Paul and tried again to get him to open up.

"Who is Jimmy, Paulie?" She still had no response and tried a different approach. "Don't worry about your accident; it could happen to any of us. We'll get you cleaned up." Paul was acutely embarrassed and humiliated by the state he was in, he looked at her under his sparse lashes and she saw tears glinting there.

"I haven't got any more trousers." He muttered. Sandy thought for a moment and then, knowing that it would meet with outrage, said

"I'm sure Oliver has some he could lend you, he must have a change in his pack," she hesitated, "I'll ask him shall I?"

"He won't let me have them, he hates me." Paul slumped again, dejected and hopeless. Sandy got to her feet and joined Oliver at the now smouldering fire.

"Good, we have fire. Maybe instead of coffee we could give Paul a bit of privacy and let him wash himself?"

"Yeah great, and then what, put his foul clothes back on?"

"Well, that's what I was coming to," Sandy, in her mind was

carefully composing her request, "we'll need to wash them out a bit first,"

"And have a half-naked idiot sitting in my tent? No thanks!"

"He couldn't help it Oliver, he's probably lived on blackberries and nothing else and when you jumped him he was terrified. Put that together and the outcome was the shits!" Oliver flung his arms up in exasperation,

"I've just about had enough of this ridiculous situation. Do whatever you want and then let's get the hell off this moor!" Sandy gave him time to control his exasperation before it turned to temper again, knowing that her next request would light the touch paper.

"In the meantime, while we are washing his trousers and getting them dry enough to wear..." Oliver who had flung himself down beside the fire, looked up sharply

"Firstly, by 'we' I hope you mean 'he' or if you must 'you' but count me out, I am not washing his shit out of his pants!"

"No, what I was hoping is," she took a deep breath "do you have a pair of trousers he can wear for a day?" Her fears were not unfounded,

"No I bloody-well don't!" She could see his face colour up even in the semi-darkness.

"Come on Oliver, we are not far from home now, you said we'd be there in another good day's hike. I'll buy you a new pair when we get there and you can burn the others." Oliver swore, a litany of expletives even Sandy would have been loath to use. Sandy waited for him to finish then asked

"Well?" Oliver spluttered and swore some more finally shouting

"O BLOODY K. You can have my shorts. They're all I've got and they happen to be new. I've already torn up my favourite T-shirt for a sling for you, lost my emergency rations and ruined my time for writing! Just make a list of anything else you might want from me and let's get it over with!"

"By that, I take it you mean yes?" Sandy said in an authoritative tone, hoping that by doing so she could brook no more argument.

"What the hell!" Oliver nearly spat at her, "I'll get them. But he'd better have washed himself well before he uses them!" He got up angrily and ripped open the tent flap. Sandy heard him cursing whilst he extracted his shorts from his pack. He flung them on the ground in front of her. "There you are."

"Thank-you." She said quietly as she picked them up. "They should fit him."

"I'm so pleased!" replied Oliver sarcastically.

"Could you put some water on to heat for Paul? He'll need warm water to shift the muck off himself and he can then use it to wash out his clothes."

Oliver didn't reply but ungraciously filled his biggest billycan with water and put it to heat. Sandy took the shorts over to where Paul sat listening to the exchange and gently explained to him that when the water was hot enough he would be able to get clean. He could put on Oliver's shorts and then he could wash out his clothes. She told him firmly that he had to do this himself as she wasn't his mummy. At the mention of his mother, Paul started and Sandy thought he was going to run away again. She took hold of his arm gently stroked his hand.

"I'll help you Paulie." She said, wondering what it was about his mother that so upset him and deciding not to mention her again, she went to the fire to check on the water.

Paul was persuaded to take off his soiled clothes and he pulled his shirt down as far as he could, his embarrassment was pitiful to see and Sandy discreetly turned away from him.

Oliver had disappeared somewhere out of sight. Paul, using Oliver's torn up T-shirt as a flannel *don't tell Oliver* managed to wash himself and his relief was palpable. It was a difficult and unpleasant task to get his clothes vaguely clean in the small amount of water, and Sandy scrubbed and scrubbed until the water was unusable. She took it away from the site and threw it into the bushes. She then filled the billy again with clean water and put it over the fire. Finally when this too had warmed she was able to rinse the clothes and wring them out.

Paul had put Oliver's shorts on and the sight of his pale hairless legs sticking out from them would have been amusing had the circumstances been different.

On Oliver's return Paul plucked up his courage to speak to him,

"Thank you Oliver." This was all he could manage. Oliver said something along the lines of "You're welcome." Paul took it at face value and a small smile flickered across his pale, grubby face. Sandy knew the comment was laden with sarcasm and resentfulness. However, seeing Paul's grateful smile she let it pass.

"Well I'm never going to use this again!" Oliver grabbed the still hot billy-can, which Sandy had put back over the fire intending to scald and sterilise it with clean boiling water. He burned his fingers but, refusing to wince, threw it as far away as he could. It bounced off some rocks and the percussion echoed for some time around the tor. Sandy raised her eyebrows in impatience at his juvenile behaviour but chose not to comment, Oliver's mood was black enough already.

They sat around the fire in an uncomfortable silence watching the darkness thin and the subtle hints of sunrise warming the colours of the moor as it innocently rose to view.

"Well we have sopping wet clothes to dry and a soppy idiot to look after. What a great start to the day!" Oliver muttered to Sandy. Paul shifted uncomfortably as he heard this and Sandy's hackles lifted. She beckoned Oliver away from the fire and when they were out of ear-shot she, with glints of anger in her eyes said

"Look, let's just cut the sarcasm. I think we all have the message that you are pissed off. So am I if you must know. But what pisses me off most is a grown man behaving like a spoilt child." Oliver turned angrily away from her, she could see the back of his neck beneath his ginger curls glowing red and his shoulder were hunched as if he were about to hit out. Unrelenting, she pulled him back to face her; "Paul is now our responsibility and let's just accept that. The sooner we all start to behave like adults the sooner we'll be shot of each other for good!"

"I can't wait!" Oliver retorted. "Let's pack up and get going!" Oliver dismantled the tent like a child taking his ball back when he had lost a game and Sandy scuffed out the fire. Paul's clothes were wet and ignoring Oliver's sour looks, Sandy draped them across the top of the pack on his back in order to catch as much warmth from the sun as possible, hoping at the same time that it didn't rain.

"Don't tell me you can smell shit!" she snapped at Oliver as he wrinkled up his nose. "They are clean. I should know; I rubbed my hands raw scrubbing them!"

Oliver checked his compass and in total silence they went on their way.

Luckily no rain fell and the day matured into one of those beautiful early autumn days with a hard blue sky and a clean ozone filled air. Oliver's mood however hung around them like a wet black cloud through which no sun could penetrate. *God knows why I wanted to stay in touch!* Sandy too had had enough of this 'adventure' and it was obvious that Paul had experienced as much as he could take. He walked silently behind them and if Sandy turned to check on him he would immediately avert his eyes. Sandy had not had the chance to try to extract anything from him about what had happened to him after he had run off. Perhaps, she thought, I'll just leave it. If he wants to tell me he will. They trudged on in an uncomfortable atmosphere, stopping occasionally for a rest and some water. Finally as the sun began to slip down the sky Oliver said

"I'm going hunting. Light a fire. I want to eat. With luck we'll be only one more night and then it's good-bye."

"Why are we stopping, there's plenty of daylight. I thought you wanted shot of us?"

"You may be the mummy of this party, washing and mommy-coddling but I am the tracker and your only guide. This is the best place to stop and to find game so just stop whining and do as I say." Oliver snapped and giving her a cold nod he set off into the shrubs, his sling shot ready and the gun across his arm. It was a horrible feeling to be looked at and spoken to in that way; they had been getting on so well before Paul turned up. Sandy felt tearful but fought them back; dislike and anger taking their place. She rummaged around for some tinder and soon had a cook-fire going. She and Paul then sat disconsolately either side of the fire and waited. Sandy tried again to coax something out of Paul but he just kept repeating the name Jimmy and would expand no further. He just sat and whimpered as if traumatised.

After an hour or so of sitting pointlessly staring at and feeding the fire they heard a shot in the near distance. Oliver must have nabbed a bird. *All we need now are some poisonous mushrooms and the day will be complete* Sandy thought sadly. She had been rather enjoying trekking with Oliver and happy in the thought that Paul was being searched for and basically off her hands. All had changed now and she and Oliver were all but enemies. *Oh Josie, I wish I could be where you are!*

Josie was surprised and thrilled when she had a reply from the High Commission regarding her enquiry of work. They had invited her to participate in a government run aid scheme for Family Planning. She accepted on the spot. She was allocated a government flat and fifty rupees a week. She moved into her new furnished accommodation, was introduced to her maid. *Really*? And began her new job of only four days a week, the remainder to spend how she would. At the job she met American and British young men and women of her own age. Sandy didn't know what she was missing; beach parties, snorkelling, even home grown weed cultivated illicitly between the sugar canes.

CHAPTER 8

WHERE THE DEVIL is he? Sandy had been expecting Oliver back ages ago. The afternoon was wearing on and she had no idea what Oliver's plans were for the night. Apart from the fact that time was wasting Sandy had begun to worry that Oliver had cleared off without them. She immediately put that thought aside as she knew that no matter how angry he was Oliver was an honourable bloke and beneath his temper and intolerance she believed he was instinctively kind. After all, his sojourn had been totally wrecked by her and Paul, no wonder he was angry. She paced back and forth, feeding the fire, sitting down then getting up again. Oliver still hadn't returned and at least another hour had gone by. This was becoming very serious. What should she do? The sky had begun to turn a pale mauve grey and there was still no sign of him. Sandy imagined that he had fallen and hurt himself but where? The question as to whether to go and look for him brought back vivid memories of the last time she had done that. She dare not wander off again. Also, she had Paul to consider. It was getting dark anyway and that was the deciding factor which made her unpack the tent.

Meanwhile, Paul had started to become very agitated and kept looking around him anxiously. Sandy reassured him as best she could that Oliver would be back soon and would be glad they had made camp. But this didn't seem to ease his restlessness. Finally Sandy made Paul look her in the eye and asked him what was bothering him.

"Jimmy, it's Jimmy" was all he would say.

For want of any other course of action, Sandy, with Paul's fumbling help, erected the tent. But even though night had all but fallen and it was becoming chilly, she was disinclined to go inside. She felt increasingly fearful and knew that sleep would be impossible. And so they remained outside, feeding the fire and waiting.

Suddenly Sandy stiffened; she had heard movement in the dark. They could see nothing beyond the firelight and Sandy realised that they were silhouetted against it. She was sure that no harmful wild creatures lived on the moor but prickles ran up her spine anyway. If it was Oliver coming back why didn't he call out?

"Oliver is that you?" she finally blurted out getting to her feet. Paul had scrambled to his feet also

"It's Jimmy!" he cried and backed up against Sandy nearly knocking her into the fire.

"Paulie, calm down." she managed to sound calm in spite of her growing fear.

"Oliver?" she called again. This time a voice answered, backed up by a shadowy figure approaching them.

"No it's not Oliver, he can't come, he's hurt."

"Are you the rescue people?" Sandy felt relieved. "Thank goodness. Where is Oliver, is he badly hurt?"

"It's Jimmy!" Paul's voice was almost a scream. "Quick, run!"

"I wouldn't if I were you" drawled the voice in a mild yet menacing tone. The figure came right into the firelight and Sandy saw a tall, rangy man with a shaven head and black stubble on his face. Her eyes locked on the gun in his hand; it looked like Oliver's gun.

She jumped back in terror.

"Who are you? Where's Oliver?" Paul was crouched behind Sandy whimpering in fear,

"Jimmy, don't hurt us!"

"That's Oliver's gun! What have you done to him?"

"Oliver's resting; he's had a long day." Jimmy smirked. "I'm going to take you to him so pack up that tent, I need it, and yes, it's Oliver's gun, kind of him to let me have it wasn't it?" Sandy had no choice and with the gun firmly levelled at them, she and Paul dismantled the tent, rolled it and secured the straps. "Put out the fire young Paul." Jimmy instructed and Paul shuffled over to the smouldering remains. Sandy pushed in front of him and bending down to the fire scooped a double handful of scorching ashes and threw them at Jimmy's face. She registered the skin on her hands immediately blister but her adrenaline blanketed the pain. Jimmy was startled as the ash flew into his face, but his reactions were so fast as to be almost a blur. He sidestepped and the bulk of the ashes flew past him. He took two strides across the remains of the fire and smacked his fist into the side of Sandy's head. Seeing stars, she slumped to the ground to the sound of Paul screaming and all was dark.

She woke later, although it was still night, it was less dark. She heard the sound of Paul screaming, and a throbbing pain in her head and neck made her want to vomit. Jimmy was sitting astride Paul who was wriggling ineffectually beneath Jimmy's knees on his arms as he pressed the glowing end of a cigarette against Paul's bared chest.

She staggered to her feet, reeling with dizziness and pain.

"Stop it!" she yelled, lunging at Jimmy. He laughed and nonchalantly brushed her aside. Sandy, tears pouring down her face fell to the ground. Jimmy released Paul and stretched as a cat might after a good meal.

"That's enough for now young Paul. Next time you'll do as I tell you won't you!" Paul, through snot and tears mumbled that he would and rolled over to sob into the ground.

"What a pathetic creature!" Jimmy laughed. "At least *you've* got some guts." He pushed at Sandy with his boot, "Get up girl we have some distance to go. Just hope for your Oliver's sake that you haven't delayed us too much."

"You bastard what have you done to him!?" Sandy cried, imagining Oliver shot with his own gun.

"Just a small bump on the head, much the same as I gave you." Jimmy replied calmly. "Now get going!" He roughly pushed Sandy and Paul in front of him and prodded Sandy in the back with the gun. "I'll direct you from the rear and just in case you're feeling brave, the gun is cocked and loaded and I can assure you a shotgun blast from this distance would make a bit of a mess of you. It would probably get both of you with one barrel." Jimmy made Paul load Oliver's back pack and the tent on to his back, the billy cans clanking together like lone members of a timpani orchestra, and roughly pushed him forward.

Having no choice but to obey, Sandy and Paul led the way, instructed by Jimmy from behind, the barrel of the gun occasionally poking them in the back. It was still not completely light, they couldn't see where they were putting their feet and stumbled often. As they struggled on, the day gradually dawned to a murky sky, grey as slate, not a hint of the glorious sunshine of the day before. All the while Sandy walked, her head was swimming and she felt nauseous. Suddenly the sickness took hold and she spewed at her feet. Jimmy thinking initially that she was trying another escape kicked her in the back of the knees making her fall on to her knees into her own vomit.

"I *am* sorry" he said "look at that, you've dirtied your jeans. Perhaps you had better ask Paul to wash them for you." Sandy felt dreadful, she knew she was concussed and she should be resting but the desire to plead a break fought with her anxiety about Oliver. It was her fault he was hurt, and guilt nagged at her. It had all started with her not paying attention on the road and then that ridiculous chase after Paul. Then it all had begun to go okay and they had been going home. Home; it seemed so far away, would she ever get there? Jimmy nudged her again in the back

"You'll have lots of time to rest when we get there, so step on it girl!"

Finally, just as Sandy's resilience was at an end, Jimmy called a halt. He unbuckled the back pack from Paul's shoulders,

"I'll keep this. You won't be needing it. But you can have these." He pulled Paul's trousers and underpants from under the straps of the pack and threw them into Paul's face. "You, Paul, see that slab of rock?" He indicated a large stone which had recently been cleared of moss and grass. A heavy rock had been laid on top of the stone. "Shift that rock and pull up the slab." There was a ring of metal set into the slab. Sandy could see it wasn't stone but concrete.

"Get your back into that and lift it up, go on, now!" he shouted angrily at Paul who stood motionless, bewildered at the order. "Now I said!" Paul bent and with difficulty rolled the rock aside, he heaved at the ring, the slab gave a little then re-settled. Paul tried again, this time he managed to lift it and slide it aside. "All the way, come on you retard." Pain shot across Paul's face at Jimmy's words,

"I'm not a retard." He stood up to face Jimmy, then, no sooner than it had risen, his bravery failed him and he bent back to the task.

The stone had covered a deep dark hole, one wall of which had a metal ladder attached to it. The ladder looked rusty and Sandy could not see where it ended. A terrified spasm ran through her, he was going to bury them alive!

"Down you go, it's a long way so hang on tight to the ladder, don't want you hurting yourselves."

"Why are you doing this to us?" Sandy pleaded, "I've never met you or done anything to hurt you, neither has Oliver." She couldn't control her fear and she sobbed and pleaded with Jimmy to let them all go.

"Not so gutsy now are you?" Jimmy sneered. Paul, who had been sobbing throughout flung himself on the ground at Jimmy's feet

"Please Jimmy, please don't make us go down there, it's dark, I don't like the dark!" It was the most Paul had said since Oliver had discovered him outside the tent. He continued "I tried to get it for you, I did I did, I'm sorry I'm sorry, please don't punish me!"

"What did you try to get Paul? The gun?!" Sandy forgot her fear in her outrage. "After I helped you and worried about you, you tried to steal Oliver's gun? For this BASTARD?"

"He made me, he hurt me, he said he was my friend and then he wasn't..." Paul tailed off in his plea and throwing back his head he howled and screamed until Jimmy smacked him across his face with a blow that whiplashed Paul's neck with an audible crack.

"Down the ladder NOW and no messing. Oliver's waiting at the bottom. Now go or I'll just push you down!" Sandy lowered herself gingerly over the edge and found the first rung of the shaky ladder, slowly and carefully, tears flowing freely she felt her way down and down into the dark. Above her she could hear Paul crying loudly as he followed her into the depths. She heard a soft grinding noise from above and a dull thud as the slab fell into place like the lid of a tomb. The faint light from above was extinguished and they were in total darkness. Paul let out a wail of terror and Sandy felt her heart-beat accelerate to a wild thumping in her ears. How far down did the ladder go? And what awaited them at the bottom? Did the ladder even reach to the bottom or would they find they were suspended in space with no choice but to let go and fall? She couldn't see where Paul was although she could hear his cries, he seemed to have stopped his descent and Sandy visualised him frozen with fear afraid to move up or down. Something soft brushed Sandy's face and she recoiled in the darkness as Paul cried

"My trousers!"

"Paul," she called "hold on, I'm coming back up for you!" Sandy began the treacherous climb back up the ladder until she reached Paul who had not moved from the first few steps down. She could feel his terror through the trembling of the rungs as she neared him.

"Try to be calm," her voice betraying her own lack of calm, she added "I'm sure he'll come back and let us out." Paul scrabbled at the stone above him, his feet slipping on the rungs, forcing Sandy to keep her distance for fear he would kick her off, or fall himself and take her with him.

"He won't, I know he won't!" His breathing was fast and shallow. His ensuing scream of fear ripped through the stale earthy air, until his breath ran out, then, gulping more into his lungs he screamed again and again until Sandy screamed back at him to stop. Shaking with fear herself, she commanded him to stop kicking and to stay still; her grip on the ladder, tenuous in the first place was being made more so by the shuddering reverberating through the rusty rungs. Paul fell silent at her angry command and his thrashing ceased, seguing into an uncontrollable trembling. Sandy's authoritative tone gradually gave him a little self-control and slowly the vibrations through the ladder lessened and his breathing, although still shallow, was more regular. Hanging desperately on to the ladder, her forehead painfully pressed against the rusting metal as her legs shook as badly as Paul's, Sandy tried to think. Edging a little nearer to him she touched his leg

"I'm here. Paul, I'm here."

"Sandy, please, please —"

"Paul, can you reach the stone?"

"No!" He wailed, "I'm going to fall!"

"Paul, hang on, please don't panic, try, please try to reach the stone, we may be able to lift it. Let me come up, we can lift together." Blindly she attempted to ease herself up the ladder to get beside Paul but it was too narrow; he screamed and grabbed her hair like a drowning man. She cried out in pain and fear as her foot slipped, swinging away from the ladder into nothingness.

"You fucking idiot!" She screamed "Help me!" Paul, instead of helping, screamed as well. Her flailing foot at last found a rung and she wrapped her arms around the ladder, panting.

"Paul," she gasped, "I'm okay."

"I'm scared, don't leave me, don't leave me please Sandy!"

"I'm here. Paul, I'm here." Although he was under-developed muscularly, Paul was still a man and thus inherently much stronger than a woman. She must persuade him to try and lift the stone.

"Try and reach the stone Paul, we must try and lift it, give it a go; you're strong aren't you." She made this a statement not a question, hoping to boost his confidence and to appeal to what masculinity he possessed. Paul shifted his feet on the ladder and Sandy shifted her fingers quickly away from his feet, and fumbled for another rung, for safety she grasped the outer uprights of the ladder and held on. Paul stiffened his body and she heard him grunting with his effort to raise the slab.

"It won't move!" he cried, his voice rising to a higher key. "I can't do it!"

"Have another go, Paul, please!" She was aware of the desperation in her voice. Paul took a deep breath and heaved with all the strength he possessed; she couldn't believe that the extra rock on top of the slab could make so much difference. *He must have rolled more rocks on top – the bastard!* The slab of concrete remained completely static with not even a hint of movement.

"It won't move! We can't get out, Help, help, help!" Paul began to panic once more. Sandy again had to shout angrily at him to make him stop. He clung to the ladder and sobbed.

"Come on Paul, you've done your best," Dejectedly she tugged lightly at the hem of Paul's borrowed shorts, "we've got to go down."

"I can't!" Paul shouted at her making her start. *Oh Christ don't get aggressive – please!* She moved down a few rungs to be away from him and tried again to coax him with gentle words. She stopped mid-sentence;

"Sandy!" from far below, Oliver's voice, muted by the claustrophobic mass of earth, floated up, "Sandy, be careful! The ladder's rusty, come down slowly!"

"Oliver!" she shouted back, overjoyed that he was alright and mostly that he was there with them. She had faith in him, he would get them out. "Thank God!" She climbed back up to Paul,

"Come on Paul, carefully follow me down".

"Nooo" he wailed, "I want to get out!" He clung with his whole body to the ladder and nearly kicked Sandy off as she tried to coax him.

"Paul! Come on!" With that she began her descent towards the comfort of Oliver's voice. When she had gone down ten feet or so she felt the ladder vibrate and Paul begin his agonizing decent, as she had hoped he would if she left him behind. Just like her little mongrel cross springer, Lilly, who refused to come when called but as soon as Sandy walked on and didn't look back, would scamper up, fearful of being left.

It was cold and dank, moisture dripped on to her, making her hands and feet slip. Sandy shivered uncontrollably as the cold penetrated through her entire body. She glanced down and below she saw a small beam of light, thank goodness at least Oliver had his torch. Then as she looked it went out. Fumbling the rest of the way down and literally falling into Oliver's arms as the ladder ended a few feet off the ground her bravery crumpled and she held him tightly whilst stifling her tears. Some minutes later Paul landed with a thump beside them.

"Oh good, you've brought Paul!" Oliver said with a half-hearted attempt at humour. "Are you okay old man?" He spoke kindly to Paul who was crouched in a miserable heap mewling to himself. He didn't answer, Sandy wasn't sure he had even registered the question.

"What about you?" Sandy still held on to Oliver as if he would evaporate "What happened?"

"I'll tell you in a minute, I've discovered a slightly drier place than this and I've sort of made camp."

"Paul tried to lift the slab but he couldn't move it, do you think you could? You're stronger than him." Sandy held Oliver's arm as he went to move off.

"Don't think I haven't tried?" He said grimly," I strained every muscle balanced on that rusty ladder; I couldn't really get any strength behind me. It felt much heavier than I remembered from moving it when he forced me down here he must have put an extra weight on top."

"There was, he'd put a big rock on top, and probably he's added to it just to be sure!" Sandy slackened her hold on Oliver, "I hope something dreadful happens to him, the bastard!"

"Watch what you wish for," Oliver muttered, "he's the only one who knows where we are and may be our only hope of rescue."

"Fat chance of that evil shit relenting and coming back for us!" Sandy ejaculated.

"Hang on, what's that?" Oliver's torch beam picked out a crumpled pair of trousers and underpants on the damp earth,

"My trousers!" Paul gathered the items into his arms almost lovingly. "I dropped them."

"Yea, they nearly landed on my head!" Sandy laughed, surprising herself that she could see anything amusing in their situation.

"God forbid!!" Oliver exclaimed with a smile in his voice. The relief at being with him again, a capable strong man, raised

Sandy's spirits. He would find a way out. Oliver led them down a passage flicking his torch on an off the walls where he had scratched marks with a stone, other passages led off and Sandy could see how easy it would be to become totally lost. Trust Oliver to be so resourceful. She would probably have meandered all over the place and never found her way back.

They came to a place where the echoes of their voices became slightly muted, indicating that they were in a small space. Oliver shone his torch around them, it was man made, there were wooden struts and cross beams and a broken down concrete block wall. Although it wasn't any warmer it was certainly drier. Oliver had made his camp, if it could be called a camp. It consisted of a parka, a sling shot and a bottle of water and his string sack. Oliver picked up the parka and wrapped it around Sandy, zipping it up to her chin and pulling the fur-trimmed hood over her head. It was huge on her and she hugged it round her freezing body in pure ecstasy.

"Thanks, I think you've saved my life." Oliver crouched beside Paul and touched him gently on the shoulder,

"Come on over here with us and we'll all try to warm each other up," Paul shrank away from him, "it's okay I won't hurt you, come on Paul, we have to help each other now." Sandy joined Oliver and Paul reached out for her, she took his icy hand and stroked it.

"You're freezing Paul, put your trousers on over the shorts and let's all get a bit warmer, then we can think straight about how to get out." With the mention of getting out, and the intimacy of Sandy holding his hand, Paul stirred, and guided by them both he shuffled in the dark to Oliver's camp. Sandy slipped out of the parka and sitting on the ground between Oliver and Paul she draped it over the three of them as they huddled closer to her. Sandy told Oliver what had happened after he had left them. He swore violently when she told him of the blow Jimmy had dealt her and again in disbelief at the torture he inflicted on Paul.

"What a bastard! However did you get mixed up with him Paul?"

"That's something we have yet to discover," Sandy muttered, "he was using Paul and threatening him if he didn't obey."

"I realise that now, and I can see why Paul was so scared, poor bugger." Oliver reached across Sandy and gave Paul a re-assuring pat on the arm, "I'm really sorry I hurt you Paul," he said sincerely, "we'll make that bastard pay somehow!" The genuine kindness in Oliver's voice opened the flood gates for Paul, he had desperately wanted to explain but had been frightened both by Jimmy's threat of retribution and by Oliver's temper.

"He made me..." Paul began his voice cracking, "he made me try to take your gun, I didn't want to, I don't like guns, he hurt me, lots of times."

"He is a brute, he followed me, I'm embarrassed that I didn't register it, I thought I was a good ranger but he has an amazing stealth." Oliver suddenly pulled away from the others and staggered into the darkness,

"What is it?" Sandy called in alarm, they heard Oliver being sick. When he had finished heaving at nothing he slumped down next to Sandy,

"I think I have a slight concussion, he walloped me across the head with something, I think it must have been a log."

"I was sick after he hit me, not competing, but I think I may be concussed as well," Sandy said worriedly, "do you feel dizzy?"

"We both are, probably, you don't get a blow to the head as vicious as we got and not suffer some consequences."

"I'm not sick, I can help," Paul offered, much to Oliver and Sandy's surprise.

"That's brilliant, thanks Paul, don't know how to thank you!" Oliver answered with deliberately exaggerated enthusiasm. "Together we'll make it, 'All for one and one for all' Eh?"

"All for one and one for all." They repeated in unison. Sandy gave Oliver a little nudge and whispered

"Well done, just what he needed."

The little group under the parka multiplied and shared their body warmth and finally, Paul's head on Sandy's shoulder and Oliver's arm around Sandy, her head resting on his chest, with the comforting rhythm of his heart-beat, one by one they fell into an exhausted sleep.

Sandy woke to find an empty space where Oliver had been, her head was on his rolled up sweater and the parka was tucked tightly around her and Paul who still slept deeply. *I wonder when he last slept.* She could hear his heavy breathing in the dark and very gently eased herself out of his sleeping embrace. However, she did not move away from the camp, having learnt her lesson previously. Neither did she call out to Oliver, knowing he was investigating their prison in hope of finding another way out and that he would return. The darkness was palpable, never had she experienced total absence of light. It was terrifying; a subterranean dungeon where one day someone may find their skeletons or maybe they would never be found. She couldn't bear to imagine her mother's anguish, never knowing what had happened to her only and very precious child. To spend the rest of her life waiting and hoping would be a torture no mother should have to endure. Sandy was beginning to become agitated and panicky, she wished Oliver would return and that he would bring them some hope. Was it night or day outside? Was the sun shining or was it moonlight? Would she ever see the sky again? She felt a desperate desire to scream. Oliver's torch flickering on and off was a beacon in the blackness and she jumped up to go and meet it.

"What have you found?" she panted. "Is there another way out?"

"Nothing so far, I'm sorry." Oliver took hold of her hand as she pulled at her hair, the torch light making her wet eyes sparkle,

"Don't despair, this is some sort of bunker, there has to be another way, I will find it I promise." He led her back to where Paul had now woken and was sitting up with his arms tightly wrapped around himself. Crouching on his haunches he explained to them what he had found. The bunker was huge and had many corridors and 'rooms', some of the corridors were blocked where the walls had buckled. He had tried to map out in his mind the layout but it was too confusing in the dark. Hoping he might smell or feel a change in the air where perhaps there was an opening to the outside he had taken any path which had seemed to incline upwards. However most of the time he was sure he had been just as far beneath the surface as ever.

"I am also keeping a close check on the time, I know it sounds odd but I need to know whether it's day or night."

"Not odd," commented Sandy, "I feel the same, but my watch has stopped, I need to feel, in some way, still in contact with outside."

Oliver was glad that his watch was a new digital one with a twenty four hour clock; it could be confusing as to whether it was daytime or night with a spring mechanism and a clock-face. It had cost a lot of money being one of the first on the market and Oliver treasured it. "It's," he pressed a button on his watch and the numbers lit up "five minutes past nine, in the morning, we've slept through the night which is good, we must try to stick to this routine to keep ourselves orientated." Glad though she was that Oliver was in charge and being positive Sandy thought she would go mad with not being able to see. It was like being struck totally blind, she felt claustrophobic; the sightlessness seemed to somehow suffocate her as well, as though she had a thick black bag over her whole head.

"I don't think I can stand this, I feel as if I'm going mad!" she burst into tears and as Oliver tried to hold her to comfort her, she thumped him wildly in the chest, "For God's sake get us out of here! We're going to die aren't we?" She choked on her tears and coughed violently. Paul, who had not made a sound throughout their exchange, suddenly spoke,

"Sandy, please don't cry" he reached out to find her in the dark and accidentally poked her in the eye,

"Ouch!" Sandy smacked his hand away, but instead of being rebuffed, Paul caught hold of her hand and held it firmly.

"You are brave Sandy," he spoke quite forcefully, his voice deeper than before, making Sandy pause in her histrionics and she turned to him wishing she could see his face, "you tried to help me, I knew you were kind. You are the nicest person I have ever met." Sandy felt Oliver sit forward, his attention caught by the sudden change in Paul, who seemed more able to express himself when he wasn't being looked at. The darkness seemed to offer him protection, like a blanket, from people's eyes in which he must often see pity, laughter, disgust and sometimes cruelty.

"Oh Paul, I wish I had helped you but look where we are, I'm sorry. I couldn't fight that man, neither of us could."

"He's a wicked man, he hurts people."

"Paul, you must tell us everything you know about him" Oliver interjected, "I'm totally confused, why were you with him in the first place?" Paul fell silent for a long while and it seemed as though he had clammed up. But, after an audible intake of breath he said

"We ran away from the hospital, he said he needed my help."

"What hospital? Were you ill?" Sandy asked him, "Was he ill as well? He seemed alright to me!" Paul suddenly became animated and hardly taking a breath he tried to explain,

"No we weren't ill but they wouldn't let us go home, they put needles in me and made me sleepy, they hurt me, they locked me in a room and tied me up. They wouldn't listen to me. I didn't do it!" He finished with a shout. In spite of the outraged noises that Sandy and Oliver made at what he had just told them, he refused to elaborate further.

Paul withdrew into his painful thoughts, how could he tell anyone what had happened to him and why he had been sent to the asylum. His righteous claims that he hadn't done it still didn't suppress the dreadful guilt he felt. He must have done something bad but it wasn't what they said he had done. He remembered shouting and hitting out at the men who came to his house but it was only because they tried to take him away. He desperately wanted to see his mummy again, she always made things right.

CHAPTER 9

PAUL HAD BEEN taken away in a big black van with bars on the windows and doors. Two stern men had forced him inside, holding his arms behind him. He had struggled and dragged his feet, kicking at the legs of his captors. His cries were ignored and the van doors closed. The walls of the asylum where they had taken Paul were green. People had been shouting and his cries joined the cacophony of noise. Hitting out at his warders in a frenzy of fear, Paul had felt something sharp stabbed into his arm. Eyes blurring with tears and a fading of consciousness he'd slumped to the ground, his last mute cry –

"Mummy!" as the world spun into a pin prick of light then vanished.

Paul had wakened to a room no bigger than the tiny box room where his mother had done the ironing. The smell of the hot iron on fresh-air dried washing was as much the smell of home as were the aromas of his mother's cooking. She would often do the laundry on a Sunday morning, the dinner cooking in the kitchen and Family Favourites playing on the wireless. For a brief moment Paul had thought he had dozed off on the settee and looked up expecting to see, through the open door of the box room, his mother rubbing the iron up and down the folded sheets and shirts, humming along to the songs.

He was lying on the floor, his own sick in a puddle by his head. The walls were closing in, "Mummy?" he whispered. No mother answered his plea. Paul had tried to stand but found that not only were his legs too weak to bear him but he was unable to move his arms; they were somehow tangled in a shirt whose sleeves were too long and vanished behind his back. He had struggled frantically, tossing his head from side to side and rolling into his own vomit as he writhed to escape from his restraints. He had screamed. He had wept and banged his head on the floor which somehow didn't hurt but bounced with a muffled sort of thud.

MUMMY, MUMMY, MUMMY, MUMMY!

Where was his mummy; the only person who could comfort him?

He barely noticed the door opening; he was thrashing and vomiting, choking and crying.

"Are you going to behave yourself?" A man's voice had asked.

"Because if you don't you can stay here like this all night." The man had been wearing a white coat and at his belt hung a bunch of keys. Paul had looked up at his cold stare and in his innocent heart he knew his life had changed for ever.

Paul was obedient when they led him to another room, they had taken the horrible shirt off him but a big man still held his arm so tightly that it hurt. There were two narrow beds in the room, they didn't look comfortable; his bed at home was soft and had a bright bedspread with pretty patterns on it. These beds had only a grey blanket and the sheets looked a bit dirty. The pillow was very flat and didn't look at all comfortable. They had pushed him in and closed and locked the door behind him. He was frightened to see that a man was on one of the beds. He was lying with his face to the wall and didn't move or speak as Paul sank down on the other bed. Paul had been glad that the man was facing the other way. He wished that he hadn't been there at all. Paul had never shared a room other than when he had curled up to his mother when he had had a bad dream. Although he felt happy when he was with his mother or with the friends he had made at his special school, he still felt lonely and worried around strangers, especially men. Men were big and sometimes spoke very loudly. They didn't talk to him like his mummy did and the lady teachers at his school; they were kind. Men talked *about* him and thought he didn't hear what they said. And sometimes bigger boys in the town laughed at him.

He had only a faint memory of a man who used to live with his mummy and him when he was very young. The only time the man had ever spoken to him it was to tell him off. He was always sent to his room when people came to visit them. He would creep out on to the landing and listen to them talking and laughing in the sitting room. If the man caught him there he would shout at him and tell him that no one wanted to see him and if he cried he was smacked. When Paul had tried to call him Daddy the man's face had gone very red and he had pushed him roughly away saying

"I didn't father you. You spastic!" Paul had no idea what a spastic was but his mummy was furious,

"How can you treat your son like that?" she had cried.

His mummy didn't spend much time in the sitting room when the visitors were there; she always said she had things to do in the kitchen. Paul knew she wasn't happy because when she thought she was alone she looked sad. But when she saw him she would smile and hold out her arms for a cuddle, so he knew it wasn't him who was making her sad. On the evenings when the man had his friends round, his mummy would always come up to him and take him gently back to his room from the landing and she would sit on his bed telling him lovely stories as he cuddled up to her. One day the man had hit Paul very hard and his mummy had run to protect him, the man had then hit her too. After that day it had been just him and his mummy.

Suddenly, his room-mate had sat up and Paul shrank back against the wall and tried to pretend that he wasn't there. When the man spoke to him he knew it was rude not to pay attention, so he listened politely but sat looking at the floor, the man spoke as though he were smiling all the time but his eyes were hard and didn't smile.

"I assume they treated you to the padded cell and strait-jacket? Usual practice for a new guest."

"Is it?" Paul had asked, wonderingly.

When it was obvious that Paul wouldn't or couldn't bring himself to tell them any more Oliver said,

"It's okay Paul; don't worry about it for now. What we need is a positive plan, something to drink and some food."

"But he took your pack!" Sandy visualised Jimmy making camp with all Oliver's gear, making a cook-fire and using his sleeping roll. "I wish I had left the billycan still full of shit!" She exclaimed "And let him cook it along with the game he probably stole from you!"

"Actually, he didn't. It's in my string bag, I had it tucked inside my parka to free up my hands for hunting and he didn't know it was there. I not only have the game but I still have the rest of the veg we harvested yesterday."

"Wow, that's fantastic, at least we won't starve!" Sandy cried, then "Well at least we won't starve today." she added quietly.

"Yea, but the problem is cooking it." Oliver sucked his teeth, "In the meantime we can have a sip of water each. I've got a full flask of water but it's got to last." He unbuckled his hikers' flask from his belt and handed it first to Sandy who took a tiny mouthful and then to Paul and allowed him a sip whilst maintaining a firm hold on the bottle to prevent him taking too much or inadvertently spilling it.

"We can't light a fire in here; we'll suffocate in the smoke. I'm going to find a place which has a higher ceiling to take some of the smoke away." He got up and taking his torch he said "Stay here and don't leave this spot. I won't be long." Paul and Sandy watched as the torch light flicked on and off until they were left once again in darkness.

Oliver followed the marks he had made earlier and set about finding the bigger chamber he had discovered before Sandy and Paul had joined him. Concentrating intensely on his route for fear of getting lost, he enlarged the scratches on the walls to avoid missing them on his return. He came quite quickly to the large chamber and shining his torch around he could see that it had been lined with blocks and he thought it must have been the centre of the bunker. Leading off from the room were other corridors and he made a note to investigate them later. *This will do,* he thought and he retraced his route back to the others.

They followed Oliver closely, Sandy holding Paul's hand. It was colder now that the space was larger; the coldness which is particular to underground; deep caves or tombs. Sandy remembered experiencing this type of cold on an organised tour of a huge cave in France. They had been in the cave far longer than the scheduled time as the guide was inexperienced and by the time they had emerged into the hot July sunshine everyone was blue and shivering. However, on that trip there had been lots of people and lights and most importantly; a guaranteed exit.

"Here we are." Said Oliver almost proudly as he swept the torch around them. "What do you think?" He reminded Sandy of an estate agent trying to sell a really crappy house. She laughed and said

"We'll take it." Then more seriously "It should be big enough not to smoke us out, but has it occurred to you that we have nothing to burn?"

"There's enough rubbish to start it, don't forget, people have used this and people always leave rubbish." This was true, Oliver's torch picked out a jumble of paper and what looked like a pile of old paper files. "This must have been the headquarters." Sandy echoed Oliver's earlier surmising, "You know what? That could mean we are near a way out!"

"Not necessarily." Oliver countered, unnecessarily, she thought, dampening her hopes. An empty feeling clutched her stomach as he spoke; they were going to die here, buried for ever.

Oliver's practical approach was on the one hand reassuring and the other daunting. He saw things as they were with no false hopes but also without despair. Sandy wished she could be more like him but her emotions were as volatile as her mother's and had always manifested themselves physically.

They gathered the paper and Sandy and Paul folded it, with difficulty in the pitch dark, into tight spills which would burn more slowly rather than just flaring up and dying. Oliver took himself off to find other more sustainable fuel and they heard a whoop of joy as he discovered a broken chair and table in one of the corridors. Judging by the weight he thought it must be made of oak which was a fantastic bonus as oak would burn almost like coal and it wouldn't smoke too much.

Oliver carefully laid the fire and struck a match, it caught and carefully he built it up until a wonderful warmth emanated from it into their very bones.

"Even if we had nothing to cook, this would almost be enough," Sandy watched the wood glow and stretched out her hands towards it, "just to have some light and to be warm again." Oliver prepared one of the rabbits for cooking, using only his rangers' penknife which he kept in his pocket, his bigger knives, along with Ali's rope and everything else of any use were in his stolen pack. Paul and Sandy sat as close to the fire as they could and stared into its flame, mesmerised as though they had never before seen fire. Suspending the rabbit far enough above the flames so as to cook it but not burn it was a problem. There was nothing metallic they could use and the small bar from the broken chair, which Oliver first tried, burned through and the rabbit fell into the fire. Oliver scrabbled it out and burned his hands quite badly,

"Shit, shit, shit!" He swore, blew on them, then he placed them palms down on the cold condensation on the wall. Whilst he was attempting to take the sting out of the burns he noticed a small heap of broken concrete blocks at the foot of the wall. "Perfect" he called, "Sandy, give me a hand." They carried the blocks to the fire and Oliver, grimacing at the pain in his hands, built two little walls either side of the fire and finished with two blocks crossways, "two mini Stonehenges" he said proudly. The space between the cross pieces was just big enough to allow the heat to reach the rabbit but small enough that it didn't fall through. Turning the meat periodically and adjusting its position, their juices flowed at the smell of cooking meat. It must have been her ravenousness which made Sandy think it was the most beautiful smell she had ever smelt. Her memories of the unpleasant aroma of rabbit stew at her grandparents suddenly seemed fictional. When the rabbit was nearly done Oliver took three medium sized mushrooms from his bag and after rubbing some of the rabbit fat over them positioned them on the now scorching hot block to cook. They each had a very small helping of rabbit, keeping some for the next meal, and a mushroom, Oliver rationed out a small portion of the vegetables, these they ate raw as much for the fluid they contained as for the food.

It was amazing how their spirits rose with the food inside them, albeit that it was a meagre repast, and having firelight to see each other by. They could almost have been camping above ground with the stars above them. "I think we should make this our camp site the smoke isn't a problem and it's stupid to keep trekking from here to there."

"Agreed." Oliver said, "We've got all our things here, so we may as well stay."

CHAPTER 10

OLIVER'S FAMILY WERE preparing to see Alistair off to university as the summer break was now over. He was in his final year of hard study and had secured a placement with an Exeter based firm of solicitors pending good results.

"I thought Oli would have bothered to get back to see me off seeing as he's been out on the moor for most of my holiday." He complained when they had loaded the car. "Bloody typical; too wrapped up in his meditating and what not!"

"I must admit," his mother, Alice muttered, "I'm surprised he's not back yet, p'raps he's lost track of the date."

"No way mother, Oli's never without his swanky watch, he knows the date and the time both here and in America probably." He slammed the boot of the car angrily. Alistair, in spite of knocking Oliver whenever he had the opportunity, valued his elder brother's approval and would never forget that horrific night in the peat bog when Oli had saved him. He was disappointed and hurt that Oliver had not bothered to get back in time to see him off, "Maybe he's gone native!" And with those words he jumped into the car and drove off, spraying the gravel of the driveway in George and Alice's faces and barely glancing behind to wave good-bye.

"Oh Ali, why the anger all the time?" Alice said quietly to herself. *Drive carefully.*

June and Tim still waited for a phone call from Sandy, but none came, neither did a letter or even a postcard. June tried to be positive and failed. Tim stoically took the brunt of her anxiety fuelled anger but spent as much time as he could out of her company. June, resenting this, found even more reasons to verbally abuse her husband and his reassurances of his love for her fell on stony ground.

"I'm contacting the High Commission in Mauritius!" June spat out one morning over breakfast, "She promised she would contact us, something must have happened to her."

"Okay why don't you do that and then perhaps you'll stop giving me a hard time." Tim was becoming less patient with his wife's temper but what made it worse was his anxiety over Sandy's safety was eating at him as well. If he showed June how worried he was becoming he knew it would send her into a complete panic. June had had periods of severe depression throughout their marriage, starting with the miscarriage of their first child, a girl. After her second miscarriage, also a girl, Tim had thought she would never recover. He had always been the one on whom she took out her mood swings, but he loved her unconditionally. He had held and comforted her during these dreadful times and had never stinted in his affections; she was vulnerable, she regarded herself inadequate as a woman, one who couldn't carry a child full term. Tim had always loved her, ever since they first met thirty years ago and he hurt with her and for her, he understood her, knowing when to take her in his arms and when to leave her alone. With the birth of Sandy, June had blossomed again, they had a healthy child and it was a girl. June had always wanted a girl, though, given her fear that she would never carry full-term; she would have worshipped a baby of either gender.

Together they wrote a letter to the High Commission in Mauritius asking them for information and begging them to trace Sandy's whereabouts.

"I don't care if she doesn't write," June lied, "as long as she's safe." She sealed the airmail envelope and was heading out of the door to the post office when Tim called her back,

"Whilst we're about it," he broached the subject carefully, "we could always check that she actually went to Mauritius."

"What do you mean?" June's voice became shrill, "Are you implying that she's run away and doesn't want us to know where?"

"Don't be ridiculous, of course I'm not saying that!" Tim was astounded that June had even slightly considered this option.

"In that case you think she's in trouble, say what you mean!" Fear showed in every aspect of June's body; her face drained to a sickly ivory white and her hands shook so badly that Tim grasped them in his own and leading her to the sofa, made her sit down, but she immediately rose to her feet again and started pacing around the room her hands fluttering like butterfly wings caught in a web.

"I don't know what to think." He replied honestly, "Let's face it June, we're both worried, you're right to contact the High Commission. I think we should also speak to the airline." At least they would know in which country to search when they had ascertained whether she had boarded the flight or not.

"Do you think we should get in touch with the police as well?" June picked up the phone.

"We could, but I suspect they won't take it seriously as she is an adult and in fact has only been gone since last weekend. They won't class it as a missing person's case, just a case of non-communication. They'll wonder why we are making such a fuss." Tim moved closer to June and took the phone from her trembling grasp, "We'll find out firstly if she is in Mauritius and that she is okay. Then we can put our minds at rest and wait for her to bother to get in touch." June, always a slim woman seemed to have lost weight in only seven days, her face, pale and drawn showed darkness beneath her eyes and she looked every day of her fifty-five years. The permanent worry lines appeared twice as deep in her forehead and her mouth pulled down at the corners as if she harboured a vile taste in her mouth.

"How could she be so thoughtless?" she broke down and rubbing her hands over her face as if she wished to scour the skin from her flesh she sobbed. "I would gladly die for Sandy, you know that. She's the most precious thing I have ever had."

"I know; I feel the same." Tim pulled her to him and held her shaking body to his. "Don't despair, please, I'm sure she's okay, just being her usual scatter-brained self. She may have taken her time to drop us a postcard, and airmail takes a few days to arrive. Once we know she's safe then we can concentrate on being outraged at her behaviour!" He tried to inject a small amount of levity into his voice and was relieved to see a faint smile ghosting around June's mouth but disappearing as soon as it was manifested.

"All I want to do is hold her again." She murmured. Together, they wrote a letter to the airline, a cheap charter company which Sandy and Josie had discovered whilst planning their holiday. Tim then donned his waterproof and walked to the village post office to send them both.

Slate grey sky, thick clouds and a cold north-westerly wind added to his despondent mood as he pulled up his hood, he looked up at the sky and the rain ran down his face.

In Mauritius the letter which Tim and June had previously written to Sandy was finally delivered to Josie's post box. As Josie had moved to the other side of the island and had informed her parents of her new address, she saw no reason to return to check her mail. She did, however, think it was very odd that Sandy had not turned up or communicated her change of plan and resolved to write to her at her home to find out why. She was busy that weekend, scuba diving, then barbecuing with her new friends.

She fully intended to write to Sandy but, well, you know how things lose their priority when you're having a good time.

Tim and June's letter lay inside the door of the hut for a couple of days but was finally torn in to tiny shreds by a nesting mouse.

CHAPTER 11

DEEP UNDER THE ground the cold and hopeless trio were trying to keep their spirits up. Oliver, being naturally the leader had spent most of the day searching for another exit from the bunker. His trips had taken him away from 'camp' for long periods leaving Sandy and Paul sitting huddled together for warmth. They had spoken little. Sandy again tried to get Paul to tell her what had happened to him but he seemed unable to. It was as if he didn't really know. It dawned on Sandy that whatever it was, it was so traumatic that Paul's mind had been unable to process it. She fell silent and together they awaited Oliver's return.

When Oliver returned from his fruitless search, the quietness of his footsteps and his heart-felt sigh as he lowered himself to the ground beside them rendered it unnecessary for him to enlighten them. They made another small fire to both warm themselves and give them some light, ate the remainder of the rabbit, supped a mouthful of water each and curled up under the parka to sleep. Each had his own thoughts, none spoke.

During the night, Oliver woke and quietly extracted himself from the parka and headed off once again hoping to return with good news before the other two woke. He took a completely different route this time and was amazed at how big this underground 'dwelling' was. From his hurried flashes of torch light it appeared to him that this wasn't just a man-made bunker, but was a natural cave which had been enlarged and utilised. The bunker must have been constructed during the Second World War. He found further evidence of human occupation by way of more paper litter and odd bits of broken furniture. Walking slowly and carefully, watching where he put his feet, Oliver was unaware of the sudden drop in ceiling height and his head cracked into a low lintel. He staggered back and his foot dropped suddenly into space. Before he could recover, his whole leg fell through and he landed straddled and in pain half in and half out of a hole. He felt frantically around him for his torch which had gone out when he fell. Luck was with him; his groping fingers located it horribly close to the hole. He clutched it to him and holding his breath he pushed the switch. It lit! The heavy duty rubber casing had cushioned it as it fell. He shone it around him. The earth floor had given way to rock. The hole in which he had slipped was a natural cavity. There was no knowing how deep it was. One thing for sure was that he was in dangerous territory. Oliver, his strong arms and shoulders straining, pulled himself out of the hole and he sat against the rocky wall nursing his leg. It was agony. Surely he couldn't have broken it; that would be the end if he had. He knew from his cadet training that a long bone break such as a femur bled internally and the patient's blood pressure dropped severely. If this were the case, he could look forward to blacking out, followed by death. In spite of the pain, Oliver forced himself to try to move his leg of its own volition. The spasm of pain which shot through him made him scream. But, he could move his leg. Feeling down his shin and shining the torch briefly on his lower leg he re-assured himself that his foot was facing the right way but his leg was swelling as he looked at it. He had to remove his boot; the flesh above it was ballooning. Gritting his teeth against the pain, he unlaced his boot and pulled it off, having the sense to tie it around his neck. The pain eased a little but not much and not for long; as the blood rushed into his foot it came back stronger. Oliver leaned back again against the wall and breathed deeply. He was sure that he had torn a ligament in his ankle. The injury resembled a rugby injury suffered by one of his mates at university. He remembered how quickly his friend's leg had swollen and now understood that his assessment of him being a wimp had been hasty.

The cure for a torn ligament was rest! Oliver laughed ruefully as the thought came to him. *Yea, I'll just put my feet up and expect breakfast in bed!*

Back at 'base camp' Sandy stirred, felt to her right and found an empty space. Not wishing to face the truth of their situation she tried to imagine that she was anywhere but there, curling up under the parka on the hard floor she attempted to go back to sleep. However, no amount of wishful thinking could change things and she finally gave into the fact that she was wide awake and exactly where she had been the day before. Having no idea of the time, or whether it was day or night she agitated for Oliver's return if only to know the time.

Oliver resisted the asinine urge to call out for help from Sandy and Paul, telling himself to be practical. There was no other option but to limp or probably crawl back the way he had come, which, he recalled, was some distance. What he must not do now is get lost. Crying out as his ankle felt as though it were being torn from his leg, he managed to stand on his good leg, bracing himself against the wall. He hopped a few steps and stopped. It was going to take for ever to get anywhere like that. He had to bear the pain and try to use his injured leg. He could favour it by limping quickly and lightly on it. If he did this, at least he would make some better headway. Whatever were they going to do now? He was no use to anyone.

Out on the moor, the new day was dawning, like a dejected water-colourist drenching his paper with his emotions; a purple grey colour-wash painted the sky. The natural hues of the moor were turned to sepia and cold rain cascaded from the sombre clouds. No birds sang, no bees buzzed and even the mosquitoes had found shelter. The only sound was the ceaseless drumming of water filling the pools and marshes, overflowing the streams and liquefying the peat. Jimmy was dry, if not warm, Oliver's little tent nestled under the lee of some rocks, out of sight. Jimmy sat contentedly under the canvas with the flap tied back, smoking a hand rolled cigarette. No one would be looking for him in this weather. He had made sure that Paul and his new found friends could cause him no bother. He had plenty of time to plan his route. He had been travelling mostly at dawn, just before sunrise and late afternoon. He had managed to nab a couple of rabbits with Oliver's gun but was chary about using it too much, partly for fear of being heard and partly because he needed to keep a good supply of shot. Up until this morning he had been able to light a fire and cook. Luckily he had eaten well last night and was quite capable of going the day with no food. There was plenty of water!

Oliver's journey back to Sandy and Paul must have taken him three times longer than his outward one. He had dragged himself along, cursing with the pain, stopping to rest when he felt faint. Thank goodness his torch had decent batteries and also that his marks on the walls were big and clearly visible with merely a flash of light. It was late afternoon when he finally stumbled into 'camp'. The shuffling, scraping footsteps coming closer and closer, accompanied by laboured breathing, jolted Sandy from her thoughts in fear. That isn't Oliver, was there someone else down here as well as them? It sounded like some sort of horror film monster and in the darkness the simile was easy to believe. She quickly hushed Paul who had also started at the sound, and they sat huddled together trying not to let their breathing become too loud. "Sandy." croaked a voice which was and yet wasn't Oliver's. "It's me." A flash of torch light swept over them and the figure followed it in a lurching, limp. "Christ, let me sit!" Oliver virtually fell to the floor and groaned.

"Oliver, what have you done?" Sandy grabbed the torch and shone it at Oliver. She could hardly believe what she saw. His leg was swollen and he had no boot on. Pain had drained his face of its normal ruddy brown which even in the torchlight had always looked healthy.

"Torn ligament, I'm sure." He groaned. "I'm so sorry." They were silent; the implications of Oliver's last words fell like icy water on their hopes.

After a long desolate silence, Sandy hesitantly asked

"Did you find anything?"

"Just a bloody great chasm!" Oliver groaned, "I thought it was going to swallow me whole." He shuddered and shifted his position in an attempt to ease the pain.

"Oh God, what a bloody fool I am, I've buggered everything haven't I?"

"No! Don't say that, you've been marvellous. All you need to do is rest it a bit and Paul and I will do everything..." She tailed off feeling pathetically inadequate.

"Yes, we'll look after you." Paul spoke from the darkness; he had been so quiet that his sudden entry into the conversation surprised them.

"Yes, we will!" agreed Sandy with forced enthusiasm. "Give me the torch, first thing Paul and I are going to do is make you as comfortable as possible, come on Paul!" Oliver handed her the torch warning her to use it sparingly and she and Paul went in search of wood. Her limited knowledge of first aid told her that sprains and such-like should be rested in an elevated position. She would build a fire to warm Oliver and try to construct a foot stool for him. It was down to her now to keep things together.

They returned from where Oliver had first found the broken table and chairs laden with wood and a bundle of discarded paper files.

"These are probably Top Secret, but, hell, tough, they're cushions now." Sandy stacked some planks up to a height of nine inches or so and balanced a wad of papers on top. "Now, gently lift your leg on top." She winced as Oliver stifled a cry as he moved his leg. Sandy tucked the parka behind his back and attempted to make him as comfortable as was possible in the inhospitable conditions.

"Thanks, that's brilliant." Oliver relaxed slightly against the padding of his parka, "I wish I had my back pack, there was a first aid kit in it with pain killers. Hand me the other rabbit and I can get it ready for you to cook." Sandy and Paul made a fire and between them they prepared a meal, carefully putting aside half for the following day. As they were eating, slowly, reluctant to finish, Paul kept shuffling and every now and then he took a breath as though he were about to speak but then seemed to change his mind.

"What is it Paul, you're fidgeting?" Sandy asked "Do you need to go?!"

"No, no, it's not that." Paul's embarrassment made him shrink into himself and Sandy wished she had been less forthright.

"Don't embarrass the poor bloke; it's something I've been able to do while I'm away from you on my recces, don't you need to pee or anything?"

"Quite frankly, I've had so little to eat and drink that I think my digestive system has closed down, I can't remember when I last did a big job. I have peed, just over there." She indicated the little alley which led off from their new camp.

"What about you Paul, have you managed to relieve yourself?" Sandy asked delicately.

"Yes, thank-you," Paul muttered. They each had their prescribed mouthful of water and warmed themselves around the dying fire.

"Excuse me please" Paul broke their contemplative silence "can I borrow the torch for a bit?"

"Okay, but don't go far and don't lose it and don't..."

"I think he's got the message!" Sandy interrupted Oliver quickly, "Do you want me to come with you or is it private?"

"Yes please, Sandy." Paul sounded relieved that she had offered. They left Oliver, Paul this time leading the way. In a matter of minutes they returned and Paul was obviously excited.

"Look what Paul has found." Sandy drew Paul closer to Oliver, the firelight was dimming now but it was adequate to see what Paul was holding,

"I've found you a crutch!" Paul squeaked like a child giving his mother her Christmas present. In his hand he held the leg and cross string of a table. It was a bit too short for Oliver but with a bit of packing it would be relatively comfortable to use.

"We can pad the top with your shorts, you'll have to bend over a bit but it is useable isn't it?" Sandy willed Oliver to agree.

"Wow!" exclaimed Oliver, "Well done, give me a few hours rest and then I'll be as good as new!" Paul swelled with pleasure and immediately removed his trousers and gave Sandy Oliver's shorts so that she could fashion a pad for the crutch.

It took longer than they had hoped for Oliver to recover enough to be able to even try the crutch, his leg was swollen up to the knee and the act of even becoming vertical was agony as the blood seemed to rush downwards exacerbating the pain. Paul and Sandy took over searching for an exit but to no avail. The small rabbits had been eaten and their water was half gone. Their despair and the lack of sustenance plunged them into long miserable silences. Sandy wept as she thought of her parents and the longing for a sight of the sky again began to drive her mad. She suffered panic attacks and lay shaking whilst Paul sat mutely at her side holding her hand.

Two days passed, Sandy had given up hope and Paul was not

competent to wander off on his own. Oliver, though still in pain and feeling weak from lack of food and water had mastered the crutch though he did wonder why he had bothered as it seemed unlikely that they would ever escape from their tomb. Their only comfort was the little fire they lit each day although even that would soon be a thing of the past as the supply of wood was running out and so were Oliver's matches.

CHAPTER 12

JUNE AND TIM answered the door to a loud knocking and June gasped and staggered back into Tim. A very young, pink faced constable holding a note book in front of him like a shield, stepped into the porch,

"Good morning, is this the address of a Sandra Williams?" June screamed and lunged towards the policeman

"Where is she? What's happened?" Tim held her as she looked about to faint.

"Please," he begged the policeman "tell us she's alright."

"May I come in please?" He looked nervous and Tim feared the worst. He opened the door fully and ushered the man inside. When they had guided June to a seat and she had collapsed into it, Tim turned to the policeman

"Well?"

"I can't tell you anything about her wellbeing or her whereabouts sir, the only information I have is that a car registered to Sandra Williams has been discovered." He referred to his notebook again and read from it like an automaton, "The vehicle was found by a man and a woman blackberry picking. The vehicle was discovered in a deep ditch and not visible from the road." He looked up from his notes and then down again "It is not clear how long the vehicle has been there. The vehicle is burnt-out; it was identified by its engine number as being the property of Sandra Williams at this address." June's face already pale, turned ashen, she gave a strangled cry

"Oh my baby, my darling!" Tim rushed to catch her as she fell forwards from her seat in a dead faint.

"I must add sir that the vehicle, on preliminary inspection, did not appear to have been occupied at the time of the fire."

"Why the fuck didn't you say that first?!" Tim furiously shouted at him, "Look at her, she's collapsed, please go and fetch some water while I call a doctor!" The policemen obediently strode off to the kitchen to fetch a glass of water, saying as he went

"There's no call to be offensive sir, I am only doing my job."

"Not very well!" shouted Tim after him. Tim rang their friend Dr. Squires at the local surgery and explained to the receptionist what had happened, she assured him that Dr. Squires would come immediately as morning surgery had just finished. They lived in a small hamlet and the doctor and his wife were well known to them both as family doctor and fellow parent. Sandy and their son Andy had attended the same school and both sets of parents had acted at various times as taxis to and from parties. Mike Squires had been a kind, comforting and positive presence whilst treating June for her post-miscarriage depressions; their friendship had deepened considerably during those harrowing times.

June began to stir and Tim handed her the glass of water. He forestalled a further outburst from her by telling her quickly that Sandy had not been in the car. She sank back into the cushions of the settee tears streaming down her face.

"Her car was probably stolen from the car park by some hooligans, the bastards!" He sat beside her and with his arm around her he smoothed her face and hair, "Mike Squires is on his way darling, I think you need some medication to help you cope with this."

When Dr. Squires arrived the policeman stood quietly to one side as he examined June's blood pressure and heart.

"You don't have to stay constable." Tim indicated that the

policeman had done his job and that they wished him to leave.

"I do have further information sir, might I speak to you in private seeing as your wife is so upset?" June's attention, luckily, was being held by Mike Squires as he instructed her as to the dosage of her pills etcetera and was not party to this exchange.

"I'm just seeing the constable out darling." He called as he walked to the front door with him. "We'll talk outside." Tim ushered the policeman on to the driveway, "What is it?" He asked anxiously. The constable referred again to his notebook,

"Well sir, there was, as I have said, no evidence of any body in the wreckage, but I must ask if you can identify some items which survived the fire. There was not much left of the vehicle as you can imagine, but some metallic objects were found which weren't part of the fabric of the car. Where was your daughter going, did she have luggage with her?"

"She was driving to the train station to catch a connection to her flight to Ostend; she would have had a suitcase and hand luggage. Why do you ask?"

"We need to identify the items found in order to ascertain whether they belonged to her and whether the car was stolen before or after she arrived at her destination." He explained. Tim's heart stopped, momentarily,

"What sort of objects?" Sandy's car was always a mobile dustbin, she never seemed worried about all the clutter which gathered between the seats; broken umbrellas, empty Pepsi bottles, discarded jackets and shoes, the list was endless.

"I think it would be best sir if you came to the station and viewed them for yourself. If they do not belong to her or were not part of her luggage, we can assume they belonged to whoever stole the vehicle which could give a possible lead on the culprits.

"And if they are hers?" Tim felt his chest tighten and suppressing a wave of panic he said "I will come as soon as I can leave my wife." The policeman drove off on his motorcycle and

Tim returned to the house. Mike Squires handed him a prescription saying

"June's calmer now, get these as soon as you can, the dosage will be on the packet." He put his arm around Tim's shoulder, "Try not to worry old man, I'm sure it's a straightforward case of theft." Tim forwent telling him of his conversation with the policeman, thanked him for coming so quickly and waved him off.

Inside the house, June, tucked up in a blanket on the settee, was dozing – the effect of the medication Mike had given her. He made sure she was comfortable and not in danger of rolling off, scribbled a note saying 'gone for prescription back soon. Love you' and left, closing the door quietly.

Tim dropped the prescription into the chemist saying he would call back in half an hour and then made his apprehensive way to the police station. He was shown into a small interview room where a different policeman joined him and invited him to sit down. He placed a large plastic bag on the table and from it he extracted some blackened objects which he placed in front of Tim. There was the broken umbrella, unmistakable by its thin, now buckled, wands, a mangled bottle opener, the old biscuit tin in which Sandy kept her tapes and other sundry items.

"They certainly look like Sandy's things, she always had a lot of junk in the car, never cleared it out..." Tim paused, a small mostly melted item caught his eye, it looked initially like a melted blob of aluminium. Tim picked it up and with shaking hands he turned it over and over. There was another blob, similar to the other but smaller. In a flash Tim recognised them. Sandy would never have left them in the car, she had packed them, wrapped in tissue paper deep inside her suitcase, and he remembered suggesting that she leave them at home where they were safe. The remains of his mother's silver backed hairbrush and her silver jewellery box sat in his hands.

CHAPTER 13

THE FORLORN FRIENDS, deep under the moor, lay curled up to each other, watching the smoke rise from their fire. Their stomachs writhed with hunger and their mouths were swollen with thirst. Their water was nearly gone in spite of the rationing of two sips each three times a day, dehydration was the biggest fear; you could live without food for quite some time but not without water. Sandy suggested bitterly that they could lick the condensation from the walls. To her surprise, Oliver praised her for a brilliant idea. Hesitantly at first, with expectations of a gritty foul tasting, muddy liquid, she ran her finger over the wet blocks and licked it off. It tasted of nothing, just water. However the thought of actually licking the wall was a bit off-putting.

"I could mop it up with my T-shirt and suck it."

"No, that's wasteful, lick the bloody wall!" Oliver croaked as he eased himself to join her, "don't be precious. If you can't bring yourself to do it you can't be thirsty enough. I know I am." With that he gathered some drops with his tongue.

"Come on Paul, get licking." The relief of knowing that there was a constant supply of moisture hanging on the walls was immense. They would never get as much as they really needed this way but it could be enough to save their lives. Though how much longer they could survive like this was questionable. They had not eaten for days now and their rush of excitement about the water soon dwindled into hopelessness. They lay listlessly as close to the small fire as they could, no one speaking; there was nothing to say which could lift their hopes.

"What a pathetic little fire," Oliver said suddenly, "what's the point of rationing the wood? We may as well bung the rest of it on and die warm." Adding "Maybe the smoke will suffocate us before we starve; it's got to be a better way to go surely?" Neither Sandy nor Paul bothered to answer his rhetorical question. Paul heaved a pile of wood onto the fire and it caught quickly, flaring up so as to light the chamber all around them. By its light they took in the view of what was to be their graves, the smoke curling up and away, "No luck, the space is too big, looks like we'll starve after all." Oliver groaned and turned away from the fire, curling up despondently; a sight Sandy never thought she'd see.

"Where does it go?" Paul asked suddenly.

"Where does what go?" Oliver answered,

"The smoke." Paul replied gesturing at the spirals making their way upwards.

"God knows, and probably doesn't care." Oliver had truly lost heart. He felt that his injury had sentenced them to die; he kicked at a stray smouldering stick and winced at the pain in his leg. Sandy's attention, however was piqued,

"That's a point, it escapes somewhere doesn't it? We've never been smoked out all the time we've lit fires here, I haven't even smelt smoke in the mornings; it would surely hang around if there wasn't an outlet somewhere!" She was excited and shook Oliver to make him sit up, "Come on Oliver, think!"

"It's probably just some fissure which leads into another space; a crack in the wall." He lay down again and turned his back to them. Sandy looked at Paul who returned a baleful smile, "Will you cuddle me Sandy? I'm scared about dying." Sandy sat with Paul's head resting on her shoulder and soundlessly wept.

They fell into a sleep filled with despair, Sandy half hoping that she wouldn't re-awaken. Oliver, who though curled up as if asleep, was wide awake when he heard it; a loud hiss followed by still more, the fire spluttered and steam and smoke rose in unison. *Must be raining. Raining!* "Sandy, Paul, wake up!" Sandy and Paul jumped and sat up in shock, what was the matter? "Listen, do you hear that?" Oliver looked excitedly at them both, "that's rain and it's coming in!" He hobbled to his feet and held his hand out over the fire, and yes, a drop of water fell onto it. His first thought was that they should catch the water to drink and he scrambled to find his bottle. It was a stupid idea; as catching the drops in the small neck of a flask was totally impractical.

"It's just above the fire; that must be where the smoke is getting out as well!" Sandy too got to her feet, gazing upwards. Oliver shone his torch and they followed its beam as he played it across the ceiling. Droplets of water sparkled in its light and fell intermittently into the flames. The ceiling was lower at this point and the water, gravity pulling it, released its hold and plopped down. Following the slight rise of the ceiling and the dribble of water with his torch Oliver located the source it was near the wall, the seepage was quite heavy and getting heavier.

The rain was torrential and accompanied by a howling wind, Oliver's tent was beginning to leak and the shelter of the rock was becoming inadequate protection from the buffeting gale. Jimmy was hungry; he had had no success bagging a fowl, the rain in his eyes making his aim poor. A great deal of Oliver's shot had been wasted and he was angry with himself over this. He should have made a move earlier and not tried to use Paul to do his gun thieving, he would be off the moor by now had he done so. The only advantage of using Paul had been the chance to get rid of him; a witness who could identify him. He had been hoping to secure the gun by stealth and to keep his existence hidden from the other two. As it was he had had to get rid of them as well. He did feel a little bit sorry that he had been forced to do away with the girl; she was only a kid and pretty at that. He shook off the feeling as easily as a dog shakes the wet from its coat. No one would tell the tale and he wasn't cursed with much of a conscience.

"It's there, that's where it's coming from!" Sandy pointed excitedly,

"The only problem is that it's up there and we can't reach it." Oliver extinguished his torch and along with it, his hope. They sank back down wordlessly and Oliver threw a stick onto the spluttering fire. "All that it's going to do is put our fire out!"

Suddenly a steady downpour of water completely snuffed out the fire, "Great. Thank-you God!" exclaimed Oliver. "Show us the way out, show us we can't reach it and then put our fire out! Thank-you God!" This was more like Oliver, Sandy thought, a good bit of temper, she imagined his face flushing with outrage and his ginger curls standing out from his head. Before she had time to react there was an ominous creaking sound in the pitch dark and something crashed to the floor. They jumped in alarm.

"What the hell was that? Is everyone okay?" Oliver called. Sandy and Paul answered him in unison that they were. Water was pouring down from the ceiling and they hurriedly moved out from under it.

"A star!!" Paul squeaked, "There's a star!" Sandy and Oliver looked up to where Paul was pointing and there it was: a lone star. As they gazed up at the outside world through the hole in the roof, a black cloud, moved on hurriedly by the gale, opened a window and through it shone a full yellow moon. A shaft of luminous lemon light flooded through the open roof on to the floor and picked out a rotted wooden trap door, its coating of grass and weeds still clinging to it like some wild wig. They gathered in the moon beam, soaking up the feeling of contact with the world again, refusing for the moment to acknowledge the underlying fact that they were still trapped and without food.

CHAPTER 14

TIM SAT RIGIDLY on his chair in the interview room, clutching the melted silver in his trembling hands. His thoughts were running wild. No matter how he re-arranged his reasoning the answer remained the same. Sandy's luggage had been in the car when it was stolen. Where was she? Had the thieves harmed her, was she also lying in a ditch somewhere as yet undiscovered? Whatever was he going to tell June?

"These are hers as well," he said quietly to the policeman, "they were my mother's silver box and hairbrush which I know Sandy packed in her case."

"My constable tells me she was travelling to the train station in Exeter, is that correct?"

"Yes, she was going on holiday." Tim's voice felt unconnected to him, he heard the words but was unaware of having spoken them.

"Would Sandra have left her case in the car when it was unattended at any time?" the detective asked. Tim's hopes momentarily rose; of course, her car was stolen when she had stopped at a service station.

"She was travelling over night by train; the station has a free car park where she was going to leave her car. Other than a convenience stop there wouldn't have been any call for her to leave her car unattended. Of course; that must be when it was stolen!" As soon as he had said it he knew it was untrue. His shoulders slumped and he looked miserably at the detective saying "If it was stolen when she was at a service station she would have rung me or reported it immediately. Oh God, something dreadful has happened to her or we would have heard from her by now, it's been nearly three weeks since she left." Tim fought to control his emotions. "I'm sorry, she's our only child, it'll kill her mother if anything has happened to her." Tim wouldn't bring himself to use the word 'dead'; that would be unbearable.

"We'll register a missing persons' file and start our enquiries immediately." The policeman stood and held out his hand to shake Tim's unsteady one, "We'll do our best to find her. If there's anything else you think we should know, get in touch." He handed Tim his card and showed him out.

He was half way home before he remembered June's prescription and thus arrived back more than an hour later than he should have had he been only going to the chemist. June was awake.

"Where have you been? You've been ages." Tim had never lied to June; there had never been any need to. He was a faithful husband and June always knew where he was at any time. The only secrets he ever kept from her were innocent ones such as what he had bought her for birthdays or Christmas. Should he lie to her now? He reasoned that it would be lying by omission which wasn't the same as a blatant lie. The whereabouts of Sandy may be discovered very soon with a perfectly plausible explanation, she was probably okay. *No*! He said firmly to himself, he was fooling himself in order to avoid the anguish of dealing with June's anguish. He had to be honest. One look at Tim's face and his trembling hands would be proof enough for her that all was not well.

Sandy had decided that they needed warmth and a new location for the fire. Knowing Oliver's matches were running low she had suggested they gather as much wood as possible from wherever they could find it and keep a fire burning, if only a small one. So, she had busied herself rummaging in adjoining 'rooms' with the aid of the now rather faint light of the torch and had stacked a sizeable pile of wood in the dry, slightly elevated section of the room, before she joined Oliver and Paul to gaze up through the opening. The night sky was hypnotic in its embodiment of the unattainable outside; the world could be glimpsed like a painting in a frame; but unlike a painting, it was real, it was tangible — but it was unreachable. Slowly the colour of the square of night sky lifted, the blue grey colours of dawn replaced the black blue of night and somewhere the sun was hoisting its glowing body to sweep the remaining shadows away. The scent of rain-washed foliage wafted down to them and they breathed it in as a drowning man sucks in oxygen on his last rise to the surface before he sinks below and his lungs finally fill with water. The darkness and dankness of their tomb was accentuated by the comparison to the freshness above them. The sheer existence of the clean outside world where birds flew and people breathed fresh air brought them closer to despair than they had hitherto been. They were doomed to see it, to smell it, to hear it, but not to touch it. For want of anything else to do they re-kindled the fire and watched the smoke escape as they could never do. What a cruel torture, it might have been better if the trapdoor had never fallen in. At least then they would die knowing they had tried everything.

"We *cannot* sit here and ignore the fact that we have a means of escape." Oliver told them, "There must be a way we can get up to it."

As the dawn shed some light into the room they surveyed their surroundings, the walls all around them were made of blocks, Oliver limped over to the wall nearest to the opening in the roof, running his fingers over it he searched for anything which could be a foothold, in spite of his injury he felt sure that he could scale the wall if there were any. It was smooth; the mortar between the blocks was flush with the blocks themselves. And the wall was slippery; wringing wet. Climbing it was out of the question. For the remainder of the day they argued back and forth about how to reach the opening; with no solution. Oliver took his penknife and attempted to cut footholds in the mortar. He managed to make some impression in them and attempted a trial climb favouring his bad leg. He managed to reach the top of his handholds and he attempted to carve more out above him, his position, spread-eagled against the wall, made it impossible for him to get any purchase with the knife whilst holding on with his fingertips of the other hand. He lost his grip and slipped clumsily to the ground. Sandy could see the pain in his face as he bravely tried to smother a cry. She felt utterly useless; she knew she had no more hope of scaling the wall than Oliver had.

June and Tim's anxieties were not lessened when they received an air mail letter addressed to Sandy. They opened it to find that it was from Josie telling of the great time she was having and wondering where Sandy had decided to go instead of joining her as agreed. A letter from the charter airline the following day confirmed what they already knew, that Sandy had not boarded the flight from Ostend and in fact had not taken the ferry plane out of England.

The police were now seriously pursuing Sandy's disappearance as a missing person but so far there had been no response to their enquiries. She had been travelling alone and at night, no-one had seen her since she had left her parents' home. Needless to say, the youths who had stolen her car remained silent. All the police had to go on was the final location of the car. Police dogs were taken to the site of the wreckage and the search radiated from there. By this time, they were not searching for a person but fully expected to find a body. The air-sea rescue helicopters were already employed on a search for two missing inmates from the asylum near Exeter and Sandy's details were added to their agenda. Rumours began at the police station that the two might be connected; the escapees were known to be dangerous. What if they had hi-jacked Sandy and killed her, dumping her body goodness knows where, and then, when the car broke down or ran out of petrol or for whatever reason, they decided to abandon it, they would naturally have set fire to it to obliterate any evidence. The search intensified.

Oliver's parents' interest was caught by the news item on the television when it mentioned Sandy's journey took her across the moor. It reminded them that Oliver should really have come home by now. They generally didn't worry about him when he went on his sojourns, which he regularly did, as they knew he had excellent survival skills, but, what if he had had an accident? Anxiety crept slowly over them.

There was increasing helicopter presence over the moor much to Jimmy's disquiet. He had hoped that it would have died down again by now, but of course, idiot that he was; they were probably looking for that couple of youngsters. He hurriedly dismantled the tent and scuffed out his fire as he heard the chop-chop of blades rather too close for comfort. He would have to make sure to pack up before light every day and hope they didn't use search lights at night. The tent was a bright blue, shame it wasn't khaki. He had attempted to camouflage it with bits of shrubs but he hadn't been happy with the result. The foliage kept slipping on the smooth sloping walls of the tent and bits of bright blue fabric shone out in the sunshine. No he would have to dismantle it before dawn every day, or not use it at all.

He daren't use the gun, he dug into the back-pack thinking he would find the sling shot he had seen Oliver using; he could have a go at hunting with that. Bugger, it wasn't there; the boy must have had it in his pocket. As for a fire, he couldn't chance lighting one out in the open. At night the flame would be seen and in the day the smoke would give him away. He had to keep out of sight. Things, he realised, were getting tricky. He needed to think carefully about his movements. Gathering up his stolen possessions he headed cautiously towards a small clump of hawthorn bushes; he could shelter out of sight under them for the time being.

As twilight filled the little window on the world, birds twittered their goodnights and flew to roost, their carefree songs seeming to mock the prisoners down below. That night they took it in turns to watch the fire and keep it stoked whilst the other two slept, Oliver's box contained just five precious matches, the fire was the only comfort they had; they dare not let it die before they did.

The following morning, Oliver who had been restless beside Sandy all night, spoke into the semi-darkness,

"There *must* be a way we can reach it!" The other two sat up, Sandy asked eagerly

"Have you got a plan?"

"Not exactly, but we can't just sit here and give up can we?"

"But it's well out of reach, we'd need a ladder..."

"The ladder! That's it; if we can dislodge the ladder we came down on and lug it here it might reach."

"What are we waiting for?" cried Sandy. "Come on Oliver, Paul can be your extra crutch. Come on!" She had leapt to her feet and was tugging at their hands as they sat there,

"We could be out today!"

They followed the scratches on the wall to the place of their first encounter with the bunker. The ladder hung there bleak and rusty, stretching up into the darkness and the immovable slab above it. The sight of it made them shiver with the memory of their fear as they were forced underground to die. But, as well as being the means of their descent into their tomb, it could also be the means of their ascent from it.

"Right, let's give it a go. It was very shaky when I came down and I suspect the fixings are pretty much corroded." Oliver staggered a little as the makeshift crutch slipped sideways.

"Be careful, for goodness sake don't make your leg any worse, we need you!" Sandy exclaimed. They all grabbed the bottom of the ladder, Paul on one side, Sandy on the other and Oliver in the middle. After a count of three they started to shake and shake the ladder, bits of mortar fell on their heads as the fixings seemed to give way.

"It's coming, keep going!" Oliver told them in between grunts. They shook and shook and more bits fell on them but the ladder stayed fixed to the wall. "Stop, it's no good, it's only moving the last bit. I'm going up to the top I may be able to prise the fixings loose with my penknife." Oliver started to climb but Sandy pulled him back,

"Don't Oliver, you can barely stand as it is, you could fall; anyway do you really think a penknife would be any good?"

"I've got to try." Oliver made to continue his climb.

"What if the ladder comes away when you're at the top? It will crash down with you on it!" Sandy was becoming fearful of Oliver injuring himself even more. "I'll go, I'm lighter than you and I've got pretty strong hands to dig with the knife. You two have got more bulk between you to hold the ladder at the bottom just enough so that it can sort of slide down to the ground if I get it loose." It was a better plan than Oliver going up and Paul was too nervous to do it. Oliver was furious at himself for his stupid accident which made him a burden to the others. He knew it was foolhardy for him to go up the ladder with a leg he could barely put any weight on but was reluctant all the same to admit his defeat. He sighed, and pulled open the biggest blade from his penknife and gave it to her telling her to hold the blade away from herself in case she should slip.

Much later, as they trudged their way, despondent and tired, back to their camp, ladder-less, no-one spoke. It had been a brilliant idea but one broken knife blade later and with cuts and grazes on Sandy's knuckles, they had been forced to give it up. They built up their little fire and had a sip of water each. They had no food and the water wouldn't last for ever. They had to find a way out or they were surely going to die. They curled up close to each other near the fire and one by one sank into sleep.

Day came and then the night fell, then day came again and the three of them grew hungrier and thirstier. They had managed to catch a tiny amount of water from the deluge which had brought the trapdoor down but it was barely enough to wet their lips. Far too quickly the remainder had seeped away into the ground. They were weary and growing weaker with every hour. They had lost track of how many days they had spent underground, but it seemed an eternity. Oliver took to playing disconsolately with his sling shot, picking up bits of stone from the floor and firing them through the hole.

"You never know," he said wryly, "I might hit a passing pigeon."

"Yea, and pigs may fly." Retorted Sandy, she no longer had the strength to hope; especially for something which was as unlikely as them being hit by lightning.

It was as though God had finally relented and decided that any sins they may have committed were absolved, for there on the edge of the opening, looking inquisitively down at them was a big fat pigeon. It cooed and fussed, preening itself and then, to their joint amazement it flew down and landed close by their original fire site. There it began to peck around, finding minute scraps of their previous meals. Very quietly Oliver loaded his sling with the heaviest stone to hand and carefully took aim. They held their breath as he drew his arm back, expecting the bird to notice the movement and fly off, but pigeons are stupid creatures and it merely glanced at them with one beady eye which blinked off as the stone hit it squarely. It toppled fluttering to the floor. Oliver, in spite of his injured leg, was first to reach it and twisting its neck he put it out of misery.

"Supper, we have supper!" He shouted in tears. Get the fire going!"

They slept again that night, wrapped up in the parka, their hunger still gnawing at their stomachs, the pigeon, fat though it was, had hardly been enough for one person; and divided into three it merely underlined their hunger.

Sandy woke to the sound of dawn; a blackbird singing its glorious celebration of a new day. A sharp frosty air from above shivered her flesh. She sat up to see Oliver, balancing precariously on his crutch, with the help of Paul's supporting arm, looking longingly at the opening above them, neither of them speaking. Sandy joined them and they encircled her with their arms.

"We are going to get out!" Oliver was emphatic, "I'm buggered if I'm giving up!"

"Paul and I are going to find as much wood as we can and as many blocks as we can carry and pile them up as far as we can. I just hope we haven't burnt all the sturdy stuff."

"I'm coming too." Sandy hugged them tighter, "We *will* survive this." They spent the remainder of the day lugging blocks from broken walls and carefully stacking them under the trapdoor. There was very little in the way of sturdy wood left, with the exception of Oliver's crutch which wouldn't really make much difference to the pyramid they were constructing, so they concentrated on the blocks. By the time they had done as much as their tired undernourished bodies could manage, the pile of rubble stood a mere four feet from the ground. Paul looked dreadful; he was puffing and wheezing, high spots of colour on his cheeks looking incongruous against the pallor of his forehead. Sandy was exhausted and breathless; also, their lack of sustenance telling on them all. Oliver sat nursing his leg which looked to Sandy as though it was more swollen than before.

"Well that's less than quarter-way up." He muttered. "God knows whether we'll find enough to reach the opening." No one answered him. They pulled the parka around them and collapsed into sleep. Exhausted though they were, none of them slept for long. Sandy woke herself by her sobbing and Oliver, who had barely closed his eyes, pulled her to him and soothed her as best he could; muttering encouraging words into her ear. Paul tried his best to comfort her as well but he was as near to tears as she was. When they realised that trying to sleep was pointless they sat up and drew closer to the fire, Oliver tossed a couple of small bits of wood on the embers and blew the flames into life.

"We have to find more blocks, this place is huge; there must be something somewhere." He stretched his long arms and, grimacing at the resurgence of pain in his leg rose to his feet.

"We're coming with you." Sandy said, and she and Paul got shakily to their feet and joined Oliver in the quest for materials.

They wandered further into the labyrinthine tunnels than they had done before, Oliver taking great care to mark their way. They were all very wary of possible dangers such as the fissure Oliver had fallen into and praying that the batteries would hold out, he played the torch light over the floor and ceiling before entering each corridor. He limped along gamely, he was suffering; every step produced a grunt or an intake of breath as he strove to conceal his discomfort from the others. Paul was insistent that he carry more than he was really strong enough to do and stayed as close to Oliver as he could attempting to provide a support for Oliver should he need it. Between them they carried all the blocks they could find, broken and whole back to their camp, journey after journey until they simply could do no more. After resting for a short while, Oliver started building on to their existing pyramid. In order to gain more height, he took some of the lower stabilising blocks and piled them precariously on top. The pile was now as tall as Oliver. However, this left a distance of his height again plus some.

"It's still nothing like high enough, and even if we do get some more height it's going to be unstable. Some of those top blocks are going to have to come down and increase the base area or the whole bloody lot is going to fall." He started to rearrange the blocks, with tired, deflated movements.

"Oliver, leave it be for now, let's talk it through." Sandy pulled him down to sit beside her and Paul. "How unstable is it?"

"Well, at the moment it's quite stable, but much higher without lateral support and it'll collapse."

"Do you think you could reach the opening?"

"It must be still well over eight feet above the top of the blocks, I might be able to reach the opening but only with my fingertips, I'm sorry, but I honestly don't think I could pull myself up with just my fingers. Maybe a few weeks ago I might have had the strength but I am bloody knackered now."

"If we can manage to build it up another foot even, do you think you could do it then?"

"Possibly, I'm willing to give it a go. I just wish I didn't have this bloody bad ankle." Sandy and Paul helped Oliver rearrange the blocks, taking any from the bottom where they didn't seem to be particularly load bearing and between them they managed to increase the height of the apex by twelve or so inches, it was a bit wobbly but with care it might do the job.

"It's getting dark outside, and we need to rest. In the morning, I'll give it a go." Oliver sank to the ground with pain filled exhaustion, "Let's try and sleep now."

The morning chorus of blackbirds, followed by a thrush's beautiful song greeted their waking ears. It was torturous.

"Right, if I make it out, I'm going to try and find you some food and water and then I'm going for help." Oliver, put his sling shot into his string bag and fastened the flask to his belt. Donning his parka he climbed slowly and carefully up the block pyramid. He reached the top and was relieved to find it didn't wobble too much.

"Here goes!" He took a deep breath and reached up, his hand grasped the edge of the opening and he attempted to do likewise with his other one. He pushed up from his feet and grabbed a handful of rotten wood which came away in his hand. The momentum of his body as it swung off balance put all his weight on his bad leg. He felt it give way under him and he tumbled down, cracking his elbows and collarbone in his descent. Sandy and Paul rushed to him and he raised his face to theirs, then, burying his head in his arms as he lay prone on the cold floor, he wept.

Sandy sat quietly beside him and gently laid her hand on his shaking shoulders as he lay, his back towards them and gave in to his grief. Paul sat a little apart, unsure what to do or say. Oliver tried to gain control of his tears and, gulping them back he sat up and gazed into Sandy's eyes,

"I'm so sorry." They sat mutely, each with the same thought, if Oliver couldn't get out what were they going to do? Paul would be no use, he wasn't very tall, he wasn't very strong and he wouldn't be any good at hunting. He would be as unable to get help as Sandy would be as neither of them knew the moor. It had to be Oliver. But how on earth would he do it now? The fall had twisted his leg and must have put the healing back by days. His self-confidence was knocked and he blamed himself. Paul broke the silence, hesitantly saying

"I might be able to get out Oliver." Oliver and Sandy turned to him, both with the same thought,

"No Paul, you'll never even reach it and even if you did get out what then? You don't know the way home any more than I do." Sandy tried to be gracious in her refusal but Paul crumpled as the recognition of his inadequacy showed in her answer.

"But someone has to go!" He said shrilly, panic creeping into his voice.

"What we need more than anything is water and food." Oliver had regained his leadership role. I can't do it but I think you could." He looked at Sandy, "If we could somehow get you out you could at least find some water, there should be plenty up there."

"We'd need to build it up at least another eighteen inches before I could even *reach* the edge and then I'd still have to get out. If I fall and break something that would just about finish us off." Sandy was amazed that Oliver could be so daft.

"I'm serious," he said, "if I can reach it from the top of the blocks, then with you on my shoulders you'd be half way out."

"But you can hardly stand let alone bear my weight on top. Anyway, the blocks wouldn't be stable enough surely?"

"I reckon that if we rearrange them so they are really solid it doesn't matter if they are lower, because with both our heights put together it would be high enough to get you out. Come on, it's still early in the day, we've got to try it, we can't lie down and die until we have exhausted every minute possibility." Oliver was right, there was no 'can't' they had to succeed.

Once Oliver was satisfied that the blocks were sound and that they weren't going to topple he climbed to the top which was now wide enough for two people to stand close together and he then beckoned Paul up beside him. Paul looked surprised and a little apprehensive but cautiously did as he was bidden.

"Paul, you must give me support, stand to my right and brace yourself against me to take the strain off my ankle. That's right. Now Sandy, put the sling shot and most importantly, the flask into the bag and come up here."

"But I can't leave you both down here. Where do I go? I don't know the way home."

The temptation to escape fought agonisingly with Sandy's conscience, to be out of this hole, to breathe the open air again. She imagined herself orienteering as well as Oliver did; striding through the moor and reaching habitation. She would then find help and rescue the others. Oliver could see her thoughts flashing through her mind, her face betraying every emotion.

"I'm not suggesting you go for help; just water and if possible food; anything edible I don't care what it is, berries, roots..." Oliver explained, "Come on, put on my sweater it's oiled wool and very warm, you'll need it!" She still hesitated until Oliver said sharply "Sandy COME ON!" She climbed up to them where Oliver, shaky with hunger and trying to favour his leg stood ready, Paul bracing him. He cupped his hands for Sandy's foot and heaved her up.

She scrambled on to his shoulders her hands painfully grasping a handful of his curls. Oliver, tall and strong though he was, found her slight weight agonisingly heavy as his injured leg threatened to betray him. Paul wedged his shoulder under Oliver's arm and braced himself to take some of the strain. Sandy managed to climb on to his shoulders but refused to stand up fully,

"I'll fall!" she cried, "I can't balance!" She still clung on to Oliver's hair until he shouted

"Let go of my bloody hair you're going to pull it out! Just take it slowly and keep focused." Sandy responded to the old Oliver's authority and slowly raised herself up to a standing position, Oliver swayed as if he were about to collapse and she shrieked. Paul reached up and held her ankles with a surprisingly firm grip,

"I've got you Sandy, you can do it!" He re-assured her. Sandy reached up and could only just reach the edges of the opening,

"It's too far; I can't pull myself up from here!" She wobbled and both she and Oliver swayed precariously, Paul tried his best to stabilise them both by wedging himself under Oliver's shoulder.

"Come down! Paul get ready to catch her." Oliver was gasping with the pain in his leg and Sandy's knee in his eye and half of his hair being pulled out on her descent didn't help his discomfort.

"It's okay," Oliver reassured her when she started to apologise for hurting him, and for her inability to stretch high enough. "We just have to build it up a bit more." He tried to inject a bit more enthusiasm in his voice than he felt. He had been sure they'd be able to get her out.

"Were you standing up completely? Was she Paul?"

"Yes, I was!" Sandy snapped back at him, "I stretched as far as I could; I'm not made of rubber!"

"Okay, okay, calm down, we'll try again when we've found some more building materials."

Sandy sat down with a thump,

"Do you really think I'd not give it everything?" She growled at Oliver.

"I'm sorry. I'm just disappointed that's all." Oliver sat down beside her, "We'll get there, we're nearly there, it's just a small setback, okay?" Sandy got to her feet,

"Come on then, let's make it work, I've got to get out of this place before I go mad!" She picked up one of the heavier blocks and threw it violently against the wall where it broke into pieces. She thumped herself back down.

"Well done, that's one block less!" Oliver shouted at her.

"Oh bollocks to you!" She shouted back.

"Oliver?" Paul poked him in the back,

"What is it Paul?" Oliver turned to face him. Paul pointed at two broken breeze blocks at the bottom of the wall near where

Sandy had thrown the concrete block. Behind them the natural wall of the bunker could be seen. There was a thin layer of earth at the bottom giving way to rock further up.

"Hey, look at this." Oliver shook Sandy by the shoulder to make her turn round. She swivelled on her bottom to face the wall. "The blocks have come loose, we may be able to prise some more away." Like an idiot, he kicked at the wall and cried out in pain. Then he picked up one of the broken pieces of block and used it like a hammer against the wall.

Another block came loose and another. He managed to dislodge six or so blocks before the wall suddenly became immovable. The space between the blocks themselves and the rock behind had been filled with concrete and was as solid as granite. The little hollow area had obviously been a flaw in the construction; the concrete hadn't flowed right down to the bottom.

"Great! Another bloody dead-end!" Oliver cursed.

"Well at least we have a few more blocks without having to go looking for them." Sandy said petulantly. Oliver had visualised breaking down the blocks of the wall in such a way as to turn it into a climbing wall which would have enabled them all to get out at the same time.

Watching Oliver in his despair and exhaustion Sandy felt shamed by her aggressive outburst; she caught hold of Oliver's arm and said quietly

"I'm sorry, that was stupid of me. Come on then let's give it another try." They carried the extra blocks to the top of the pile and managed to raise it by eighteen inches or so, still making sure it was stable and large enough for two people to stand on it as before. Again Sandy wobbled her way into a standing position on Oliver's shoulders, taking another handful of his curls with her. She stretched up and grabbed the edges of the opening; she pulled herself up to her fullest height and found that she was looking at the world again.

"Can you get out?" Oliver called in a strangled voice as his leg throbbed and pain tore through him.

"Hang on, I think I can." Using the muscles in her arms and shoulders, which heaving crates of milk had developed, she pulled herself up until she managed to hook her elbows over the edge scrabbling for a handhold. Grasping a bunch of heather in her one hand she pushed hard with the other until she lay sprawled out on the sopping wet ground.

"I'm out!" She cried in jubilation. There was a cry from below and swivelling around so that she could see back into the hole, she looked anxiously down and saw Oliver and Paul sprawled on the floor, a pile of blocks scattered around them. Oliver was nursing his leg and groaning with pain. Paul moved to crouch at his side.

"My God, what happened? Are you alright?" screamed Sandy.

"I'm okay," he replied to her concerned call, "sodding blocks slipped!" He was in agony; but he fought the urge to cry out. As Sandy watched, Paul hugged Oliver, "You are so clever!" He squeaked. Paul then carefully helped Oliver into a more comfortable position, gently arranging the parka to give him some support and padding against the hard floor.

"Well done Sandy, well done!" Paul did a little jig and clapped his hands, a huge grin spread across his face which was now as gaunt as a corpse.

"Thanks Paul, I'm fine now." Oliver smiled up at him and Paul beamed with pleasure. "Sandy, see what's what up there, if you can fill the flask that would be brilliant," Oliver called up, "but be careful!" Sandy stood up and gazed around her, the frost was sparkling on the shrubs and grasses and autumn berries glowed in the clean sunlight as though varnished.

"Oh my God, it's beautiful!" she exclaimed. She felt like a blind person whose sight had been miraculously restored. The air which she inhaled deeply bit at her lungs and tingled in her nose;

it was cold, but such a different sort of cold to that of below ground that it didn't seem cold at all. Her whole body, though weak, felt truly alive, an inner strength gave her an energy which she didn't have before and she swore to herself that she would not rest until they were all safe. Being early in the day, she had hours of daylight at her disposal, firstly, water had to be found and then something, anything, for them to eat, but she knew that she dare not waste the day; another night without water could be disastrous for them.

"I'm going to look for water," she called down, "there should be plenty after all that rain." Within a short time of searching, wading through the sopping foliage, she came to an area which seemed wetter than the rest, just as she was about to venture into it she paused, it was too green, Oliver had warned her to be careful and with good reason; this looked suspiciously like moss. There were some other plants amongst the moss, what did Oliver call them? Bog bean or something. She remembered that they spread under water and took over marshy land. Turning away to find more solid ground she noticed some curly greenery with a reddish tinge which looked very like the plant that Oliver had pulled up. She pulled some up and stuffed them into the bag. A little further on the ground became firmer and stones showed through the turf. She glanced back to her starting-point, she dare not lose sight of where that was, selecting a landmark of a small berry clad hawthorn tree which was near the opening she moved onward. The turf had become thinner and the terrain more rocky. Sandy climbed over a jumble of stones and, to her delight found a big puddle of rainwater pooling in a concave rock. It looked clean, cleaner than the water Oliver had given her on their first meeting. She crouched down and filled the flask, drank it all very slowly and filled it again. Tucking it safely into the bag she headed back to Oliver and Paul.

"I've got you some water and I think I've found some edible

stalks." She called down, "Get ready to catch the flask." Oliver and Paul held the parka out like a safety net and Sandy tossed it down to them.

"Before we drink it all," Oliver cautioned "we have to consider whether we can get it back up to you for a refill."

"You will have to throw it up and hope I catch it, there's no other way." Sandy replied.

"Oh for Ali's rope!" Oliver sighed. "Okay we'll chance it, throw down the stalks and I'll see if they are edible and if they are you could get us some more, we probably need vegetables more than we need meat." Oliver drank half the bottle of water and Paul downed the remainder too quickly his stomach griping with shock.

"Paul grab this." He stretched the parka between them again as a safety net in case Sandy missed the catch, "It'll smash if it hits the floor." He looked up at Sandy, "Ready?" Sandy tensed, waiting for the throw. Up it came; a strong and accurate throw, Sandy caught it easily. She threw the stalks down to Oliver who called back up that they were indeed the same as he had pulled earlier; pleased that she had picked up some of his imparted knowledge of foraging.

Sandy retraced her steps to replenish the supplies. *I wonder if I could use this*, she pulled the slingshot from the bag and a handful of stones from the ground and, loading the sling, she selected a rock a short distance away. Aiming, as she had seen Oliver do, she let fly the stone, it landed bang in the middle but the strength of hit was so feeble it wouldn't have killed a fly. She tried again and then again, each time her aim was perfect and the strength increased. Realising she had not yet returned with the water and greens she stopped practising and packed the sling back into the bag. Sandy delivered the goods to her trapped friends and waited for instruction from Oliver as to what she should now do.

“I’ve been practising with the slingshot; I think I could catch something with it.” She called down. “Even if it’s only a snail!” She added quietly.

“That would be fantastic!” Oliver replied “Hide down in the foliage and wait quietly until some game comes close enough, it could be a longish wait but have the sling ready loaded, okay?”

“Will do, see you later with supper!” As Sandy went off to hunt with a renewed hope of their survival, she suddenly realised that in feeding Oliver and Paul, she had completely forgotten that she would not be feeding herself. Oliver obviously had forgotten this also. In order for her to partake of the food she would need to be back down with them, there was no way they could throw the cooked food back up to her. It was like pulling the plug on a lovely warm bath and filling it with cold water. Also, what would she do for shelter that night? Sandy’s buoyancy of only a moment ago deflated, why was this happening to her? The dramas in her life had hitherto been mostly emotional dilemmas over boyfriends, never had she imagined being in this sort of predicament. For a while she just sat on a rock and with her head in her hands tried to think calmly and practically. A fluttering of wings made her look up, a pair of partridge had landed not ten feet away and were busily pecking around, beady eyes flicking up now and then and their heads twitching from side to side as they cocked their heads, alert to any dangers. Sandy immediately put aside her self-pitying thoughts and quietly took the slingshot from the bag and a decent sized stone from her little pile she had collected, holding her breath she let fly, there was a squawking and a panic filled flapping of wings as one bird took off in the clumsy un-aerodynamic way that only partridge have. Sandy’s disappointment at what seemed like an abortive shot was suddenly replaced with joy as she realised that she had actually killed one of the birds. It was killed outright, thank goodness, which meant that she didn’t have to wring its neck, something she wasn’t sure she could bring herself to do. She gathered it up and stuffed it into the bag and fairly galloped back to the men. They heard her coming; she was singing at the top of her voice, mostly out of tune but singing all the same. Oliver looked at Paul and raised his eyebrows.

"Either she's gone bonkers or she's happy. It's hard to tell with Sandy," Oliver looked up as Sandy's smiling face looked down, "what are you so riotous about?"

"This!" she cried and dangled the fowl over the edge, "Catch!"

"Bloody hell, well done! I knew you were a fast learner, now down you come and we'll eat."

"What do you mean down you come?" Sandy was horrified, she couldn't go down there again and remain trapped, one partridge wouldn't keep them going for long and then they'd be in exactly the same situation as before.

"We got you up once we can get you up again, silly!" Oliver called excitedly, "We've built the blocks up again, they're more secure than they were, I hope. Slide over the edge and hang yourself down, it'll lessen the distance for you to drop. Come on, we'll catch you."

"Okay, but not just yet," Sandy replied, her spirits restored once more, "I'm going to see what else I can find for us, back soon."

The daylight could only last another hour at the most, the sun's colours were seeping into the clouds lying like chiffon along the horizon, a heavy dew was falling and the temperature was beginning to drop. Sandy shivered in spite of Oliver's sweater. She would give herself an estimated half an hour and return. The thought of descending back into the dank hole depressed her, but at least there was a fire going down there. With that thought an idea sprung into her mind; the wood must be running short down there, she would collect firewood. For the rest of her time above ground she gathered dead sticks and a couple of armfuls of prickly scrub, depositing them at the hole, and even dragged back a fair sized dead thorn bush which had finally given up its tenuous hold in the thin covering of soil allowing itself to be blown down by the wind. As the chiffon blankets shredded themselves into wisps of pink and dispersed like thread veins into the darkening sky she made her last trip back to the hole in the ground.

"Watch out below!" she called, "Timber!" Oliver called up to her, impatience and anxiety in his voice; each fighting for supremacy

"What have you been doing? It's nearly dark; don't ever stay out so long again!" Sandy was fleetingly taken back to childhood when she had found her mother agitating on the steps of their house. Sandy had been at the park with some older children playing on the swings and had been enjoying herself so much that she had not noticed it was getting late.

"Sorry Mum, I've didn't notice the time!" She replied light-heartedly to Oliver.

"Seriously Sandy, I was beginning to worry, come on down now." Oliver sounded so much like her father that she was brought back to reality. *I'm being childish* she thought. After throwing down the firewood she had gathered, following Oliver's instructions she hung and dropped towards the pile of blocks below, landing safely in, not Oliver's, but Paul's arms. He held her briefly in a tight hug before releasing her.

"You've done well." Oliver said, "But you must never be out there in the dark on your own, it's dangerous enough in daylight. From a purely selfish point of view, we can't afford to lose you; you're our only hope of survival."

"I'm sorry, I got carried away, I'll be more sensible in future." She replied contritely. There was a lot more meat on the partridge than on the pigeon and for want of a container to boil the stalks they grilled them over the fire.

"They tasted better than when I boiled them and I can't say I enjoyed them much raw!" Oliver smiled at Sandy. His previous desolate thoughts put behind him, he had renewed hope; Sandy was a real gem.

"Now I can get out, why don't I go for help?" Sandy asked Oliver. "I can use a compass if you tell me what direction to go in."

"No Sandy, I don't want you wandering on the moor on your own, for a start, if anything happens to you we're done for and also we need you to keep us supplied with food. We're okay for the time being. When I can walk better we'll think again."

And so their lives continued, every day Sandy was hoisted up to the quickly changing autumn world and each day she returned with water, food, and as necessary, wood. Oliver's injury was slowly mending and he could now walk without the crutch for small distances albeit with a painful limp.

"If we're going to live here we ought to give it an address," Sandy said one evening after they had eaten the rabbit she had caught, "how about Rose Cottage?"

"More like Dunroamin!" Oliver countered.

"Oh yes. Very good, but a teeny bit defeatist don't you think?" Sandy laughed.

"I know I know!" Paul joined in, "Bag End!" His mummy had read him the 'Hobbit' years ago and he had loved it that so much that he had insisted she read it again. Later, when he could read himself he re-read it and almost knew it by heart. "They lived underground!"

"Brilliant Paul, but how about 'Baggins Hall'? That's a bit less final, if you know what I mean, do you agree Oliver?"

"Absolutely!" Oliver immediately seconded the name; he also had been a fan of 'The Hobbit' and later of 'The Lord of the Rings'. His book of 'The Lord of The Rings' had fallen apart with so much reading and he had sellotaped it together and preserved it on his shelf of favourite books.

And so, Sandy continued her daily sorties from 'Baggins Hall', witnessing the autumn palette of fruitful oranges and reds gradually change to more sombre hues of misty grey and brown.

She noted the falling leaves and the stark outlines of the naked thorn bushes. The fat purple sloes; split with the first frosts had fallen to sow themselves ready for the following spring when they would join the kindergarten in the protection of their parent trees. The autumn was giving way to winter, what did it hold for them?

Oliver's leg was finally useable and one evening he gathered them around the fire saying

"Sandy, we need to find help. We can't spend the winter here, if it snows heavily we'll have no fuel and hunting will be impossible."

"I can't do it, I don't know where to go," Sandy answered him pitifully, "why can't we hoist you up; now you can walk, you know the moor, do you still have your compass?"

"Yes I do. My leg is ninety per cent healed that's why I'm saying this now. I don't want to leave you both on your own, but I think it has to be me who goes. I know my way and I am used to the moor."

Paul and Sandy were silent. They knew he was right, but the idea of being left alone scared them both. Oliver was the natural leader, they needed him.

"Yes, it has to be you, we trust you; I don't trust myself." Sandy conceded. "Let's try it now, you can do a big hunt for us, in this cold the food will keep. You've a much better chance of getting help than we have." Oliver knew this was true and now that his leg was much better he would be able to move swiftly, especially if he had only himself to look after on the journey.

"Tomorrow, first light, we'll try it."

The following morning as the dawn light filtered down to them they put their plan into action. Oliver armed himself with his slingshot and flask; he gave his penknife to Sandy so that she would be able to prepare the food he brought. Sandy grimaced at the thought of skinning and gutting the game but having watched Oliver many times she knew how to do the grizzly task. He was keen to get on. Oliver knew it would be extremely difficult for him to get out. He couldn't reach the opening from the top of the blocks and the only option was for him to use Paul as Sandy had used him. However, Paul's height and strength were substantially less than Oliver's. Could he support Oliver's weight?

"I can do it Oliver!" Paul insisted and began to clamber up the pile.

"Okay, good man, Sandy can you give him some support do you think?" It took two attempts before Oliver even got to Paul's shoulders and both times he collapsed under Oliver's weight.

"I *can* do it! Try again Oliver please!" Paul pleaded.

"Have a rest for a minute Paul. Then we'll try one more time." Oliver was beginning to despair.

"Why don't I sort of make a support for Paul, if I bend over like this," She braced her legs and placed her hands on her knees, "Paul can transfer some of the weight by putting his hands on my back. If you can balance without help long enough to reach the edge you could do it." No other bright ideas came to them and so they tried it. Finally, with many ouches from Paul, Oliver clambered on to his sloping shoulders and with a final heave pulled himself out of 'Baggins Hall'. Oliver hunted all day and foraged for meat, greenery and mushrooms, being experienced, he was far more successful than Sandy at finding the succour and by nightfall he had stocked their larder with two brace of partridge, a pheasant, three rabbits and a heap of roots and mushrooms. He had also managed to find some late blackberries, well past their best but still edible. Scrub and sticks and dry grasses, logs and peat also lay stacked in a dry corner.

"If I come back down to eat and sleep tonight, do you think you could get me up one last time Paul?"

"We'll manage it if it kills us!" Sandy answered. So Oliver, apprehensively lowered himself back down dropping with a slight wince on to the blocks where Sandy and Paul steadied him as he landed and surveyed his gleanings,

"It's not as much as I would have liked but if you ration it you'll be okay for at least a week." He said, "But I am worried about water, I'll leave you my flask full up but I can't do more than that. Just go easy on it and if you're desperate there's the seepage from the walls." They ate a frugal meal then slept. Sandy cuddled close to Oliver; he wrapped his arms around her to keep her warm and to comfort her as he heard little sniffles from her as she dreamt. *I'll be back.* He promised her silently.

Oliver was first to wake and he gently stirred the other two,

"It's time I was off now." He said. He reiterated all the instructions he had given the previous day and underlined the necessity to keep the fire going. He gave Sandy a couple of flints which, if the fire failed and the matches were used up, God forbid that should happen, she might be able to use to strike a spark. He hoped that it wouldn't come to that as he knew how difficult it was to start a fire with flints, never having managed it himself. "I'm sorry but I really need to take the parka if I'm sleeping outdoors, but you keep the sweater, it's oiled wool and, you may have noticed, pretty warm."

It took it out of Paul and he was gasping by the time they got Oliver out of 'Baggins Hall's' front door and with a final wave and reassurance that he would be back, he vanished from the square of light above them.

CHAPTER 15

OLIVER'S FATHER WAS concerned, not overly concerned, but the nagging memory of Alistair's near death in the bog haunted him; the image of his youngest son sinking into the morass repeatedly flashed on his inner eye. Oliver was experienced and careful; surely he would come home soon, laughing at their anxiety.

June and Tim, however, were desperate. Absolutely no sightings of Sandy had been reported she seemed to have vanished completely. The police had had no success either in tracking the two who had escaped from the asylum; they were now convinced that the two incidents were linked in some way. The television and radio broadcast images or descriptions of the two escapees and of Sandy with appeals to the public for information and warnings not to approach either of the two dangerous fugitives.

Oliver's father, a fit sixty year old, decided he was going to look for Oliver.

"No you don't" Alice warned him, "there are convicts loose, and you're getting old my love. Oliver is sensible enough to avoid any contact with them, anyway, the moor is huge they are probably nowhere near each other." She smacked him heartily on his back, "Don't be an old woman, he'll be home soon, mark my words."

Jimmy, an ex-army corporal, was not bothered by the stringent conditions. Having spent time on manoeuvres on this very moor, he had known the old bunker, having spent time in it during the war. He also knew there was very little chance of them escaping from it. He grinned to himself. As a young man he had been feared by boys and girls alike and when he had left to join the army, many hoped he would never return. Unfortunately for the man he later shot for 'looking like a German' with his illegally smuggled service pistol, he came home unscathed, and meaner than ever. On his arrival home his behaviour had been so aggressive that he had been locked up at the local police station on more than one occasion for violent behaviour. The locals were sure he was insane; and then, when he had shot that poor man, the whole community had spoken against him resulting in him being sectioned under the mental health act pending his trial for murder. There was no doubt that he was guilty and only a few years earlier he would have probably been hanged, capital punishment had only just been abolished in 1969. The future for Jimmy would therefore be life imprisonment at Dartmoor prison or, if he was deemed insane, incarceration for life at a mental institution. After his stay in the asylum he knew which he would prefer should his bid for freedom prove a failure. Thus, cold nights and poor shelter out in the open were a luxury to Jimmy and he was content to let things die down before making a foray into any form of civilization. He would bide his time.

Their first night without Oliver in 'Baggins Hall' found Sandy and Paul with mixed feelings. On the one hand Sandy was excited by the thought of Oliver rescuing them; she had great faith in his ability to do so. And on the other, she felt lonely and vulnerable. Paul, sweet though he was, did not bounce off her personality as Oliver did. He tended to regard her as a big sister or surrogate mother in spite of his being older than her by, Sandy estimated, five years or so. It was difficult to tell his age as he still possessed the smooth skin and loving dependency of a child. They sat together eking out the food sensibly and restricting their intake of water.

"Oliver will save us." Paul trustingly said.

"Yes he will," she replied, "then we can all go home and get on with our lives." She couldn't wait to walk through her parents' door and throw herself into their arms. She forced herself not to dwell on what must be happening to them at the moment. They must by now know that she is lost and probably they think she is dead. Sandy felt her eyes prick with the onset of tears. She refused to let them come. It had fallen once again to Sandy to look after Paul and she must show herself to be stalwart and resilient. She glanced at Paul in the firelight and saw tears rolling down his face.

"Paul!" She cried, moving closer and hugging him to her, "Don't cry, I know it's been horrendous these last weeks but it'll all be okay you'll see."

"I can't go home." He fell against her and sobbed. "I don't know what to do!" Sandy realised that the closer they were to being rescued, the closer to the surface Paul's traumatic memories came. She remembered his reaction in the tent when she had first mentioned home and his outburst when his mother had been mentioned. She had to wring these memories from him; she couldn't help him until she had learned everything that had happened.

"They took me away from Mummy! She didn't stop them, she just lay there and they took me."

"Paul, start at the beginning. What happened first, before they took you away?" Paul looked beseechingly into Sandy's eyes and her heart went out to him.

"Tell me about your life, your home, your mummy and then I will understand and be able to help." That night, Paul intermittently sobbing and crying for his mother, told Sandy his story. Patiently listening and not interrupting him for fear he would withdraw from her, she took his tale into her heart.

He told her of his wonderful mummy and the house they had shared and how it was surrounded by a pretty garden which had lots of flowers in it. The teachers at his school had been kind to him and he had been happy. His face darkened as he told her of the man who, Sandy deduced, had been his father and who had hit his mother.

"I tried to kick him hard when he hurt Mummy, but he hit me again and I cried." His face lightened again when he remembered his mother throwing all the man's things outside and telling him to go away, "He was horrid, he didn't love Mummy like I did. I was so happy when he went." That had been when Paul was only a child; the story of growing up with just his mother animated him as he told it. They had obviously been a very happy family. Even when Paul had become a grown-up he had stayed living at home, his mother wanted him to stay and he was happy to do so. As he had become more of a man he had helped his mother in their garden, digging the vegetable patch and mowing the lawn. He also helped in the house with cleaning and other heavier chores. She had never again allowed him to do the ironing after he had left the iron on a sheet and nearly caught the house on fire; he chuckled at this. And so the night wore on. Paul had never before spoken for so long in Sandy's company and, yawning discreetly, she let him talk into the night. She still hadn't discovered what had traumatised him and she was prepared to stay awake for as long as was necessary to find out.

The moor was illuminated by a brilliant full moon and Oliver travelled well into the night before he stopped to shelter and grab some sleep. Tucking himself under an overhanging evergreen oak tree, the branches of which formed a canopy over him, he made a bed of ferns and pulled the hood of his parka snugly around his face and slept immediately. His good progress had exhilarated him and the physical exercise had tired him. He slept soundly and woke refreshed, if hungry, at first light. The day was fine, sharp and bright; he hoped it would remain so and not turn to rain or worse, a ghastly fog. He got up from nature's bed and immediately set off, plucking some late berries from a bramble and only stopping once at a stream to drink and freshen his mouth and face. The relief of freedom made him want to whistle as he strode on. His thoughts, however, were never far away from his friends back in that dank hole. If he ever met up with that bastard Jimmy, he would surely kill him. Of that he had no doubt. Oliver's fiery character truly reflected his colouring. He was quick to burn at injustice and acerbic if crossed. But his temper had never induced him to strike anyone except in self-defence as had happened once when, as a child, some thugs had thrown him off his bike, kicked him and bundled him into a patch of stinging nettles. His face scarlet with anger and his green eyes flashing, he had seen them off with two well-placed punches.

"Well done my boy!" His mother had praised him as she rubbed dock leaves over the red welts on his bare legs, "They won't do it again." And she was right. He smiled at the memory; his mother was quite capable of seeking out the culprits and giving them a 'seeing to'. *I wonder who I take after*. Deep in his thoughts and memories Oliver didn't at first see the figure who skulked parallel to him but some thirty feet away and partially concealed by the bushes. A crack of a broken stick called him back and he was immediately alert. Suspecting that it was a person and not an animal who had made the noise, Oliver cast around him to see if there was anything he could use as a weapon. If it was a person, he had a pretty shrewd idea who it might be. *Now, you bastard, just let me get my hands on you!*

Jimmy, realising he had been seen came out into the open, in his hands he held Oliver's gun, cocked and pointing straight at him. He didn't speak but levelled his aim and without hesitation loosed both barrels at Oliver. The distance may have had something to do with Oliver's lucky escape as the shot dispersed a little as Oliver flung himself to the ground. Split second decisions had to be made, should he play dead or rush the bastard while the gun was empty. He decided on the latter and with a cry a banshee would have envied, Oliver rushed across the space between them for all the world looking like a rampaging Viking of old. Jimmy, not expecting this reaction as he thought he had the upper hand, hesitated and then turned and ran. He hadn't been able to re-load the gun and without the element of surprise, he, at fifty-five, wasn't sure he was a match for this big ginger burning mass of anger in a hand to hand combat, in spite of his army training. So he ran and Oliver chased him. Oliver, being the younger and fitter of the two in spite of being weakened by lack of food, easily shortened the distance between them, screaming obscenities all the way. Jimmy dropped out of sight. What the hell was he playing at, hide and seek? Oliver didn't lessen his pace in case Jimmy was attempting to re-load, but he approached more warily, circling around the spot where Jimmy had disappeared, hoping to come at him from an unexpected direction.

"Help! For God's sake help me!" Jimmy's voice, infused with terror reached Oliver's ears. *I'm not a fool; it's a trick.* But the fear sounded genuine and was becoming more frantic. When Oliver reached the source of the cries, he saw Jimmy; he was sinking fast. Oliver's first thought was humanitarian, save him. But how? He had no rope and he was damned if he was getting any closer to the edge of that mire. He took Ali's rope! Oliver turned away without a word, he didn't want to witness the scene but his ears told him to the last second of bubbling cries what was happening.

He sat trembling and nauseous, trying to justify his lack of aid. Even a man as wicked as Jimmy shouldn't die in such a vile way.

Once he had recovered a little from the nightmarish scene, his instinct for survival kicked in. He surmised that if Jimmy had been nearby then so must his tent and belongings. If he had them back it would make such a difference to his chance of success. He ran his eyes across the landscape but no little blue mound beckoned him. Reasoning that Jimmy must have packed it up in order to travel, he set off in the direction of where he had first seen the man. He scouted around for a long time and despaired of finding it. Thirsty, he looked for a water supply and finally after walking far away from the place where he had first sighted Jimmy, he found a beautifully clear stream running over limestone rocks. He scooped some into his mouth and it was as pure as he had ever tasted. Refreshed, he continued his search. If he could find even his backpack it would mean he could use Ali's rope to rescue Sandy and Paul, if he could find his tent as well it would mean they had shelter whilst they travelled. However, he could spend hours if not days looking for where Jimmy had stashed them and not find them, thereby wasting precious time and possibly precious life. Sandy and Paul only had enough food for a week and very little water. He decided to give it another half hour of searching and no more. If he hadn't found anything by then he would go on. Oliver considered how Jimmy had been adept at both tracking him and survival on the moor, he obviously had been experienced in this sort of thing and Oliver tried to put himself in Jimmy's mind. The stream was the first clue; any camper would pitch his tent close to such a water supply. But, assuming that Jimmy had not wanted to be seen, he would dismantle it during the day, even if he stayed in the same spot that night. It was beginning to make sense. The tent must be hidden somewhere in this vicinity. It would doubtless be camouflaged; all he had to do was think like Jimmy. He found it, tent, back-pack, billy cans, the lot! They were cunningly concealed not far from the stream, under fern fronds and grass, in a slight dell, which, when packed with his possessions and covered, disguised the hollow, merging it into the rest of the surrounding area.

"Yes!" He whooped out loud. "Sandy, Paul, here I come!" And without waiting a second longer he loaded himself with his gear and turned back towards 'Baggins Hall'.

Paul had finally finished the telling of his ordeals to Sandy and they slept where they had slumped, Paul's head cradled in Sandy' arms as he wept.

CHAPTER 16

THE POLICE REGRETFULLY called off the search for Sandy. They had searched by helicopter and on foot; there was no sign of her. June and Tim's lives had changed irrevocably. What was there left to live for? June wanted to die and tried to persuade Tim to join her in a suicide pact. She was beyond comfort, all her life she had fought against fate which always seemed to defeat her until Sandy was born. She felt then that finally she had served her karma and life would be kind to her. Now all was lost. If her darling daughter was dead then she wanted to be also. Tim, although emotionally destroyed would not consider this finality.

"We don't know!" He tried to reason with June. "They haven't found her but that doesn't mean she's dead!" She wrenched herself away from him, refusing to listen,

"I want to die!" Was all she would say. Tim was scared to leave her for a minute, she had been hysterical but now she was coolly calm. This was more worrying than her screaming anguish. Mike Squires called daily and administered her medication and often a sedative in order that Tim could get some rest.

"Do you want me to admit June into hospital?" Mike asked kindly, "She would be monitored twenty four hours, maybe in time she will value her life again."

"No, I couldn't do that to her. Let me try in my own way." Tim thanked him sadly.

Oliver needed to stop; it was getting dark but he didn't want to delay, in his excitement of finding his gear he wanted to get to the others as soon as he could. But his common sense told him to rest while it was dark. Sandy had plenty of food and firewood. She would be okay for another night. He didn't bother with the tent as he wanted to up and go with speed as soon as dawn broke. He made do with just his bed roll using his parka as a pillow, and curled up in a soft mound of grasses. He rose with the blackbirds the following day glad to do so; the bedroll had smelt of Jimmy and cigarette smoke. He had almost heaved on breathing Jimmy's rank smell and had it not been so cold he would have abandoned it. As he approached 'Baggins Hall' he caught sight of Sandy's landmark hawthorn tree, stripped by birds of its berries, standing out forlornly skeletal. He was so excited he could barely stop himself from shouting out. Instead, he thought he would surprise them. Creeping up to the 'front door', he took from his back-pack, Ali's rope. He looped it around the hawthorn tree, securing it firmly with a clove hitch and quietly lowered the other end down to the floor where Sandy and Paul lay curled together. He then, supressing a growing fit of childish giggles building up inside, lay on his stomach looking down at them and waited for them to wake. Paul was the first to open his eyes; he looked at the rope dangling down and rolled over closing his eyes again. Then, as though the visual image had had a delayed reaction in reaching his brain, he sat bolt upright, shaking Sandy awake with his sudden movement.

"What is it?! She asked him timorously; without Oliver there she had been very jumpy.

"Look!" Paul pointed up. Sandy looked at the frame of sky above which contained a silhouette with lots of curls standing out from its head like broken springs.

"Oliver!" she shrieked, jumping up, "What...?"

"I'm back!" He called, "And guess what, I'm getting you both out!"

"How did you find a rope?" Sandy started firing questions up at him.

"I'll explain later. Get yourselves together, bring the food and don't forget the flask." Sandy and Paul gathered their few bits and pieces including the penknife and the game and stood waiting at the bottom of the rope.

"Right, Paul you first, tie the rope around your chest under your arms and tell me when you're ready. Paul fumbled with the rope and Sandy helped him. She wasn't much good at knots in spite of attending guides (so she had tied quite a lot of them). Oliver took the rope end which he had looped around the tree and, puffing a bit, he winched Paul up to the surface. In the daylight Oliver was shocked at the man's appearance; he was grey, not a speck of colour in his hollow cheeks. "Well done Paul, a bit of fresh air for you eh?" Oliver still hadn't managed to find quite the right way to speak to Paul and he overdid every nuance.

"Me next!" Called Sandy from below. "Get a move on!" She too rose to the surface on the rope clutching the food and the flask. Oliver's Aran sweater, once white, was as grimy as her face; she gave him a massive grin as she emerged into the early, peachy morning light. To Oliver it was a more beautiful sight than the golden orb rising behind her. Sandy linked her arms with the men's and they turned towards her giving themselves a massive group hug.

"Before we go," Oliver said seriously, "we ought to make this safe." He looked around them to find something with which they could cover the hole or at least indicate that it was there. Their experience of that dank dungeon was not one they would wish on anyone else. The grass and weeds would knit themselves together in time concealing a trap door through which any unsuspecting hiker could fall. Together they lugged a dead tree branch and placed it across 'Baggins Hall's' front door and heaped other sturdy branches on top.

"I wish I had a flag or something we could put up to mark the place." Oliver said,

"How about your shorts!" Sandy asked mischievously.

"What my new shorts!" Exclaimed Oliver, "Actually, I don't think I'll be wearing them again, so okay." They propped a tall branch amongst the others and Oliver, sadly cut a couple of holes in his shorts and threaded them on to the branch where they flapped limply in the breeze. "Right, let's go." He hoisted the backpack and tent on to his shoulders and started off.

"Wait!" Sandy called out, "I've forgotten something!"

"What could you possibly have forgotten? You didn't have anything other than the clothes you're wearing." Oliver looked concerned, he really didn't want anyone to venture back down there again, a stupid accident could jeopardise everything.

"I forgot to write 'Sandy Woz 'ere' on the wall!" Oliver cuffed her lightly across her head and said with a laugh,

"Idiot!"

"How long do you think it'll be before we get home?" Sandy asked Oliver as they walked side by side, Paul following closely behind.

"We're nearest my home so we'll head there, should get there tomorrow or the day after." Oliver explained that he still lived with his parents in their farmhouse which was virtually adjoining the moor and that from there they could telephone her parents and the police to report what had happened to Jimmy.

"What has happened to him? And how did you find your tent? You haven't told us anything." Sandy asked. Oliver heaved a sigh,

"Jimmy's dead. He fell into the mire and I couldn't save him." His conscience pricked him as he remembered turning away as Jimmy's cries were suffocated by the sucking bog, he reasoned with himself that he had been unable to help but he also knew that he didn't want to save him. The excuse that he had no means with which to aid Jimmy eased his guilt and he was grateful for it.

Oliver recounted to them his confrontation with Jimmy and told of the cold-blooded way in which Jimmy had tried to murder him and of how a red haze had come over his eyes as he taken up the chase. He chose not to linger on the description of Jimmy's last moments, it was unnecessary to burden the others with the image.

That night, as they slept jumbled up together in Oliver's tiny tent, Oliver woke the others crying out "NO!" he was trembling and soaked with sweat. The other two started up,

"What's the matter?" Sandy cried, all the fears of the last few weeks racing to the surface again.

"Ali!" Oliver shouted. His shout seemed to shake him out of sleep and he sat bolt upright, the faint moonlight through the fabric of the tent illuminating his face with a ghostly blue tinge. His eyes were wide and full of tears.

"Whatever is it Oliver?" Sandy took him into her arms.

"It was a dream, it's okay." Oliver wiped his face with the back of his hand and shivered. "Sorry, did I shout?" His voice shook and was thick with emotion which he tried to hide from her.

"Loud enough to wake the dead!" Sandy said. "Are you okay now?"

"Yes, I'm okay, go back to sleep." However, Oliver's dream stayed vividly with him, he fought off sleep for fear it would return. He had dreamed of Jimmy struggling and calling out, the terror in his eyes sending shivers down Oliver's spine, he had run to help and then Jimmy's face had become Ali's and he, Oliver, had turned away. Ali had cried "Oli help me!" His last word had been a mere bubble of sound. Oliver had turned back to the mire and Ali had disappeared.

Oliver had left the tent when Sandy awoke and Paul was sleeping soundly, his hands tucked under his chin, and Sandy wondered whether he had been sucking his thumb. She quietly slipped out of the tent and wandered over to where Oliver stood silently, with his head bowed as if in prayer. He looked up and gave her a warm, if slightly forced smile.

"Are you alright?" Sandy asked him as she took his arm, she had to tilt her head back to look him in the eye, her five foot four dwarfed by his six foot four. His hair shone red-gold in the low sun, its curls hung over his forehead and corkscrewed around his ears.

"Yea, I'm okay, just a bit drained." Oliver looked down at her and releasing his arm from hers he draped it around her shoulders. "Looking forward to getting home?" He asked her with an attempt at normalcy.

"You bet! But, Oliver, we must talk about Paul."

"I was thinking that. He hasn't said a word since we left 'Baggins' and he seems to droop with every step we make." Sandy knew what was tormenting Paul and now, when he was sleeping she had a chance to update Oliver on what he had told her through that long night. After listening to his heart-rending account Sandy had been thrown into a dilemma. Paul had to return with them, there was no other option, but what on earth was going to happen to him then? "Did you get any more out of him when I was gone?" Oliver continued.

"Yes, he told me everything. Let's sit down over there out of earshot and I'll tell you." They sat close together on the springy turf, Oliver's arm still around her shoulders; she moved closer to him and briefly outlined Paul's happy life with his mother. "But," she took a deep breath and sighed it out, "we have a big problem; Paul has been accused of murdering his mother."

"What!" exclaimed Oliver,

"It's true. Not that he did, but that he has been accused. I know you thought badly of him when you first met him, but," she pulled away from Oliver and fixed him with a direct look, "I can't believe it of him, can you?"

"In all truth, no. I can't imagine him hurting anything; I should think he would step over a snail if it was in his path."

"Quite. But apparently someone found him hitting his mother as she lay on their hall floor and they called the police. According to Paul he had come in from the garden and she had been lying there, not moving. He tried to wake her up but she must have been already dead though he didn't realise it."

"The poor bugger!" Oliver groaned, "So, now he's alone with no one to look after him."

"Yes, and he's at the mercy of the authorities, with his disability he's assumed to be simple or worse; a lunatic. People can't cope with 'different'. Not only is Paul 'different' in character to the normal man but he looks different as well. He is a prime scapegoat and target for bullies. Anyway," she continued, "he panicked and shook her and smacked her face and that was when the neighbour arrived, Paul thinks it was the woman who had only recently moved in next door, the door was still open, and from what she saw, she thought she was witnessing a murder. Paul didn't know what had happened to his mother except that she had some blood on the back of her head. But what made it worse still was the woman had seen him appearing to bang his mother's head on the floor and swore that he was behaving like a madman. That's putting it in my words. He is still too traumatised by the whole thing to be coherent. Personally I suspect that she had fallen down the stairs and was killed outright."

"That would be my assessment based on what you've said, but how on earth did he end up out on the moor with Jimmy?"

"I'm coming to that," Sandy got up and began to walk away from Oliver as she felt herself well up. There was a lot to tell Oliver and it didn't get any better, she needed to get herself together, she had come to love Paul in a sisterly way and she was both pained and outraged at what had been done to him.

Oliver came slowly up behind her and she turned and buried her face in his chest, his warm masculine scent, and his kindness released her tears and she let them flow.

"You don't have to tell me it all now," he said gently "we'll have time to talk later when we make camp and Paul is safely tucked up in bed."

"I'm worried that the closer we get to people the odder Paul will behave. He's terrified of going back to the asylum and of facing up to the loss of his mother." She dried her eyes on his shirt front and gave him a sad but cheeky look as he raised his eyebrows at her using him as a handkerchief.

"Asylum?" Queried Paul, "I thought he said it was a hospital."

"Only in the sense that they wore white coats and I believe they had a sign or something on the gates that said Mental Hospital or some such, a eupemism for loony bin. I need to tell you the rest so you are aware of what we're dealing with." They returned to the grassy spot where they had sat previously and Sandy told him about Paul's incarceration in the asylum.

"It appears that they classed him as criminally insane, at least, that's how I interpreted it. Because of his hysteria and grief he was uncontrollable. His behaviour when the police came was manic because of his inability to express himself and his panic was exacerbated by the woman screeching over and over, 'I saw him, he killed her!' He had screamed that he hadn't done it and he had screamed for his mummy. They called the asylum and they took him away to wait for his trial. He needed kindness and comfort but he was strait-jacketed and sedated and treated like a serial killer. That was where he met Jimmy."

"That bastard!" Exploded Oliver, "He was truly evil!"

"Yes, he was, and cunning and manipulative as well." Sandy warmed to her anger. "He apparently befriended Paul when they were room-mates, pretended to look after him and gained his trust, which wouldn't be hard to do." Sandy recalled the way Paul had first clung to her in the tent, 'I like you, you're kind'; he had given himself into her care like a dog responding to the slightest sign of affection. "Jimmy had made sure that Paul wasn't bullied by the other in-mates and always managed to acquire good helpings of food for him. Paul fell for it totally. So when Jimmy told him that he could see how unhappy Paul was, being locked up, because he was unhappy being locked up too, and that he knew how they could leave that horrid place, Paul became his puppet."

"So, Jimmy had worked out a plan of escape which would only work with Paul's acquiescence." Oliver continued for Sandy. "What was it?"

"One evening the doctor was doing his rounds, administering sedative injections to unruly in-mates and he came into Jimmy and Paul's room on his own. It appears that under Jimmy's instructions, Paul had been behaving badly, screaming and crying and thus had been given a sedative for the previous few nights." Sandy paused, "Remember, I'm putting this together from the jumble of information I got from Paul. I like to think I am more lucid than he is. Jimmy, on the other hand had been behaving without reproach, he had even been helping with the more pathetic creatures in there. In fact he had helped hold Paul down each night when he had fought against having the injection. Remember, Paul was completely under Jimmy's Svengali-like control and played the part to perfection. After all it wasn't hard for him to do because he was distraught anyway. It's cunning and makes sense, the doctor was off his guard when it came to Jimmy, who, pretending to go to the aid of the doctor as Paul struggled, had instead grabbed the medication he had on him and stabbed a massive dose into him. Paul said that the man 'went to sleep straight away and fell over'. Jimmy then put on the doctor's coat and his white cap and calmly walked out of the room with Paul in front of him. He held Paul's arm twisted behind his back as if he were controlling an outburst and they just walked out of the door."

Oliver asked. “Why was the door unlocked?”

“All the inmates are locked in their rooms, or cells would be a better name, at night so security would be slacker, staff changing shift and all that. I’m only surmising, but whatever the reason, they were able to leave the place.”

“And no one asked them where they were going?”

“No, apparently there’s a punishment block in the grounds where Paul had been put when he first arrived. It was probably assumed that the ‘doctor’ was taking him there. The security kiosk at the gate was attended by an old man, probably a retired person earning a bit of extra and Jimmy clouted him around the head, took the raincoat off him and gave it to Paul for him to wear, the raincoat was dark, do you remember it? He was wearing it when we first saw him. Jimmy took off the white coat and left it in the kiosk, grabbed a donkey jacket that was on a peg and they just opened the gate and walked out.”

“That’s behaviour more fitting of a commando, to keep your cool and to indiscriminately bash an old man over the head is not the behaviour of a normal civilian. What a monster!” Oliver’s eyes flashed. “Well he got his just deserts!”

“Paul’s awake.” Sandy shushed Oliver as Paul crawled out of the tent. He stood up and looked around for them,

“Over here.” Sandy called. Paul came slowly over to them and Oliver said heartily,

“Sleep well Paul?”

“Yes thank you.” He didn’t look rested; in spite of his apparently deep sleep he had dark shadows under his red rimmed eyes.

“Cheer up it might never happen!” Oliver was doing it again, completely the wrong thing to say. He meant to be kind but just couldn’t quite get it right.

“Let’s have some breakfast.” Sandy quickly interjected. She gave Oliver a withering look and was mollified to see him looking shamefaced.

Whilst they were eating the cold remains of last night's meal Paul spoke directly to Oliver

"Where are we going?"

"Home..." Oliver began but Sandy cut him off,

"We are going somewhere safe Paul, and when we get there we are going to look after you." Paul looked lovingly at Sandy,

"Do you promise? Cross your heart and hope to die?"

"Yes Paul, I promise." Sandy wondered how she was going to be able to keep this promise but she was determined she would try.

Later that evening at their new camp site, when Paul was sleeping, Sandy and Oliver crept away from the tent and continued their conversation of that morning.

"I've been thinking," Oliver jumped straight in as soon as they were far enough away, "that violence at the asylum you described, they won't necessarily know that it was Jimmy and not Paul who's responsible."

Sandy nodded as he was speaking,

"I've been worrying about that as well, what if one of those men has died, it would be a definite murder charge then, and no one left to accuse but Paul."

"Exactly what I was thinking." Oliver tugged at his hair, and Sandy couldn't help but watch fascinated as the curls sprung back.

"I love your hair!" She said completely apropos of nothing.

"Why thank you." He replied with a faint flush of pink rising up from his neck. "But let's be serious, what are we going to do with Paul?"

"We have to keep our word that we'll help him. He has to have legal help."

"The other problem" Oliver said "is that we will have to tell the police everything. And they're bound to arrest him again."

"Can't we hide him until we find someone who can act for him?

Or we could swear to keep him sort of under house arrest until his trial, he can't go back to the asylum especially if any of those men has died, his life would be absolute hell!"

"Christ, I don't know what to do!" Oliver paced about, opening his mouth to speak as he thought of something and then thinking again swallowing whatever he was about to say and pacing some more. "By the way," he changed tack, "what did he tell you about his running in front of your car?"

"Oh yes, he said that Jimmy had forced him to run out to try to get me to stop, he was going to hi-jack the car, but when I didn't stop in time and hit Paul, he must have hesitated, probably because things weren't going to plan and then he missed his chance because I ran after Paul. I think what must have happened then, is that Jimmy found that I had taken the keys with me, it's an automatic thing isn't it, to take your keys? I did it instinctively; I've still got them in my pocket. So he probably assumed I would do the sensible thing and come back to the car when Paul didn't stop. Or rather, what a man with no conscience would do; abandon an injured man. So he probably waited for a while, confident that he would be able to get them off me and take the car when I returned. However, when I didn't come back he decided to follow me, but what with the time lapse and then the fog he temporarily lost track.

"Thank God he didn't hi-jack you, knowing now what a cold blooded bastard he was I don't think you'd be alive now if he had." Oliver hugged her tightly to him and repeated, "Thank God!" Sandy hugged him back,

"Yes, thank God!"

"His tracking skills were pretty good though, he found all of us pretty quickly, must have been following us all the time without us realising it. I'd lay a bet that he was no stranger to the moor."

"I suppose that's why he made for the moor after escaping, rather than trying for London or Bristol where he could disappear among the crowds, or stowing away on a ship from the harbour at Exeter and going abroad or something." Sandy mused,

"Don't forget, he had the encumbrance of Paul, he wouldn't want to have him tagging along; he'd stand out like a sore thumb. He was probably keeping him alive just as long as he could use him and once he had served his purpose by stopping your car. I'd lay a bet he intended to kill him and where better to do that than on the moor!"

"But why did he track us after he'd missed his chance with the car? He'd got rid of Paul; he would have been less noticeable on his own and he would have stood more chance of getting to a big city?" Sandy queried.

"All I can think is that he intended to find you and get your keys off you and then he would have been off. But when he finally caught up with you I'd already found you and he realised that not only did I have camping gear which would have been very useful to him, but I also had a gun. That's when he decided to make Paul do his dirty work for him. Did Paul say how they survived after they escaped? They must have been sleeping in the open for some time and what did they do for food?"

"He said they slept in barns, under hedges, wherever they found shelter. They stole bread, eggs and milk off an unoccupied milk float and vegetables from a farm and fruit from an orchard. Then, when they were on the moor and the food ran out, they starved. That was when Jimmy had the idea to hi-jack a car. He probably couldn't believe his luck when he found us and discovered that you had all the kit he needed, especially the gun." They sat quietly for a while, thinking it all over. Oliver turned to Sandy,

"You know, I reckon Jimmy had training in combat; he certainly had no qualms about killing. I don't think for a minute anyone will think it was Paul masterminding their escape. We don't know why Jimmy was in the asylum do we? He wouldn't be there if he was a harmless normal person. I'll bet he's killed before and not necessarily when he was in uniform!"

"You may be right, he was about the right age to have fought in the war, and that bunker – he knew exactly where it was." Sandy exclaimed. "We know Paul didn't kill his mother, all we have to do is prove it."

CHAPTER 17

THE DORMER WINDOW in Alistair's attic room at the farmhouse glinted with the last of the rays of the setting sun. He put his study papers aside and pushing his chair back, rose and stretched. It was the mid-term break and as his final exams were only a term away he was dedicating himself to work. Oliver's absence, instead of irking him had begun to worry him. He had never been away so long before. His parents were also becoming more anxious, and hearing on the news bulletins that the search for the other missing people had been called off they had begun to wonder what on earth was going on. They couldn't recall when a coincidence such as this had ever happened before on the moor. Surely they weren't connected? Finally, giving in to their anxiety they decided between them that they would report his absence if he hadn't returned by the weekend.

Alistair wandered over to his window and gazed out at the fast fading light as dusk cast its haunting colourless cloak over the moor. He pulled his blind down and immediately let it shoot back up, whirring as it hit the top of the window frame. He thought he saw shadowy figures approaching in the distance; he turned off his light to get a better view of the outside and yes, they were still there. Three people,

"Mum, Dad!" He shouted as he rushed down the stairs, Oli's home!" Oliver's tall figure with the backpack and tent on his shoulders was unmistakeable.

Alistair, Alice and George collided at the door in their rush to be first out. Oliver and his companions, a small girl and a clumsy looking man followed him through the gate, the girl was holding the man's hand and seemed to be partly coaxing and partly pulling him along. As they drew closer to the light, the sight of the reluctant man's face made Alice gasp,

"It's one of those escaped convicts!" She hissed in George's ear. "What the devil is Oli doing with him?" The girl retained a firm grip on the man's hand and Oliver dropped back and took his other hand. Together they approached the family who, having been on the point of rushing to hug Oliver now stood hesitantly in a group.

"Mum, Dad, Ali, meet Sandy and Paul." Oliver said nonchalantly as though they had merely been out for the evening and not been missing for nearly two months. He gave his mother a 'don't say anything' look as he saw her scrutinising Paul.

"Oli, thank God you're back." George strode forward and hugged his son and then turned to Sandy and Paul, "Come on in all of you, Ali put the kettle on, or should we crack open the champagne?" His bonhomie was a little forced and Oliver said quietly to him as he took him aside,

"It's okay dad, I'll explain later." They filed indoors and into the kitchen, Sandy still holding the man's hand. "Dad, the first thing we must do, even before a cup of tea, is 'phone Sandy's parents."

"Of course, of course, they must be worried sick, you're the girl they've been looking for aren't you?" He turned to Sandy and led her, still holding Paul's hand into the hall and said, "Take as long as you want, I'll bring you a cuppa, how about you Paul, do you take sugar?" Paul nodded and smiled hesitantly,

"Yes please, I take sugar, thank-you." In the kitchen Alice, a true farmer's wife, was already at the stove. She had dug out a ham and potatoes, fresh greens and bread and was laying the table for six. George and Oliver sat with Alistair by the fire in the sitting room enjoying a mug of beer, Oliver having expressed a preference for alcohol rather than tea.

"I'll tell you everything in a while, but it'll take some time and it's complicated." He said when George prompted him, "But you must understand that Paul is not a criminal, he is harmless and needs our help. However, tonight you must make sure that all the doors and window are locked or he may try to run away."

"Why?" Alistair exclaimed, "If he's not a criminal why should he want to run away?"

"Because he's scared." Oliver stated baldly. You can't have missed the fact that he's Down syndrome, he's confused and in shock, he's been through a lot and we've promised to help him."

"Mum, it's me!" June staggered at the sound of Sandy's voice on the 'phone. Struck mute with shock she lowered herself into the chair by the 'phone and gasped for breath.

"Mum?" Sandy's voice came tinnily through the receiver dangling from the wall.

"What is it?" Tim rushed up to June as she slumped barely able to get her breath,

"Sandy!" She whispered, "It's Sandy." Tim, immediately thought the worst, Sandy's body had been found.

"No!" He whispered, "Please tell me no."

"She's alive!" June gasped, Tim grabbed the receiver and shouted "Sandy is that you?!"

"Yes dad, it's me, I'm okay. I'm safe now." After tears of release had been shed on both ends of the line Sandy told them where she was and that she would get Oliver's father to give them instructions how to get there. "Dad, don't tell the police yet that I'm back. I need to speak to you first." She refused to elaborate any further telling him it was too complicated but not to worry, repeating that she was safe. George gave Tim directions to their farm and thanking him, Tim hung up. He grabbed his coat from the hook by the door saying,

"Come on let's get going, I'll just lock the back door and get the car keys." Tim came into the hall with his car keys in his hand, to find June, already in her coat, replacing the telephone receiver on the hook,

"Engaged." She said. He raised his eyebrows in question; "The Squires, I was going to tell them the good news."

"We'll ring them tomorrow, come on darling." Tim took her arm and they went out to the car, Lilly, Sandy's scruffy spaniel terrier cross, in tow.

Oliver and his 'guests' sat with his family at the huge pine kitchen table and ate like starving people, which in fact they were. Wine was opened and the warmth of the Aga soon had them feeling extremely sleepy. Oliver, for once managing to say the right things, hinted strongly throughout the meal at what luck it had been to find Paul and that without his help they wouldn't be here. Sandy smiled to herself at his white lies and Paul's demeanour visibly relaxed as he glowed with pleasure at Oliver's praise. Although he was sure that he hadn't really been much help it was wonderful to hear his name once again spoken with affection.

Sandy's parents had a good hour's journey before they came to Oliver's home, its lights blazing out in the dark, a celebratory declaration of joy. June could barely control her excitement. She jumped out of the car as soon as they stopped.

"We've brought the dog, I hope that's okay, we couldn't leave her on her own." Tim apologised to George, as he caught June up at the door.

"Come on in. Hello mate." He rummaged Lilly's ears.

They were ushered into the warmth of the house by George, who immediately led them into the sitting room where the 'lost trio' were slumped together on the big chesterfield sofa, half asleep, they had instinctively cuddled closer to each other and it made a moving if slightly odd tableau. Sandy was between the two men, her head resting on Oliver's shoulder and her hand in Paul's, whilst he snuggled up against her. Oliver's arm was around Sandy' shoulder and his head rested sideways on the top of her spiky hair. June grasped Tim's arm at the sight of Paul cuddled against Sandy,

"Who's that man?" She hissed at him.

"Mum!" Sandy broke free from the others and she and her mother clung to each other, their tears flowing unchecked. Tim flung his arms around them both, his eyes glistening. Lilly bounced up and down, as if to say

"And me, and me!"

George brought refreshments to everyone and they basked in the joy of reunion.

Then the questions started. The whys, the hows, the whos.

"Mum, Dad," Oliver and Sandy both started to speak, Sandy took the floor, "Mum" she started again, "it's late, we're all safe but exhausted; as must you be. It can wait. I promise we'll tell you everything tomorrow." She added hurriedly, "In the meantime don't contact anyone else please. I'll explain tomorrow."

"You must all stay here tonight." George looked towards Alice, who unhesitatingly nodded her agreement,

"There's plenty of room, Oli if you share with Ali, Sandy can have your room, Paul can have the single guest room and Tim and June the double." Once the rooms had been allocated and everyone shown the bathrooms etcetera, the guests retired to bed. Alice had given them clean towels and assured the trio that there was plenty of hot water for them to take a bath each. Sandy had grinned saying,

"Yes, we're pretty filthy aren't we?" Alice, in her down to earth way said

"Yes, you are and those sheets are clean!" She took Sandy's hands in her own, work roughened hands, smiled kindly at her and added, "There's foam bath or lavender oil if you prefer, have a good soak. Sleep well." When everyone was out of the room, Oliver took George aside and said,

"I want to sleep down here," he put his hand up to forestall his father's questions, "remember what I said about Paul?" His father nodded.

"Yes, I do. Okay then, I'll double check the locks before I go to bed and make sure no keys are left in them, Goodnight son, it's good to have you back." Oliver had a good relationship with his father who treated him with the respect of an equal. George trusted Oliver's judgement on most things and although it bothered him, he felt sure that Oliver knew what he was doing. Alistair was quite relieved that he didn't have to share his single bed with Oliver's bulk and after giving him a 'manly hug' he too retired to bed. Oliver, using the downstairs bathroom had a rather quicker bath than he would have liked as he wanted to be finished before the house had settled just in case Paul should think to run away.

Paul's room was quite small but prettily decorated, it looked like a lady's room and this fact comforted him; his mummy's room was pretty. The bed had a floral spread on it and the pillows had frills at the edges. He felt dirty, he was dirty! He looked at himself in the mirror and turned away in disgust. For weeks now he had been looking at Oliver' face; handsome even in torch light, and Sandy's pretty smile and strangely spikey hair style, he had almost forgotten what *he* looked like. The face that looked back at him was pale; Oliver's had always looked slightly bronzed and had colour in his cheeks. Sandy had become pale living underground and she had got thinner as well but she still had looked pretty and never ugly as he saw himself now. He looked into his reflected eyes and saw deep misery. He couldn't bear to look at it any longer. Sitting on the side of his bed he tried to draw the image of his mummy's face from his memory but all he could see was her lifeless eyes and he wept.

Sandy waited until the parents had all used the bathroom, just for a light wash and tooth clean, saving the water for the filthy three, she tapped on Paul's door,

"I'm going for a bath Paul" she called; "do you want to go first?" Paul brightened a little at the sound of Sandy's voice,

"It's alright, ladies first." An expression he had picked up from his mummy, when she had been teaching him how to behave in company. Sandy smiled at his rather prim response,

"Okay, I'll try not to be long." It was pure heaven to soak in the huge bath, she put some foam-bath in as the old Victorian tap gushed out hot water, the soothing lavender scented steam rose up and filled her senses. As she soaked with her eyes closed, she created images of cottage gardens and bees buzzing around the bushes and the sun warming the fertile soil. She must have dozed a little because when she heard Paul's nervous tap at the door she realised that the water was distinctly cooler than it had been.

"Sandy?" Paul whispered from outside, "Are you alright?"

"Oh, I'm so sorry Paul" she called, "I must have dozed off, just give me a minute to rinse my hair and it's all yours." *Thoughtless cow!* She berated herself. In a flash she was out of the bath, and had cleaned her teeth, vigorously, with the new toothbrush Alice had left with her towels and, wearing the over-large pair of pyjamas, again laid out by Alice in her room, Sandy exited the bathroom full of apologies to a patient Paul waiting on the landing.

"It's alright Sandy," Paul insisted, "I didn't mind." He gazed at her, her skin fresh and clean and her hair standing out in wet spikes from her head, she was, to Paul, the most beautiful thing he had ever seen. She touched him tenderly on the cheek,

"It'll be okay, you'll see, I'll look after you. Enjoy your bath." Paul was in love.

In the guest room Tim and June lay in each other's arms, overwhelmed with relief. For a long while neither spoke, their closeness saying it all. Tim was beginning to doze off when June, pulling away from his embrace, whispered

"When you and George were talking in the kitchen, did he say who that other man was and what he's doing here?"

"No," muttered Tim sleepily, "I'm as much in the dark as you. I don't think George knows who he is either. Go to sleep, and stop worrying."

"It's just that he looks a bit odd and he was all cuddled up to Sandy."

"Darling, they were all half asleep!" Tim was now wide awake and becoming irritable, "For goodness sake just be grateful she's safe and stop finding things to worry about!" He turned away from her on to his side saying "They promised us an explanation in the morning so just be patient will you?"

Oliver slept fitfully half expecting to see a shadowy furtive Paul creeping towards the door, but thankfully the house remained undisturbed until he heard the whistler kettle proclaiming loudly that tea was on the agenda. George fulfilled the kettle's promise and he arrived with a strong cuppa. Oliver swung his stiff, tired legs round and sat up, making room for George to sit on the sofa beside him.

"Don't suppose you slept very well did you, long shanks?" George took in Oliver's pink rimmed eyes, the green irises flecked with tiny sparks of gold almost identical to his beloved Alice's. "You need a haircut my lad." He said playfully pulling at Oliver's rampant curls.

"I think I'm going to grow it into an afro!" Oliver teased.

"Wrong texture, any longer and you'll look like Little Lord Fauntleroy." They drank their tea saying little else, the joking having merely disguised the necessity for serious talk. "I'll just pop a cup up to mum and leave you to get dressed and then we can go for a stroll before breakfast."

"All will be revealed dad, give mum a kiss from me."

Sandy woke to the comfort of a soft sprung mattress and downy pillows, the warm weight of the blankets and bedspread over her feet felt almost too heavy; having slept with no cover save a share of the parka for more nights than she cared to think. Oliver's bed-roll had stunk so badly of Jimmy and his cigarettes that none of them chose to use it on the way home. Oliver had brought it home never the less, though why, he wasn't sure. Maybe the police would have a way of determining that Jimmy had used it, he wasn't sure, he'd ask Ali. Sandy went to the bathroom and, finding it free, washed and cleaned her teeth. When she returned to her room to put her filthy clothes back on, miraculously, Alice had, like a fairy god mother, left some jeans which had obviously belonged to one of the boys when they were younger, a voluminous shirt and an equally large sweater. Tim and June, in their hurry to get to Sandy had not thought to bring anything with them. The house around her had wakened and very soon she heard a tap at her door, June entered and immediately hugged her daughter so tightly that she had to beg to be released.

"I couldn't sleep, I was frightened it had all been a dream and you were still lost." June was on the verge of tears again and Sandy pinched her playfully to ease the emotion building up.

"See, you're awake and I'm here." She looked at her mother, she was thin and pale and looked older and her hands trembled when she lifted them. "Oh mum, I thought I'd never see you again!"

"Who's that other man? I'm sure I saw something about him on the news. Are you sure he's not dangerous?"

"Mum, he's fine. We'll explain everything, promise." June muttered something about his looks and *I hope so*. Sandy sighed, and put her arms around June hugging her tight,

"Don't worry any more mum, I'm safe now."

They all gathered in the kitchen for breakfast. Paul was the last to arrive and shyly took his place beside Sandy.

"Good morning Paul," George greeted him kindly, "did you sleep well?"

"Yes thank-you." Paul answered, aware that everyone was looking at him he stared down at his plate of bacon and eggs that Alice had placed in front of him.

"Paul and I are going for a stroll after breakfast, Ali has told us you have some unusual chickens and we're going to see them, aren't we?"

"That'll be nice." June commented lamely. "But I thought you were going to tell us what happened to you." Oliver had asked Sandy to take Paul out of the house for an hour or so in order that they could up-date the parents and discuss what their next move should be. She had been reluctant as first, wanting to be in on the discussion, but Oliver reasoned that she was the only person he really felt safe with. She understood and agreed with him, but made him swear that no action would be taken without her knowing of it. She shot her mother a look of impatience and June fell reluctantly silent. As soon as Sandy and Paul were out of the house the questions flooded out.

"Hang on, hang on!" Oliver held up his hands, "If you can bear to leave your questions for a minute, I'll tell you, in detail all that has happened to us and all that has happened to Paul."

Oliver sat them all down in the sitting room and for a full hour spoke of his chance meeting with Sandy and then Paul. He omitted his bad behaviour over Paul when he first encountered him and glossed over Sandy's irresponsible behaviour when she had wandered off. He told them of their attempt to get home, only to be thwarted by Jimmy. An explanation of how Jimmy was connected to Paul couldn't be avoided and he recounted the information that Sandy had extracted from Paul when he had left them in 'Baggins Hall'. Ali laughed when he told them the name they had chosen for their underground home,

"You and your hobbits!" He teased.

"Actually it was Paul who thought of it; his mother read him 'The Hobbit' when he was a boy."

"What! That man was going to leave you there to starve?!" June was incredulous. She had, like most people, never met a truly bad person, the worst sort of cruelty or meanness she had encountered were small spiteful gestures or being snubbed in the street, she couldn't imagine how anyone could be so cold blooded.

"Not only did he intend us to starve but when I met up with him later he tried to shoot me — with my own gun!" Oliver had not yet reached the part of the tale where Jimmy had perished but now it had come; "Jimmy ran away when he missed me, he let off both barrels and I took the opportunity to chase after him knowing he didn't have time to re-load," Oliver paused, "he fell into the mire."

"What did you do?" George glanced fleetingly at Alistair, who had blanched,

"I couldn't save him, he had stolen my gear along with," he hesitated before calling it Ali's rope, "the rope." He shuddered, "There was nothing I could do."

"Damn good riddance!" Alice said stridently, "After he'd tried to kill you I'm surprised you even considered rescuing him!" Silence fell in the room, Oliver's family drawn together in the memory none of them would forget.

"Anyway," Oliver shook the shivers from his spine, "he's gone and that was when I went back for Paul and Sandy and here we are." The time had now come to decide what they were going to do about Paul.

Following Oliver's account of Paul's experiences it was unanimously agreed that he had been unforgivably wronged and that he needed help. That was where they drew a blank. Firstly, the police would have to be told sooner or later that Sandy had been found but the question whether they had to be told about Paul's discovery at the same time produced a heated debate. June, whilst expressing pity for him, was more concerned about being embroiled in something which delayed her having Sandy back and resuming their lives. Alice, a gutsier person by far, than June, was adamant that they could not let Paul be sent back to the asylum. Oliver questioned them whether they had heard on the news after Paul's escape anything about the doctor and the security man, if they were killed or seriously hurt as this could have ramifications on Paul's situation which was bad enough already. None of them could recall having seen or heard anything about a death resulting from the men's escape, and it was therefore assumed that neither had suffered any ill effects; reasoning that reports of murder would not have been forgotten. Oliver was relieved on that score at least.

"Well, all we have to do is prove that a) Paul is incapable of violence and certainly of murder and b) that the neighbour was mistaken and hysterical."

"And how on earth are you going to do that?" George demanded, "The only witness appears to have been the neighbour, other than Paul. And more to the point is what do we do with him in the meantime?" No one could think what to do. June and Tim talked quietly together on the sofa, snippets of their conversation, reaching the ears of the others, mostly centred on June's desire to get Sandy home. After a while Alistair stood up and facing them said

"May I make a suggestion?" Heads turned towards him expectantly, "You are aware I assume that I am studying criminal law?"

"Really?" Tim looked up admiringly at him. "Yes, and I have an idea." Ali paused organising his thoughts, *he looks like a barrister already* Oliver thought proudly. "I suggest that for the moment we tell no one about anything."

"But we can't keep it quiet once Sandy comes home everyone will know she's okay and..." Tim objected, disappointed in Ali's idea, he had hoped for a legal minded solution, not a game of subterfuge.

Alistair, pausing for effect said

"May I continue?"

"Off your high horse Ali, you're not in court yet!" Oliver chided him, "We're all trying to find a solution so we're all entitled to express our thoughts."

"I'm sorry Tim," Alistair immediately apologised, "My idea may not appeal to you and June but I suggest that, as we are pretty isolated here, Sandy and Paul should stay with us for a while." June was about to object, she was dying to have Sandy back to herself again. But Tim said,

"Go on, Alistair, tell us why that wouldn't just be putting off the day when we have to declare her found."

"In the meantime, I have some very clever and experienced contacts at university. I'm due to return in a week but I could go sooner, in fact it would be better if I went before term restarts as I wouldn't have timetable pressures to cope with." Sparks of comprehension showed in his audience's faces, "I'll put the situation hypothetically at first, to this one guy I know who's got a brilliant mind. Then if, hypothetically, he comes up with something I'll put it to him in reality, he's a practicing barrister when he isn't a visiting lecturer and he may even fight our case for us."

June looked at Tim anxiously,

"What about the Squires?"

"You haven't told anyone yet have you?" Alistair could see his plans coming unravelled before they had even started.

"No, but our friends, June's doctor and his wife have been marvellous, they have known Sandy all her life and are as distraught as we have been, we have to tell them!"

"Yes we must" June added, "how can I pretend to them; lie to them, I can't do it Tim."

"You could stay here for the time being, then you wouldn't have to speak to them, they would think you've gone away." Oliver suggested.

"We can't abuse your hospitality any longer, especially as you are going to be looking after Paul."

"And Sandy." Added Alistair,

"But we could possibly go away for a while." Tim looked to June for agreement, "We could see if that cottage in St. Ives is available, the one we stayed at last summer, it's out of season so it shouldn't be a problem."

"No." June was adamant, "Well, yes, we could go away to avoid other people but Mike and Sylvia have to be told."

Alistair sighed,

"Can they be trusted to keep it to themselves?"

"I doubt it." George joined in, "If he's a doctor and a 'pillar of the community' he won't want to jeopardise his career by keeping information about a suspect from the police." They had reached a stale-mate.

Sandy and Paul had meandered around the farm looking at the chicken, the geese, the barns and anything else Sandy could find. In the end she had run out of reasons to keep him outside and it was getting chilly,

"Can we go in now please?" Paul asked, "I need the toilet."

"Of course, come on." Sandy made sure they made a fair amount of noise as they came in to the warmth of the Aga heated kitchen. "Off you go then, I'll just tell the others we're back, maybe there'll be coffee and biscuits if we're lucky." She popped her head around the door of the sitting room, "We're back." She said, unnecessarily; they had been heard. The sitting room occupants looked collectively guilty and despondent. Paul was heard approaching the door and everyone shook themselves into nonchalant postures, appearing to be chatting aimlessly to each other.

"Paul, come and sit by the fire, you look frozen, Sandy's kept you out for too long." Alice beckoned him to take her seat by the crackling logs.

"Oh no, I'm very well thank you, ladies first." Paul replied declining her offer. Oliver disguised a laugh, at Paul's sweet gesture, with a cough.

"Who would like some coffee?" He got up and gently pushed Paul into his vacated chair.

After they had drunk their coffee, George suggested to Tim that he might like to see round the farm. Guessing the reasoning behind the offer, both Tim and June said that they would love to. Alistair and Oliver offered to join them. Alice declared she would start preparing lunch and would Sandy like to help? *Bugger* thought Sandy; she wanted to participate in the discussions that were obviously on-going.

"Paul's very good in the kitchen, maybe he would like to help you." She said pointedly to Alice, who, picking up on Sandy's undisguised pique, turned to Paul,

"Is that so? How about giving me a hand peeling the spuds?"

"Yes, I'd like to do that." He answered happily. Already, Paul felt quite comfortable with Alice, the matriarch, it was like being with his mummy. She had ordered him about like Alice was doing, in a firm but kindly way. Sandy rushed to catch up with the others.

"Well?" She demanded immediately on catching Oliver up who had lagged behind for her.

"You may well ask," replied Oliver, "Ali has a good idea, but there's a problem with your parents." They deliberately fell further behind the others while Oliver up-dated Sandy.

"Oh I see," she thought for a moment, "I reckon we could trust the Squires, he's due to retire this year and he's a super bloke, really understanding and down to earth."

"Hmm, if you're sure, if they betray us the whole plan is shot." Oliver wasn't totally convinced.

"Let's catch up." She replied, already burning to have her say. Instead of the heated debate she expected to find, the others were walking in silence. She caught her mother's arm and fell into step bedside her.

"Any thoughts mum?" She asked,

"We're divided at the moment," June answered, "It's Mike and Sylvia..."

"I know, Oliver told me. But I think, under the right circumstances we could tell them." Her comment caught the attention of the others and they stopped and waited for her to continue.

"Oliver has told me about your not being able to go home without everyone knowing I'm safe, so, why don't you book up the cottage and then invite the Squires down for a weekend break with you?"

"And kidnap them?!" Alistair couldn't resist the quip. Sandy grinned at him,

"That's a good idea, but what I thought was, get them away from home territory, relax them and then, very carefully draw them into the plan." She looked around at their unconvinced expressions, "Old Mike is a sweetie and no stick in the mud, let me talk to him and then let him meet Paul, I'm sure he will keep quiet. After all he can always deny having known I was safe. If you are away from home it's quite plausible that you haven't been in touch with him."

"Other than not telling him at all and possibly losing his friendship, we can tell him and then lose his friendship!" Tim said exasperatedly, "What have we got to lose!"

"If he lets us down you know what will happen to Paul don't you?" Oliver wasn't happy about involving the Squires at all, "A secret's a secret until two people know it. We have already seven in on it and that's excluding the main protagonist: Paul."

"Yes but we are all personally involved so that makes us just one." Sandy retorted, "And I trust the Squires, they are extremely kind people."

"Shall we put it to the vote?" George asked.

"I vote No!" Alistair exclaimed. "But you do as you think best. I'm going back to university tomorrow to put my idea into practice. The sooner I do that the better."

"I need to think on it for a while." Tim looked at June,

"I do as well; I'm not sure what to do." So, the problem still unresolved they trooped back indoors.

June and Tim quietly discussed the situation as they got ready for lunch.

"I'm not happy with keeping this sort of secret Tim. I'm sure if they hand Paul in to the police, they could still try and clear his name. At least Sandy needn't be involved then. He needn't necessarily go back to the asylum need he? Couldn't he be held in a local police station?"

"Don't let Sandy hear you say that darling! I don't think you understand; she's spent a long time with Paul and she has seen how disturbed he is. I think he's innocent of murder, don't you? He needs protection and George and Alice are doing all they can for him. Alice is a saint." June bridled at this praise of a woman who she had instinctively disliked, well not exactly disliked, but certainly hadn't warmed to.

"She's just enjoying being in charge!" June snapped. Tim was used to June's possessiveness of her small family, this included him as well as Sandy, and she jealously held their affections close. She added "I don't know why you think she's so special!" Tim ignored her slandering of Alice,

"Come on love, I know you want Sandy to yourself, so do I after all the worry we've had with her missing, but you know Sandy, she won't let it go now." They decided to book the cottage anyway and they would consider further whether to involve the Squires. George offered the use of his 'phone and the booking was made for Saturday the following day.

"At least it will give us some time to think and we will be out of touch with anyone who doesn't know we are there." Tim was uneasy about involving his friends; June was uneasy about *not* involving them. However, they decided to travel back home early the next morning, hoping they didn't run into the Squires, quickly pack a suitcase, and drive down to St. Ives to collect the key to the cottage that afternoon.

Oliver and Sandy met by arrangement later in the morning; Paul was busy with Alice, learning how to make bread, and his happy floury face was a masterpiece in concentration. Sandy playfully tossed some more flour at him and they exited the back door into the garden with his giggling in their ears.

"He's a lovely man, so easy to please; I won't let him go back to that asylum." Sandy took Oliver's proffered hand and they wandered down the path to the garden seat by the fish pond. Sandy closed her eyes and let the flickers of sunlight reflected off the water play across her eyelids.

"He's happy here," Oliver commented, "and he's really taken to mum."

"She's just what he needs at the moment; a mother figure," Sandy opened her eyes and turned to Oliver, "what if he stayed here and we changed his appearance a bit and his name. You're isolated here and in a month or two you could sort of integrate him into your family; a cousin or something. I could declare myself safe and not say anything about him or Jimmy!" She was getting excited, "I could just say I got lost when my car broke down and I tried to take a short cut. You don't have to explain yourself as you're just a hiker who found me when I had hurt myself!"

"How do we account for the length of time it took me to get you home? We can't pretend it took weeks to get from there to here."

"Hmm, good point... Of course! You fell and tore your ligament didn't you? We don't have to tell anyone where it happened. No one could travel with that sort of injury."

"True, but it still wouldn't take us as long as it did, don't forget, I could walk within a week or so of doing it." Sandy was a little deflated, but not for long,

"We could always say that we fell in love and were so enjoying our time together that we completely forgot about anyone else."

"But that would paint you as a selfish, inconsiderate bitch; which you certainly are not!" Oliver didn't like the idea of her or indeed, himself, being portrayed in this way.

"I know, but the people who matter know the truth and in time everyone else will forget; they all have their own lives to lead."

"It's an idea," mused Oliver, "let's think it through a bit more before putting it to the others."

"Mum and Dad are leaving tomorrow; we have to talk to everyone this evening at the latest." Sandy jumped up; full of enthusiasm at her plan and Oliver pulled her back down beside him,

"They won't like it." He warned her.

CHAPTER 18

IT WAS TIME to involve Paul in the discussions. A preliminary meeting with June, Tim and George, whilst Alice kept Paul occupied ended with some enthusiasm for the plan from George but Sandy's parents were not happy at their daughter's character being besmirched. George had a hasty chat with Alice whilst the bread was baking and Paul had been despatched to clean himself up.

"What do you think my love, would you be prepared to look after him?"

"Yes, I would, at least it would give Alistair some time for research and the police could close Sandy's case. In time people forget." Alice replied without hesitation. "Also, they're never going to find that Jimmy; as far as the police are concerned, they both might have perished on the moor, especially once winter closes in."

"I thought you'd agree." George regarded his wife fondly, "In fact Paul could be a real help on the farm, as well as in the kitchen."

Over lunch, Alice, as she was piling more food on to Paul's plate, said casually, "Would you like to stay with us Paul?" Paul's face lit up and he gazed at Alice with supreme gratitude,

"Oh yes please, I would like that. And Sandy too?" He turned his pale blue eyes to Sandy with longing.

"I can stay for a little while, but I'll have to go home for a bit to report ouch!"

Oliver had kicked her shin under the table to stop any careless talk. “Sorry, I had a bit of cramp,” she improvised, “I was saying, yes I’ll come back after I’ve sorted a few of my possessions out.” Paul looked a little disappointed but his gratitude at Alice’s invitation shone through.

“That’s grand, you’ll be a great help to us.” George enthused, “We’ll have to get you a load more clothes, work clothes for the farm and smart stuff for other times, but, just for the time being you can borrow Oliver’s.”

“It won’t be the first time!” Oliver looked at Sandy and she looked at Paul and the three of them, remembering Paul’s humiliation remained quietly complicit, ignoring the questioning glances around them.

June searched out Alice to thank her for the hospitality and unsuccessfully attempt to pay for their keep.

“I wouldn’t think of it!” Alice put her hands behind her back in refusal of the offer, “It’s all home grown and we have plenty to share.”

“So, what are you and mum going to do? Are you still going to the cottage?” Sandy and Tim were alone in the sitting room,

“Yes, we are, we need some time to get our heads around all this.” Tim answered, “Why don’t you come too, just to relax and recuperate a little?”

“I’d love to dad, but I need to make sure Paul settles and don’t forget I’m still missing! Come back this way on your way home next week and pick me up. I’ll have prepared my story for everyone by then.”

Early the following morning Sandy’s parents waved a reluctant goodbye to her and set off home. When the car had disappeared into the distance Oliver led her away to their seat by the pond.

“I think we may have a problem with your mum.”

“Oh, don’t worry about her, dad’ll pull her round. She’s just nervy; anything which is chancy or out of sync with everyday life sends her into a spin.”

"What about these Squires, why's she so keen on involving them?" Oliver found it a bit odd that she kept on about them, "They're not related or something are they?"

"No, they're just friends. Mike's been mum's doctor for ever and he looked after her through two miscarriages before I was born. She dotes on him. And his wife, Sylvia is always there for a good gossip or a shoulder to cry on."

"I'm sorry to hear your mum had miscarriages; that must be why she's so possessive of you. By the way, Ali 'phoned last night, late. He's meeting his master-mind barrister today. Fingers crossed!"

"I'm still not sure how we are going to play that part of events, in order for the barrister to fight Paul's case, Paul has to be declared found. Then, while he's waiting for the trial or whatever, he'll be in custody again. He'll think we've betrayed him and God knows what that will do to him!" Sandy turned to Oliver pleadingly, "Can't we just hide him here for as long as it takes for it all to blow over?"

"I've had the same thoughts, I wonder if the clearing of Paul's name could be done posthumously."

"But he isn't dead!"

"I know, silly, but if it was assumed that he was dead, on the moor, frozen in the cold or sunk in a bog, Ali's barrister could perhaps call on character witnesses like Paul's old teacher to testify to his gentle nature and clear him of the charges. Then, maybe six months or so after, Paul could be 'found' and he would be a free man."

"That's a fantastic idea!" Sandy squeezed Oliver's arm, "Ask Ali what he thinks, tell him to keep everything hypothetical for the time being."

"So, the complete plan," Oliver and Sandy told Alice and George, "is to firstly hide Paul here and make sure no one sees him. Secondly, Ali's gathering legal advice on how to clear Paul's name. Thirdly, we declare Sandy safe and get our story right for the police. And fourthly, we make sure that Paul is presumed dead, lastly we clear Paul's name 'posthumously'."

"Well, that's some plan, let's hope we can pull it off." George said shaking his head.

As luck would have it, on their arrival home June and Tim found Mike Squires walking up to their front door,

"Leave it to me." Tim parked the car and hallooed Mike,

"You've just caught us; we're going away for a few days."

"Looks like you're just coming back!" Mike joked half-heartedly.

"Yes, it does doesn't it, we had gone about ten miles, and then June said she couldn't remember whether she had turned the cooker off!!" Tim improvised hastily.

"Best to be sure. Have you got enough pills June?" He leaned through the car window to give June a peck on the cheek.

"Yes I'm fine thanks Mike." She sounded forced, a little stiff Mike thought, but, given their situation it wasn't surprising. He wished them a safe journey, made no enquiry of their destination and strode off down the road. June and Tim hurriedly packed a case and left within half an hour.

"I feel dreadful, looking Mike in the eye and not telling him." June said miserably, "I wish to God Sandy had never gone after that Paul, she'd have been sunning herself in Mauritius all this time."

"It's no good, we can't undo what's done, anyway within the week Mike will be told. His relief that Sandy's safe will be all that matters, he doesn't need to know anything else and I'm sure we can tell it in such a way that Sandy doesn't come over badly." He drove a little too fast around a bend and June demanded him to slow down,

"Do you want to get us killed?" She snapped "That would be a lovely homecoming present for Sandy I'm sure!"

"Sorry, darling, I was planning the story in my head and wondering how long we could stretch Sandy's injury; probably suffering concussion when she fell and then Oliver's torn ligament, the maths took over my concentration." Although June supposed she felt sorry for Paul, she didn't have the same amount of compassion for him as the others did, she found his physiognomy unpleasant and the way he looked at Sandy unnerved and vaguely repulsed her. *I wish he had died!* She immediately rebuked herself for her uncharitable thought, but couldn't deny the truth of it. The only thing that mattered to June was her family, it was a small family with just the three of them, June's sister and a few cousins scattered across the county but Sandy was precious to her; June wanted it all to be over and Sandy back at home with them. She didn't like any of their plans if they delayed this happening. "I feel terrible not telling Mike, they're such good friends; I think we *should* tell them," June said miserably.

"We promised." Tim said adamantly. But June continued,

"I don't know why they're making such a fuss over him. It's not as if he's family. Just some mental defective Sandy happened to get stuck with!" Tim gave a sharp intake of breath and glanced sideways at his wife. He couldn't believe what he had heard. He bit his tongue and drove on, June sitting sullenly by his side.

Back at the farm, Sandy and Oliver took Lilly for a run across the fields, the winter wheat was already poking little spikes of green through the soil and from a distance the field looked like a green carpet. Closer up, however pools of muddy water hung in every dip.

"It's a bit mucky, we'll have to give her a hose down when we get back; she'll love that!" Sandy watched Lilly, tearing like a released caged animal, after scents which only her nose could detect; head down tail wagging furiously, oblivious to anything else. "I've missed her, she's such a character; makes me laugh."

"I miss our old collie, Nipper, he died earlier this year and we haven't had the heart to replace him yet." Oliver laughed as Lilly, misjudging a leap, somersaulted and landed, still running as if nothing had happened.

"You remember I mentioned to you that Paul had a dark raincoat?"

"Yes, what of it?" Oliver looked puzzled,

"Well he didn't have it later did he?"

"No, he was shivering, but maybe that was in fear of me!" Oliver wondered what Sandy was getting at.

"And you remember I told you that Jimmy had a donkey jacket?" Oliver nodded, "Did you see if he was wearing it when he shot at you?" Oliver thought back, reluctant to recall those last moments of Jimmy's life,

"I don't think so, no he was in a shirt, I remember now, it was sunny and quite warm, no, he definitely wasn't wearing it. Why are you asking?" Sandy answered him with another question,

"Did you see it anywhere nearby, for instance when you found your pack and your tent, did you see anything which could have been a jacket but didn't recognise it as such?"

"Hang on, you're losing me." Oliver was bemused by Sandy's questions. "Why do you want to know?"

"Because," Sandy beamed with excitement "if the raincoat and the donkey jacket were both to be found in the same area and by a peat bog, the authorities might just put two and two together and..."

"Pronounce them both lost, feared dead!" Oliver finished for her.

"Yes! So when do we go?"

"To find the coats?"

"Of course, what else?" Sandy was nearly bouncing with the idea she had formulated. "We could take Lilly with us, or maybe not, she's a bit manic, I don't want her running off and drowning herself."

"No just as well not. She'll be okay here with dad, he adores her already. The only problem is that although Jimmy's jacket is probably in the area where I met him, we have no idea where Paul's raincoat could be." Oliver took a bit of steam out of her, but not for long, in a flash she replied,

"We'll ask him!"

"Okay, we can try, he probably won't remember though." But Sandy couldn't wait to start.

"LILLY!" She hollered making Oliver jump with the sheer volume of sound issuing from her diminutive form, "HERE!" Lilly unglued her nose from the ground and came bounding back to sit at Sandy's feet waiting for her treat. Sandy tore on ahead of Oliver and he had to call to her to hold on a moment, this was another thing that had to be approached carefully.

"Wait, Sandy, let's plan things a bit before we go rushing in."

They got back to the farm to hear a lot of noise coming from the bathroom downstairs; Paul was squealing,

"Ouch, It's gone in my eye!"

"Hold still, it's nearly done!" Alice's exasperated voice answered.

"What's going on?" Oliver asked George who was leaning against the wall outside, grinning broadly.

"Wait and see." He laughed, "Poor old Paul!" After a lot more squealing from Paul and the sound of running water, Paul and Alice emerged from the bathroom. Paul was pink in the face and rubbing his eyes, Alice followed him with a towel which she was attempting to rub over Paul's hair.

"Wow!" Oliver exclaimed "You look like one of the family!" Paul immediately stopped complaining,

"Do I?" He beamed,

"Yea, those curls are just like mine except, luckily for you they're not bright ginger!"

"I did wonder about dyeing it as well," Alice puffed with exertion but perhaps that can wait 'til another day."

Alice had permed Paul's hair; its lankness was replaced by soft curls which fell around his face and over his collar. His hair had grown quite considerably during their time on the moor and Alice, instead of cutting it to tidy it up, had decided to start his planned disguise.

"Now he's Peter, our nephew from London; and your cousin, Oli." She prompted Paul, "Who are you?"

"My name is Peter and I am staying for a bit." Paul replied parrot-like.

"That'll do for now." Alice smiled, "We'll work on details later while we're getting dinner, okay Peter?" Paul didn't immediately respond and then, realising she meant him said,

"Oh, yes, thank you Auntie."

"Brilliant!" Oliver hugged Paul, or rather, Peter, saying "Good to have you visiting, Cousin Peter."

"We must use his new name all the time now so we all get used to it." Alice added. "Now *Peter*, with curly hair, you let it dry naturally and don't brush it or it'll go frizzy," Alice told him, his eyes never leaving her face he took in his instructions obediently.

Oliver and Sandy went into the kitchen for coffee, chuckling over Paul's transformation.

"He looks brighter; less Down's somehow," Sandy observed, "the curls cover his funny ears and all in all he looks more 'normal'."

"True, as long as he keeps a low profile and doesn't have to talk to anyone; that could give him away, at a glance he looks like just any old bod."

Over lunch, Sandy explained to all of them, including Peter, what she and Oliver had thought of doing. Peter wasn't very happy at being 'dead' but once he realised that it might save him from going back to that horrid place, he readily agreed to try and help.

"Can you remember where you last had your raincoat Paueter?" Sandy still had to do a double take before using his new name. Peter knew exactly when he had lost it because it was when he was agonising about whether to try and find it that Jimmy had found *him*. He also told them he had put it on a rock to dry in the sun, and that there were lots of big rocks there as well.

"How soon after he found you did you come to our tent?" Oliver was pretty sure he knew the little tor Peter was referring to, and just had to confirm the timing; to make sure.

"He made me do it that night, I didn't want to..." Peter began to whine but Sandy cut him off

"We know that Peter, don't fret." She turned to Oliver and said angrily "He was a bloody cunning piece of shit!" Sandy wasn't averse to giving vent to her feelings with expletives, irrespective of the company she was in. Her parents had despaired, June blushing with embarrassment when Sandy came out with 'bugger', 'shit' or 'arse hole' in company. Her language had deteriorated further during her four years at college and June had given up on her daughter ever becoming 'lady-like'.

Oliver put his hand over Sandy's clenched fist on the table top,

"Calm down, dear, we know that, don't fret!" He mimicked her "Go on Peter." Peter told them that he had left the raincoat and then walked for a bit and eaten some blackberries and that Jimmy had discovered him soon after that. "I reckon I know exactly where he left it." Oliver said, "It'll still be there, and if we can find Jimmy's donkey jacket we can put plan B into action. I know he was wearing it when he shoved me down that bunker, did he have it on when he brought you to join me?"

"I'm pretty sure he did." Sandy recalled the dark figure

straddled over Paul's prostrate body, it certainly wasn't a shirt-sleeved one.

"We just have to hope that he didn't discard it between then and when I found him, though I can't see why he would, he was no fool." Oliver felt that they were ready to go searching.

"By the way, what was Plan A?" Sandy asked cheekily.

"I've no idea but Plan B sounds better." Oliver laughed.

That evening, when Alistair made his nightly report by 'phone, Oliver explained what they were going to do. Alistair was impressed with Sandy's thinking. He had made some progress with his hypothesis and had also been researching Down syndrome; reinforcing their unanimous assessment that people with the syndrome were intrinsically gentle and loving. He felt that, given breathing space, he could present a case for Paul/Peter's innocence.

Reassured, Oliver and Sandy planned to venture back into the moor on Sunday; the following day. Oliver spread his map of the moor out on the table and marked the two places where he was pretty sure they would find the items they needed. Sunday morning they were up early but Alice had beaten them to it, she was busy packing lunch boxes with food.

"This time we're going prepared, no need to hunt or forage; mum's packing us cold meats bread, milk, and anything else she can find in the cupboards. You'll have to take a pack, just hope you're strong enough to carry the entire contents of her larder."

"You'll need warm and waterproof clothing as well Sandy," Alice came into the room with a bundle of items ranging from a hooded parka she said was hers and would nearly fit Sandy, waterproof walking boots which, with thick socks, fitted Sandy perfectly, a fisherman's knit sweater and a pair of gloves. "You can never tell when the weather is going to change."

"Tell me about it!" Sandy replied, "Fog, torrential rain, frost, I've experienced them all in a few weeks. It was like all the seasons rolled into one!" Oliver, practised in the art, packed all the other essentials, torch with new and spare batteries, a second torch just in case, his compass, map, two sleeping bags, (not his old one) etcetera. Finally, and with almost a loving care, he stowed Ali's rope snugly in his pack.

"You'd better take this." George handed Oliver his shot gun. "Though I sincerely hope you don't need to use it."

"Thanks dad, I doubt I will; now that Jimmy's gone and with all this nosh I won't have to hunt."

Sandy gave Peter, George and Alice a hug saying "We'll be back in a few days, four at the most, that's right isn't it, Oliver?" He nodded.

"Hopefully, before your mum and dad come at the end of the week."

"What do you want us to tell them if they 'phone?" George was sure that June wouldn't approve of this latest expedition.

"Just tell them we've gone out for the day, hopefully they won't ring and it'll be a fait accompli by the time they get here." Sandy's thought mirrored George's. She wasn't being unfair to her mother but she had always felt it better to keep her mum in the dark over some of her activities and this was certainly one that fell into that category.

Alice and George watched their tall ginger-headed son and his small pixie-like companion walking purposefully out of sight. They raised their hands in a farewell and a blessing as the hikers turned the bend at the end of the lane vanishing from sight.

Peter and Alice got on well in the kitchen and during the first couple of days of Oliver and Sandy's absence he learned how to make fairy cakes which he decorated with hundreds and thousands and then couldn't wait to eat. He also helped Alice prepare some hams for smoking and had even helped with the bramble jelly she was making, tasting it with a spoon before it was poured into the glass jars and securing the paper lids with rubber rings whilst they were still too hot to handle. In the afternoons when he wasn't learning to be a cook he went out with George and Lilly, who didn't mind with whom she walked as long as she could run wild. They walked the boundaries of the farm, George pointing out the various crops and animals as they went. As it was late autumn, the harvests had been taken in and the fields prepared and sown. The itinerant workers who turned up each summer picking fruit in exchange for food and a bed in the barn, converted for use as a bunk-house, had all moved on. They had the farm to themselves for a few months. Peter was safe from prying eyes and gossip for the time being.

CHAPTER 19

SANDY AND OLIVER made excellent time, knowing exactly where they were heading first. Oliver led them safely across a landscape familiar to him and they made their first camp well before dark. It would only take them a couple of days to find the raincoat; the bigger problem was the donkey jacket: had Jimmy died with it on? Oliver was sure he hadn't but memory sometimes plays tricks. As if to buoy their spirits, the evening was balmy for the time of year, the downside was the abundance of mosquitoes swarming by the hundreds around their heads. Oliver lit a strange green coil which gave off a smell reminiscent of marijuana of which Sandy had partaken a little whilst at college.

"Are we going to get high on it?" She joked.

"What naughty secrets are you concealing?" Oliver replied, "It isn't pot, so don't get excited!" The fumes from the coil helped a little at keeping the mosquitoes at bay and they ate their first evening meal on the moor for which they hadn't hunted, in relative peace. Their existing mosquito bites however, itched them to distraction.

"Damn, I should have remembered the repellent cream." Oliver said scratching his now un-bearded chin.

Beside a log fire, or in wicker chairs around the Aga while Alice cooked, George and Peter chatted. Peter told him about his mummy and their home together. He never spoke of his last memory of her. George recounted humorous tales about the boys when they were young which made Peter laugh. They used his new name constantly in order to drum it into both his and their minds. His curly hair certainly had changed his appearance and healthy food and affectionate company had given him some colour and vivacity. He was no longer the greasy-haired misfit who had been led into their home that night, but a relaxed and to all appearances, happy young man who suffered a little from shyness.

They rehearsed his so called family history as Peter, George's fictitious brother's son; whose wife was having an operation and had asked if he could stay with them, just to be on the safe side. They didn't worry overmuch about him meeting anyone though; they were isolated and people seldom called. Alice baked her own bread and they had milk from the goats, vegetables and meat from the farm. The only person to come to the farm was the postman in his van and that wasn't every day. George suspected that in order to make his round shorter and so that he could get off home early, the postman stockpiled their post and made at the most two deliveries a week. Thus it was that Wednesday morning, when Peter was busy washing up the breakfast things while Alice changed the sheets on the beds and George was milking the goats, the door, on the jar, was pushed open and a head in a peaked cap peered into the kitchen,

"Post!" He called and, catching sight of Peter, "Is the missus in?" Then, looking inquisitively at Peter he asked, "D'you work here then?"

"Nno, I live here." Peter stuttered; flustered by the sudden appearance of a stranger he backed away and rushed out of the kitchen door and up the stairs to Alice.

"What's up Peter, you looked flushed?"

"There's a man downstairs." He almost hid behind Alice and she took hold of his hands,

"Don't panic, stay here, I'll go and see." Alice ran down the stairs and into the kitchen to find the postman standing by the door, he looked as if he were about to say something but changed his mind and touching his cap he turned to the door.

"Thank-you Bert, quite a pile today, been building up again?" Bert had the decency to look bashful, touched his cap once more,

"'Morning Missus."

"'Bye then." Alice replied, "Give my best to Jean." Bert and Jean had married soon after leaving school and had both worked at the post office since then. They were incurably nosey and dreadful gossips, Jean had access to all sorts of private information about savings accounts and Bert tended to notice the type of letters people received; whether they were official and if they used red ink, meaning they were overdue bills, or personal post from abroad (that would be old so an' so, left in a cloud) and so on. They were tolerated by the locals who mostly laughed off the gossip which filtered out from the post office. However, on his way back to the sorting office, Bert was wracking his brains. And when he met up with Jean for lunch he said

"I didn't know ole Alice up at the farm had a spastic son!"

"She hasn't, at least as far as I know, unless she's had him in one of those homes and out of sight. Why d'you say that?"

"Well, this morning I met a bloke up there, in their kitchen, quite at home he was, he looked a bit odd and he said he lived there and then did a runner up to Alice and didn't show his face again while I was there."

"That *is* odd." Jean was thoughtful. "Did she say anything about him?"

"No, just behaved like normal, sent her best to you and that was it."

Wednesday afternoon Oliver and Sandy arrived at the tor and there, stretched out on the rock, just as Peter had described it, was a dirty charcoal black gabardine raincoat.

"Eureka!" Oliver gathered it up, stuffed it in his pack and they set off again, following the map, in their quest to find the donkey jacket. Oliver was not looking forward to once again visiting the place where he had heard Jimmy's last bubbled cries. He still couldn't shake his dream from his mind. He was a little subdued and Sandy wondered why. After the discovery of the raincoat he had been so jubilant. So, hesitantly at first, Oliver told her about his dream and the recurring nightmares he had had since rescuing Ali from the peat. Sandy caught hold of his hand and squeezed it as they walked and he talked, he squeezed hers in return. She listened quietly and he felt a weight lifted from him. He hadn't told anyone of the countless nights he had woken calling Ali's name, shaking and sweating. It was a relief to have spoken of it at last.

"We'll be home by Friday I reckon." He said more heartily, as they erected the tent that night. "Once we have found the jacket and left them both in a compromising position we can make tracks." The temperature, after the bright day, dropped considerably as they built their fire, this time for warmth only and they huddled thankfully around it. Alice's parka and boots were snug but the frosty air crept in.

"Whoever would want to live in a town with lights everywhere" Oliver gazed up at the stars "when there's such beauty in a night sky just waiting to be appreciated?" The white gold moon glistened as though frosted, the North Star shone brilliantly and every point of the Plough was visible. There was enough light to see the bushes and small trees around them and on the horizon the moon and starlight picked out Paul's tor, giving it the appearance of a giant mushroom. Loathe to go to bed on such a lovely night, Oliver and Sandy built up the fire and let themselves relax, absorbed in the peace of the moment. The shadow of an owl, silent as a ghost, glanced across the moon, a rustle in the undergrowth as a small rodent scurried to hide from those incredible eyes, nature without man; it was intoxicating. Oliver leaned in to put more fuel on the fire, shuffling in closer to the warmth and Sandy. He lay back and resting his head across her legs he asked

"You don't mind do you?"

"No, I can play with your curls." Sandy laughed.

"You can't keep your hands off them can you? Haven't you still got the ones you yanked out in 'Baggins Hall'?" Reaching into his parka, he pulled out his penknife, "Here you are, some of your very own, you can play with them all the time, all clean now, and smelling of shampoo." He sliced off a long strand and dangled it between his fingers where, catching the light from the fire it gleamed like copper.

"I can't believe we've been strangers, friends, enemies and then friends again in just two months!" He mused, "Let's hope we stay friends."

"I have no doubt of it Oliver; I think finally we are on the same wave-length. I can't imagine not being friends with you, not now, after all we've experienced, and we also have a common goal don't we?"

"We certainly do. Dear old Paul, what a shit I was to him! I don't think I shall ever really forgive myself for my behaviour." He sat up and looked into Sandy's moonlit eyes, "Never again will I be so judgemental."

"We've both had an epiphany!" Sandy replied "What an education in humanity. I think I'll go to university and take a degree in sociology or should it be philosophy?"

"Teach it more likely!" Oliver laughed. "Sandy, on a more serious note, I am worried about your mum's obsession with the Squires."

"She'll be okay, dad'll sort it, he's more down to earth, mum's a bit neurotic, I hate to say, but she *has* been through a lot so I suppose it's only to be expected." As the night deepened they chatted about themselves and their lives before they met. Oliver recounted some hilarious tales from his teaching days when three girls fainted when dissecting a worm and they laughed helplessly at some of the questions he'd been asked in human biology lessons. He had a girl-friend, Susie, at the school who taught English and it was she who had encouraged him to write. He supposed they were still a couple if she hadn't given up on him after such a long period of non-communication. After Tom, other than fleeting flings, some of which Sandy was a bit ashamed, she had not had a deep relationship. Her memory of her time with Tom and his anguish when she had left him was something she didn't want to discuss with Oliver or indeed, anyone. No matter that she knew there was no going back, deep in her heart she kept a place for him.

"I'm not worried about settling down yet and I don't want to be straitjacketed, I want to travel and live a bit and I want to paint. Hell I'm only just twenty three."

"I don't think you'll ever really grow up, I mean get old and staid, I reckon you'll be just as reckless as you are now, you'll be wearing jeans and spiking your hair when you're sixty!"

"Just stay around friend and make sure you're proven right."

"I will, now I think we need to sleep, we've got a bedroll each this time, such luxury!"

On reaching the stream near where Oliver had encountered Jimmy, they went directly to the little dell where Oliver had found his gear. The jacket was there hidden under bracken just as his backpack and tent had been. They took the two coats to the edge of the mire. The raincoat they spread close to the edge of the bog so that it vaguely floated over and into it. They lay the donkey jacket on the ground as if it had been shrugged off in a hurry.

"How does that look?" Oliver asked Sandy, "Does it look authentic to you?"

"Yes, I think so." Sandy answered.

"Let's get away from this place." Oliver said with a shiver. "I don't want to hang around." His imagination showed him a body sunk deep with outstretched hands, and it appalled him. They turned away and set off in the direction of home.

"How are we going to make sure someone finds them?" Sandy asked after they had walked a while in mutual silence. This aspect had escaped their thoughts when they had made the plan.

"Oh God, that's a point." Oliver stopped and scratched at his mosquito-bitten head, the ginger curls springing around his fingers in a way which made Sandy itch to play with them. "It has to be an apparent stranger; we can't be connected in any way. Who could it be? And it must be soon; before winter. Nobody with any sense hikes the moor in the winter except the army on their survival manoeuvres."

"How about an anonymous 'phone call on a bad line from a 'phone box, a lone hiker, nearly fell in the bog, we can give him a Scottish accent, that's a good long way from here, the line is too bad to make out his name and it gets cut off as he tells them his address, they won't bother trying to contact him as there wouldn't really be any need and anyway Scotland's way up there!!" Sandy was talking faster and faster, she gesticulated pointing vaguely northwards her wild imagination carrying her along.

"By Jove, I think she's got it!" Sang Oliver, "You ought to write detective mysteries!"

CHAPTER 20

TIM AND JUNE felt claustrophobic sitting indoors at the cottage. In the evenings in an attempt at homeliness they lit a fire in the open grate and sat, pretending to read the books they had brought with them, but both of them knew the other's mind was elsewhere. Every day they walked over the cliffs and along the beach, anywhere rather than staying in a close uncomfortable atmosphere. Out in the open they could remark on the sky, the sea, the weather, they attempted to behave like an ordinary couple on holiday. But always, the conversations were but a step away from Paul. They fell to walking in silence during their late afternoon strolls along the beach, as each time the subject was raised an argument simmered. June's silence was one of petulance as Tim persistently refused to involve the Squires. Tim's silence was pensive. He had found himself in a dilemma; he wasn't sure about the way the Tregowens and Sandy were going about the problem of Paul, but he couldn't think of an alternative without Paul being re-arrested. Having met the man, he had no doubt in his mind that he was innocent of murder. However, June, although reluctantly prepared to believe Paul's innocence, was adamant that there was another way to deal with it without involving Sandy, but the only way she could come up with was to turn Paul in. Tim was sick of hearing her harking on about the Squires,

"Why are you so keen to involve them? What benefit would it be to anyone?" He asked her in exasperation after yet another stale-mate conversation.

"Mike would know what to do!" She exclaimed, "He wouldn't be dragged along in this hair-brained scheme of theirs!" Tim sighed,

"We promised darling, and I will not break a promise." June huffed and walked ahead of him along the beach. He let her walk on; reasoning with her was getting him nowhere. She was sitting on a rock staring out at the sea when he caught her up. He sat beside her and draped his arm over her shoulders; always the protective and loving husband he generally ceded to her wishes, but he was finding their differences of opinion hard to reconcile. They sat there for a long time watching the rolling waves crash on to the rocks on the headland and listening to the hissing of the receding water, draining through the fissures and pebbles on its way back to the sea.

"If only life could be as simple as this."

Tim hugged her frail shoulder tighter as she leaned into him.

"Tim, I can't stay here a moment longer!" She added. Tim, very surprised at the suddenness of her change of thought, but unsurprised by the thought itself quietly agreed.

"Me neither. Let's go back to the farm and Sandy. Maybe they'll have some good news."

"I suppose we could always ring them and speak to Sandy?" June mooted, then, changing her mind, "No let's just go."

The next morning, on the Thursday, they handed the keys in to the agent who enquired if everything at the cottage had been satisfactory and wondered why they were taking their leave so soon, especially as they seemed to be having an Indian summer, which was most unusual in November...

"Yes, thank-you, everything was perfect. We're leaving for personal reasons."

"Christ Alice!" Cried George, "There are three police cars coming up the lane!" Alice grabbed Peter's hand

"I'm not going to hide you Peter, remember PETER, YOU'RE MY NEPHEW!" She spelt it out slowly. Peter shook with fear. "There's no point hiding him George, they'll turn the place upside down and they'll find him. If we behave innocently and stick to our story..." They heard the cars pull up outside, unnecessarily making the gravel fly and before the policemen had got out of their cars Alice opened the front door, George and Peter standing beside her.

"Whatever is going on?!" She took the initiative, her eyes flashing and her face flushed, "Just look what you've done to my gravel!" She shouted at the officer who was approaching the door. Over his shoulder she saw the other cars disgorge their occupants some of whom fanned out behind him while others ran to the back of the house. She was distressed to see that some of them were carrying guns. The officer approaching was momentarily nonplussed at her response to his carefully planned raid. In his experience people tried to run away. He lost some of his swagger. Then pulling himself up to his full height which wasn't much more than Alice's, he said

"Madam I have reason to believe that you may be sheltering a dangerous criminal; a murderer", his eye fell on Peter and he shouted,

"There he is men, arrest him!" They rushed forward, knocking Alice and George to one side and grabbed Peter by both arms, forcing them up behind his back so that he was bent double.

"Auntie!" He cried, tears streaming down his face, "Auntie, Uncle George!" Alice's face turned puce with genuine anger, and it wasn't an act; she felt murderous towards the policemen. Whether Peter was Paul or Paul was Peter, was irrelevant; they had no right to treat an unarmed man in this way. She and George strode into their midst,

"How dare you!" George thundered at the officer in charge,

"How dare you come here and manhandle my nephew?! What's your name and rank *sonny*? Your career will be over by the time I've finished with you!" He turned to Alice, who was bristling with rage at his side,

"Alice take Peter inside and comfort him." To the men holding Peter he said, coldly and calmly,

"Let go of my nephew; immediately!" They looked at the officer in charge, hesitantly relaxing their hold on Peter who was sobbing with fear, he gave a barely perceptible nod and they let go of Peter who rushed into Alice's arms, where he buried his face in her hair and wept.

"Now, call your men together and put those bloody guns away. I demand an explanation!" George looked down on the officer from his six foot five advantage, "And I want it now, on this spot, from where you are standing. I can assure you that I am not going to invite you in."

"I'm sorry Sir, there seems to have been a mistake."

"A mistake you call it do you? Well I call it assault!"

"Well Sir, from the description we received from our informant, this nephew of yours matched that of an escaped suspect who was being held at a mental institution pending his trial for murder." He recited.

"And by that you mean that any unfortunate man afflicted with Down syndrome is automatically a suspect!" George spoke coldly with ice in his eyes. The policeman looked down at his boots which seemed to be shuffling of their own accord,

"It may appear so Sir, but I can assure you that we only have the best interests of the public in mind." All through the interview he had spoken as if from a text book on how to be a policeman and George's patience was running out.

"Are you a married man, officer?" The officer said that he was, "And do you have children?" Yes he did, "And are they all fit and normal?" They were, "Then you are a lucky man. Go away and do some homework on the syndrome and thank God for the lovely but misjudged people that they are." He turned his back on the officer and strode into the house, shutting the door firmly behind him.

Alice was holding the trembling Peter in her arms,

"I didn't do it!" He sobbed.

"We know you didn't, love." Alice held him close as a mother would and slowly his sobbing abated and she lowered him gently on to a chair. "We'll not let them take you away, we'll look after you."

"Bloody jumped up little squirt!" George was still fuming at the way the police had behaved, "It was as if they were arresting an IRA bomber!"

Later that night when they had calmed Peter and put him to bed, they sat by the fire, its soft flickering flames and the perfume of burning apple logs, restoring them to some form of sanity. Alice lay back in her chair, exhausted from spent emotion, breathed

"That was dreadful."

"Yes, it was, but I hope it'll be the last we hear from them." George replied.

"You were pretty intimidating darling, I just hope he doesn't seek revenge for his humiliation in front of the others."

"We can only hope that our anger came over as that of injured parties and not just a lot of bluster."

"I don't know about you, but I really felt like his auntie, I felt as though I was protecting one of my own. I've grown so fond of him, George, I can't believe he has only been here a week, it feels as though I have known and loved him for ever." She faced her husband who was nodding his agreement, "When all this is over, do you think he'd like to live with us permanently?"

"I've no doubt about that. Rest assured my love, he loves you like a special aunt, that's obvious."

"I'll just check the doors and stoke the Aga, off you go to bed, I'll be up in a tick." George raised his long form from the chair and running his fingers through her now greying auburn curls; he kissed the top of her head, and went into the kitchen. Alice heard him shaking the scuttle into the Aga as she wearily climbed the stairs.

It was earlier than George and Alice normally retired and so when June and Tim's car drove into the yard they were greeted by dark windows, no lights were on save the light over the front door which George had forgotten to turn off.

"What shall we do? They all seem to be in bed." June was surprised by this as when they were last here it was past eleven before they went to bed.

"Perhaps we should go and find a B & B somewhere and come back in the morning." Tim suggested and he put the car into reverse to turn it around. Suddenly a light came on in an upstairs room, George and Alice's, June remembered it was at the front of the house, and a face looked out of the window.

"The police haven't come back have they?" Alice sat up in alarm,

"No, unless it's an unmarked car, hang on, oh no it's Tim and June!"

"What the devil are they doing back so soon?" Alice was whacked, the last thing she needed was guests especially at this hour, especially Tim and June! "Sandy and Oliver; they're going to want to see Sandy. What are we going to tell them?"

"The truth." George was as annoyed as Alice at this late visit but he had no choice but to let them in. "But not tonight!"

Plastering a forced expression of welcome over his face, George opened the door to June and Tim who were apologising before they had even crossed the door step.

"We're so sorry to arrive so unexpectedly, we just couldn't switch off." June said as George kissed her cheek and ushered them inside,

"No, no, it's fine; we've had a long day and decided to have an early night. Your room is ready for you; the same one as before," then, remembering his manners he added "have you eaten?"

"Oh yes, please don't worry about food, we had something on the way." Tim was feeling awkward; it was obvious that their arrival was not entirely welcome.

"Would you like a cup of cocoa or tea?" George stifled a yawn.

"No, we'll just go to bed, I'm so sorry to do this to you George, thank you for being so polite about it." Tim picked up their case from the hall floor and they followed George up the stairs. After seeing them to their room and wishing them goodnight, George headed back to his own room; seeing the door to Oliver's empty room, where Sandy slept, was open, he hastily closed it. It was en route to the bathroom and he would rather save the problem of the discovery of her absence 'til the morning. He had had enough drama for one day.

God help us!

Alice and George, being farmers, as were their parents and grandparents, always rose early and after doing the usual early chores, sat together drinking tea in the kitchen, dreading June's descent from her room expecting to find Sandy.

"She's going to be difficult you know!" Alice understood the dreadful strain that June had been under all the while Sandy had been missing having experienced similar fears when Alistair had run off. She could easily imagine the overwhelming grief she must have felt when they thought Sandy was dead. But she was completely different to June in character, and found it hard to cope with *unnecessary* histrionics; after all, Sandy was safe now.

"We'll just have to deal with it. Oli and Sandy should be back any time soon, just keep your patience and we'll cope." George took her hand in his and squeezed it reassuringly.

Soon after this, steps were heard from above, water ran for a bath and they took deep breaths to prepare them for the guaranteed onslaught from June when she discovered Sandy gone.

"Sandy not up yet?" Tim asked jokingly, "She's always been a sleepy head."

"Sandy's gone on a trip with Oliver, they should be back today." George replied evasively.

"Oh, where?" June asked "I thought she was meant to be in hiding while this business with Paul was being dealt with."

"Actually, that's what they're doing." George looked at Alice for help. She sighed, resigned to the fact that it was no good beating around the bush.

"They have gone out on the moor..." She didn't finish her sentence

"What! Why ever do they want to go back out there for?" June was horrified; to her the moor had become the place of nightmares, the hell on earth where she had nearly lost her daughter. "And you let them go?!" Tim reached to June to try to calm her,

"Darling, let Alice speak." She shrugged him away. Striding over to George and Alice she accused them of irresponsibility and lack of concern for her daughter, demanding that George immediately went to get them back.

"June!" Tim stepped in, "Please control yourself." He was embarrassed and annoyed at her behaviour. "Just sit down and listen will you!" He took her quite forcibly by the arm and pushed her on to a chair, "Alice, please forgive my wife, she has been through a lot."

"Hmm," Alice didn't immediately reply, she felt anger building up and was trying to control it. Yesterday had been a traumatic day for them and in particular for Peter and her patience with June was thin; would the woman at least let her explain? When she finally spoke she addressed Tim, coolly and precisely, holding her hand up to ward off June's attempted interruptions, she explained exactly what Oliver and Sandy were doing. She ignored June's outbursts and continued until she had finished with

"Oliver is an experienced trekker, he knows the moor like no one else and I would trust him with my life."

An icy silence filled the kitchen, June and Alice shot daggers at one another across the room. Neither woman had warmed to the other on their first meeting and now, with their altercation their lukewarm 'friendship' had frozen.

June stood up and left the room, as she entered the hall she turned and saw Paul or *Peter* as they said he had to be called, standing hesitantly at the foot of the stairs. She thought his hair looked ridiculous and that he still looked dim,

"You!" She snapped at him, "It's all your fault!"

Alice flew out of the kitchen on hearing this and was caught by George before she had reached June; the expression on her face was murderous. As she came to an abrupt halt with George's restraining arm she shouted,

"Have you no compassion, you self-centred cow?!"

"We're leaving." Tim moved to his wife's side, "We will go along with your plans; I don't think we have much option. We *do* have compassion but I think it's best if we communicate either by 'phone or through Sandy. Thank-you for your hospitality." He led June out to the car and returned to fetch their case. George walked with him on to the drive and beckoned him to come with him to the nearby barn.

"Just give me a moment before you go Tim." They entered the barn and closed the door behind them, the flecks of straw dust floated in the sunlight filtering through the wooden slats. It was quiet and warm, the smell of hay and straw heady in the enclosed space.

"I'm sorry." They both attempted to apologise on their wives' behalf. George stopped Tim with an upheld hand.

"Tim, Alice is a fiery character, but normally she keeps it under control. She has grown to love both your Sandy and Peter. She is the sort of woman who would fight for those she loves. There is no way she would have allowed Oliver to take Sandy back out there if she thought she would be in danger."

"I know that, but June has been through hell these past weeks and she just flipped."

"We hoped they'd be back before you returned and then it would be over with." George thought this sounded deceitful and hurriedly continued, "Stay tonight, they'll be back tonight or tomorrow. We can try to get the women to make up."

"I don't think that's wise, although June is desperate to see Sandy, I think it best we leave. Just one request; please ring as soon as she is back."

"Before you go then, please let me explain Alice's reaction over June's comment to Peter. Maybe you could tell June on your way home what I'm about to say." George sat down on a bale of straw, his long legs folding up in front of him cricket-like, he pulled a stalk from the bale and chewed on it, Tim lowered himself down likewise on to a bale and facing George he nodded to him to proceed.

George told Tim of the traumatic events of last night, before he and June had arrived, explaining also that they had been the reason for his lack of welcome. He told Tim of the inhumane treatment Peter had received purely because he had the physical characteristics of Down syndrome and of Alice's outrage spurred purely by compassion and a growing love for Peter. He told him also of his forcing the police to back off and of the tense moments before the officer called his men back. Tim listened quietly and empathetically to him, shaking his head in disbelief at George's account of the weapon wielding forces surrounding his home.

"So Tim, Peter is family now."

"I understand, George, thank you for telling me this. We'll go now, but we'll be in touch and maybe when all this is over June and Alice may become friends again."

"Let's hope so."

CHAPTER 21

OLIVER AND SANDY returned jubilantly to find a sombre atmosphere at the farm. George seeing them coming had walked out to meet them.

"Success dad!" Oliver called to him and launched into his account as soon as they met. Sandy trotting alongside noticed that George wasn't his usual bluff self and that he didn't seem to be paying much attention to Oliver. She gently nudged Oliver and indicated discreetly, George's bowed head and distracted manner.

"What's up dad?"

"Hm?" George looked up, "Sorry, what were you saying? I was miles away."

"Yes you were, what's the matter?" Oliver asked again.

"Oh, it'll blow over I'm sure."

"What will blow over? Come on dad, what's happened?" George's shoulders sagged and he looked tired and melancholy.

"I don't know where to begin, a lot has happened while you've been away." He steered them down the lane away from the house and to a five-bar gate at which he stopped and leaning his elbows on the top bar he told them as concisely as possible all that had happened since Sunday morning.

"And now Peter thinks everyone blames him and he has gone into himself, barely talking even when he helps Alice in the kitchen."

"Oh mum!" Sandy couldn't help the tears, "Poor mum, I feel dreadful, I'm so sorry George, and PauI I mean Peter; he was doing so well."

"Alice is distraught, we all are, we hoped that you'd be back before they came and on top of the police raid, the timing couldn't have been worse."

"It was all going too well I suppose something had to bugger it up!" Sandy and Oliver were bitterly disappointed that their mothers had fallen out although it had been apparent from the start that they were never going to be close; they never thought it would come to all-out war.

"Come on back home." George shook himself, "Maybe your presence will cheer Peter up Sandy. Oh and by the way, ring home as soon as you get in."

"Peter, Alice, they're back!" George called as they came indoors. Alice came hurriedly from the kitchen but Peter remained behind.

"Peter!" Sandy called, "how about a welcome hug?" Peter came to the edge of the door frame but no further, he wouldn't look them in the eye.

"Okay, mountain, I'll be Mohammed!" Sandy took the few steps to Peter and before he could retreat she caught him in a hug, Oliver joined her,

"Kettle mum!" Oliver commanded and Alice willingly obeyed casting a hopeful glance at the three friends as she turned on the tap. After she had made the tea, a sign from George told her to leave the three together. She followed George to the seat by the pond and they waited in silence. After some time George said firmly,

"They've been through hell and back together; pulling each of them in turn back from the brink, if they can't mend this bridge then no-one can."

With their return to the farm, Peter began to recover his confidence, but it was a slow process. Oliver and Sandy spent as much time as possible with him and they talked about what they had endured in 'Baggins Hall' Oliver making much of Peter's contributions, exaggerating as necessary. When they were alone they planned their next move. Sandy would have to 'be found' soon but Peter needed to be handled carefully as her leaving may throw him back into his depression. Firstly, they decided, the coats had to be found in order to close that particular chapter.

The 'phone in the police station rang and the desk constable answered it. It was a very bad line, muffled and crackling, he had a job to hear the caller's voice clearly; it sounded like a Scotsman with a severe cold. Through the crackles he made out something about the moor and coats and falling in peat bogs. He called his superior to the 'phone,

"Hello! Can I take your name please?" He scribbled down something on a pad which looked like MacDonald and after many requests of "Could you repeat that" he wrote a map reference on his pad. "Thank you very much Sir and now if you would kindly give me a contact address and telephone number... hello, I'm sorry I didn't catch that, hello, hello?" The connection had finally given out.

Back in the 'phone box Sandy and Oliver collapsed against each other in fits of laughter. Oliver crackled the stiff paper bag once more and put his handkerchief back in his pocket.

"Och Aye the Noo!" He laughed.

"Old MacDonald had a farm!" Sandy sang, "Why MacDonald?"

"It's the only Scottish name I could think of." They hugged each other, still laughing.

"Well that's it; done. Let's just hope they take it seriously."

Peter seemed oblivious to all the planning and activities the others were doing to clear his name. He had become contented with his life at the farm and proved to be a big help with the milking of the goats and fetching fresh warm eggs from the chicken coops. His face filled out and he looked healthy. Alice's heart warmed more and more to him, every day. The sight of his sweet smile as he carefully carried the eggs across the yard and his gentle way with the goats as he talked to them whilst pulling the teats, the milk spurting into the bucket, brought tears to her eyes.

"Oh George," she said as they watched him in the goat shed, "how could they believe he would hurt anyone? Just look at him, he's as gentle as a mother with a new-born." She bristled suddenly,

"I will never forgive that woman for saying those things to him!" She only ever referred to June as either 'Sandy's mother' or 'that woman', she thought her the most selfish, spoilt woman she had ever met.

"Now, now, she's only trying to protect Sandy, don't forget that she had to cope for weeks, thinking Sandy was dead," George placated her, "and now she's back safe she wants to take her away from it all, try to understand darling."

"I think it's more her trying to protect herself!" Alice replied ungraciously.

Time went on and they waited anxiously for any news. Sandy hopped about in an unrelenting state of urgency, rushing to the television at news time and grabbing the local and national papers as soon as Oliver bought them. Finally, weeks after their disguised 'phone call to the police, an announcement on the local news said that the search for the fugitives had been called off after the inquest had arrived at a verdict; missing, presumed dead. Apparently a hiker on the moor had reported finding clothing partially submerged in a peat bog and it was thought to have belonged to the two fugitives who had escaped from a mental institution earlier that year. This was followed by an interview and statement from the chief constable.

"It is thought that the two dangerous fugitives, who escaped from the secure institution for the criminally insane, have met with a fatal accident on the moor. It would appear from the evidence found that one of the men fell into a peat bog and the other, presumably attempting to save him, perished also. Clothing, matching the description of the items stolen from the staff at the hospital was found at the scene. We have yet to decide whether or not to attempt to retrieve the bodies of the men. These mires are extremely dangerous places and we are reluctant to endanger the lives of our police or those of the army if we feel it to be an unnecessary course of action." The programme ended with flashing reporters' cameras and questions being thrown at the spokesman which he refused to answer, saying that a full report would be broadcast in due course.

"Now we have to hope that they swallow the bait completely and close the case against Paul." George remarked to Alice as they breathed a sigh of relief at the news. "Even if they do try to exhume the bodies, they'll find Jimmy's which surely will indicate that Paul's is in there as well but sunk deeper." Paul was no more. He would from now on be known only as Peter Tregowen, a nephew of Mr. and Mrs. Tregowen at Moor Lane Farm. His future seemed secure and a great weight was lifted from them all. Alistair insisted that he continued to try to clear Paul's name 'posthumously' and they agreed wholeheartedly with this.

After a few days of deliberation and anxiety, they all decided that it was time for Sandy to 'be found'. She rehearsed her story with Oliver and telephoned her parents to tell them she was coming home. She pleaded with them to say as little as possible to anyone including the press in case they should let slip the truth. Promising Peter she would be back soon to visit she hugged George and Alice and Oliver drove her to her parents' house. Arriving late at night they would avoid any local attention and in the morning she would contact the police. They thought it best that Oliver went with her; as he was responsible for her rescue he would have to be interviewed by the police and they didn't want it to happen at the farm for obvious reasons.

CHAPTER 22

LOST STUDENT FOUND SAFE AND WELL

Sandra Williams, an art student who has been missing for six weeks and feared dead has turned up at her parents' home. She is said to be in good health despite spending many days and nights out in the open. She was found unconscious and delirious and suffering from concussion by hiker Oliver Tregowen. It seems that her car broke down and in an attempt at a short-cut she became lost when a thick fog descended. Mr Tregowen brought her safely home in spite of tearing a ligament in his leg when he too slipped on wet rocks. They survived by foraging for food and apparently at one point were near to starving when Mr Tregowen was unable to walk and hunt. She says that they ate a lot of blackberries! Sandra had no idea that there were convicts loose on the moor and says she saw nobody except her rescuer. The Police deny having stated their belief that the incidents were in any way connected and commented that they were extremely glad for the family that Sandra was safe.

Sandy and her parents put the local paper aside.

"Now it's down to Alistair to clear Paul's name." Sandy stretched and lay back against June's shoulder. "It's good to be home mum."

They settled into a routine, Oliver visited her, but more often she visited him. She either took the train and Oliver would meet her at the station or he would sometimes drive and pick her up in his car. The insurance people were being difficult about payment on Sandy's car as she had abandoned it and they maintained that the fault lay with her. She missed the independence of having her own transport but had no money to buy another car even an old banger. Tim insisted on fighting her corner with the insurance company assuring her that he would win in the end. So she just had to be patient. Peter pined for Sandy when she was away, much as he loved Alice, he longed for Sandy's visits. The fondness between the trio had strengthened rather than waned and no matter what the future held, Sandy could never imagine it not involving both Oliver and Peter. Following on from the inquest on the fugitives, an inquest was held on Paul's dead mother. The finding was death by a blow to the head with a blunt instrument. The suspect now believed to be deceased, the case was closed and her body released for burial. They kept this information from Paul, his beloved mother had gone long ago for him and opening his wounds would not benefit him whatsoever.

Sandy and Oliver discreetly ascertained where and when the funeral would take place and quietly slipped in at the back of the church to pay their respects and by proxy, Paul's. They slipped away again before the service had finished.

They were finally free from scrutiny and a huge sense of calm descended on both families. Alistair rang regularly with updates but everything was moving too slowly. The professor wanted to compile a water-tight case in favour of Paul's innocence. It was difficult because it all had to be based on character references as the only witness to his mother's death refused to help him, saying she had seen what she had seen and that's what she had told the police. Yes; she was new to the area and didn't know Paul or his mother, but that was irrelevant, she knew what she had seen, and so on and so on. He had given up on "that ignorant woman". Alistair quoted the professor's words, and was concentrating on Paul's teachers and friends of his mother. He was also researching the syndrome and speaking to specialists and doctors on the subject. It would, he told them, take a fair bit longer for him to feel he had enough to present a case. Then, Alistair reported, he had to apply for a hearing and who knows how long that would take. They had no option but to wait.

Sandy continued to alternate between her parents and the farm. When she was at the farm she missed her mother and when at home she missed them all at the farm. She was like a moth with two flames, attracted by one and then being seduced by the other. The atmosphere at home was a bit tense, she noticed, June forever begging her to stay longer and Tim seeming to want her to go back to the farm. She heard them talking in low voices well into the night and strove to hear what they were saying but without actually eavesdropping at the bedroom door, she was unable to discern the words.

Christmas was fast approaching and as she neared the farm on her latest visit and surveyed the stark, naked branches blowing like skeleton limbs against the grey December sky she was overwhelmed by a deep sadness. She was greeted fondly by the family and should have felt cheered, but in these darkening mid-winter days she felt a darkening in herself. She knew she had to spend, wanted to spend, Christmas with Tim and June but the Christmas spirit just wasn't there; friction shot like electricity throughout the house and Sandy had no sooner entered it than she wanted to leave again. She felt guilty every time she left to return to the farm, telephoning her mother as soon as she had arrived just to tell her she loved her. June's 'I love you too, so does dad' instead of easing her guilt somehow increased it.

Sandy searched out, not Oliver, but George; she wanted to talk to someone about how she felt and George seemed the least emotionally involved.

"What's up lass?" He asked, "Is all the waiting getting you down?"

"Yes, it is, but it's not just that," she didn't know where to start; she hadn't formulated her feelings into words before and now, when she had a kindly ear, she couldn't express them.

"It's trying I know love, it'll not be much longer I'm sure."

"I know. I just can't wait 'til it's all done and we can get back to normal. But," she hesitated, "it's mum and dad, they don't seem right, I feel awful, it's all my fault!"

"It's been a traumatic time for us all, but mostly for your parents, they are still reeling from the shock of thinking they'd lost you, give them time, and give yourself time, once Peter's name is cleared, and I have every faith in Professor Small, it'll all come right I'm sure." They talked about the row that Alice and June had had and Sandy apologised for June, George waved her apology away, attempting to justify June, he said she had been overwrought at the thought of Sandy back on the moor and Alice had just had that harrowing episode with the police.

"Don't you worry about those two, they'll make it up in time I'm sure." He gave Sandy a reassuring pat and some of the worry faded from her face.

"Thanks, for listening to me George." As she walked away, still emanating sadness, he hoped his reassurances would prove true. But somehow he doubted it.

Sandy went home for Christmas. The day was taken up with cooking, present giving and the obligatory after lunch walk to 'help it go down'. Sandy, Tim and June strolled along, with Lilly tugging at her lead, heading for the park where they met neighbours and exchanged Merry Christmases with them all. Many stopped for a word or two, mostly in order to express their happiness that Sandy had been rescued by that kind young man, and was he the tall red-headed young man who came to visit? Knowing looks passed between couples when they mentioned Oliver's visits and Sandy laughingly thought, no chance mate. Sandy went to bed that night feeling much happier; they had laughed at the dreadful jokes in the crackers and Tim had watched television with his arm over June's shoulders, the fire had crackled in the grate and it had felt as though the last few months had never happened.

On Boxing Day, Aunt Gillie and Uncle Stewart visited and the day progressed much like Christmas day had. They waved them off late that evening with "Drive carefully; remember you've had a few drinks!"

"That was a nice visit." June said happily as they had crackers and cheese for a night-cap. "Thank goodness they didn't ask too many questions." June longed to tell Gillie the truth about Sandy's time when she was lost but Tim had expressly forbidden her,

"You know what a blabber-mouth she is!"

"I beg your pardon; you don't have to be rude about my sister!" June had taken the comment in good heart as she well knew that Gillie could never keep anything to herself. But she still hankered after telling the Squires, however, she kept that thought to herself. The Christmas holiday was going well, the atmosphere relaxed and homely; Sandy was relieved and thought back to her conversation with George, he had been right; it was only tension in the aftermath of nearly losing her. Everything would be alright.

The following evening the Squires had invited them round for drinks, Sandy asked if she could plead a hangover or something. She really didn't want to be questioned about anything, and Mike was a very astute man, she was frightened she would let something slip. However, it was June who Tim was most concerned about, would she take Sylvia aside in the kitchen and tell her what she's been longing to tell her but had sworn not to? Before they left, agreeing that Sandy could stay home, he pinned June against the wall in a fierce kiss.

"What was that for?" June exclaimed, flushed with pleasure and surprise.

"Just to remind you that I love you." He said and repeated the embrace. "But on a more serious note, if you say anything about Peter to the Squires that's the last kiss you'll get from me." He said this with a laugh in his voice and was relieved that June took it light-heartedly, but behind his laugh his resolve was firm, one hint of a betrayal and he would whisk June out of the Squires' door before she could even say goodnight.

June behaved herself and the evening went well, rather too much wine was drunk and Sandy heard them come noisily up the stairs, stifling their laughter. Happily, she rolled over and slept peacefully.

The following morning, while her parents slept in, Sandy telephoned Oliver to ask how everyone was and to see what, if anything, they had planned for the New Year.

"I trust you'll be spending it with us?" He asked, "You've had Christmas at one home, it's time you visited your other one."

"Yes please, I could do with some younger company, spent too much time with aunts and uncles and elderly neighbours."

"Pick you up from the station tomorrow?"

"See you, bye!"

June and Tim were going to the New Year party at the Squires' and were quite happy for Sandy to go back to the farm.

"There's snow forecast, when do you plan on going? The railways always seize up at the first snow flake, and you know what the roads are like around Oliver's place."

"Tomorrow dad. Oliver's meeting me at the station."

Sandy left her mum and dad with a lighter heart than she had come home with and bounced happily into the kitchen on her arrival at the farm. George caught her eye and gave her a wink which she returned. Alice caught the exchange,

"What are you two conspiring between you?"

"It's just our little secret!" He gave Sandy another obvious wink. Alice grinned, and said laughing,

"Shift your arse." And slapping him out of her way as if she were shooing an errant chicken from the kitchen, she put the kettle on the Aga.

Peter, stood, as always when Sandy had been away, shyly; watching this exchange and laughing in his giggly sort of way at Alice's removal of her husband from his favourite place, in front of the Aga, resting his behind on the rail along its front.

"Peter, give us a hug!" Sandy knew this was the best way to bring him out of his shyness, forthright was better than coaxing.

"And did you have a good Christmas?"

"Oh yes, it was lovely, Auntie Alice gave me lots of lovely presents." He suddenly looked sad,

"Why the long face then?" Sandy asked.

"I didn't buy anything for her, or anyone." He replied, "I haven't got any money and..."

"Now, now, Peter", Alice cut in, "you're being silly, what did you do for us on Christmas day hmm?"

"He cooked most of the dinner, helped decorate the tree, brought loads of logs and coal in and, well, the list is endless." George said for him when he bashfully looked at his feet. "The only complaint I have is", Peter looked up worriedly from his shoes, anxiety clouding his eyes as if they burned with a desire to cry, "that it let that lazy lump Alistair stay in bed longer than he should have!" The relief, followed by amusement, floated like projected images across Peter's face whilst Alistair made offended noises in the corner at being called a lump, lazy he accepted, but a lump!

The snow came on New Year's Eve. It started sometime during the night and by the time they woke nine inches had fallen, and it was still falling. Peter insisted on milking the goats and worried that they might be cold, taking a couple of old blankets with him he waded across the pristine snow and disappeared into the shed where he stayed for such a long time they began to wonder what he was doing. George pulled on his boots saying he was going to do the rounds and invited Oliver to come too. They grabbed their coats and gloves, a shovel each and set off to check on the other livestock. When they had completed their feeding and watering they ended up at the goat shed where they found Peter sitting on a stool, chatting away to the nannies as he milked them.

"Nearly done?" George asked him. Peter started, the snow had muffled their steps and he had been so engrossed in his favourite task he hadn't heard them come in.

"You made me jump!" He squeaked, his voice always rose an octave when he was surprised or frightened. "I nearly knocked my bucket over." He had nearly finished his milking but George asked him why it had taken him so long. "Nancy and Daisy were cold and I had to cuddle them with the blanket." He explained. George and Oliver turned away to hide their amusement, the goats were hardy and had never before shown that they suffered from the cold.

"Alice should have breakfast ready, let's get back before Ali eats it all." George took one of the buckets and Peter carried the other and they followed the smell of bacon back to the kitchen.

CHAPTER 23

1972 HAD ENDED and the cold winds and snow of January 1973 blanketed the country. Sandy was marooned at the farm. June and Alice had still not met since their disagreement and it seemed likely that no common ground would be found. It was a shame Tim thought, the rest of us get on fine. He had tried to reason with June, but she was immovable. She seemed to positively hate Peter and blamed him for everything. She refused to listen when Tim reminded her that he was a victim not a perpetrator.

"I don't care!" She shouted at him one day when he was trying so very hard to pave the way for peace, "He's revolting, and he's got his eyes on Sandy all the time. He's a dirty pervert!"

Tim finally lost his temper

"Alice was right; you have no compassion!" After all these years of living with and loving June he had never thought her to be lacking compassion. But, he realised, it had always been directed at her and she had soaked it up like a dry sponge. All the histrionics, the 'depression', justified though they were at the time, now seemed to Tim like a selfish cry of "ME, ME, ME!" He looked into her flinty eyes and thought, *I never knew you.* He left the house and walked through the snow not knowing exactly where he was going. Finding himself in the Squires' street he considered knocking on their door, changed his mind and meandered on.

When Tim walked out June remained stunned in her chair, unable to believe that the man who had loved and protected her for as long as she could remember had suddenly turned on her.

Could their whole life together be dismissed in one short sentence? She tried to reason with herself that it was her love for her daughter which had made her so damning of Paul, or whatever they were calling him now. Surely Tim knew that? Surely he didn't put a stranger's wellbeing before his wife's happiness! She recalled her words and tried to regret them but the regret was false. It was true, Paul *was* responsible for all that had happened to Sandy, and thus responsible for the anguish she had suffered over those weeks, how could Tim ignore that? As far as the accusations against Paul were concerned, she, like the others, believed them to be wrong; she fully understood and sympathised with the man's predicament and supposed she was glad that he was now safe, but she wanted to distance herself and her family from it all. Sandy's strong friendship with the Tregowens meant that she spent more time there than at home and June resented this, also it meant that Paul was able to moon after her and ogle her. June imagined him accosting Sandy or spying on her in her bedroom and she shuddered at the thought.

Late that night, when June, angry and saddened had finally gone to bed, Tim returned home. She heard him in the porch, shaking the snow from his coat and stamping it off his shoes. She was undecided whether to go and meet him or to remain in bed and feign sleep. She listened to him climb the stairs and waited for the bedroom door to open and for him to come to her, put his arms around her, kiss her and tell her he was sorry and that he understood. She longed to feel the warmth of his kiss contrasting with the cold of his face from the night air. Tim walked quietly past their shared bedroom door and she heard him close the door of the spare room.

June woke early, it was Sunday. All through their married life Tim had unfailingly brought her a cup of tea in bed on a Sunday morning, this morning she knew he would not. Never before had they slept in separate rooms, never before gone to bed on a row.

She got out of bed and dressed in warm clothing, slipped down stairs and, pulling on her boots and coat, hat and scarf, she quietly opened the back door and walked out into the grey light of dawn.

She had decided to visit her friends, the Squires. As she walked through the new fall of snow, a lone figure on the deserted streets, she made up her mind; she was going to tell them everything.

At the Jones' farm, oblivious to the drama at her parents' home, Sandy had dragged Oliver and Peter from their beds (Alistair, home for the Christmas break, in language borrowed from Sandy's repertoire, had refused) and, as the early sun painted the snow, like children, they built a snowman.

Tim had heard June go out and suspected he knew where she was going. He decided to go after her as once she started pouring her heart out to Sylvia's sympathetic ear the floodgates would open and everything that George, Alice, Oliver and Sandy had done for Peter could be rendered pointless. This was not the only fear in his mind as he hurriedly got dressed; perverting the course of justice, harbouring a suspected criminal, deliberately giving false information to the police, all of these crimes put together could mean a prison sentence for some; or all of them. This would include June and him also. And Peter would become Paul again and be locked up for life. *The secret had to be kept.* June wouldn't have thought that far ahead, in her, Tim heard the word in his head, 'pathetic' need for sympathy, she would cry on Sylvia's shoulder and Mike would fuss over her. His anger rose again, he almost wished her to go ahead just to see the realisation dawn on her that she could end up with a criminal record; having been being party to what was happening. But he couldn't let that happen to the genuine caring family that had taken Peter's problems upon themselves. Neither could he let dear little Sandy down after all she had been through. *My God what a stupid woman my wife is!* If he could catch her in time he would have to swallow his pride and his gall and take her sobbing back home and life could go on, as usual but it could never be the same.

Tim ran, slipping and sliding on the snow covered paths and arrived at the Squire's house just as the door was closing behind June. He strode up to it and knocked loudly, it was opened immediately by a dressing gown clad, worried looking Mike with Sylvia, also in her dressing gown, behind him.

"I'm so sorry we've got you up at this unearthly hour Mike," he took June's arm firmly and attempted to lead her back to the door. "June and I have had a misunderstanding. Or row, if you prefer, but I'm sure you don't want to hear all about it." He held June's arm more fiercely as she attempted to pull away, "We're going home aren't we darling." It wasn't a question.

He forced himself to show her some affection, "You missed your Sunday morning cup of tea in bed." June hesitated in her bid for freedom from Tim's grip, indecision showing on her face. Tim took the opportunity to release his grip and instead he wrapped his arm around her shoulder, "Come on darling, I'm sorry. Let's go home and leave these poor people in peace."

"Why don't you come round later for dinner, when you've patched things up?" Mike asked heartily, "We'll be dressed by then won't we Sylvia?" He laughed rather lamely at his quip, "See you about seven?"

"That'll be nice, thanks Mike, we'll ring later to confirm." Tim led June out of the door and into the street, "Before you say anything," he shushed June "I'm sorry. Okay?" He forced the apology through his gritted teeth.

When Tim had safely delivered June home, he bade her sit down whilst he lit a fire in the sitting room, and made them both some tea. He was as attentive as he could be and June, having always been doted on by Tim, took his gestures as genuine. Once the fire was roaring away and they both were clutching mugs of tea, the chill of their morning walk slowly fading to a memory, Tim stood up, his back to the fire and spoke.

"Had you thought it through?"

"Thought what through?" June was genuinely puzzled.

"The ramifications of what, I suspect, you were going to do."

"I only wanted some comfort." June said pitifully, making Tim cringe.

"We promised we wouldn't tell anyone."

"But they are friends!" She exclaimed, "They wouldn't tell."

"We don't know that, and a promise is a promise." June started to protest but Tim talked over her,

"Do you want Alice, George, Oliver, Alistair, Sandy, you and me to go to prison?!" He attempted to keep his voice level but it rose in anger with every name he uttered. "And do you really want to see an innocent, vulnerable man locked up in a 'loony bin' for the rest of his life?"

"What do you mean, prison?!" June was shocked.

"Open your eyes June, we have all been involved in misleading the law, Alice and George in particular have told blatant lies to the police; how do you think that would sound in court? And do you really think the Squires would stand behind us, would they want to be associated with law-breakers?" June burst into tears. Normally Tim would have immediately held her and smoothed her hair, telling her all would okay. He stood unmoving and unmoved.

"I didn't think." June sobbed. *No you never do if it's not about you!* Tim hated himself for the way he was feeling towards June, but after all these years his eyes had been opened and he didn't like what they now saw.

Then, recovering herself she blurted,

"We'll not be in trouble if we're the ones to report him."

"What?!" Tim was horrified that she could even consider reporting Peter. But June was getting a head of steam up now,

"Sandy's been led by the Tregowens, she's a good girl and she wouldn't break the law. They're the ones who have persuaded her to go along with it all. She could tell the police that she wanted to hand him in but she was stopped by them." Tim stood open mouthed in disbelief at what she was saying, he didn't attempt to interrupt; he just didn't know where to start. His wife whom he had thought he knew and had been certain he loved for thirty years was mouthing off like a demented harpy.

"It's that Alice, she's the one who's to blame!"

Tim left the room and walked, hat and coat-less out of the front door. Coming to a 'phone box he rang the Squires and apologised but June had a migraine and they wouldn't be coming to dinner. He then walked aimlessly around the park and finally into the pub on the green where he nursed a pint whilst staring morosely into the fire.

Very late that evening he returned home and went straight to the spare room. He had not eaten anything and his stomach had turned at the thought of food. He had had a couple of pints but no more. He lay in the bed, his mind whirring. He was unbelievably heartbroken; what a waste his life had been, how could he not have seen what a vicious monster lay beneath the sweet, vulnerable surface June had presented. If she really cared about anyone other than herself, she wouldn't even consider doing what she suggested. Sandy, whom she claimed was her only reason for living seemed to have taken a back seat in her concerns. She would chance her only daughter being embroiled in a court case just to satisfy; Tim thought, what was she going to satisfy by her actions? Then, in a flash, he realised; it was pure spite at Alice.

In the morning they met like strangers in the kitchen. Tim told her there was tea in the pot and took his own cup out to the conservatory where he sat surveying the blanket of snow still covering the garden. It all looked so clean, so pure, unlike his life as he now saw it; contaminated by vile thoughts.

June made no attempt to join him at which he was relieved. He remained in the conservatory and watched the blue tits attacking the peanuts hanging from the bird table with a hunger driven ferocity. The starlings hanging on for dear life to the fat ball on the cherry tree branch would normally have made him smile; he felt his face would crack into tiny pieces if he even attempted one now. At last, he heaved himself up from the seat and, taking a minute to compose himself he entered the kitchen where June sat very still, her cup untouched on the table in front of her.

"June." She barely glanced at him. "June, we must talk."

"What is there to talk about? You obviously don't love me. I'm sorry I can't be more like your sainted Alice!" Venom had begun to take over from the pathos of her first sentence. This helped Tim in his response. When he had seen her sitting disconsolately at the table he had begun to feel remorse for what he was about to say. But, hearing that aggressive note in her voice brought his anger back to the surface. He held it in check; instead, he spoke calmly and kindly,

"I think we need a break from each other."

"I thought you were going to say that." June slipped again into the role of the wronged party. "Shall I move out or you?" She looked up at him with tears in her eyes and Tim nearly took her in his arms. Instead, he steeled himself and said,

"If you want, I'll rent somewhere and you can stay."

"No, I don't want to stay here on my own. I'll go and stay with Gillie. I'll go as soon as the trains are running." She stood up and with tears coursing down her face, gave Tim a look of such despair that he had to turn away to hide his own tears.

CHAPTER 24

THE SNOW PLOUGHS were out, creating massive sculptures at the sides of the roads as their V shaped blades carved their way through the drifts.

"I really should be getting home." Sandy said as they watched them. "The trains should be running by now." After an earlier telephone conversation with her father she was feeling guilty for living off the generosity of the Tregowens.

"You really can't sponge off them for any longer." He had said, "You have to get a job."

"I've been living off the money you gave me dad," she justified herself, "anyway, I've been helping on the farm so it's not been sponging really." She added, "I offered Alice some money for my keep."

"And she refused it as you knew jolly well she would!" Tim admired Alice and George, and rather envied them their independent, if hard, way of life. His job as an accountant had paid well and their standard of living was good but he was bored; seriously bored, with everything his life had become.

"Okay dad, I'll come home and sign on the dole!" She snapped angrily, "Maybe I'll get a job at the petrol pumps if I'm lucky." Her fine art diploma didn't exactly give her any prospects of a job; she had been hoping to put this dilemma off until she had returned from Mauritius in the spring.

"There's still time for you to take up the teachers' training place you were offered." Tim had persuaded her to apply for this as 'another iron to her fire'. A snort was all he received in reply.

Sandy told Alice and George that she had been 'summoned home' as she put it. She felt at ease on the farm and loved the way of life but she did miss her mum and dad, especially her mum. Fussy and over-protective though she was, June was her special person. They agreed that she should spend some time with her parents, especially as they had been through so much, adding that they would miss her and that she was welcome any time. Oliver promised to visit often before the advent of spring demanded his input on the farm. Peter looked tearful but brightened a little when Sandy promised to ring him often.

The following day, Oliver took her to the station and waved her off.

Alistair was excited; his professor had telephoned to say that he had given the case some deep thought and was keen to take it on.

"I had to lie a bit..."

"A bit! Oliver exclaimed, "It's *all* lies."

"On top of the main lies, he asked why I was so keen to pursue it and I said I had a cousin who had had to virtually go into hiding when the newspapers published Paul's picture last year, after the escape from the asylum. I told him that he was being bullied in the street and called a mother murderer. He was in danger of being really hurt and so they had taken him to stay on the farm."

"That was a bit chancy Ali, I thought we wanted to keep Peter off the radar." Oliver said.

"I know it was but he wasn't wholly convinced that I wanted to do it as ex-curricular study when my finals were so close. But," he continued, "he immediately recognised my personal interest and said that he had heard of incidents like this as well.

"What does he practice? George asked, "Is he a defence barrister?"

"Mainly, yes, but he's done divorce cases, litigation, all sorts. The biggest advantage is that he's human; he has a heart. Anyway, he wants to visit us."

"When? What shall we do with Peter?" Alice asked anxiously.

"We don't have to do anything with him, he knows he's here, that's the reason he wants to visit; he wants to meet Peter." Alistair gave his mother one of his withering looks. "He's doing research on Paul at the moment and hopes to interview his old teachers and friends of his mother, and then he's planning to come directly here. It'll probably be the week after next. It fits in well as I'm due back at university the following week."

Sandy was met at the station by her father. It was immediately evident to her that he was pre-occupied and not his usual self. He barely spoke on the drive and replied to Sandy's chatter with nods and grunts. He looked a bit tired and slightly unkempt, which was unusual for him.

"Are you okay dad? You seem a bit miserable, is mum okay?" She added, sitting forward, she worried about her mum, she had had many bouts of depression and Sandy wouldn't have been surprised to hear that she was on medication again, bearing in mind all that had happened.

"Your mother's gone to stay with Aunt Gillie for a while." Tim refused to be drawn on the matter saying, "I'll explain when we get home." Sandy was confused, why had her mother gone to stay with her sister when she knew Sandy was coming home? Was she angry with her? Surely she couldn't be *that* angry as to push off without saying a word! She agitated all the way to their house, but Tim said he didn't want to discuss it whilst he was driving and so she had to wait, her anxiety increasing with every mile. Their house, usually a welcome sight, radiated emptiness; the absence of her mother in their home where she always, unfailingly, welcomed Sandy with open arms, was like a blow to the stomach. It was as if her mother had died.

"Why?" She demanded of her father as soon as they had entered the home which no longer felt like home "What have I done?"

"Oh Sandy, my love," Tim hugged her in his tubby bear-like embrace "you haven't done anything." There was moistness in his eyes as he spoke, "Your mother isn't angry with you. It's me." He strove to put himself in the wrong in Sandy's eyes, the effort was crucifying him. He adored his daughter and couldn't bear the thought of her turning against him. But, knowing Sandy's love for her mother, he had to find a way of excusing June for Sandy's sake. "We have decided to separate for a while."

"No! You can't have! Why dad, what on earth has happened?!" After finally being re-united with her parents she could see it all being torn asunder. "Oh dad, what's going on? I can't believe this. I can't stand it!" Sandy tore herself away from Tim and rushed to her bedroom, slamming the door behind her and collapsed in tears on her bed. He left her to cry it out and when, eventually she emerged he gently embraced her and sat her down beside him.

"We had an almighty row." He decided to say it bluntly, after all, couples *did* have rows; there was nothing sinister in that. "We couldn't find a common ground and didn't make it up like we have done in the past. We were like a couple of icebergs by the time we decided to separate. We weren't talking, we avoided each other and neither of us could back down. So, I suggested to your mum that she took a holiday with her sister while we both simmered down." He was playing it down considerably, for Sandy's sake; but he knew that the mine-laden field which now separated himself and June would never be crossed. He knew that unless June could change her attitude he could never again love her as he once did. He also knew that June would never change. He had realised during the last weeks that she had always been the same but his love for her had made him blind to it. Tim no longer loved June. It felt strange to him to admit to himself that a flame as strong as theirs had been could suddenly be extinguished. He tried hard to re-kindle it, if only in memory, but it was truly dead.

"What did you row about?" Sandy asked the question Tim was dreading. "Was it anything to do with me?" Tim knew she would instinctively think it was in some way her fault, children in a marriage break-up, being the physical and emotional link between the parents, always felt they were to blame whether they were twelve years old or twenty. It *was* in fact to do with Sandy, but indirectly; what had actually been the cause were the events stemming from her meeting with Paul; they had exposed a deep unfathomable flaw in his marriage.

"All sorts of things, I can't remember how it started." He lied. He wondered whether June would be as evasive as he was being, when she talked to Sandy, or would her self-pity induce her to seek compassion from Sandy for the way Tim had treated her. *Time will tell* he thought. *I have a clear conscience.*

That evening Sandy spoke on the 'phone to her mother, Tim discreetly listened to the one sided conversation being held in the hall. Sandy hadn't closed the sitting room door so he wasn't eavesdropping. He could hear tears in Sandy's voice but the conversation appeared to be sane and he breathed a sigh of relief when she put the phone down. She joined him in the sitting room.

"I'll visit mum at auntie Gillie's when she's settled in, she doesn't want me to come yet she said she's too upset." There was a lot unsaid in that comment, Tim knew, but Sandy seemed to be a comforted a little by her conversation with June which had apparently re-assured her that she wasn't to blame.

"Dad," She hesitated, "Will you be okay if I go back down to the farm?" He had sensed this was coming; she needed the security of Oliver and his family,

"Yes, love, I'm fine." In fact, he welcomed it, he needed time to himself. There was no doubt in his mind that his marriage was over and decisions would have to be made; painful ones; it was better Sandy was away from it all for the time being.

CHAPTER 25

SANDY HAD BEEN at the farm for two weeks before she had a call from her mother. Although she had been busy helping out with chores and, having brought her art materials with her this time, sketching and painting; she thought constantly of her parents, even dreaming of them. She still couldn't understand why June hadn't got in touch sooner and she still harboured the suspicion that it was somehow her fault. June asked her to come and stay with her at Auntie Gillie's and was expecting her within a couple of days. Sandy didn't want to go to Gillie's, she wanted to go home and find her mum and dad like they used to be. She had tried to persuade June to go home but June had said

"Not yet darling, please come, I miss you." What could she do but go? Gillie's husband met her at the station, though she would have been happier to walk as it was only a mile to the house. Although she was quite fond of her uncle she really didn't want to have to talk to him. Her mother greeted her with love as usual but it was all a bit restrained. Sandy hoped it was because they were not on their own, but even when they were left alone when Gillie and Stewart went shopping, June remained too distant.

"Mum, why won't you talk to me?" Sandy pleaded with June, "What's gone wrong?" All June would say was that it was too complicated and personal. That sent Sandy off on a tangent,

"Dad hasn't been having an affair has he?" She was aghast at the idea.

"Good Lord no, or if he has he's been very good at hiding it. No darling, he hasn't strayed, it's just that we have a problem between us, it doesn't involve anyone else." Sandy thought her mother was behaving too calmly and asked if she was on medication. Her mother denied it saying she was sad, not depressed, it wasn't the same thing. However, her behaviour, Sandy thought, was too matter-of-fact. She seemed just switched off. This didn't improve during Sandy's stay and she could get nothing more out of her mother about what had driven her parents apart.

June kept hinting to Sandy that she should distance herself from the Peter case.

"Why do you have to spend so much time with them?" She whined.

"I like them mum, I *love* you but Oli and I get on so well and Peter's such a dear..." She didn't have time to finish her sentence before her mother shocked her into silence by launching into a damning assault on Peter and his being the cause of all their anguish. Sandy knew that the *facts* were true. Had Peter not run out in front of the car she would not be sitting here; she would be having a good time in the sun. But, that was something which could not be undone; she and the two men had been thrown together in the worst circumstance she could imagine. They had come through; they had bonded with un-breakable glue. Could her mother not see that? Nothing would make her withdraw her support or lessen her fondness for them.

"I don't want you going back there," June started pacing about, her face getting pink with her growing agitation, "he leers at you, surely you've seen it! Or do you encourage it?" Sandy was stunned "You know he's sub-normal," June hardly took a breath, "he could rape you, he *is* male I presume, with all the necessary parts?!"

"Mum how dare you!" Sandy's face, now as flushed as June's showed utter amazement and shock at the way her mother was talking. "Peter is the sweetest person I've ever met. I will NOT hear you speak like that about him!"

"Now you sound like Alice. She seems to have stolen your affections from me as well as that man!" Sandy had never heard her mother talk in this way before, she couldn't stand it. In tears of hurt and outrage she ran from the room.

The following day Sandy left, her mother held her tight as they said goodbye,

"It's only because I love you so much." She pleaded with Sandy to understand.

"I love you too mum, with all my heart but don't do this to me. I don't want to have to choose between you and my loyalty to my friends." Sandy returned to the farm via her home where her father was staying until he could find somewhere to rent or buy. Tim had been careful with his money throughout his career and they had put quite a bit aside. He intended to buy a small cottage out of town and June could do what she wanted with the house; sell it, rent it out, he didn't really care. All he knew was that they would never live in it as a family again. Sandy told him about her fall-out with June. She was very distressed about it. Her love for June could never be extinguished; but June had forced her to choose, she shouldn't have done that. Sandy had chosen loyalty.

Tim didn't dissuade her from returning to where her loyalties lay, he said he wished he could come with her.

"Why don't you dad?" Sandy's mood brightened,

"I have too much to sort out here. But if I'm welcome maybe later okay?"

Oliver met Sandy at the station and she told him of the problems at home. He wasn't as surprised as he might have been, having seen the friction growing between them. He said he was sorry to hear it and asked if she thought they might make it up again. She shook her head sadly,

"No, I don't think they will, I never thought they would ever not love each other."

On the way home Sandy updated him on her family crisis and he listened sympathetically,

"It's up to them to sort themselves out; you can't do anything but show you love them both." When they were approaching the lane leading to the farm Oliver turned off and headed towards the village.

"How about a pint?"

"Yea, why not? We seem to spend all our time at mine or yours." They pulled into the car park of the Red Lion and were pleased to grab the comfortable seats by the log fire in the inglenook.

"Do you realise that this is the first time we have gone to a pub without a member of either family since we got home?" Oliver relaxed into the soft upholstery of his chair.

"You're right, I've been so churned up over mum and dad and so involved in Peter's case that I honestly hadn't noticed. What a relief to be away from it all for a bit. I could almost imagine I was a student again with no worries except how to pay for my pint of mild.

"Tell you what, why don't we, Peter, you and me get away from everything for a bit, Ali's got things in hand with the professor; he's visiting the end of next week. I'm not needed around here much at the moment, to tell the truth I miss the quiet of the moor."

"Where do you want to go?" Sandy asked slightly apprehensively, she suspected he was about to suggest they went trekking again.

"Well we could always go to that cottage in St. Ives, the coastline's stunning, especially in the winter."

"What about Peter, we're meant to be keeping him out of sight aren't we?"

"Yes and no. Don't forget that the local police already know he exists, as Peter, my cousin and the more we behave as though he really *is* my cousin, the more people will be ready to accept him as such."

"I think that's a brilliant idea, I'm sure Peter would love it." Sandy downed the nearly full pint glass of bitter in about three gulps.

"You drank that like a professional! Another?" Oliver swallowed the remainder of his and sauntered up to the bar.

"Same again Oliver?" The barman asked, "Your little friend must have hollow legs!"

"Yea, she is a bit deceptive." Chuckled Oliver, glancing over his shoulder at Sandy who was sitting gazing distractedly into the flames.

They arrived back at the farm a little tipsy just in time for dinner. Sandy didn't talk about Tim and June; she wanted to forget all about them for a while. After dinner, Sandy and Oliver sought out Peter as he was bedding down the goats,

"How would you like a few days away with us Peter?" Oliver asked. Peter looked fearful, "It'll be okay, cousin," said Oliver, patting him affectionately on the shoulder, "we don't need to worry about you being seen; now you're family."

"What about Daisy and Nancy?" Peter caressed Daisy's head lovingly.

"They'll be here when you get back, dad will look after them while we're gone, or that fat lazy lump Ali could shift himself for a change." Oliver laughed kindly at Peter's concern for his charges.

"Do you think auntie would mind?" Peter's interest was piqued, he loved being with Alice but Oliver and Sandy treated him like one of them, they even called him 'mate' sometimes and it made Peter glow inside to have real friends.

"Absolutely not, she'll be glad for you to have a break; you seem to do all the work around here, slave labour is what I call it.

Seriously though, mum loves having you around but she did hint a while back that it would be nice for you to have a change of scene." Sandy glanced enquiringly at Oliver who winked and barely perceptibly shook his head. They left Peter to finish bedding down the goats and walked back to the kitchen.

"I'll have a quick word with mum; tell her what she's meant to have said."

Alice was a little concerned at the suggestion,

"It's a lovely idea Oli, but are you sure you want to parade Peter in public, up until recently he was a wanted man and we don't want to stir up any suspicions?"

"There'll be hardly anyone about mum at this time of year and anyway, as I said to Sandy, the more blatant we are about him being a member of the family the less notice people will take of him." George was keen on the idea, saying it would

"Do him good to get some sea air and a bit of hill walking; build up his muscles for all the work we'll have lined up for him when he gets back!"

Tim gave Sandy the contact details over the phone and they booked the cottage.

"Shall we take Lilly or do you think she's happier on the farm?" Oliver was packing the car and hovering over Lilly's little bed.

"Oh let's take her, she loves the beach, we'd better check first though if dogs are allowed at the cottage. A quick 'phone call to the agents confirmed that it was fine as long as no damage was done and stressed that dogs were not allowed in the bedrooms.

"There are a lot of sheep on the hills down there, make sure she doesn't chase them or they'll shoot her." George warned them sternly, he rather wished they would leave Lilly with him; she was great company on his rounds of the farm. Sandy and Oliver chose not to see the disappointment on George's face when they said they were taking her.

The car was loaded, Peter in the back, flushed and excitedly nervous, with Lilly sitting on him and plaguing him with kisses and Sandy and Oliver in the front. They waved goodbye and off they drove.

"We're all going on a winter holiday..." Sandy began singing in her usual tone deaf manner,

"Belt up!" Oliver said, "I can't stand Cliff."

"Me neither." She answered.

"Admittedly, he does sing better than you!"

"I like him!" A little voice came from the back seat.

"Belt up Peter!" They called in unison over their shoulders.

Later, when they returned to the cottage after dinner at the local pub, and Peter was relaxed, dozing with Lilly curled up on his lap, Sandy and Oliver wandered into the kitchen to make some coffee.

"Animals have a good judge of character don't they." Sandy was the one with whom Lilly usually cuddled but she had made a flying leap onto Peter's lap as soon as he had sat down. He had stroked her gently and instead of her usual manic wriggling and chewing she had tucked her head under his arm and begun to snore.

"You've only got to see how the goats react when he comes into the stall to see that." Oliver agreed.

"So tell me what's been going on with Professor Small, has he made much headway or is it all pie in the sky?"

"Oh yes, he's making great strides, you'll hear all about it next week when he comes over. Don't look so sad Sandy, come here." He held his arms open for her and hugged her, her small form felt so vulnerable; he was amazed at how incredibly strong she had proved to be both physically and emotionally throughout their horrendous time on the moor. What a bummer to come home to her parents' break-up. "You've still got them you know, it might be different but they're both still there for you."

"I know, but it's such a shock. I still can't really take in it." She looked up at him "And it's all my fault."

"It's not anyone's fault, just circumstances, you were behaving like a decent person, foolhardy, but decent, when you tried to help Paul. Do you really wish you had done otherwise?"

"No I don't, I just wish mum could understand. I've tried and tried to explain to her that I have to see this through and that it doesn't change my love for her and dad."

"She knows that."

"No she doesn't. She said that Alice had stolen my love from her, and she resents my putting my loyalty to Peter above her needs."

"It seems like that now, but a mother's love doesn't just go away, she'll understand in time I'm sure." Sandy withdrew from his hug, and sat down at the kitchen table. She scratched at a bit of dried food on the wood until it flicked off on to the floor.

"Thanks for trying to help Oli."

"You know *we're* all here for you as well; the whole family, and Peter. When all this is over it won't be the end of the friendship. Our home is yours whenever you want it."

They took their mugs of coffee back into the sitting room where Peter still dozed, and they sat quietly to drink it. The clock in the hall chimed 10:30,

"Time for bed I think." Oliver gently shook Peter and after Lilly had been popped out for a last minute pee she reluctantly got into her little bed in the kitchen and, tucking her nose under her tail resumed her interrupted sleep.

When Sandy had left her aunt's home, June was thrown into a dark pit. She had begged her to stay but Sandy had been hurt and angry. Gradually June slipped into deep depression. Gillie was very concerned about her lack of appetite and the length of time she spent in her room away from her and Stewart. She decided to telephone Mike Squires. Mike said he would drive over as soon as he could get away. He explained that his partner was off work and he had to cover for him so it wouldn't be that weekend. He told Gillie to ring her own doctor if June was in real need and to give the surgery his contact number if they needed to speak with him. Would it be alright if he brought Sylvia when he came as she always had a rejuvenating effect on June? Mike reassured them that he would bring her a prescription for her usual meds just in case. On his return home that night, he mentioned to Sylvia the call he had received about June.

"Poor June, she has been through hell, should I go on ahead just to be a comfort to her?" Sylvia and June had become very close over the years and she was the one June always rang if she was feeling low. Gillie, June's sister didn't appear to have much spare time. She ran her own business and was on goodness knows how many committees.

"No, don't do that, I can't get down for over a week, I think you'd been putting too much on Gillie's hospitality if you went now."

The cottage at St. Ives was situated facing the coast, the views over the rocks into the often boiling sea were ever changing. Sandy joined Oliver by the garden fence as he stood taking huge breaths of the sea air.

"We'd better do a shop for food, then how about a cliff walk? He asked. "I've planned a route which won't be too taxing for Peter. Lunch at a pub and home again for dinner. How does that grab you?"

"Sounds good. The weather looks settled doesn't it? No need for waterproofs?"

"Be prepared for everything, that's my motto. Anyway, the wind's chilly so hat and gloves on."

Peter looked like the abominable snowman by the time they had layered him in warm clothing and a huge bobbly hat.

"Oli, take a photo of us, go on!" Sandy grabbed Peter by his huge glove and snuggled up close to him. Oliver snapped a couple of shots of them, laughing as he did so; they were so wrapped up they looked twice their normal size.

The walk took them along the fenced cliff walk, gaining altitude as it went. The wind *was* chilly, but the sun bright. Flashes of light sparkled on the water beyond the surf. They climbed as high as the path took them. Looking back towards the town with the panorama of the sea below they sat with their backs to the wind and drank the flask of coffee they had brought with them. Sandy kept Lilly on the lead for fear she would chase a bird over the cliff top. There were too many gaps in the wooden fencing through which she could scramble.

"Tomorrow we'll go to the beach and you can have a swim!" Sandy told her.

"Thanks mum!" Lilly replied.

"Did you just have a conversation with your dog?" Oliver turned to Sandy with a grin.

"Of course, we have long conversations don't we Lil'?" Lilly agreed.

"Daisy and Nancy talk to me too." Peter said, joining in the fun. "They told me when they were cold."

"There you are!" Sandy kissed Lilly's happy little face, "You're not normal Oli."

"I won't answer that. I'm hungry for lunch and a pint, let's go." Oliver unfolded his long legs from under him, gave Peter and Sandy one of his hands each and heaved them up to their feet as though they weighed nothing.

They arrived back at the cottage as the sun was dropping to the west leaving a seething volcanic orange mass behind it. The temperature was dropping in time with the sun's descent.

"I'll get some logs in and light a fire, what shall we eat?" Oliver grabbed the log basket on his way through the cottage.

"I'll knock up a cottage pie shall I?"

"Oh yes, that's my favourite." Enthused Peter. "Can we play a game after?" Sandy had taught him how to play draughts which he loved and often won. Tonight however she was determined they would play scrabble. They'd keep it simple so as not to discourage Peter.

"That was a bloody good cottage pie if I say so myself!" Sandy belched accidentally loudly.

"Sorry!"

"I knew a bloke who could belch the National Anthem; he needed a pint of lager first though." Oliver replied. Peter collapsed into laughter which ended in a bit of a coughing fit. Sandy thumped him on the back until Lilly joined in licking his face until he begged a reprieve. The following days at the cottage took them for long walks both over the cliffs again and along the beaches. Only one day did it rain but that didn't stop them from going out. They dried off in front of the fire and played scrabble once more. Peter was learning quite well and with a bit of contriving from Oliver, managed a triple word score which won him the game. Finally, their holiday was over and apart from Peter developing a slight cold, they all returned to the farm with healthy glowing complexions.

CHAPTER 26

THE SQUIRES ARRIVED. Gillie had told June they were coming and she was torn between anxiety and relief. At last, someone who would understand her. She got dressed with care and presented herself to them wan and tired but joyful to see them. They all went out for a drive to a country pub for lunch in order to lessen Gillie's work load. After which Stewart and Gillie went shopping, discreetly leaving the visitors alone with June.

"What's been going on June?" Mike went straight to the point; that was what she liked so much about him. June, slight in build had lost more weight than was healthy and her trim figure had become thin rather than slim.

"Tim wants a separation." Mike opened his eyes wide in surprise,

"That, I can't believe!"

"It's true; it's all to do with that Paul!" There, she had said it. It was out!

"Who's Paul?" Mike was confused. There wasn't a Paul in June's family and he knew Sandy's rescuer was called Oliver.

"He's that Mongol man, Down syndrome or whatever you call it. The one accused of murder!" She felt the tension building and draining as she said it, she would get Sandy out of that mess, if Oliver had to be sacrificed to do so it was a pity; as she rather liked him. But that Alice and her holier than thou ways had really got under her skin.

"I think you had better start at the beginning June." Mike

moved to beside her on the settee and held her hand kindly. She flushed inwardly with pleasure that he was there to listen to her and hopefully help.

June poured out the whole story to Mike and Sylvia, dwelling on the length of time it had taken the Tregowens to let them; Sandy's own parents declared she was safe! How inconsiderate and cruel of them to do that, all for the sake of some misfit. Mike flinched at her terminology, that and her use of mongol in such a derisory tone had touched his sensibilities. However, he gave her leeway as she had been so upset by Sandy's disappearance.

"How do they know for sure that he's innocent?" Asked Sylvia.

"Down's people aren't usually violent, they're usually happy, gentle people. Of course there could always be the exception." Mike wasn't sure where all this information was putting him. He rather wished that he hadn't heard it.

"I've seen him, I've seen him ogling Sandy and leering at her, always ready for a hug. It makes me squirm to think of her getting anywhere near his ugly body." June started to get up but Mike pulled her down again.

"Calm down June, Sylvia dear, get us a cuppa or something would you?" June wouldn't be calmed, now she had started she was going to get it all out of her system.

"And that Alice! She called me a self-centred cow! She's so full of herself; lady bountiful, refusing any money for our keep. She's turned my own daughter and husband against me. All I cared about was Sandy's safety I wanted to hand him over to the police right away but things had gone too far, Sandy was too involved." She leaned back in her seat, her breathing fast and shallow.

"Ah, tea." Mike said with a sigh of relief as Sylvia carried a tray in. "Stop talking for a while and let's just drink our tea." As soon as she had finished her last mouthful, June was back in full spate.

"She's got two healthy boys a loving husband what more does she want? She's taken my daughter away and turned Tim against me and not satisfied with that she's taken on the role of mother or aunt to that Paul." She turned to Mike and pleaded "Oh Mike isn't there something you can do?" Mike had seen this coming; she always believed he could move mountains, God knows he had moved enough for her! Much as he was fond of June especially after seeing her through her post-miscarriage depressions, he was a little taken aback at her vitriolic attack on this woman Alice. From what he had gleaned from the tale, she sounded like a good hearted country wife. The sort who always had time for you and a cake ready baked. However, the intrigues of the story worried him. What they had been doing and were still doing was blatantly against the law. June's confidence that he could in some way extract Sandy from it and paint her white was misguided. There was no way she could be blameless any more than the rest of them. The involvement of the professor surprised and interested him. He would find out some more about him.

"June, I can well understand why you're so upset. It's been a night-mare for both of you, but you must try to be positive. I suggest, for the moment, you don't say anything about it to anyone else." June nodded; the considerate tone of his voice had soothed her. "And," he added, "the last thing you need to worry about is Sandy's love for you. That is set in stone." June noted that he didn't mention Tim's.

They left June feeling relieved and only a tiny bit guilty. She was sure she was doing the right thing.

On their drive back home and well into the evening, Mike and Sylvia talked over what they had been told. Initially, both had great sympathy for June and Sylvia was outraged on her behalf that Tim had abandoned her after all she had been through.

"We don't know the whole story, Syl, you know what June's like, she has been so used to coming off worse in life that she expects it and almost invites it." Mike needed to know more.

He was disturbed by June's perception of a man like Paul and the viciousness in her voice when she spoke of him. *There but for the grace of God...* He thought, the fear of giving birth to a defective baby was paramount in every pregnant woman's mind and June had been quite old when she had finally given birth to Sandy. Somewhere deep in her subconscious that fear was still hiding and meeting Paul had brought it to the fore. June seemed to actively hate the man.

"I'm going to see Tim, and then he and I will visit them all at the farm. I want to know exactly what's what before I do anything else." Sylvia agreed that he should do this and they decided that it would be better if she stayed at home, they didn't want to look like a delegation.

CHAPTER 27

ALTHOUGH SANDY WAS unhappy about her parents, her mind was focused on Peter's case. She tried to fill in the time of waiting for the professor to fix a date for his hearing by continuing to draw and paint and, to his joy, gave Peter a self-portrait sketch which he immediately pinned on his wall.

"Now I can talk to you all the time." He said lovingly.

"Was that a wise move Sandy?" Oliver asked her later.

"What harm can it do?" She replied, "He's in love with me, I know, but he also knows that I am very close to you." She looked at him cheekily. "Well, we are close aren't we?"

"Yes we are. But, you know how innocent Peter is, it would be easy to inadvertently mislead him and that would be cruel. I know what you're going to say; you wouldn't ever hurt him, how could I even imagine such a thing, but... just be careful that's all."

Oliver had had the photographs developed of their holiday and the family had laughed heartily at the bundle of clothing which Peter insisted contained him.

"We can only see your nose!" roared George "And that's only because it's so pink!" They pinned the funniest pictures on the cork board in the kitchen and Peter was allowed to pin some of the more flattering ones (in particular those of him with Sandy) on his bedroom wall.

That evening news came from Professor Small; he had lots to tell them and he made arrangements to come over that weekend when he was free from his court appearances.

Sandy and Oliver were at the pub when Professor Small arrived just after lunch on Saturday.

"We've got a guest." Alice told them as they walked into the kitchen. "Ali's professor is here and he's taking the case."

Professor Small was anything but small. He towered over even Oliver and George, Sandy felt like a hobbit as he bent forward to shake her hand. He must have been in his forties but his prematurely grey hair made him look older. Not only was he extremely tall, he was round, well, not round like a ball but, Sandy imagined, if one saw a silhouette of just his torso, it would be impossible to discern which was the front, the back or the side.

"I'm very pleased to meet you Sandy," his voice was unexpectedly soft with a gentle Devonshire burr. His eyes twinkled as if at some hidden secret. "I am just reporting to the others on my interviews with people from Paul's past." Sandy joined the others in the sitting room and Alice brought her a cup of coffee and some home baked biscuits. Professor Small lowered himself carefully into the largest armchair, crossed his enormous legs and continued.

"As I was saying, I managed to track down Paul's old school teacher, retired now, but still sharp as a knife. She remembered him and his mother very well. She told me about the dreadful father who had finally left after making Paul's life unpleasant and she didn't stop telling me what a loving relationship Paul had with his mother. She said he was a loving boy to anyone who would allow him to be." Sandy stopped herself just in time; she was about to enlarge on Paul's relationship with his mother, whoops!

"Were you going to say something Sandy?" This man was unnervingly observant.

"No, no, carry on." Sandy's face flushed and Oliver pressed his knee against hers as a warning to keep her mouth firmly shut.

"This lady put me in touch with the parents of another Down syndrome child from the same class as Paul. They were kind enough to meet me and expressed sorrow at Paul's death. I must admit I felt very awkward; they were sincerely grieved. They had lost their son a few years ago from leukaemia and it's not in my nature to lie." He paused and swept his penetrating gaze over the gathering, grunted to himself and continued "However, unprompted, they declared that they couldn't believe Paul capable of hurting anyone least of all his mother. The woman remarked on how, even after Paul had grown up and was no longer at school, she would see him shopping with his mother, holding her hand and always smiling. In turn I interviewed other members of the locality where Paul lived and the answers were the same; harmless, sweet, a bit dim but okay (from a local lad). The only person who refused to talk to me again was the neighbour who reported him to the police. She merely shouted at me go away and mind my own business. I was interested to discover that a character reference was not sought and none of the other neighbours were interviewed. They only heard of Paul's mother's death and his arrest when it appeared on the news, most of them being at work at the time of the incident." Professor Small leaned back in his chair, which creaked ominously, looked up at the open door where Peter had appeared and said,

"Hello Paul, come and join us."

There was a collective intake of breath and various corrections of "Peter, his name's Peter" fell like confetti around them.

Professor Small chuckled and a huge grin spread across his face,

"Alistair, I hope you don't take me for a fool!" There was a silence so heavy that it seemed all the air had been removed from the room and they were floating in a vacuum. Finally, Alistair stammered,

"Of course not Professor..." He tailed off, the deception had implied distrust of the professor and he floundered in his attempt to justify it.

"Don't bother trying to concoct another story, Alistair, you haven't the time, or, I may add, the natural ability to lie." He stood up, his height accentuated by their low stations in the soft chairs. "I had my suspicions from the start but I was intrigued. Why did this rather introverted young man want to champion the cause of someone unknown to him? Oh yes, the story of the cousin was very good, but, I thought to myself, where is all this altruism coming from? The answer is in front of me now. I think, given some time I could tell you the story of your involvements, lacking details of course, but just line the protagonists up and what have you got? One: a girl lost on the moor, two: a Down's man missing on the moor, three: a hiker who miraculously finds the girl, four: a man matching Paul's description suddenly moves in with the family of the hiker, and finally: you, Sandy appear on the doorstep. QED." He stood facing them all, a serious expression replacing his grin of earlier. "Who'd have thought, by looking at you all, that you were, one and all deliberately perverting the course of justice? I'm amazed you have got away with it so long." He added, "It doesn't take a legal mind to work it out, just simple observation. If this came to court you wouldn't stand a chance!"

George stood up, as tall as the professor but lacking his bulk. He looked Professor Small in the eye and stated clearly.

"Yes, we are all guilty and I regret none of it, not one tiny bit!" Alice also stood, followed by the others and they all faced the professor and waited for him to speak. He stood looking at them all, scrutinising them; staring into their eyes one by one. No one turned away or lowered their eyes. The unanimous, unspoken decision to stand firm to their beliefs linked them and enclosed them like a shield.

They were shocked when the professor threw his head back and roared with laughter.

"Come on in Paul, he repeated, let's get to know each other." Then looking around him and seeing the family and Sandy still standing rigidly fixed in one position, he added "If I'm going to clear his name *posthumously* I shall need some more facts." He roared with laughter again muttering between his guffaws, "Brilliant, first class, such loyalty, I almost wish I'd been fooled!"

The gang of lawbreakers had just increased in number. Small was going to do his utmost to force the courts to hold a 'posthumous' trial and he was going to defend the 'deceased' himself. He needed more time though before he dared go to court. He hoped to get back to them the following weekend with the results of his interviews.

Then, taking leave of absence from his lecturing duties for a few days he headed back to Exeter and then to the asylum.

CHAPTER 28

TIM HAD FOUND a place to rent with the option of buying. It was not that far away from the farm. He tried to kid himself that this was accidental but in his heart he knew that it wasn't. He recalled his feeling of peace when he was at the farm, in spite of the tension surrounding them all. His parents had been country folk; it was in his blood. His work as an accountant had deemed it necessary to move into a town, albeit a small one, but he had never really taken to living on a busy street. He wouldn't miss their house one bit. June was welcome to it. The removal of his possessions he could do in the back of his car, there was no need to hire a company. The cottage was at present furnished and if the vendors wanted to sell the furniture with the house Tim was quite happy. His home comforts were not high on his priorities.

Thus, when Mike Squires drove up to his door and rang the bell no-one answered. Mike returned home, planning to telephone later that evening.

Tim had moved into the cottage. The telephone, at his request had been re-connected and the first thing he did was ring Sandy.

"Dad, what are you doing? What about Mum?" It was a door closing on her family life when he answered,

"We're never going to get back together, I'm sorry love."

"Oh dad how could you?" Oliver heard her distress and came into the hall,

"Tell him to come over." He instructed Sandy, "He's probably got no food in yet and we've got tons." Tim heard Oliver and was profoundly grateful to him. It wasn't food he wanted but sane and normal company and in that he included Peter.

"If it's okay with you darling, tell him I'd love to."

"Have you told mum where you are?" Sandy cornered him as soon as he walked in.

"Of course I have, we're not enemies my love, just not compatible any longer."

"How is Mum? I feel dreadful; I left in such a mood. Do you think I should ring her?"

"All in good time, she refused to talk to me when I rang but I left a message with Stewart. He said she was okay but depressed." He mentally rolled his eyes, how many times had she really been clinically depressed and how many attention seeking? He pulled himself up immediately; regretting such thoughts. He had loved June deeply and he knew her depressions had been genuine. He imagined himself in her position after losing two babies; he'd have been unconsolable he told himself.

"Mike has prescribed some medication for her if she needs it."

"Has he been to see her?" Sandy's heart fluttered at the thought of June using Mike as a release for her worries. After Sandy's last conversation with her mother, that scenario looked more and more likely.

"Actually, now you mention it, I'm not sure if Stewart went and picked up the prescription or Mike delivered it." Tim's hackles rose in fear and potential anger. June had become so virulent God knows what she would do with Mike as a captive audience. He resolved to keep quiet for now but tomorrow he would find out.

"June, Mike's on the line wanting to speak to you." Gillie called up the stairs. June rushed down the stairs and took the 'phone

"Hi Mike, yes I'm feeling a lot better thank-you. It was good to talk to you. Tim? Oh yes he's moved out, I have his address and telephone number if you want it." Mike at the other end of the line wasn't sure if her lightness of voice tinged with excitement was a good or bad thing. He told her that he would also like the address of the farm as he was thinking of dropping by.

"Oh good, then you can see what I meant about that mongol." Mike winced, "And that self-opinionated woman." Yes, thought Mike, I can see for myself my dear June. Whatever had come over her? He'd known her for donkey's years and had never heard her be so unselfconsciously vitriolic.

Firstly Mike attempted to ring Tim but there was no answer so he decided that irrespective of whether he had raised Tim or not, he would drive over to his cottage at the weekend and then to the farm. George and Alice had invited Tim to stay with them until he was settled in the cottage and much as he would have liked to, he refused; he had put on them too much already. However he did agree to stay for dinner the evening Professor Small was due as he wanted as much as any of them to know what progress he'd made.

The weekend arrived and so did Professor Small seeming larger than ever in his sheepskin jacket and hat. They had dinner in the kitchen where it was snug by the Aga and then retired to the roaring fire in the sitting room. George brought out some brandy to 'keep the chills away' and they sat expectantly waiting for his update.

The doorbell rang.

"Whoever can that be?" George grumbled as he left the warm fireside. A man's voice could be heard introducing himself.

"My God, it's Mike Squires!" Tim blanched and Alice bristled. Alistair said

"I knew it!" Sandy looked at Peter who had turned ashen. She went over to his chair and sat on the arm, her arm resting on the back,

"Don't worry, Peter, I'll look after you." She whispered so only he could hear.

"You'd better come in." They heard George say, in a resigned voice. Mike walked into a room filled with people, all glaring at him. With the exception of Professor Small who rose out of his chair, towering above them all and came forward to shake his hand.

"Good evening, Dr. Squires, do take my seat by the fire. You have come at just the right moment." Mike looked bemused but sat where he had been invited. "George may I presume to make the introductions?" George nodded. "I am Professor Small and these fine folk are George, Alice, Oliver and Alistair. And here is Peter previously known as Paul." Mike nodded politely in all their directions saying,

"I'm sorry, I don't wish to intrude but..."

"It's a bit late for that now." Alistair cut in.

"Ali, watch your manners!" George reprimanded him. "You're all treating this man as though he were here to do you harm. May I tell you from my extremely brief conversation in the hall just now, that is not the case." Although Sandy had always been sure that Mike wouldn't wish them harm; at hearing it confirmed she literally sagged with relief nearly falling on top of Peter who squealed as she grabbed his curls to steady herself.

"I know what that feels like!" Oliver laughed shaking his own curls around his head.

"If you're sure you're safely seated now Sandy, shall we begin?" Professor Small looked around him, "Before I fill you in, has anyone got any questions or doubts about what we are doing?" He looked at Mike who replied that as far as he knew, what they had been doing was breaking the law. After allowing the muttering to die down he added that that side of it was none of his business, but he was interested in Peter's case; as a doctor.

The professor had spoken to the staff and indeed some of the in-mates at the asylum and had some good and some bad news. His profession and his demeanour coupled with his size tended to make people take him very seriously and he had little difficulty in securing interviews there. Some of the staff were utter brutes, relishing their power over the hapless inmates. Unnoticed, he had witnessed through a partially open door, one poor man who was obviously mentally impaired being subjected to slaps and punches, his assailants grinning all the time. He had been outraged. After leaving here, he had thought to himself, I am going to expose this and see those responsible damned. However, the majority there were decent people and these were the ones he gleaned most from. They told him of Paul's utter misery and of his weeping for his mother, insisting all the time that he hadn't done it. These members of staff were inclined to believe him and one of them had even had experience of the syndrome in his own family. They were all prepared to take the stand for 'poor Paul' as they called him. The mention of the other escapee, Jimmy, gave them the shivers. The whole staff there had considered him scheming and dangerous. They had been amazed at how the doctor attending Paul that night had been fooled by him. However, there were members of the staff who were determined that Paul was dangerous and mad. When asked how they had arrived at this diagnosis, they cited his ravings and thrashings and hitting out at the staff when he had first arrived and again later just before he escaped. Only one doctor had been prepared to speak to Professor Small and he was incredulous that a man of the Professor's standing was spending his energy and, no doubt expensive, time to clear Paul's name.

"He's dead, no relations, what on earth is the point?" He had asked. "You won't get paid for it!"

"Justice!" The professor had roared.

The evening wore on, everyone had questions to ask. The brandy bottle slowly emptied and the fire died down. It was time for bed. Ali had no choice but to share his bed with Oliver who was as unkeen as him and eventually all had been allocated a room.

"Lucky I'm going back to university next week, I'll have a bed to myself again, Ali moaned as he squeezed into the single bed alongside Oliver.

Professor Small indicated to Mike to stay behind and everyone else retired to bed.

"Well?" Small asked of Mike when they were alone.

"Need you ask?" Replied Mike.

"That's good." Small shook his hand. Tim and Mike bade him farewell and drove the short distance to the cottage.

"Thanks Mike, I'm sorry not to have confided in you but I made a promise." Tim explained.

"And you honoured that promise Tim. I wish I could say the same for June. She has developed a hatred for the whole family, I can't make her out. Her references to Paul made my hair stand on end."

"That was where our breakdown started." Tim said sadly.

"I am a doctor, and I've dealt with mothers of Down syndrome children and with the children themselves, *and* when they've become adults. They have many physical weaknesses, heart, lung, sight, hearing, all their faculties are slightly impaired. And yet," He paused showing an emotional side which Tim had never before witnessed, "they are all such happy people." He added, "Your Sandy is a credit to you, she has taken on a difficult task based on simple human compassion and decency, you should be proud of her."

Mike returned home that day but demanded that Tim keep him informed of progress. He didn't make contact with June.

CHAPTER 29

IT BEGAN TO RAIN, typical February weather; heavy downpours washed the remainder of the snow away and the fields became waterlogged.

Professor Small telephoned to say that he felt confident he had a case and mentioned Mike Squires' willingness to give evidence as a doctor who had treated patients similar to Paul. So far he had half of Paul's street vying for the chance to clear his name and a specialist in genetics all willing to take the stand. He had also managed to talk off the record with the coroner who had dealt with Paul's mother's death and put it to him that it was possible that the blunt instrument might have been the newel post and that it was accidental death. Indeed, had they even examined the newel or the steps, for blood or hair? He apparently had refused to comment on this, but, the Professor thought, *the seed had been sown.* Some members of the staff from the asylum were also prepared to speak out, not only on Paul's behalf but also to expose the sort of treatment some of the inmates received. This could mean that they could lose their jobs but they were prepared to chance it. Most of the inmates who had been subjected to cruel taunting and physical abuse were not capable of putting their case and generally their cries of complaint were disbelieved. It had appeared to the professor that it was not only the patients who were frightened of these bullies but also the more compassionate members of staff were as well. Apparently they had for some time been discussing whether they should expose some of the cruelties they had witnessed but weren't confident they would be believed and that subsequently, they would themselves be exposed to bullying, ostracising or contrived dismissal. The interviews they had had with the professor had firmed their resolve that they should act. Professor Small said that he had promised the potential whistle blowers that the case would not rest with the clearing of Paul's name, as he was determined to take the evidence of maltreatment to the highest levels of the Government. He still hadn't secured a date for the case; they just had to wait.

"I don't have a home anymore." Sandy suddenly blurted out when she was walking Lilly with Oliver. "Mum's still at Gillie's and dad's in that pokey one bed cottage. I can't go to our old home just to be there all on my own." She shushed Oliver's 'our home is yours' "But it's not! It's yours; I will only ever be a guest. I don't even earn my keep. Alice won't accept any money from dad; I feel like a bloody parasite." Oliver didn't know how to reply. What she said was true, with the exception of being a parasite. He had watched Sandy becoming increasingly morose over some time now; since Tim had moved into the cottage. He was a little surprised that Tim had bought a cottage with only one bedroom. Did he think that Sandy would move back in with her mother? Or had he not even considered the question at all? It appeared that June was determined that she didn't want to move back into their old home but had made no effort to either sell or let it. Sandy definitely didn't want to stay with her at her aunt's place. Poor kid, she had no job and no home. No wonder she was so low.

"I'm really pissed off!" Sandy spoke again, more heatedly. "I just don't know where I'm going." She looked near to tears, of anger or unhappiness, Oliver wasn't sure.

"And Paul's case, it's taking for ever to arrange."

"I know," Oliver at least could comment on this, "Ali pestered the prof again but the answer is always, 'low priority'."

"So this could go on for months?"

"Possibly even longer than that. Because he has been declared dead, there isn't any urgency, apparently, especially as there are no relatives involved. To the courts it's just a formality."

"Lucky Peter seems pretty much unaware of all that is or isn't happening."

"True. As long as he has his goats and you and mum he's content." They walked on over the fields which now had a good six inches of wheat growth. At the gate to the neighbouring field Oliver stopped and wrapped his arms around Sandy. "I know it's hard but you must try to be positive. Firstly ask yourself what exactly you want from your parents, if anything. Then ask yourself what you would like to do with your life. This business with Peter can be put on the back burner for a while. Honestly. There's nothing we can do except wait. No harm is going to come to him now and you have to think of yourself. Sorry to sound like a Dutch uncle, but I'm worried about you."

"I know I've been a pain recently, I'm sorry, it's a sort of anti-climax feeling, like a kid after Christmas is over."

"Why don't you paint more? The work I've seen is really good, though I'm no expert."

"That's a back-handed compliment!" Sandy smiled at last.

"No, what I meant," Oliver smiled fondly back at her, "is that you may be able to sell some paintings at the gallery in St. Ives, you remember, the one we looked in when it was closed?"

Sandy perked up,

"Yes. The work in there wasn't half as good as mine!"

"That's more like the Sandy from 'Baggins Hall'!"

"The tourist season starts in the spring; they are really busy from then right through the summer. If you could get some work done over the next couple of months; local scenes for pot-boilers and some of your more zany work, you may be sold out by the

September when it tails off, *and* in pocket. You could then insist on paying mum something for your keep which would stop you feeling like a parasite." He looked down at her now animated face and ruffled her hair.

Sandy started to paint, she was out of practice and the pressure she put on herself to put together a good portfolio resulted in more paintings being scrapped than kept. She began to become very irritable, even with Peter who said he loved every one she did. He cried out with genuine alarm as she tore yet another sketch in half and flung it to the floor.

"Why did you do that Sandy? He wailed. "It was lovely!"

"You have no idea Peter!" She snapped back at him "Just go away!" He retreated to the kitchen where Alice comforted him with 'artistic temperament' and other explanations for Sandy's behaviour. She was beginning to wish Oliver hadn't made the suggestion.

Tim called at the farm quite regularly; usually invited by Alice for dinner. He took Sandy aside one evening when they had all eaten,

"Are you okay? You've hardly spoken to me."

"What do you think dad? Of course I'm not okay. You and mum between you have landed me practically homeless and you don't seem to have even noticed!" She turned on him, anger sparking in her eyes. "You know if it wasn't for Oliver and his family and my loyalty to Peter I'd bugger off a long way away from both of you!" Tim was taken aback at her attack; he had thought she was where she had wanted to be. He had surmised that she and Oliver were a couple and hadn't considered having her home to live with him. He honestly thought she wouldn't want to.

"I thought you were happy here." He replied, "You are boyfriend and girlfriend aren't you?"

"That's neither here nor there dad. It's the principle of the whole thing. You assume that Alice and George are virtually adopting me like Peter. I've been given no choice in the matter. I bloody well don't want to live with Auntie Gillie and her moronic husband and mum hasn't even bothered to ask me if I would!"

"I'm sorry Sandy love; I've misread the whole thing..."

"You didn't even bother to read it let alone *mis*-read it. You buy a crappy little one bedroomed cottage with no space for me and then spend most of your time here for dinner and whatnot. How about inviting the Tregowens for dinner at your place for a change?" Tim was speechless. He had never been spoken to by Sandy in this disrespectful manner. He wasn't sure whether to be angry, hurt or contrite. "I suppose you think it's all my fault, just like mum does?"

"Now come on Sandy, there's no need to be so vitriolic. If you've got a problem with me then at least have the decency to talk it over in a civilized fashion." He realised he was angry. "No I don't say it was your fault, but had things not happened as they did I think your mother and I would not have fallen out."

"I knew it!" Sandy screamed at him "You do blame me. Well sod you both." She stormed out of the room without a backward glance.

George caught her as she fled headlong up the stairs to her room.

"Sandy stop!" He commanded. She halted half way up a step; George was a man who commanded respect. He stood squarely at the foot of the stairs and motioned for her to come back down. "Whether we wanted to or not, Sandy, everyone has heard your exchange with your dad. I think we need to nip this well and truly in the bud now before it escalates any further." Sandy's face was flushed with anger and became more so with embarrassment. She reluctantly descended to the hall and George, followed by Alice, took her arm and led her back into the sitting room, where Tim sat white faced and looking very much alone. George bade them sit. Tim started to speak but Alice put a calm hand on his and he fell silent. George paused for a while before he spoke; then, standing in front of them with his back to the fire he began in a quiet, calm voice,

"We've all been thrown together under most unusual circumstances. Circumstances in which fate gave us no choice. If you believe in fate you will say that it was pre-ordained. If you don't believe in fate you'd describe it as an unfortunate set of coincidences. Whichever way you see it the facts remain the same. We have rescued one person and two have fallen by the wayside. Would this have happened under any other circumstances? We don't know. But it *has* happened and we must attempt to make the tragedy as bearable as possible. Sandy, Oliver and Peter underwent an experience which I still find hard to imagine and they have come out whole and bonded as friends for life. Alistair has shown his worth as a budding solicitor. Alice has proven herself to be an unfailing strength and has supported them all with unrelenting love and care. However, poor June has found the whole thing destructive; in her mind, robbing her of that most precious thing, her daughter, whom she thought she had lost but had found again. Tim has lost the love of his life. Now, do we tear to shreds the good that has come of these events or do we attempt to knit together the frayed ends of the broken parts?" Silence greeted him. He saw Sandy fidget in her seat and Tim start to rise from his. He and Alice left the room with no more words.

Tim left for home later that evening, his eyes pink and his farewells muted. Sandy walked outside with him to the car. They embraced. Sandy pushed her small frame tightly against Tim's comforting chest and held him tight.

"I'm so sorry dad." He kissed the top of her head

"I love you, my darling little girl. Don't ever forget that."

CHAPTER 30

"JUST PACE YOURSELF, do a bit when you feel in the right mood then leave off for a bit." Oliver stood back from the easel and surveyed the canvas on which Sandy was sketching out her scene of the harbour. So far it was looking good, a little more traditional than she liked to paint but a possible tourist eye-catcher. The tutors during her four years at art college had drummed into the students to 'push boundaries'; awarding the highest grades to the most outlandish pieces in her group. They had been scathing of anyone who painted as they termed it, 'like Beatrix Potter'. Sandy didn't paint like Beatrix Potter but she had always preferred to paint the landscape with her own interpretations of mood and colour and resented being forced into a mould which was not true to herself. The more ridiculous the project, the higher the grades they achieved. Sandy seethed at the power the tutors had to make or break and for the first year she had resolutely stuck to her principles. However, finding no praise for her efforts and the threat of being kicked off the course forced her to succumb to the pressure and join the flow. After achieving a creditable 2:1 in her diploma she had ceremoniously burnt her portfolio.

"I'm getting into it a bit more now. I just have to forget who I am and think of money." She stood back with Oliver and scrutinised what she had done. "It's okay. I'll do some little watercolours as well for the cheaper market and then, when I can afford it; I'll go back to being me."

"Do you need to go and do some sketching for more material?"

Oliver leafed through her sketch book. “We could drive over there tomorrow if you like; take another walk on the beach.”

“Yea, good idea, I’ll tell Peter to get up early and we can make a day of it.”

Peter was up very early because he wanted to check on his precious goats before leaving. They found him in the stall saying goodbye to them.

“What’s the matter with your voice? I thought it was someone else in here, it’s dropped an octave.” She smirked at Oliver and whispered “Maybe something else has dropped as well!”

Oliver smothered a laugh with a cough and catching his breath, replied

“Disgusting woman!” Peter, oblivious to being the butt of humour coughed a bit to clear his larynx

“I woke up like it, I sound like you now.” He grinned at Oliver.

They had a successful day out and thoroughly explored the area for interesting views. Whilst Sandy sketched, Oliver and Peter meandered around the shops and finally ended up at the pub where they had arranged to eat lunch. They downed a pint each in the warm, if slightly fuggy bar. Peter’s voice was still croaky and he liked the sound of it, although a bit of a sore throat accompanied it.

“Sounds like you’re coming down with a cold old man.” Oliver commented. “Better get some throat sweets when we’ve had lunch.” When Sandy joined them she was shivering from sitting on benches or stone walls and her fingers were quite blue.

“Brrr it’s bloody cold out there; let me get next to that fire.” She looked happy though “I’ve got loads to be going on with.”

Out of the blue, June telephoned the farm. Alice answered it and made a supreme effort to be civil. Unfortunately, June was not quite so subtle.

"I want to speak to Sandy." June said bluntly to Alice

"As you wish." Alice replied tartly and called Sandy to the 'phone.

"Mum, how are you?" Sandy had missed her mum and had been longing for her to make contact. She would have 'phoned June herself but argued that it was better to wait until her mother was ready. Alice carried on making lunch in the kitchen hoping the conversation would go well. She picked up snippets through the open door and as Sandy's voice became gradually more and more shrill, she ceased pretending to be busy and blatantly listened to her half of the exchange.

"I don't want to visit you *there*. Why can't you go home and then we could spend some time together away from other people?" There was a pause as Sandy listened to her mother's answer,

"No mum. I'm not coming to Aunt Gillie's, I'm sorry but I want to see you on your own. Don't you want to be with just me?... Why won't you?... Look mum, I miss you so much, please meet me at home?" Sandy sounded near to tears.

"Don't you care about me anymore?" There was a longer silence this time, then, suddenly Sandy shouted down the 'phone,

"How can you say such horrible things? It isn't his fault you and dad fell out!" There was another pause, much longer this time and Alice held her breath; she waited to hear Sandy's reply but all she heard was a loud sob and the receiver being placed quietly back on the hook. Alice went into the hall – Sandy had gone.

Peter had come in from the goats and was busy decanting the milk in the kitchen. To be out of earshot, George telephoned Tim from his office.

"Tim, I'm getting straight to the point. Sandy is distraught. She and June seem to have had a falling out on the 'phone. Alice only heard one side of the conversation obviously, but Sandy went off with the dog immediately afterwards and has been gone for ages."

"I'll come over." Tim left immediately. When he arrived Sandy still had not returned.

"From my short time of knowing her," George ventured, "I have to say this is not typical behaviour, she normally blows her top and stomps around until she simmers down."

"You're right. Whatever has June said now?"

"Well, I'm sorry to say, but I think it was about Peter again." George sighed. "Why does she hate him *so* much? I know she blames him for the horrific time you both had when Sandy was missing but that's over now; Sandy's safe and Peter's no threat to her and Sandy's relationship."

"If June would only stop and think, she'd realise that she is crucifying Sandy; she feels guilty enough as it is and I haven't helped." Tim scanned the horizon for any sight of Sandy. "Wherever has she gone?"

"She'll be back, in her own time," George assured him there was nothing dangerous on his land, like deep lakes or cliff edges, "but something has to be done about June."

"As soon as Sandy is back safely I'm driving to see June." Tim's feelings for his wife were no longer those of mere dislike.

Sandy returned, quietly, she entered by the kitchen door and took Lilly's food from the cupboard. The dog seemed subdued as well, she kept glancing up at Sandy as she ate, her tail wagging spasmodically in an apologetic sort of way as though she had done something wrong.

"It's alright Lil, it's not you." Sandy crouched beside her and smoothed her hot little head. Lilly thanked her with a dog food flavoured lick. Normally this would have produced an 'ugh' and a laugh from Sandy but she merely wiped her face with the back of her hand and continued to stroke Lilly. Tim came to find her. His chubby face full of concern, melted with love for his daughter as she looked up at him. The sadness in her eyes was heart-breaking. He felt his anger building inside him.

"My love." He knelt beside her and the dog. Alone in the kitchen he pulled her into his arms. She smelt his familiar smell, and his unshaven chin rasped against her cheek. Closing her eyes she could imagine she was a small child again and everything the way it once was.

Tim left the following morning. He didn't phone June to say he was coming. He drove fast and angrily. On the way he stopped to ring Mike who agreed to meet him en route.

"I need your support in this Mike. June has become totally unreasonable." Over a very quick lunch he explained to Mike what had happened and how he needed to make June consider Sandy over herself. "I don't care anymore what she thinks of me but damn it all Mike, how can she do it to Sandy? It's unbelievable; when she thought Sandy was dead she wanted to die as well. Now Sandy's safe she doesn't seem to give a damn about her. I don't understand what's got into her!" Mike said hesitantly,

"I don't like to say it Tim, but subconsciously, her 'I want to die' was a cry of 'what about me?' She wouldn't have realised it herself at the time as she was so distraught over Sandy, but had she really wanted to die she wouldn't have broadcast it. She would have just done it."

"Hello Gillie,"

"Tim! Is June expecting you? She didn't say." Gillie gave him a light kiss on his cheek. In spite of his leaving June, Gillie was still fond of Tim; she wished they could sort it out. Maybe that was why he was here. She invited them in, "Hello Mike, lovely to see you."

June's reaction to Tim and Mike's surprise visit shocked them all. Tim was expecting a lack of welcome, this was to be expected but he was speechless at her anger.

"What the hell do you want? Has your sainted Alice upset you?

Or has Peter/Paul murdered her thinking she was his mother?!"

"My God June!" Exclaimed Mike, "Get a grip on yourself!"

She spun round to face him

"And you Mike, after I poured out my heart to you. I thought you'd understand after all I've been through. You haven't contacted me or even left a message with Gillie. Have you joined the 'Peter' brigade as well?"

"June, dear, you seem to forget that Tim has been through the same period of anguish as you have." She cut him short

"I haven't forgotten. That's why I can't understand or forgive him for siding with the person who has destroyed our lives!"

"He hasn't destroyed them! You have!" Tim was seething "If you hadn't been so goddam selfish and so unutterably cruel about Peter, we would still be together and I would still love you. I don't understand you June." His large frame seemed to shrink as he lowered himself into a chair, "I thought I knew you, every nuance and mood. I've loved and cared for you from the minute we met. Have I been mistaken? Tell me please, is this the real you?"

"My question exactly." She replied. "Is the real *you* a man who puts the feelings of a complete stranger, a misfit at that, before the feelings of the woman he says he loves?" She stood over him bridling with anger and perceived injustice. Tim said nothing in reply, his face was flushed and a look of extreme sadness clouded the anger in his eyes.

Gillie, seizing a slight break in the accusations flying back and forth, stepped between them.

"Tim, I still don't know why you are here. Surely it wasn't just to have a fight with June?"

"No, it wasn't. I didn't want a fight. I came to beg her to consider Sandy and to give her some peace of mind. Sandy feels that June doesn't care enough about her to make a home for her. You realise that Sandy is living as a permanent guest at the Tregowens because her mother won't move back home to be with her? She wants to live with her mother. She loves you June, it's a mother she wants, not an auntie or even a father, but a mother!"

June, tears smarting her eyes, leant forward in her chair and put her hands to her face,

"Are you so stupid as to think I don't want that as well? I want with all my heart to have Sandy back. But I can't go back to our old house, it isn't home anymore."

"Well you can't stay living here. Why don't you let the bloody place or sell it and move somewhere new, make a home for you both?" June looked up tearfully,

"I can't do it on my own." Tim had always handled their affairs, managed the money and employed plumbers and the like. June had been a housewife, unversed in anything but being a wife and mother.

"I'll do it all for you if that's the only problem. All you had to do is ask." Tim had, in his emotional breakup with her, forgotten how hopeless June was at life in general. No wonder she was staying put with Gillie and Stewart. She was being looked after and didn't have to do a bloody thing.

"Alright," she said through her tears, which failed completely to move Tim, "put the place up for sale and find Sandy and me another home."

"I'll do it straight away." Tim said thankfully. He would have some good news for Sandy when he returned home.

"Then," June added "she needn't have anything more to do with that Paul and his '*family*'!"

"Your mum's agreed to sell the house and buy another one." He told Sandy on his return. "She says she can't bear the thought of living in our old one."

"I can understand that." Sandy didn't feel as emotional about the thought of living in their old house as June did; she still had the love of her father and she could see him any time. But she knew that the happy memories would haunt and suffocate her mother.

"Thanks dad. At least I can have a room again which is really my own." Tim didn't mention June's parting words. He hoped that time would sort it all out. Sandy went to hug him but his hair tickled her nose and she let forth an almighty sneeze.

"You nearly blew my head off. Bless you." Tim hugged her anyway.

The atmosphere at the farm improved dramatically now that Sandy was happy. She had a way of influencing everyone's moods just by being there.

February ended and Sandy's portfolio was growing nicely. She took a few days off drawing when her cold developed into a chesty cough as her eyes were steaming and she felt 'like shit'. The cold was determined to spread throughout the household and one by one they succumbed. Alistair came home for the half term break,

"Cushy way of life; being a student!" Oliver teased.

"You should see the amount of work I've got before you say that!" Retorted Ali. Then as Peter sneezed five times without stopping, "Bugger me, you've all got colds, I wish I'd stayed at university."

"How is the prof getting on?" Sandy asked him hopefully.

"Much the same. He's happy with his case but the date hasn't been set yet. He's trying his best to chivvy it along but he has to play it a bit cool."

Tim found a small but pleasant house for June, a sensitive distance from their old one and put an offer in for it, pending their own sale. After a bit of bargaining the offer was accepted. They were given a month in which to confirm it as and when they had an offer on their house, after that the new house would go back on the market.

"Have you had any interest dad?" Sandy asked him every time

he spoke to her. She hadn't visited June at Gillie's yet but now things with the house were moving she thought she might suggest it.

"I'm sure she'd love it," Tim was hesitant, "but why don't you wait until you can move in together properly?"

"Okay. If you think that's best. I'll give her ring tonight anyway."

Mike came down at the weekend to visit Tim.

"How are things with the house purchase? Do you think June will ease off on her Peter vendetta?"

"I doubt it, that's what worries me. If everything goes to plan and the house sale goes through, Sandy will move in. But there's no way she will stop visiting the farm or lose her affection for Peter, and if June starts on again trying to prevent her from visiting it'll all blow sky high."

"Hmm, just what I've been thinking. Do you want me to get Sylvia to try and talk some sense into her?"

"Would you? Thanks Mike, I appreciate that."

"Honestly darling, I don't know how to approach June." Sylvia dithered, "I haven't spoken to her since we visited and I don't feel I know her anymore."

"I know, I feel the same, but I did offer your help to Tim. Give it a go will you love?"

June was frosty when Sylvia rang suggesting they meet up for lunch. She offered to drive over to Gillie's and they could chat like they used to. June sounded defensive. The lack of contact from Sylvia had hurt and offended her. Neither Mike nor Sylvia had bothered with her. She had been so distraught and had been sure they would take her side; they had always been so kind and understanding before. June refused the invitation. *She's sided against me too I can tell.*

CHAPTER 31

TAKING TO HEART what Sandy had said about his eating at the farm and never inviting them back, Tim decided he would book them all in for dinner at the Red Lion, if they were willing. He didn't have room enough to cater for seven people and, being honest with himself, he didn't know if he was up to cooking for that number. Mike was invited also, making eight in total; definitely too many to accommodate. Tim had spent many lonely evenings at the pub and he and Bert got on quite well. Bert didn't resemble the typical country landlord; he was a tiny man with a face a bit like a mouse and in spite of the many pints he sank, there was no evidence of a beer gut. He was always smartly dressed as was Rosemary, his wife. Even when the pub was crowded out with locals Bert managed to keep track of everyone's orders and never forgot what 'the usual' was for any of his regulars.

The Tregowens were thrilled at the invitation and they all met up for pre-dinner drinks at Tim's before descending on the pub. Alistair and Oliver ragged Peter about his newly curled hair; as it had been growing out he had been subjected to another perm, administered by Alice.

"Hi man, where's your hippy flowers and beads?" Alistair pulled a curl out and let it spring back. "Are you really happy looking like Oli?"

"Leave him alone, he looks great!" Sandy laughed "We're getting him some flares for his birthday."

"Oh, when's that?" Ali asked. "How old will you be Peter?"

"It's the first of March and I'll be twenty six!" He replied happily. He was looking forward to his birthday; mummy had always made a big cake for him and Alice promised to do the same.

"Mad March Hare!" Ali joked. He was more than a little tipsy and enjoying himself immensely.

"Everything okay Tim?" The landlord was clearing the plates away.

"Lovely thanks, Bert. Could we have a couple more bottles of the red?"

"Coming right up." He signalled to Steve, his son who was attending the bar of the family run pub.

"How's your mum?" He turned to Peter, "Recovering okay?" Peter looked aghast. All conversation at the table died. It had been a long time since he had said 'I didn't do it!' but George could see it forming in his mind as all the colour drained from Peter's face.

"Still poorly I'm afraid." He answered quickly on Peter's behalf. "Peter's staying with us indefinitely, and Sally will probably move down to convalesce when she's out of hospital." He added "It's a blessing Bert, he's such a help on the farm: don't know how we managed before."

Bert cast a glance at Peter's still ashen face "Sorry if I upset the lad," he patted Peter on the shoulder, "I'm sure she'll be right as rain in no time. You must be missing her eh?" Peter nodded, tears in his eyes, he was about to speak but Oliver butted in,

"How about that wine Bert?"

"That was an unfortunate name you conjured up," Alice whispered to George when Bert had left them in peace, "you realise that's his mother's name." She gave a slight nod in Peter's direction.

"Shit!" George said under his breath.

Gradually they all regained their composure and with Sandy and Alistair's help Oliver managed to divert Peter from his thoughts with more teasing and general chatter about the farm and his precious goats. But his giggles still didn't disguise the haunted look on his face.

When they had all been turned out at closing time, Tim and Mike made their way back to the cottage. Tim had bought a camp bed which he intended to use and offered his bed to Mike.

"Goodnight old chap, thanks for the meal." Mike said sleepily as he climbed the dog-leg stairs to Tim's room. "Oh by the way, remind me to have a listen to that boy's chest tomorrow, I don't like the sound of it. He may need some antibiotics."

Peter squeaked when the cold stethoscope touched his chest and then his back. He breathed in and out again as Mike instructed but it made him cough.

"You've got a bit of an infection my lad; I'll give you a prescription for some penicillin." Mike left Peter to do up his shirt and joined Tim in the farmhouse kitchen,

"I'll make it out for you Tim as you're my patient and Peter can't be registered, having no medical health number. Hope that's okay?" Tim nodded. Mike addressed George and Alice,

"He has slight arrhythmia as well, it's not uncommon in Down's people. I'll give him something that will help with that as well."

Tim and June's house had a purchaser, they had knocked them down a bit but, as Tim had bargained heavily with his purchase it evened out. It was time for June to take control of her life. Sandy was equally excited and apprehensive about the move. She hadn't seen her mother since she had left in anger and her recent telephone conversations had been stilted; full of unsaid hints. However, since the news that the house was going to be sold, June had sounded more relaxed. And as the date for exchange of contracts drew nearer she had become more animated, saying she couldn't wait until she had Sandy back with her again.

The exchange was delayed, some legal technicality to do with the searches. Sandy was able to stay for Peter's birthday without having to run the gauntlet with her mum.

True to their promise, Oliver and Sandy bought Peter some bright green flared trousers, and for a laugh, some hippy beads. Alice baked a cake with loads of icing and 'HAPPY BIRTHDAY PETER' in piping on the top. Alice bought Peter some slightly more sensible clothing and his own draughts set. Alistair sent Peter a funny card with goats on it and a big box of chocolates. A birthday card arrived from Professor Small much to the surprise and pleasure of them all. In it he had enclosed a sealed letter addressed to George in which he told them that a date had been set for Paul's case and saying he would be in touch by 'phone with the final details.

The day had begun bright but with a cold wind, however, in the afternoon the wind dropped and Oliver and Sandy decided to take Lilly for a long walk. Peter asked to come too and they all wrapped up well, Peter in his new parka with its furry hood pulled snuggly around his face grinned happily and begged to hold Lilly's lead until they reached the fields.

The cold must have been the reason; they hadn't walked up any hills or even walked very quickly, but Peter became badly out of breath and began to cough. When they got him home Alice was furious with them.

"He's overdone it!" She glared at Oliver, "You shouldn't have stayed out so long!" She sat Peter close to the warmth of the Aga and made him a mug of chocolate, administered his heart pills and told him to rest. Peter's breathing improved after a while; the pills regulated his heart rhythm and Alice relaxed a little.

"On his birthday as well!" She berated them, "Thank goodness he seems alright now, but just remember he's not like you Oli!"

Professor Small rang during the week to tell them the date of the hearing. It was to be in three weeks' time. He sounded confident and extremely pleased with himself that he had managed to get it earlier than he had thought.

Easter was early this year and Alistair's four week holiday break began. He arrived home with a mountain of final work and a thesis to complete looking slimmer and a bit stressed.

"I'm sitting my finals next term and I'm a bit worried. I've been so preoccupied with Peter that I've let things build up. I've got to get at the least a 2:1, Morley and Brown won't employ me if I get any less."

"You'll be fine, love." Alice hugged him. Alistair pulled quickly away in case she decided to kiss him as well. Life continued as normal as they counted the days to the hearing. Well, nearly normal; the stress of waiting was beginning to tell in little ways. Alice spoilt the bread and swore it was Oliver's fault for opening the oven. Sandy tore up every drawing she did

"It's crap!" The date of exchange of contracts had finally been set and Sandy was becoming increasingly anxious about moving in with her mother. She found it hard to believe that she was worried about living with her mum; the person she loved more than anyone. She should be eager and ecstatic that finally they were going to be together; but she wasn't. That in itself was upsetting her. She felt guilty; her mother had put herself outside of everyone's affections with her attitude to Peter. Sandy still loved her but had chosen her friends over June when she had pushed her too far, knowing she would make the same decision again were the scene repeated, but a rift had been created in their relationship; would it ever heal?

On the plus side Professor Small telephoned to reassure them of his confidence that he could clear Paul's name and Mike rang Tim often and they met up as old friends do. Neither mentioned June.

Tim suggested that Sandy go with him to their old house to

help him pack up their possessions as June couldn't be expected to do it all on her own.

"We'll do the big stuff and your things. Gillie can help June sort her personal bits." Tim had organised a removal firm for June. He had done everything that was required of him, willingly. June had thanked him stiffly in a way which indicated that she thought it was no more than he should have done.

It was more emotional than Sandy had anticipated; she had spent her whole life in this house, her bedroom held memories of every stage, from childhood through teenage pop idols, school girl crushes and lost loves. Her fencing trophies lined the shelves alongside her books; there was 'The Lord of The Rings', falling apart just like Oli's. Digging in her wardrobe she found her fencing gear, the leather glove stiff with dried sweat so that it resembled a curled hand. Her foils and sabre stood in the corner with the mask on a nail above them. She decided that she would definitely find a local club and take it up again. In a moment of nostalgia Sandy pulled on the plastron and jacket, slipped the mask over her face, picked up her foil and immediately found herself assuming an on guard position. This had surely been the most exhilarating sport she had ever tried, and she had been bloody good at it. The memory of beating the county champion in Nottingham sent a glow through her. Shame it had been a local contest and not a championship one. Unlike other sports, men and women fought each other as well as single sex bouts. It was brilliant beating the men, their reach and strength giving them no real advantage over a woman if she was skilful enough and agile. Sandy's advantage was her diminutive size and her speed. One man complained that he kept missing her because she was 'as small as a Chinese wrestler's jock strap!' A strange sort of compliment! Deep in the back of the cupboard she discovered her old mask, second hand when she had bought it. A deep dent at eye level, the mesh slightly fractured but unbroken, sent a shiver of recollection through her. She had lunged, fencing a beginner, and instead of parrying, her opponent had used a stop shot. She should never have let him through her defence but, he was a beginner and she had been too complacent.

The mask had stove in and she had felt the mesh on her eye lid. Thankfully it had gone no further.

There in cardboard boxes were all her school folders, essays on Hamlet and the war poets, projects on the Impressionists, Renaissance art and Cubism. Sketch books and calligraphy exercises, illuminated scripts, still life drawings and more drew her deeper into her memories and deeper into sadness. Tim called up to her asking how she was progressing which thankfully snapped her out of melancholy and into positive action.

"Getting there!" She called back and shoved her memories unceremoniously back into the boxes.

Finally she and Tim had packed all the breakables in tea chests and soft items in plastic bags. Everything was ready. The cleaners Tim had hired would give the place a scouring and leave it welcoming for the new owners. Before they left, Tim took a final reading of the meters and turned off the water, electricty and gas.

"What date are we exchanging dad?"

"The thirtieth. That's next Wednesday. Then the removal men are coming immediately to take all the stuff."

"I'll come back then to help mum. The hearing is the third of April. I want to be back at the farm for that day. I hope mum won't kick up!"

They drove back to the farm in a subdued mood. This was the final chapter of June and Tim's marriage and their life as a family.

Oliver greeted her with his usual welcoming hug and as always, they gravitated to the kitchen.

"Where's Peter?" Sand looked around expectantly.

"He's in bed; his cold's a bit worse so I decided to cosset him for a day or so." Alice explained, "It was hell's only job to stop him doing the goats but it's cold and draughty in the stall and he will spend too long in there fussing over them." She ushered Sandy to the door,

"Go up and see him, he's bound to have heard you arrive, he does miss you so when you're not here."

Peter's stay in bed extended to more than a couple of days; his cough was no better. George had lit the fire and it crackled comfortingly taking the chill off the unheated bedroom. Peter had smiled wanly at him and thanked him very much in his usual sweet manner, his gaze immediately reverting to Sandy's drawing on the wall.

"I think he needs another course of penicillin, I'll give Mike a ring and see if he can come over." George said to Alice as she was making up some tasty snacks for Peter; his cold seemed to have taken away his usual enjoyment of food. "He's due for a repeat prescription for his heart pills anyway." When he realised that Sandy was back, in spite of feeling poorly, Peter insisted he wanted to get up and come downstairs with the family.

"It can't do any harm; he must be lonely and bored up there on his own." Alice allowed him to come down only if he stayed in the warm, "No sneaking out to visit those goats!" She told him sternly. "If you're really good I may get Oli to bring them into the kitchen for a quick visit."

Peter promised to behave and then, once he was downstairs pestered Alice until she said,

"Oh for goodness sake, Oli get Daisy and Nancy. If they poo in the kitchen Peter, you can clear it up!" Peter readily agreed to clean up any mess.

"You are a dear. I didn't mean it." She looked lovingly and him and he smiled shyly back. Peter looked poorly; his face had an unhealthy flush and his cough left him breathless. He was cheerful though, being amongst the family was far better than isolated in his room, pretty though it was.

Mike came down at the weekend and checked him over.

"The infection's back. I'll increase the dosage." After a few days of the new medication Peter showed definite signs of improvement and was keen to get back to looking after the goats and helping Alice in the kitchen. However, within a very short time of taking the last dose he seemed to become much worse than he had been. Alice insisted this time that he stay in bed and, as the weather was still very wintery she filled two hot-water bottles with boiling water, wrapped them safely in their covers and tucked them in with him.

"Thank you Auntie." Even the act of speaking seemed to exhaust him. He lay back and closed his eyes. "Sleep for a while my love, it's a great healer." She kissed his forehead and hurried downstairs.

"Mike I'm so sorry to bother you but Peter is worse again, do you think you could find time to come and see him?"

"I'll come directly after surgery. Expect me at about seven."

That evening Sandy was surprised and a little wary when her mother rang. She didn't often telephone the farm as she hated having to speak to Alice or even George. They weren't due to move until Wednesday and it was only Friday, Sandy hoped nothing had gone wrong with the sale. June and Gillie had been back to the house the previous week to pack the remainder of her belongings, hurriedly and in a tear laden atmosphere she then had returned to Gillie's to stay until they took her to her new home to meet up with Sandy.

"Sandy, I miss you please come and see me." She pleaded at the end of a rather stiff conversation in which Sandy was so careful in what she said that she hardly spoke at all.

"Why now mum, we're moving on Wednesday and I'll come up then."

"I thought you could come and stay here until then, Gillie would love to see you."

"I can't mum, Peter's ill." Her mother actually rang off without saying goodbye.

Mike arrived as promised and went directly to Peter's room. He listened to his chest again and asked them the colour of his phlegm. Peter had a high temperature and Mike instructed them to bathe his forehead with cold flannels to try to bring it down.

"I fear he's developing pneumonia." Mike said later when they were downstairs.

"He's quite fit otherwise; your home cooking has built him up well. He has every chance of shaking it off. Unfortunately I can't be of much help anymore. He needs to get through it with his own immune system."

For days, Peter's condition remained much the same, no worse and no better. They kept him in bed and he lay there listlessly whilst life went on around him. He ate little; even Alice's carefully prepared trifles and puddings that Peter loved, couldn't tempt him to take more than a few mouthfuls. He had asked Sandy to pin her picture nearer the bed so that he could see it better and he spent most of the time gazing at it if she wasn't in the room with him. One or more of them sat with him throughout the day. At night, Sandy and Alice slept with their doors open in case he called for them, neither of them able to sleep soundly for fear they would not hear him.

The exchange took place on the houses and Sandy was due to move.

"I can't go. Peter needs me here." She told her father when he came over.

"I know love, June will just have to cope, after all she has Gillie. I'm certainly not going." The Wednesday came and went. There was no communication from June, Sandy wasn't sure if this was good or bad. For now, she really didn't care either way. Peter needed her more than her mother did at this time, and here she was going to stay.

Sandy was woken from her light sleep by horrendous bubbling coughing from Peter in the room next door. She rushed into him and helped him sit up in bed to ease his breathing. George and Alice soon joined her having been woken also. His face was shiny and wet with sweat and he could hardly get his breath. They sat with him wiping his forehead until 6am when George felt he could ring Mike Squires. Mike set out immediately but it was nearly 8am before he arrived. The chest infection had turned to pneumonia. All they could do was help him sweat it out; there was nothing more Mike could do.

"Even if we got him into hospital, he would get no more than we can do for him here." He said sadly, "just stay with him." The family took turns to sit with Peter night and day, wiping his forehead and holding his clammy hand as he strove to breathe. He agitated when Sandy wasn't with him, so she stayed by his bedside for longer periods than the others. She held his hand and talked to him whilst her head nodded with tiredness. When he was awake he gazed lovingly into her eyes but mostly he lay motionless, occasionally tightening his weak grip on her hand.

It was the morning of the hearing, Professor Small rang briefly to say he was on his way to court and to wish him luck. Not that, in his opinion, he needed it.

Peter's breathing was becoming more laboured and between them, they raised him further up against the pillows to alleviate it and he smiled wanly in thanks. The day wore on and his chest bubbled and rattled with the accumulation of liquid in his lungs. They sat by his bed constantly. Peter fell in and out of sleep, his breathing agony to their ears. Sandy held his moist hand in hers and talked soothingly to him as he lay listlessly with closed eyes.

Suddenly he pulled his hand out of hers and his pale eyes focused on her face. He pointed to her sketch and she unpinned it from the wall and gave it to him. He clutched it to him and gazed lovingly at it, then, raising his eyes to Sandy he reached out for her hand. His grip tightened, then loosened and still gazing into her eyes he became still.

Paul's name was cleared and he was pronounced innocent posthumously, the verdict on the death of his mother was amended to death by misadventure.

They buried him beside his mother under his own name.

Tim and Mike came to the service but June did not.